PENGARRON DYNASTY

PENGARRON DYNASTY

Gloria Cook

Severn House Large Print
London & New York

This first large print edition published in Great Britain 2003 by
SEVERN HOUSE LARGE PRINT BOOKS LTD of
9-15, High Street, Sutton, Surrey, SM1 1DF.
First world regular print edition published 2002 by
Severn House Publishers, London and New York.
This first large print edition published in the USA 2003 by
SEVERN HOUSE PUBLISHERS INC., of
595 Madison Avenue, New York, NY 10022

British Library Cataloguing in Publication Data

Cook, Gloria
    Pengarron dynasty - Large print ed.
    1. Cornwall (England) - Social life and customs - 18th
        century - Fiction
    2. Domestic fiction
    3. Large type books
    I. Title
    823.9'14 [F]

    ISBN 0-7278-7227-3

Except where actual historical events and characters are being
described for the storyline of this novel, all situations in this
publication are fictitious and any resemblance to living persons
is purely coincidental.

Printed and bound in Great Britain by
MPG Books Ltd, Bodmin, Cornwall.

*To my brothers, Raymon and Ted,
and my sisters, Sandria, Sylvia and Rosemarie,
and their spouses*

One

The house in St James's Street, London, was well ablaze. Dense smoke and bright flames were curling out of all the downstairs windows and the screams of terror inside were competing with the noise of cracking and falling timbers and splintering glass as the windows exploded.

Rounding the corner from Jermyn Street, Luke Pengarron and his servant broke into a run.

'God help us, Jack, Lord Longbourne's house is on fire!'

They flew up the debris-strewn front steps and kicked and battered on the door. Anxious onlookers and ghoulish spectators were gathering, all too afraid to help.

When the door finally crashed open under their combined weight, the two men fought their way upstairs. There were signs that the house had been ransacked. Choking on the smoke and scorched by the terrible heat of the flames, they tore into the drawing room.

Luke gave a groan of anguish and pushed Jack back out of the room.

'We can do nothing for Lord Longbourne. He's dead.'

Stabbed through the heart, the particular mark of retribution of the Society. No knife protruded from the wound, and the flames, starting their deadly dance on the young peer's feet, would burn away all evidence of the assassination. Two male servants who, no doubt, had gone to their master's aid also lay dead.

'Sophia! We must save her!' Jack bawled above the din of the steadily collapsing house.

They heard screams coming from further along the corridor. Sophia Glanville was trapped in her room.

Without thought for their own safety Luke and Jack ran on through the inferno, leaping over the gaping holes left by burnt-away floorboards, thrusting aside anything in their way, even if it was on fire. When they got to Sophia's room they found it had been barricaded. Heaving aside a heavy marble table, they burst in through the door.

Sophia and her maid, both coughing and choking, were huddled together on the far side of the room, next to an open window. Flames were eating away the centre of the floor and more tall, spiralling darts of orange-red were riding the bedposts and its flowing drapes.

'Come to us!' Jack yelled to them. 'We'll

lead you to safety.'

'Alex! Where's Alex?' Sophia cried, her fine face blackened by smoke and frozen with fear. 'There were men, their faces were masked.'

'Get her out, Jack. I'll take the maid,' Luke ordered, winding his neckcloth round his face so he might breathe better.

Jack skirted the flames and wrapped his scarf over Sophia's mouth and nose. Freeing her from the clawing grasp of the maid, he began to lead her to the door. Suddenly a heavy bedpost was blasted ceiling high. On its descent it sheered sideways, striking Jack on the head and cutting him down. Sophia shrieked and knelt beside his unconscious form.

Luke acted quickly, dragging Jack and Sophia out to the corridor. He ran back to fetch the maid.

With her arms up to protect her face she was sidling past the treacherous hole in the floor, but on reaching the doorway and faced with the full violence of the conflagration, which, like some malevolent beast was greedily devouring the floors and walls, she stood petrified with fear and refused to shift.

'If you don't come now, I'll not be able to come back for you!' Luke bawled at her.

She blubbered hysterically as he tried to force her to move. Then she lashed out at him in panic and terror, raking her nails down his face, ripping out the bow that tied back his black hair.

It was a losing battle. After a moment's thought he lunged at Sophia where she crouched over Jack, covering his face with her skirts to fight off the suffocating effect of the smoke. Snatching the diamond necklace off her neck, Luke thrust it down the front of the maid's bodice and left her to her fate.

The main staircase had completely burned away. Flames were leaping several feet up in the air. Yanking Jack up off the floor, Luke shouted at Sophia to hold on to his coat. Edging along the corridor, he made for the servants' stairs.

There was a hideous scream; the maid was burning. Sophia shrieked her name.

Bitter smoke blotted out everything. Luke and Sophia stumbled their way down the narrow, twisting stairs as fast as they dared. A female servant lay dead, murdered, at the bottom. A sudden roaring whoosh of red-hot flame cut off the next flight down to the kitchens. They were on a tiny square of landing and Luke knew there was a window at one end which they could smash and climb through to the mews below where the carriage and horses were kept. It was their only hope.

Feeling along the wall until he reached the window he broke the glass, using the curtains to protect his hands. Putting his coat over the sill to lessen the danger from splinters, he pushed Jack over, feet first, then held him out at full length and let him drop the short distance to the cobbled ground. Grabbing Sophia round the waist, he thrust her out after Jack in one swinging movement, shouting, 'Jump!' Then he threw himself out after them.

Sophia was on her feet, rubbing a painful arm. Her voice was a rasp, 'Are you hurt, Luke?'

He shook his head, coughing harshly. Allowing himself a second to gulp in much needed air, he swung Jack over his left shoulder. Sharp pains stabbed at his right shoulder and arm, the legacy of a childhood injury, now aggravated by the rescue.

Ignoring Sophia's pleas to be told if Lord Longbourne was alive, he ran with his charges through the back alleys until a churchyard was reached. A vandalized tomb, recently stripped of its dead by body snatchers, would have to do as a hiding place.

It would soon be dark. Luke prayed, as he eased his tortured lungs, that Sophia would stay securely out of sight, with Jack in her care, until he fetched his and Jack's things from their lodgings.

Then he must get them away to Cornwall.

Two

'Can I come in, m'dear?'

'Yes, of course, but I wish you wouldn't climb up the stairs by yourself, Bea.'

'Day I can't manage a few stairs, I'll let 'ee knaw!'

'I was only thinking of your arthritis,' said Kerensa, Lady Pengarron. The unconventional attitudes of Sir Oliver, Kerensa's husband, allowed the old nursemaid many liberties.

'Ahh! Thought I'd catch 'ee doin' that,' Beatrice rasped, staring cross-eyed at the miniature portrait Kerensa was holding. The painting was of Luke, heir to the Pengarron estate, who, twelve months ago, had left home in a temper and had only written twice of his whereabouts and circumstances, trusting all other communication to acquaintances who happened to be travelling from London to Cornwall. 'E'll be all right, my 'an'some. Aint nothin' you can do to bring un 'ome any quicker.'

'I know. But he'll come home for the baptism, won't he? Luke wouldn't miss such an important occasion for his brother's child, the first of the next generation. I know he and Kane weren't on good terms when last they met, but surely Luke's still not bearing a grudge.'

With her iron-grey hair escaping her lace cap, her apron coming loose, Beatrice's frailties, her weight and her fondness for the gin bottle gained mastery of her and she sank down on the blanket chest at the foot of the bed. Kerensa whipped back a supporting hand, for Beatrice might very well slap it hard.

Leaving Beatrice to reclaim her breath, Kerensa studied Luke's likeness again. He favoured his father in looks. The same dark brooding features and the same restlessness Oliver had borne when Kerensa first knew him. Luke's bearing was not as proud owing to his stiff right arm and shoulder, the result of an act of wilful disobedience. His eyes, deep-set and clear black, displayed the pain and frustration of sitting for Olivia, his elder sister, who had been forced to resort to an incredible array of inducements to get the portrait completed.

Luke's frustration came as no surprise; Kerensa knew her son through and through. It arose from his disability and being confined to a desk instead of being out and about doing the more masculine pursuits enjoyed by his father and brother. But there was something else portrayed in Olivia's clever brushstrokes: a soul-deep sadness. Guilt came to Kerensa, she had not noticed the sadness before.

The late afternoon sun beamed over where Beatrice slouched, banging a fist against her drooping bosom to loosen phlegm, intermittently humming and hawing to herself. A sharp goldenness strangely illuminated the peculiarly ugly slattern; a scene from myth and fable, incorporating dark suggestion, except Beatrice was on the side of goodness and happy endings.

'Goodness sake, stop worritin',' Beatrice swiped foul-looking dribble off her many chins with the sleeve of her none too clean dress. She smelled none too sweet either, from the sweat of her exertions and her reluctance to use the washbowl.

'Luke writ 'ee 'e was comin' 'ome didn't 'e? And bringing Jack along with un, and don't start off about 'e too. We all know you miss un as well. Grown men, the both. Time you let 'em be so.' Kerensa failed to hand Beatrice a handkerchief. 'And don't 'ee dare start yer fussin' over me!'

The observation that some of the elderly regressed to a second childhood passed through Kerensa's mind. 'We only received a relayed message from Luke, as you very well know.'

'Well, either they'll come or they won't.

14

Still be a baptism. Kane's boy's a dear little soul, ed'n 'e?'

Kerensa parried Beatrice's shrewd look. 'You got vexed with me yesterday for talking too much about Harry.'

'Well, if I can't say nothin' right for thee today, I'll be off and git meself a blessed drink. Not 'nough time t' yerself, that's yourn trouble. Too bleddy young.' Beatrice was off on one of her favourite themes. 'You was too young when Oliver forced thee to be 'is bride, youm too young to 'ave so many children and far too young to be a gran'-mothur! Youm still a little maid.'

'I've been a wife and mother these past four and twenty years. I'm approaching my forty-second birthday. Not too young to have a first grandchild.'

'And Luke and Jack and the rest of 'em–' Beatrice wagged a gnarled finger – 'baint too young to be leading their own lives.'

'Are you saying I interfere in their lives? Kane, Luke, Olivia and Kelynen? Cordelia too? Do you think I smother my dear little Samuel?' Kerensa was steeped in passion, dark colour creeping up her neck and flushing her finely sculptured face. No one but Beatrice would dare suggest she behaved in any way detrimental to her children or Oliver's niece, Cordelia, who lived at the manor. Wasn't a mother supposed to guide her offspring through the dangers and

15

vagaries of life, keep the peace between them, make sacrifices on their behalf? Worry herself half to death on occasion?

'Ais, I am. You brung Kane 'ome from the market as a tiny liddle ill-treated infant.' Beatrice counted on her worn-out fingers. 'You bore three 'ealthy babies, then lost dear baby Joseph t' the typhus, God rest un, then you brought forth young Samuel just two year ago, and you fuss and fret on 'em all day long! And yes, you fusses over that other liddle maid too. G' us some shade, m'dear, can't see nothin' in this brave sunlight.'

Kerensa usually had the curtains drawn at this time of day to preserve the ancient furniture, she drew them herself today.

'You can't expect me to surrender a close hold on Samuel yet.' Kerensa flaunted her rights with flowing sweeps of her hands. 'And you can't really say I smother him, Cordelia lays claim on him every chance she gets. And if I do happen to run a maternal eye over Jack, it's because he was just a twelve-year-old stable boy when I married Oliver. There was only you and Jack here when I first stepped over the threshold.'

Beatrice searched her mistress's face. Seventeen-year-old, working class Kerensa Trelynne could still be detected in every angle of her exquisite face and well-honed body. Her auburn hair shone with vitality, as did her grey-green eyes. She was forever

16

fresh and young, full of grace and wholesomely beautiful. She had a bold spirit which enriched, inspired and excited those in her company. Beatrice knew it was said in mock seriousness about herself that she should be dead and decently buried by now, but she reckoned she owed her nature-defying eighty-nine years to Kerensa's liveliness and devoted care. Her love for Kerensa outreached her affections for Sir Oliver or any of their children.

'All I can say tes a good job youm not with child again ... yet.' She grinned wickedly, indicating the huge four-poster bed, graced with sea-blue and jade coloured damask drapes. 'Spend too much time in 'ere. Need t' get abroad a lot more and do somethin' for yerself. Time you 'ad a life of yer own.'

Kerensa looked at the bed and was gloriously transported back to a few hours ago, when she had felt the passion and heat of Oliver's body, his perfect touch, his worship. Always his presence dominated every part of the manor house. She had come to love, deeply and passionately, the man who had arrogantly forced her into marriage over a parcel of land, as he had come to love her. Not yet had they reached a stage of comfortable companionship, of taking each other for granted.

'I've more than enough to keep me happy, Beatrice.'

17

'What? Visitin' yer children or folk like that thar dressed up mare, Lady Rachael Besweth'rick, or charity work. When are 'ee goin' t' do somethin' fer yourself?' In her vehemence Beatrice was spitting in all directions.

'There's nothing more I want out of life, Beatrice,' Kerensa said firmly. 'Now, my dear, before you settle and drop off to sleep I'd be grateful if you'd slip away somewhere else. Be careful of the stairs. I must see to the arrangements for the reception. Oliver's so pleased Kane's agreed to have it here instead of Vellanoweth.'

Beatrice was obliged to accept Kerensa's aid in the struggle to get to her feet. 'Ais, tes only right an' proper every Pengarron be brought back 'ere after the church. Course,' she added meaningfully, 'it'll mean Oliver 'aving one or two people under 'is roof 'e won't wish 'ere at all.'

'No one will be looking for trouble, certainly not Clem.'

Beatrice let out a snorting chuckle.

Kerensa closed the door and went to her dressing table. From a china trinket jar she produced a tiny ornate key. Listening first to be certain no one else was about to disturb her, she opened the bottom drawer where she kept the things she treasured. She pulled out a plain wooden box. Unlocking the lid she carefully took the contents into her hands.

Wild flowers of every season lay carefully preserved within the pages of a small book of bitter-sweet poetry. A folded kerchief, once belonging to a young farm labourer, and a lock of his blond hair delicately tied with blue ribbon. She brought these things to her nose. Could she still detect the essence of youth, hope and cherished dreams, when she had walked and talked on moor, cliff and seashore, and planned a different, perfect future with another man? Loved another man?

These were the love tokens Clem Trenchard, the son of an estate tenant farmer, had given her many years ago, when she had lived in Trelynne Cove. Oliver's selfish scheme to own the cove and make it part of Pengarron land and the cunning of Kerensa's criminal grandfather had destroyed their plans. Clem had since married twice, produced issue from both wives and moved far away in the county.

Beatrice was right; Oliver did not want Clem in his house. In fact he had already complained about it, but Clem was baby Harry's other grandfather; Kane was married to Jessica Trenchard, Clem's daughter. Clem had every right to attend the baptism and the reception. It was more than two years since Kerensa had last seen him, when they had said their private goodbyes in Trelynne Cove and he had moved to the parish of St Cleer, on the Bodmin Moor, with his then pregnant wife Catherine, to a farm of their own. Their twins, John and Flora had been born three weeks ahead of Samuel. Clem and Catherine were due to arrive today at the parsonage. Indeed, Harry's baptism was to be quite a family occasion. Catherine's brother, the Reverend Timothy Lanyon was to perform the ceremony, and he was married to Olivia, Kerensa's eldest daughter.

Kerensa gazed at her reflection in the mirror. Why had she kept these things Clem had given her for such a long time? Had she not placed him in a compartment in her heart labelled affection, a love lost and secretly treasured? It was time to let Clem's things go, not to throw them away, that was too final, a sort of betrayal. She would take them to Trelynne Cove, place the book of dried flowers and the kerchief in the sea to float away – give them to nature. The lock of blond hair? It would be hard to let this most intimate of gifts go. Was Clem's hair still as silky and fair? She would find a particular spot in the sand and bury it down deep, feel it was still close to her.

She focused on Luke again. Then fell into thinking how good it would be to see Clem once more.

There came a sudden thud, a bump and an exclamation of fright.

'Beatrice!' Kerensa bundled the love tokens back into the box and then the drawer. Feeling guilty for allowing the elderly maid to descend the stairs unaided, she dashed out of the room to help her.

Three

'Jack.'

'Yes, sir?'

'We'll start off again in an hour. It will be good, will it not, to have our feet back on Cornish soil?'

'Yes, sir.'

'Don't sound so dispirited. I've promised that everything will work out for you. And call me Luke, we've been through so much together I shall never see you as anything less but my most trusted friend.'

'You do me an honour, Luke.' From Jack's profound expression, it was obviously an honour he felt he deserved.

'Do eat. Granted, the fare doesn't look at all appetizing but it's the best we've had put in front of us for many a day.'

Luke and Jack, the Pengarron estate's head

groom, were breakfasting in a small inn, situated some distance from the main thoroughfares, on the outer reaches of Plymouth. The shabby confines reeked of stale ale, pipe smoke, the fug of tallow candles and body odours, but they were dim and appreciably private. The planked door was heavily scratched and pitted, as if recipient to a number of kicks and knife blades, and the two men warily scrutinized every coming and going. The patrons included workmen and farm labourers, the occasional sailor or merchant, and quiet travellers like themselves.

Luke and Jack kept a whispered conference, knowing that they themselves provided an extraordinary sight, both bearing bandages on their hands, scorched and blistered in the fire. Jack also had a dressing across his forehead.

'Has the lady risen from her bed?' Luke's voice was hoarse from the lingering effects of smoke.

'No. She spent the darkness in nightmares again. She's worn out and went straight to sleep after the maid brought up her breakfast.'

Jack gingerly broke off a chunk of tough, greyish-coloured bread but did not carry it to his mouth. Luke was devouring the cold meat and duck eggs like a hungry dog, but Jack had no appetite, although this had nothing to do with his split bottom lip and bruised chin. Every so often he was overcome by a wave of nausea, an outbreak of sweat. When he held his head up, the inadequacy of the dressing revealed a gash on his left temple, the flesh red and purple and swollen.

'Unfortunate for us to have had to pass so many days in the saddle, but to travel by post coach was a risk we could not take. We need to be circumspect.'

Jack remained quiet, still not eating but drinking from his tankard of porter.

Luke surveyed Jack's temporary disfigurements and the similar ones on his own hands. His chest ached from a cracked rib and he braced himself as the need to cough overwhelmed him. He wiped at his mouth in disgust. Would he never get this foul taste of smoke out of his throat? He sipped his porter, savouring this more soothing burn as he swallowed.

'My mama will not be pleased with me, Jack. When I talked you into accompanying me to London, I promised her I'd look after you. We're both returning exhausted and dishevelled and injured. I apologize for the miserable times you've had. Horses are your forte, not acting as a manservant ... and our other activities. I took you away from your little cottage a sober Methodist and have turned you into a hearty imbiber, and worse.

We planned to look over stock for the horse stud, and never did. Nor did I look up my cousins; Miss Cordelia will not be pleased with me.'

'You're not responsible for my conscience, Luke, and I enjoyed many a day in the capital. You didn't talk me into anything, I wanted the adventure. And we promised her ladyship t' look after each other.' Jack's thoughts drifted. 'She's going to ask questions, and so is Sir Oliver.'

'I know, I know. Stop worrying. They can't do anything to us, we're grown men, for God's sake! It's vital we keep to our story, Jack.' Tension made Luke's stiff shoulder ache. He wheeled it as much as the disability allowed, and rubbed it near the collar bone.

'I'm not about to forget a thing. A nobleman and all his servants are dead. Butchered.' Jack's eyes, nearly as dark, and equally as drawn and under-shadowed as Luke's, gravely indicated the poky, bleak bedroom directly above them, and he shuddered, dropping his voice even lower. 'And Sophia was left to burn alive. We should never've got involved with those people.'

'It was I who got involved with them, not you. The fact is Sophia's alive and practically unscathed. As for ... he knew he had a death sentence over him, and of his own making. I warned him not to make threats against those particular gentlemen. It's terrible

24

about the others, but all we can do now is put it behind us. And Sophia must never forget to use her real name, Alicia, from now on.'

'She won't. We both have a new name,' Jack said sombrely, wiping sweat off the back of his neck and gulping down the last of his beer.

Leaning forward Luke touched the arm of the servant, some fourteen years older than he, who had helped him learn to ride as a boy, and was now his confidante. 'You are pleased about that? History has it that you were only a thieving urchin, with nothing save a first name when my father gave you a home and employment. Now you have a legal identity. Does Jack Rosevear not suit you?'

'That part suits me.'

'Damn it, Jack.' Luke shifted uncomfortably. 'You're what, thirty-six? Have you never wanted a wife, children, the regular comforts of a woman?'

'Not this way.' Jack massaged his tired eyes.

'I'm sorry about that but there was nothing else to be done. We both swore to Lord Longbourne that if anything untoward happened to him we'd protect her. The lady is with child, and she has nothing and no one except for the two of us. I couldn't marry her myself, any wife I take would be noted in high society and it might soon be realized who she really was. Granted, you're worlds apart, but so were my parents and their marriage became successful, you'll not find a happier couple.'

'There's no comparison with my arranged marriage, Luke.'

'And yet you have a care for her.' Luke's eyes glinted over the rim of his tankard.

For the first time in over a week Jack worked up a smile. 'You know I do. But she'd never have married me if it weren't for her predicament. She might end up resenting it. I'm afraid she'll feel trapped.'

'You're worrying unnecessarily, she took little persuading to agree to my suggestion.'

'She was in shock, Luke. I know only too well what can happen when you're not in full possession of your mind. I've let the devil into mine, done so many things against my nature and my faith.' Jack ducked his head when one of the Methodist evangelists who had come into the inn caught his eye. 'And it don't rest easy now I'm nearing home.'

'Alicia has lived in humble circumstances before. You know this, she confided in you during those tête-à-têtes you shared with her.'

'Being an impoverished squire's daughter is a lot different to being a groom's wife.'

'But she won't be living in poverty as your wife, Jack. You have my word all will be well. Just leave it to me. You do trust me?'

26

'You know I trust you with my life.'

'Well, then. Now rouse Mrs Rosevear and let us be on our way.'

While Jack mounted the dirt-laden stairs to awaken his bride, Luke paid the bill and went outside to wait for the horses to be saddled. He would not go back inside. He craved fresh air and open spaces for evermore, he felt, after spending the ten days since the fire choking on the effects of smoke in his lungs, and staying in scabby accommodation.

Their progress to Cornwall had been slow. Jack had found riding difficult at first, the terrified and grief-stricken lady had needed comfort. Luke had been terrified himself that those who had committed the arson in the quiet select house in St James's Street would discover that Sophia, witness to their crime, was alive and slay her, and he and Jack also for saving her. Someone from the Society would have stayed and watched the house burning, would have seen him and Jack forcing an entrance. It may have been noticed that he had returned to his lodgings and left again almost immediately, taking his and Jack's luggage with him. Apart from his disorderly appearance, hopefully, no one would think this particularly unusual, as it was well known in the circles they had frequented that he and his servant were about to return home for his nephew's baptism. Pray God, no one from that unforgiving, seedy set saw him and his little party after that.

With luck, Sophia would be thought to have perished, as he had planned when giving her necklace to the maid. Luke had no regrets over his part in Sophia's survival. Seldom had he met a more likeable, courteous, sympathetic young woman. He had enjoyed her company in London, and in the hours Jack had been charged in escorting her hither and thither, so had he.

In the light of day, far away from the murder scene, it almost seemed an horrific dream. Cautiously, for he must, Luke took a breath of air and looked about.

Mid spring. It used to be his favourite time of year: flower-sprigged verges and hedges; benevolent sun; alluring skies and vibrant clouds; wildlife astir; promises afloat; treasures beckoning. Feet away was a humpbacked stone bridge coated with emerald-green algae, atop a swift river. Two pink-faced children were sitting on the lush grassy bank playing with a ginger kitten and a piece of string. A delightful scene. Something his sister would long to capture on canvas. But Luke gleaned no pleasure from it.

Nothing held any value, had any reason or prospect for him, not since the bitter quarrel with his elder, adopted, brother, when reality had broken in, mocking him as to what he truly was. Heir to a title and a prosperous estate maybe, he was also a cripple, lacking in manhood, denied the coveted regimental career his father and brother had taken for granted, doomed to light tasks and writing reports. Half measures, ultimate non-accomplishment.

A long day's ride and by nightfall he would be home to familiar sights, familiar pursuits, monotony and predictability. Home, to the family bosom, to his parents' blissfully happy marriage, to siblings with two healthy arms going about their usual splendid business.

He would be expected to croon over Kane's child. Damn Kane, for being so fulfilled. Kane had his own expanding farm and a wife whose free spirit suited him perfectly. Damn Kane, for pointing out that day he could have something similar if he stopped behaving like a spoiled brat and channelled his restless energy into something more fitting than gambling and womanizing. Kane, whose real parents had been an unmarried brothel bitch and a deserting wayfarer, had no right to speak so. Luke would not tolerate a recurrence.

Then there was Olivia, the elder to him by one year. She also had everything she wanted, including a doting husband who indulged her foolish passion for painting.

And sixteen-year-old Kelynen, his father's favourite, who toted an annoying boisterous dog everywhere she went. Beatrice would be being Beatrice: drinking, soothsaying, smelling, swearing. There would be the same boring obedient servants and submissive tenants. The same batch of young ladies ruthlessly parading their accomplishments before him in the hope of becoming his wife. A return to all the old ways and soul-draining sameness.

There was really nothing for him to do at home. He would likely be an old man before he came into his inheritance, and even then there would be no challenge left for him. In the few years before his marriage, his father had rebuilt the estate from near ruin, and although Sir Oliver was many years senior to his mother, he wore them like a man of youth and vigour.

The one dream Luke kept in his heart, that did not involve the Pengarron estate or any of his expected duties, and which only Jack knew about, would be ridiculed if he ever brought it to light. He could not bear that.

Ignoring the anguish of his burns, Luke felt about in his coat pocket and brought out a letter from Cordelia. It would be good to see his little cousin again. He had missed her, but pray God she had found herself a husband and wasn't about to resume shadowing his heels like a faithful puppy.

The adolescent playfulness and demands of a puppy could so easily become tiresome.

Hell's teeth! Hot-faced and grinding his teeth, he stalked on to the hump of the bridge and stared down into the waters. They swirled bracken-brown, thick and dull. No bed of weeds or stones was visible, nor the dark reddish earth of this fertile county of Devon. Why not spare himself all those naked grey years ahead? Leap in, let the river carry him away to be dashed to death on some blessed rocks or to drown in its deceptive depths. He was going to drown anyway. In despondency. In nothingness.

He was going home. To the same old frustrations and his sense of worthlessness.

Four

With a sense of irony, Clem Trenchard looked out of the window of the ivy-clad parsonage at Perranbarvah. Before his marriage to the parson's sister he would have had to enter by the back door, and this was the very room where Kerensa had stayed in the month leading up to her enforced marriage. He had spent many desperate hours staring up at this small-paned window pining for her.

Clem heaved the window up on its protest-ing sashes and stuck his blond head out. The smell of the sea. Wonderful! How he had missed it. Gazing down the steep hill to the fishing village, he listened to the steady drag of the tide creaming over and then receding from the shore. Gulls chattered and showed off their expertise on wing. He had missed the gulls too, but the moor he now lived on offered an interesting variety of bird life.

Thanks to the gentle touch of the sun the grey-green waters were sparkling, flirting with the senses. See, look, the calm English Channel seemed to be hinting, my depths are as safe as a harbour on which to make a living. The inhabitants of the tiny cob cottages below knew its deception. A month ago, those artful waves had turned into an unnegotiable monster, encouraging its cruel sister, the south-west wind, to surge up into a tempest out at the Ray Pits, where it teased and taunted three of Perranbarvah's vessels for several maniacal hours, before finally crushing and splintering them into oblivion. Only two crew members from one of the luggers had been rescued by those frantic, foolhardy and courageous enough to sweat out the storm and attempt a rescue.

Clem heard the crows cawing in the churchyard. Here, here, the black harbingers of doom gloated; here lie the smashed putrid bodies of the six who were recovered. Clem hated crows, the dark bastard-birds who ate the seeds of his crops, who fed on the corpses of his prey-slain beasts; given the opportunity these crows here would devour the remains in the graves they were swanking over.

Timothy Lanyon had written to his sister about the tragedy, and Catherine had wanted to leave the moor and offer comfort to the sorrowing widows and orphans. But that province was Mrs Lanyon's now. Did Kerensa's daughter do well in this respect? Certainly, Kerensa would have made haste to the bereaved. Beautiful, compassionate Kerensa, her arms held out to soothe, to ease the burden. Such a glorious compensation.

The luggers, thirty to forty feet in length, that had survived the storm were shored dejectedly on the shingle. Fresh paint gleamed on the repaired timbers. Clem knew all the folk he could see below going about their usual business, dressed in black. The fishermen were preparing for the night's launch, tarring ropes, mending nets, stowing baskets, checking line. Another trip to the Ray Pits. Clem sensed them praying for their safety and good catches. Many in the small fishing community held to the fervour of the Methodist connection. Their faith and a certain amount of optimism pointed to their expectation being high, for added to the fine weather there was a 'fair old sea running'. Their grief and depression, however, were almost tangible, rising mournfully on the salt-laden air.

The bedroom door opened and Catherine joined him, placing her arm round his waist, staying silent. She was a handsome woman with snow-white skin, a charitable heart and a quiet charm. She overlooked Clem's melancholic moods and honoured his frequent need for solitude.

They joined in respectful homage to those who had lost their lives and those below who had lost their kin.

Finally, Clem said, 'It's all so very cruel, may God have mercy. Are the twins settled in the nursery, Cathy?'

'Yes, my dear, they're both asleep at last. I've ordered Lydia not to leave them. They would have stayed settled at home.' Not a reproach, but in the short time since arriving in her former home, Catherine now wished they had not brought the children with them for the forthcoming event. She felt a need to keep track of Clem while back in this parish, where Kerensa Pengarron lived.

In the two years at Greystone's Farm, Clem had rarely mentioned her name, yet Catherine knew, that all too often, she was inside his head. Already, she felt the invisible bond that he shared with the flame-haired lady of the manor placing a stronger grip on her husband. Clem had been so eager to come. Instead of being slightly distant, closed and guarded, he shone, he was animated. Catherine tried not to resent it – she had not entered this marriage blind to Clem's yearnings – but she wanted every bit of him to herself.

'I like my children near me,' Clem said.

Catherine wound her littlest finger around his, just one of her many gestures of understanding. She took comfort in his statement. Clem was a loyal family man and she was the mother of two of his children. 'The nursery is very well done, no doubt my brother will be hoping for a child of his own soon.'

'Pleased to be back here, are you?'

'It's very pleasant. My room was the one next to this. I enjoyed the sea view.'

'Miss it?'

Catherine took heart. He had lost interest in the view and was looking steadily at her. 'Not particularly. I swapped the view for the fields and valley of Trecath-en Farm and then for the beauty of the moors. I have you and my beloved family and feel myself the most fortunate of women. Have you missed Trecath-en, Clem?'

'No, but I've missed the sea.'

'You must take the opportunity of its nearness.' But not Trelynne Cove, she wanted to add. It was a special place to *her*.

'I will. What think you of the bed? Shall we

knock two of the farm's bedrooms into one and buy such a giant?'

Clem was gently pressing his fingers on the softness of Catherine's neck. With nothing to do until they were due to dine with Jessica and Kane in the evening, he felt a desire for his wife. Intimacy between them was long overdue. The twins' recent attack of croup, and the unexpected gales of two weeks ago, resulting in damage to farm buildings and early crops, had seen to that. And Catherine was watching him, trying as she sometimes did to get inside his thoughts; she knew the reason for his lighter spirit. Making love to her would put her off guard, release him, at least for a while, from her probings. 'We're also s'posed to be resting after our journey.'

Catherine moved the tiniest distance away from him. 'Clem, my brother and sister-in-law are at home. What if they hear us?'

'What if they do?'

He was nuzzling behind her ears, his breath inflaming her skin and her inner regions, distressingly so. Catherine was elated that his thoughts and desire were for her. She desperately loved this good-looking man of the lower orders, who sometimes liked to tease her with his roughcast ways, but she was a creature of right, of etiquette, of modesty.

'Well, I—'

Clem took her to the bed.

'Clem, don't you think we should wait?'

Smiling, he threw his riding coat to the floor, having no care for the finer clothes he wore from the elevated state of this second marriage. 'I want you now, Cathy.'

His hands were on her and he was kissing her mouth.

Dazed by his intensity, she allowed him to position her on the bed and lie over her and lift her skirts. While he was freeing himself and seeking her, she was praying the bed would not creak and incriminate them. The moment they were joined as husband and wife, when she indeed had all of him to herself, she gave way to his dominance and set her passion for him free.

'You are going abroad, Clem?' Olivia Lanyon enquired, having followed him to the parsonage stables.

'I am. If it's agreeable with you. I thought t' look at Trecath-en Farm, spy on the new tenant, see what he's doing with my old fields.'

'You're perfectly free to go where you will. I am concerned only that you are comfortable. With Catherine still resting, I'm unable to ask her.'

Clem viewed Olivia with impatience while enjoying the spectacle of her standing quite still, allowing the wind to catch her red hair. She was so much like her mother in

37

colouring and femininity, but the resemblance ended there. She had Pengarron's overbearing stance and disdain in almost every gaze. He had heard her giving orders to the staff in a curt manner, flustering the housekeeper, Nancy Wills, who was a nice little body. Catherine thought her selfish, she complained after every letter of Timothy's that it seemed all Olivia wanted to do was paint – hardly a suitable pastime for a vicar's wife.

Giving her a short bow, Clem mounted the black stallion – a superior piece of Pengarron horseflesh – brought to him by the parsonage groom. He was allowing his own mare, Tally, to graze in the parson's paddock.

Nearly two miles on and he made the border, a high hedgerow of earth, rock and hawthorn which ran between Trecath-en and Ker-an-Mor, the Pengarron home and stud farm. Honeysuckle weaved in joyful disorder through the long grasses, as did cow parsley, pink ragged robin and nettle flower. He felt unemotional to be back on his old land, this wasn't what he had been loathe to leave behind.

He raised his wide-shouldered, lean body in the saddle to inspect the fields. Oats, barley, wheat and animal feed were in their infancy, not tall enough yet to be swayed in the light winds, but healthier in comparison to those of his own fields, advanced more by the kinder climate here in Mount's Bay, tucked in as it was on the south coast. Barring treacherous weather, in a few weeks the fields would be aburst with harvesters – men, women and children; tinners, fisherfolk, drifters, locals without permanent jobs, earning a little something to offset their families' hunger pangs. His brother-in-law would count his tithes and the conceited owner and landlord of the estate would count his profits. Damn him.

Clem trotted down Trecath-en's steep valley. He stared at the silent trio of elm trees on the river bank, where he had seduced and impregnated his first wife, Alice, once Kerensa's personal maid. He had come to love Alice, buried now in Perranbarvah's churchyard, although not in the passionate way he had, and still did, love Kerensa. His feelings for Catherine were not destined to eclipse those either. Nothing ever would.

Before Alice's time, he had sat under these elm trees with Kerensa planning their future, holding hands and kissing chastely. It had been enough just to be with her. They would have had many children. Been so happy. Together always and forever.

That last day, saying goodbye in Trelynne Cove, he had asked her to remember him with more than affection. He had not given her time to answer before striding away, his heart in pieces again, for the second time in his life to face the future without her, pretending to himself that his pregnant wife and the new farm miles away on the moor would finally purge his pain and sense of isolation. But without Kerensa, his soul was doomed to grieve and fester in bitterness, at times with hatred, for the man who had stolen Kerensa away from him.

He lived with a little hope. Kerensa had embraced him warmly during their last meeting, clung to his hand until the last moment. Did she still love him? So many times she had told him that she always would.

There was no point in looking at the farm buildings. He had chosen to leave them and move on with his life. It had become unbearable to dwell any longer under Oliver Pengarron's sufferance and egotistical, watchful black eyes. Let the new tenant, Bennets was his name, so Jessica had written, keep his privacy. Clem missed Jessica so much. He had seen her only a handful of times since vacating Trecath-en, on brief visits to her home when he was sure Pengarron must have known of his imminent arrival and ensured Kerensa would not be there. Jessica had come only once to his farm, on Catherine's confinement. Thank God, she had married Kane Pengarron, their baby gave him reason to see Kerensa again, and he liked Kane; he had no Pengarron blood in him.

Heading the stallion back up the valley, he rehearsed what he would say to Kerensa when next they met, in the little stone church at Perranbarvah. For Catherine's sake and to put Pengarron off his guard, he would be respectful and discreet. Kerensa would know how he felt about her by the secret messages in his eyes.

At the top of the valley, a man on an equally good horse was closing the boundary gate. The stud breeder. The Lord of the Manor. His daughter Kelynen was with him, her black retriever bounding along close behind.

The two men glowered at each other in mutual despite.

'You are trespassing on my property, Trenchard, and have a care with that horse,' Sir Oliver Pengarron said coldly.

Clem lifted his tricorn hat, inclined his head a fraction. 'My humble apologies, Sir Oliver,' he replied insincerely. 'Good day to you, Miss Kelynen.'

The girl, whom he had delivered in his and Alice's bedroom, after Kerensa's premature labour, following an attack by footpads on her and Jack near Trecath-en, was fully a woman now. Not much like either parent in looks, she bore an air of confidence as befitted her status, but not, Clem was pleased to see, the boorish condescension of her father.

He had always been closely interested in the child, baptised with the name Kerensa had asked him to choose for her. Pengarron and Kerensa had been briefly estranged at the time, and Pengarron only ever called her Shelley, derived from the French name Michelle he had chosen for her, on his return from Brittany.

'Good day, Clem,' she replied politely, then glanced at her father as if to read his thoughts.

'Shelley, you go on ahead,' Oliver said firmly. 'I shall be but a minute.'

When she had moved out of earshot, he turned his sharp eyes on Clem. 'Be sure you conduct yourself appropriately under my other daughter's roof, Trenchard.' Oliver appraised his old rival's fine apparel and confident manner. 'You look well. Moorland air obviously agrees with you. How goes your wife's and your son's farm?'

Clem's face clouded over. The bastard. Bastard-crow! So, it was straight in on the attack. To belittle him with the fact that it was Philip's wrestling purses and the one thousand pounds settled on Catherine which had bought him his new position.

After ten disrespectful seconds, Clem spat, 'Harry's as much my grandson as yours.'

'He bears my name.' Oliver smiled grimly under constricted eyes.

'Even so, the Almighty won't hold back his

42

angels from watching over him. And,' Clem also had a sword with which to pierce the other man's heart, 'he has my blood in him, not a drop of yours, Kane being sired elsewhere.'

Oliver rested his large hands on the pommel of his saddle and leaned slightly forward. 'Kane has done well in his own right. You never will, Trenchard. You'll never have the means to get anything you really want.'

So, as always, everything came back to Kerensa. Clem recalled again her last show of affection to him.

Slowly replacing his hat, nudging his mount with his knees to move along, Clem mouthed in a scathing manner, 'See you in church, m'lord. My regards to Kerensa.' He heard Pengarron's angry intake of breath and laughed to himself.

Oliver stole upstairs to the master bed-chamber. He had a present for Kerensa, an exquisite diamond bracelet to give her on the day of the baptism, to wear as part of their own private celebration of the event.

He smiled at finding the bottom drawer of her dressing table slightly open and things protruding from it. Kerensa kept the things she cherished in there and had likely hidden away a gift for him. He pulled the drawer out further to rearrange the things and close it properly. He did not want any surprise she had in store for him to be spoiled for her.

A river of shock, distaste, hurt and betrayal rushed up his spine.

It was unbelievable! Lying crammed in amid the miscellany of empty perfume bottles, good-luck charms, babies' milk teeth and first-hair clippings, was a box, and in the same way in which he had found the drawer, it was not quite closed. Something fair was sticking out of it at the corner. The tips of a lock of hair. No one in the family had such colour hair. There was only one explanation for this and it sent the world he thought he had delighted in for so many years of devoted love and honour, crashing down, splintering his heart. Reducing him to a fool, a blind, deceived fool. Other things that complemented the lock of hair were also in the box, things which he had come across during the first fateful year of his marriage, while nursing Kerensa, fearing he was losing her to foul-water poisoning.

For all these years, Kerensa had kept the things Clem Trenchard had given her as a lovesick youth. No, damn him! Trenchard had never been lovesick. He had loved Kerensa in the same way as he did, with a man's love, all-enduring, uncompromising, everlasting. And Kerensa had been in love with him. Still was, if she had needed to keep his love gifts and take them out and look at them.

Had she been holding them, just a while ago, to her breast? Regretting the outcome of the past? Wanting Trenchard, longing for him? Just how much was Kerensa looking forward to seeing her old love at their grandson's baptism?

He went to his dressing room and threw the bracelet into a closet, then strode downstairs. He knew where Kerensa would be at this time of day.

She was in her private sitting room. Busy with the menu for the baptism, she put it aside at once and rose to share an embrace with him. They sat on the sofa.

Kerensa gazed at him. He was holding her very tight.

'The Bennets family are all well.' He anticipated her first enquiry as to how his day had gone. Kerensa felt she had a duty for the welfare of the entire parish and estate. 'They send their thanks for the lace you sent over for the elder daughter's wedding.'

'Let's hope all goes well for the ceremony next month. Where's Kelynen? The dressmaker arrived for a fitting for her dress for the baptism, but as usual she had slipped away to be with you,' Kerensa said vexedly, yet could not help smiling.

'You are so good not to begrudge the time she spends with me. She's taken a kitten to the hut. It was blinded in one eye after an

45

unwise encounter with one of those fierce cats that always seem to be about Trecathen. Jacob Bennets was about to put it out of its misery, but Shelley pleaded for it. With the help of one of Beatrice's potions the wound should soon heal. She'll have to find a home for it elsewhere, of course, I can't be doing with constantly watering eyes.' Oliver looked thoughtful. 'Our daughter is full of compassion as well as being intelligent and talented. She takes a keen interest in all the affairs of the estate. She could very likely run it as efficiently as any man.'

'I know, Oliver. Beloved, I can't see why she shouldn't do something to help run the estate. It's what she wants.' Kelynen had implored Kerensa that very morning to impress this fact upon her father.

'Luke will be home shortly and it would not do for him to see his younger sister, barely out of childhood, taking over his occupation. We may well have a hard task getting him to settle as it is, if his mood has not improved.'

'But otherwise you'd have no objections?' Kerensa ran a delicate finger along Oliver's strong jaw, then down his throat and lower still.

He caught her finger. 'I haven't given it much thought.'

Kerensa smiled into his eyes. 'But you will?'

'I shall consider Shelley's daydream. Now, let us speak of other things. I've just had strong words with Michael and Conan. They've allowed Jack's high standard in the stable yard to slip disgracefully. I've given them until the end of the day to rectify matters. Thank goodness Jack will soon be back.'

'You're sure of that, Oliver? You've received word?'

'No, but Luke had better not scorn his obligation to be at Harry's ceremony or delay much longer in returning Jack to his duties.'

'If only he'd kept in touch more,' Kerensa lamented. 'When, at last, he comes home I hope he'll not be in an ill humour. I hate it when our children are on bad terms.'

'Kane will not allow his brother's churlishness to continue, but it is to be hoped Luke will have had a change of heart. In that, I mean, that he'll have purged his restlessness and is ready to resume his duties.'

'We can only wait and see, but let's be hopeful. Beatrice implored me today not to fret so much over the children. I suppose she's right.'

'Is she? Should a woman not be concerned almost entirely with her family?'

Again there was that sharpness and Kerensa eyed him quizzically. What had happened to put him in a bad frame of mind? Oliver was a complicated man, given to rapid mood changes. He seemed always to have too much energy, which he channelled into hard work and advancement, or social activities, where he was happy to mix either with gentry or people of Kerensa's own class. He ran the estate with precision, endurance, and a keen sense of duty, and expected everyone else, no matter how lowly their position, to do likewise. While he overlooked the occurrence of a poached rabbit to feed the empty bellies of a deserving family, he never ever suffered a fool, a liar or a lazy workman, but she thought the misdemeanour of the stable boys unlikely to be the cause of his present ill humour. He seemed cool towards her. So far he had offered none of his usual kisses and endearments.

'Speaking of Beatrice, she slipped on the stairs today. She landed on her backside, and thankfully that's well padded, but I think it's time she had a room downstairs before she has a serious accident.'

'Good idea.'

'Oliver, are you tired?'

'Not at all. Why do you ask?'

'I just thought – it doesn't matter.' He seemed to be waiting ... She asked, 'Has anything of particular interest happened today?'

He stared straight into her eyes. 'I saw Clem Trenchard. Yes,' he repeated, piercing her again with his black eyes, 'I saw Trenchard.'

Kerensa thought she knew the reason for his disquiet. 'Oh, where?' She tried to sound impartial, but felt a flicker of excitement at the thought of Clem actually being here in Mounts Bay. She regretted the emotion, for the severity of Oliver's gaze told her he had sensed it.

He answered as if he had something bitter in his mouth. 'He was skulking about Trecath-en Farm, trespassing as if the Almighty Himself had given him permission to do whatever he wished.'

Her next question was asked a little anxiously. 'Did unkind words pass between you?'

'Naturally.'

'Oliver, I don't want there to be an atmosphere on the day of the baptism for Kane's, Jessica's and Harry's sakes.'

'Then you must hope Trenchard's behaviour gives no rise to unpleasantness.'

A few minutes ago, as if touching something vile and contaminated, he had secured the farmer's lock of hair back in its hiding place and closed the dressing-table drawer firmly. He would not reveal to Kerensa that he knew of her secret hoard. But he would be watching her, to see if, indeed, he had the need to feel as devastated as he now did.

He smiled at her, as if he was as content as when he had risen that morning. 'Now, my dear love, how long until dinner?'

Five

Hours later as dusk fell, three riders, weary, hungry and travel-stained, hobbled into the stable yard.

The two men of the party looked all about them, bewildered.

'Where is everyone?' Luke said.

Jack could see enough in the thickening gloom to be satisfied that everything outside the stables was in good order. Not that at this moment he cared much. Was it really only a year ago he had mounted a Pengarron mare and ridden off with Luke, excited by the fact he was to see something of life at last? Luke, accusing him of being an old spinster and a dullard, had roused his sense of adventure. By God, how he wished he had not.

Yet he could not really say he wished that, otherwise he would not have met Alicia.

It was a relief to toss away the reins tormenting his blistered hands, and place his feet on familiar ground. Approaching his

50

wife, he gently rubbed her gloved hand.

Her body snapped upright. 'What? Where are we?'

Luke, breathing in the tangy-sweet air, heard the fear, the miscomprehension in her voice. 'We're safe at last, Alicia, and thankfully at the end of our journey. We'll go inside and eat and get warm.'

Michael and Conan, who had drifted off to sleep due to their extra labours, crept forth from their accommodation over the stables.

'Hello, who's there?' Michael, the slightly braver of the two, and Jack's acknowledged next in command, called out cautiously.

'What the hell have you been about? Come and take our mounts at once,' Luke snarled at their half-hidden figures. 'Is his lordship at home?'

'Oh, Mister Luke! Jack!' Michael simpered, leaping into full view and bowing again and again. Conan followed, thrusting his own head down low. Michael said, 'We're some sorry not t' be here ready for 'ee, sir. And no, sir, his lordship's over the stud, for a foaling. Her ladyship and Miss Kelynen and Miss Cordelia are gone too.'

'Thank God for that,' Luke rasped under his breath. He broke into a fit of coughing. The two stable boys watched wide-eyed, as he hacked and gasped for a full minute while Jack vigorously patted his back.

Next instant, Luke was barking huskily,

'What are you two standing about for? These horses are not in good form but do your best for them. Tomorrow, put the pony out to pasture. Don't you dare send anyone to inform Sir Oliver we're here. Come along Jack, bring Mrs Rosevear into the house.'

'Yes, sir,' Jack reverted to the use of Luke's proper title in the presence of the stable boys. He made no response when Michael said he was glad to see him back safely. He would rather have gone straight to his cottage, reached by a short walk behind the orchards, but he knew Luke would not be argued with. He gave his arm to Alicia. Statuesque, but like a wraith in the dark, she could only stumble a few steps. Luke helped guide her along to a door which opened on to the long corridor that ran to the kitchens.

'Mrs O'Flynn! Come at once, if you please!' He shouted for the housekeeper, risking his sore throat. 'We're in need of assistance.'

Polly O' Flynn, plain clothed, steadfast and efficient, wife of the estate gamekeeper and head forester, was there in a moment. Luke noticed she had stepped into middle age during his absence. Her cotton-capped hair was now completely grey, her jawline no longer firm, a pound or two of weight was added about her hips. A strange melancholy seeped into him. It was only a little thing to see a change in a servant, but it was more

52

than just change. It was ageing, and it was irrevocable. What other unpleasant surprises lay in wait for him?

'God in heaven is merciful!' Polly exclaimed, bending at the knee. 'Her ladyship will be that pleased you're both home safely, and in time for Master Harry's baptism. I suggest you go along to the library, Mr Pengarron, there's a fire lit against the chill in there. I'll see to your needs at once.'

She turned to Jack. 'Your cottage is in proper order, Jack, all ready for your return.'

Luke thanked Polly, who hastened away, then he had to wait for Beatrice, dangerously out of breath, to come upon him and his party. She instantly gleaned the story from the men's appearance and their near-fainting female companion.

' 'Ad a feelin' you wus about to spring yourself on us. 'Ome at last then, and brung trouble with 'ee too by the look of it. Tes some wonderful to see 'ee though, boy.'

He refused to be hugged by her, something he had never done before. 'You can see the state we're in. Bring medicines to the library.'

Unused to this sort of rebuff the old woman was perplexed for a time then, grumbling about her 'poor ole legs' and declaring ' 'e should've said please!', she shuffled away to her newly allotted ground-floor room.

53

'This way,' Luke said testily, heading off a disapproving look from Jack, who saw his treatment of Beatrice, at the least, as a woeful lack of good manners. Sometimes Jack's correctness and honesty made Luke feel small and worthless. 'We need to get cleaned up before my parents arrive back.'

Fronting a line of servants, primed by her to be unobtrusive, Polly knocked on the library door and entered. Like the entire house, the room was panelled in dark Pengarron oak. Cosy and draughtproof, furnished for comfort rather than ostentation, the room was lined from floor to ceiling with books, on any subject that had taken the family's fancy.

Luke had ordered many volumes himself: classical literature, medical and natural history, diaries, mythology, poetry, the arts, philosophy, theology. He had always meant to wade through them, but rarely had he taken a book off the carefully catalogued shelves. Now he observed them with interest and a sort of hunger. They would be very useful, if only ... No, it was best he kept those thoughts, that longing, at the back of his mind – it would be deemed a silly venture.

Hot beef broth, bread, cheeses, cold meats and puddings, cordials, red wine and canary were laid out on the long table. Luke rectified his earlier misdemeanour by enquiring after the health of Polly's young son, Shaun, then resuming his acquaintance with the manor's cook, Ruth, and head housemaid, Esther King, and Cherry, his former nurse-maid and now young Samuel's. He allowed Polly to introduce a couple of new under-lings, a boot boy and a footman. Jack gave all four women a warm hug.

When they had gone to their usual duties only Polly remained, and moving about economically, placed more logs on the blaze. Surreptitiously, she eyed the woman Mr Luke had referred to as Mrs Rosevear, where she reclined a few feet away on a sofa, which had been pushed up close to the huge stone fireplace. Cushions had been placed behind her head and shoulders and under her feet. The men had laid their coats over her, but still she shivered. There were no apparent wounds on her person but she rubbed at her right arm as if it troubled her.

'I'll fetch some blankets for the lady, sir.'

Jack stood with his back to the fire, hands clasped behind him, until the heat was too fierce for his scorched flesh to bear. His moderate, rather narrow face wore an ex-pression of trepidation. He and Alicia being here was not sensible. Her presence should be kept low-key.

'Perhaps I should take Alicia away with me now, Luke.'

Helping himself to wine, Luke gave a shrug.

'Whose is this house, Jack? Luke?' Alicia whispered, incapable of a higher tone, for the harrowing episodes of the last week and more had sapped her strength.

'We're in my father's house, Pengarron Manor,' Luke replied soothingly. 'Jack will take you to your new home shortly. It's small and barely adequate compared to what you are used to, but I'll arrange to have every comfort put in place without delay.'

'You are too kind, Luke. You also, Jack. I can never repay you both for all you've done for me. All you tried to do for Alex,' her voice faltered and Luke shied away, grim faced.

Polly came back with soft wool blankets and traded them for the men's coats. She detected the smell of smoke on them. Mrs Rosevear was wearing a plain dress and a brown cloak. The hood was pushed back and her hair, shining honey-gold in the flame light, was breaking free from a neckerchief Polly recognized as one of Jack's. Her shoes were at odds with her clothes, made from some fragile gold-coloured stuff and high-heeled, more suitable for a smart social occasion. Her face, half hidden by a delicatel y shaped raised hand, appeared neither commonplace nor noble. She appeared to be on the early side of twenty. Who was she with? Both Mr Luke and Jack seemed familiar with her.

'Will Mrs Rosevear require anything, sir?

Nightclothes? Help in retiring?'

'Clothing, yes. See to it personally, please, Polly.' Luke's severe bearing forbade further probing.

Polly left again and Luke swore profanely at another knock on the door. Esther King carried in Beatrice's box of medicines and the old woman followed eventually, puffing and blowing and complaining, 'All this biznuzz will be the end of me.'

'I'll tell you all about our misfortunes on the morrow, Bea, I promise. And if you see my mama before I do, I forbid you to say anything to her. You've no excuse, you're sober for once.'

'Damned cheek!' Beatrice hid her hurt by twisting up her ugly face and pointing an accusing finger. 'Goodness sake! When 'ave I ever spoke out of turn, eh? Tension enough in the 'ouse as tes. Youm only goin' to add to it.'

'What's the matter?' Luke demanded.

'Find out fer yerself.'

Luke and Jack exchanged wry looks. Beatrice hesitated. Luke and Jack had always been on close terms but this new affinity suggested something deeper, deeds done and secrets shared.

Luke went to the door, opened it for Beatrice, then lowered his head to kiss her on the cheek when she got there. Pacified, for in all probability Luke would confide in her more than in his parents, she shuffled off down the corridor, muttering to herself.

Jack looked down at Alicia. Her eyes, glittering like huge dark gems in the firelight, betrayed perplexity and anxiety. For much of their long journey, made arduous by their aches and pains and need for secrecy, she had slept or had longed for sleep. Luke had seen fit to drug her against hysterics for the first part of the way. He had done this against Jack's protests. Had he known Alicia as well as Jack did he would not have used this resort.

Alicia, or Sophia Glanville, as he had known her for many months, was strong and brave, intelligent and resourceful. And tender-hearted, kind and friendly, and a good and willing listener. Jack had fallen in love with her some time ago.

He crouched down beside her, tucking the blankets around her more securely. 'Don't worry about Beatrice, she likes a bit of trouble but she's completely harmless.'

Alicia grasped his hand tightly and, because it was her touching him, he did not feel the sting of his burns. 'Are you sure she's not a witch? She looked straight into me. She'll know.'

'You must forget all that superstitious nonsense,' Luke said forcefully but not unkindly, 'Forget everything that fortune-telling wretch at the countess's private theatre show ever told you. She was an actress after all, and a charlatan. Anyway, are we all not very much alive? And who can hurt you now? You are under my protection and Jack will constantly be at your side.'

'I'll get you some broth,' Jack said gently. 'You'll feel better when you've eaten.' Patiently, wanting only to see her sit up straight and be as composed as he'd known her before, he helped her consume half of the bowl's contents and take a few sips of wine. Refusing the glass Luke offered him, he swore privately never to betray his convictions again.

Luke downed two glasses of wine, poured a third and ripped a plump leg off a chicken carcass. Eating on his feet, he shared out the ointments, salves and tinctures into two lots. Buttercup salve for burns, comfrey for bruises, soapwort to soothe inflamed flesh, a gargle for the throat.

'I have no need of them, Luke, my arm is just a little sore now. I just want to rest, lie on a soft clean bed. I'm so tired.' Alicia yawned, and gazed pleadingly at Jack.

'We should go before Sir Oliver returns,' Jack said, suddenly wanting nothing less than being under the scrutiny of the baronet's eagle-sharp eyes.

'You'll have to carry her. I'll get a lantern and light your way,' Luke said. 'And for God's sake, act naturally.'

Act naturally! With death and shame behind them, and he with a wife of a higher class brought home with him. Jack let out an almost hysterical laugh.

'The lady will remain until we've been introduced,' came a strong, authoritative voice from the doorway.

Luke whirled round, hurting his stiff arm, and met the direct stare of his father's stern eyes.

'Welcome home, son.'

Kerensa pushed past Oliver and rushed to Luke. Paralysed with emotion, he embraced her tightly, burying his face against her neck. Angry with himself for putting his feelings on display, he finally found his voice. 'It's good to see you again, Mama.'

When he let her go, his eyes were damp and he felt ashamed. Ashamed to be seen crying, ashamed to come back home a failure. His father was the next to be embraced, then Kelynen and then the tiny Cordelia, and by the time he had given his final hug he had buried his feelings away deep inside.

Jack was welcomed home, but in view of his bandages handshakes were not exchanged.

'Michael informed us of your and Jack's injuries,' Oliver said, pushing Luke down on a chair and taking his son's wrists to study his wounds. 'Tell all.'

Luke and Jack glanced at each other.

Luke spoke, 'There was a fire at the inn we stayed in on the first night of our travels home. It was only by God's grace we escaped alive. The lady is Alicia, Mrs Jack Rosevear. Jack has taken a surname.'

Oliver raised his black brows.

Tearing her eyes away from Luke, Kerensa exclaimed, 'You're married, Jack? Really? How wonderful. We're very pleased to meet you, Mrs Rosevear. It's terrible you had such a perilous start on your journey down here.'

Alicia tried to rise but Kerensa was beside her, perching on the edge of the sofa, bringing a candlestick near so she could gain a clearer view of the groom's wife. She was astonished at the extent of the fearfulness staring back at her. Flawless skin over fine cheekbones, a lovely mouth and perfect poise spoke of refined living.

'My dear, is there anything I can get you? You're obviously in shock, unwell. You and Jack must stay here for the night, mustn't they, Oliver? We insist. Thank God, you're all safe, thank God.'

'I am in your debt, Lady Pengarron, Sir Oliver,' Alicia said in her well-modulated voice. 'I'm just dreadfully weary. I'm happy to be wherever Jack is, his cottage will do us very well. I'm afraid my clothes were all destroyed in the fire. Your housekeeper is kindly finding me something to wear for the night.'

'We shall raid our clothes presses for you,' Kelynen interjected.

Oliver was standing at the back of the huddle, his mind on something learned at a gentleman's coffee house in Marazion earlier in the week. Surely his son and his groom had not been involved in something so sordid, deceitful and dangerous? Yet Luke had a reckless streak in him, he was headstrong and rebellious, his disability was proof of it. It was hard to believe it of Jack, but he and his wife were distinctly mismatched. 'Was anyone unfortunate enough to have died in this fire, Luke?'

'The landlord's son and two of the guests perished, Father,' he replied immediately.

'I see.' Oliver's penetrating eyes fell on Jack, who made a jerky movement backwards. A guilty reaction? 'Her ladyship has offered you and your wife our hospitality, Jack. You shall receive it. And I shall have a long talk with you by and by.'

Again Jack and Luke's eyes met. 'About what, may I ask, m'lord?'

'You may not. The lax manners of the capital city will not do here, Jack Rosevear.'

'I'm very sorry, sir.' Jack looked down.

Kerensa shared Oliver's suspicion that there was more to Luke's story but now was not the time for more interrogation, and not with Kelynen and Cordelia present.

'I'll ring for Polly to prepare a room for

Jack and Mrs Rosevear. Sit down everyone. Luke, I'm sure you'll be interested to hear all about the precious little nephew you've not yet seen.'

Six

On the other side of Mount's Bay from the Pengarron estate, at Gulval, up on high ground and surrounded by lush landscape, was Vellanoweth Farm, the home and property of Captain Kane Pengarron, Kerensa's adopted son. The sprawling, well-kept house and husbandry buildings faced the bay, all vantage points from which to view St Michael's Mount, a small island a short distance out in the green waters.

On the summit of the Mount was a castle, once a monastery, once a fortress, now inhabited by titled gentry, and this graceful structure, parts dating back to the twelfth century, had been in sight for most of Kerensa's journey to the farm. To her, the castle maintained an other-worldly quality and inspired her to rein in her pony just inside Vellanoweth's farmyard and, with a company of hens pecking among the cobbles, she compared her life and her family's to the world of legend and superstition.

At the beginning of her marriage, Oliver had been the wicked overlord. And while the subsequent years had been mainly happy and fulfilling, all too often, cruelly and unexpectedly, a goblin or a witch had sought to destroy her or her marriage, and once, in the person of an evil, effeminate sea captain, had almost destroyed one of her children. Now Luke was home, still as restless and bad-tempered as a sprite, and as lost as a prince on a quest for some unattainable treasure, his sense of undervalue as strong as before, and hiding a secret.

What lay behind the tale of the mysterious Alicia Rosevear? An innocent maiden or a sorceress? Luke acted as if he had rescued her from a dragon. She had certainly weaved a spell over Jack. He was besotted with her and she showed an affectionate concern for him, but there must be more to their union than this. Kerensa was sure the fine-faced, sweetly mannered young woman played the greater part in the secret both men were keeping.

Looking up at the blue mantle of sky where brilliant white clouds glided cheerfully, she prayed long and hard to ward off anything or anyone about to spring out of the mists of darkness and threaten her or her beloved family's happiness again.

Kerensa felt the gentle warmth of the sun,

tasted the sea-fresh air, and slipped into the tranquillity that was always in this place. She loved it here. She was calling on the one child who welcomed her presence at any time. Kane never saw her weekly visits as being too often, her advice or concern as interference. She was allowed to make as much fuss of Harry as she liked. Having had such a terrible start to his own life – for the first two years he had been brought up in a brothel, starved and beaten – Kane believed one could never bestow too much love on a child. The high-spirited Jessica was of the same mind, and, Kerensa thought, still smarting at her ill-spent morning, had never accused her of smothering, impeding or suffocating her or Kane.

Kerensa's hopes of an intimate family breakfast had been crushed. Oliver had risen before first light, declaring he had important business and would go straightway to Keran-Mor Farm and eat with the estate steward, Matthias Renfree. Luke bolted down his food, stating impatiently that he had no time to linger and answer more questions; apparently it was a matter of some urgency for him to see Jack and Mrs Rosevear settled into their cottage. Hearing her father was abroad, Kelynen immediately took off after him, rebelliously refusing to eat a morsel. Cordelia, uncommonly in a strop, had asked Esther King to take her breakfast up to the nursery, where she would eat with Samuel. Kerensa knew this was Luke's doing. He had only given her passing attention since his return, even pushing her arm away when she sought to link it through his. Kerensa hoped Cordelia's infatuation for Luke had not turned into something stronger. She had felt she had no other choice but to allow Cordelia to monopolize Samuel all day.

If everyone else was so intent on their own agenda then perhaps she should take Beatrice's advice, even if Oliver did not approve, and think more about herself and not place all her hopes and dreams in others.

'Mornin' m'lady,' Ben Penberthy, Kane's amiable foreman, stocky and dark in the typical Cornish build, appeared from an outbuilding and took charge of her chestnut thoroughbred. 'Cap'n and missus 'ave just gone out ridin', lookin' over the livestock.'

Kerensa was disappointed and kept a hand on Kernick's bridle. 'Have they taken the baby with them, Ben?' Jessica's marriage into the gentry had given her no pretensions and she usually took Harry with her everywhere, tied to her body with a shawl.

'Not this time, m'lady. Young Master Harry's tucked up in his cradle.' Ben was all grins. 'Got someone special watching over un t' day.'

'Oh? Someone I know?'

'Aye, missus wouldn't leave un with just anybody.' Ben seemed intent on keeping his secret and, happy at not having a wasted journey, Kerensa left him to his private amusement.

Kerensa let herself in through the front door, tossing her feathered hat and kid gloves on the side table in the passage. Where was this someone special? She made quiet investigation. There was no one in the pleasantly furnished parlour or dining room, or Jessica's cluttered sitting room or Kane's spacious den. All the windows were open and Kerensa was heedful to close each door carefully to prevent a sudden bang and awakening Harry. The kitchen staff were busy baking bread and pies, and after bidding a friendly good morning to the cook and housemaids, red faced and respectful in the heat, she withdrew and crept up the stairs.

The first floor of the house seemed to be slumbering in peace. The door to Harry's nursery was ajar, and mesmerized by the calm, Kerensa peeped through the space and listened. She could see her grandson's fair silky hair above the light covers, the gentle rise and fall of his sturdy little body as he slept soundly. Harry's watcher must be silently about her work, perhaps folding linen.

Kerensa called out softly, 'Hello, it's

Harry's grandmother. Can I came in?'

There came a careful tread from within the room and the door was opened wide. Illuminated in the delicate golden light streaming in through the lace-curtained window panes, a figure appeared. Tall, fair, blue-eyed, tanned, handsome. Smiling beguilingly.

'Clem!' she gasped, a hand automatically stretching out towards him. 'You're Harry's watcher.'

'Kerensa,' he said. Just her name. He looked her over, looked into her, drank her in, breathed her into the substance of him, where she would always be. Could a woman become ever more beautiful? Grow more vital, youthful and divine with each passing year?

He claimed a hold over her reaching hand. Tenderly, he kissed her cheek.

'My dear Clem, you look so well.'

'And you, my precious love, look so beautiful.'

'I can't believe you're actually here.'

'Nor I you. I've dreamt of this moment, hoping and praying that when I saw you again we'd be alone. Two years is too long, far too long, to go without the sight of you and the sound of your voice.'

'I've missed you, Clem.'

'Life's been empty without you, Kerensa.'

They could share sentiments like this, connected in the special bond of their old love.

To Clem, it was no liberty to place a delicate touch on her face. He did not have to tell her he loved her, and to his everlasting joy he was confident the love she had said she would always keep for him was still there.

He led her to the cradle. 'Come, let us look at our grandchild.'

They knelt side by side and gazed down at the sleeping baby. Kerensa ran a finger along Harry's brow. Strong, fair features were already set in the tiny contented face. 'Isn't he just gorgeous? And so much like you. We never thought we'd have a grandchild together, Clem.'

'He's got my blood in him, Kerensa. Your soul.' Clem placed a loving hand on Harry, as if blessing him. 'He's the most precious child in all the world.'

'Yes, he is.'

She looked into Clem's face. Clem's gaze came round to her. He was precious to her too. Her first love.

'I'm so glad you're here, Clem. Stay as long as you can in Mount's Bay.'

Seven

Alicia Rosevear was sitting on a weathered bench in the apple orchard, which had become her favourite place.

On every day she came here, she formed silent prayers for Lord Alexander Longbourne's soul, ending by gazing down at the private memorial she had made to him, a small mound of stones arranged in a circle, symbolizing the eternal circle of their love.

In an effort not to weep, she talked to him in her heart. Please, beloved, don't mind too much that I married Jack. I had to do it for the sake of our baby.

Alex's excesses and gambling debts had cost him his life, leaving her alone to care for their child. Thank God, he had formed a friendship with Luke Pengarron. The two young men had found much in common, seeking pleasure at a furious rate, scorning anything considered commendable, right and proper. Alex, boyishly handsome, well set and starry-eyed, had thought he could indulge in wantonness forever, but Luke, thank God again, was something of a realist, admitting that his escape from conformity and duty was for a limited time only. And Luke, so she had thought, dreamed of something unobtainable, something he accepted, although not with good grace. And for Luke's own good there had been Jack. Quiet, dependable Jack.

It had been with much silly amusement that Alex had mimicked Jack's Cornish accent. Alicia had found it soothing, she had admired his honest, simple statements and innocent outlook. Alex had belittled his stern expressions and tut-tuttings. On more than one occasion Alex had fallen down drunk on their bed, declaring, 'Did you see his face, Phia? How does Luke stand it? Bet the poor fellow will get a good few Bible verses muttered down his ear tonight.' It was Alex who had brought Jack's keenness on her to her attention – something she had not minded. Alex had held no concerns over Jack passing away many long hours with her while she'd waited for him and Luke to return from the gaming clubs.

Alicia was four months pregnant and beginning to show. It was assumed their marriage had taken place before the baby's conception. This pleased her, for Jack's sake, and she could think of no one better as substitute father and protector for her baby. Dear, kind Jack, now he was home and settled, he was expressing an interest in the

71

baby. Unfortunately, so was the hideous crone that Luke and his family and Jack were so fond of; the disgustingly smelly individual who referred to her as Mrs Jack and looked her up and down as if she was a creature unknown to God or science. The old servant was proclaimed to be an expert on child-bearing and had announced the baby would be a 'cheeil'. Alicia hoped she was correct and it would prove to be a girl, inheriting none of her beloved Alex's weaknesses.

Last night, after waking screaming from another nightmare of the fire and Alex's gruesome death, she had lain in the comfort of Jack's arms, in the double bed that Luke had procured for them.

'I'm sorry, Jack. I keep you awake every night and you have to start your work so early in the mornings.'

'I don't mind,' he had replied softly. 'Do you want a drink of water? Or a drop of Beatrice's camomile tea? 'Tis soothing.'

'I just want to stay awake, Jack.'

'There's no need to be frightened any more, Alicia.'

'I can't help it. I fear for my life, and yours and Luke's, and I'm so afraid for my child. Its existence could be used as a ransom to call in Alex's debts. It's unlikely his younger brother, the new Lord Longbourne, would pay, but if he did and he were to demand Alex's child in return, I couldn't bear it. Or as a warning to others, the Society might kill the child.'

'Nothing like that's going to happen, Alicia, believe me. Have faith.' He had rubbed her arm, and she knew he would like to have turned the affection into something else.

'You're so good to me, Jack.' In the candlelight, lit to help chase away her terrors, his eyes were warm and caring. 'I've not been a wife to you at all. I don't cook your meals or do anything for you. And you've been patient with me – you know what I mean.'

'I'm happy to wait as long as you want. You're still grieving for Lord Alex.'

'I'm grateful for your compassion. You deserve more than I can give you.'

Jack had cleared his throat, but even so his voice had come husky and a little shy. 'I'll be happy for the rest of my life if you give me no more than you already do.' He had kissed her cheek then and ventured a soft kiss on her lips. Then retreated.

Remembering Alex's perfect, long, deep kisses, she was caught unawares by grief again and sobbed throughout the rest of the night.

As she sat in the privacy of the apple trees, she felt guilty about denying Jack his right to the fullest use of the marriage bed. She had lost so much, escaped so much, and gained so much, in having a wealthy protector and an understanding husband.

She forbade a further time of weeping by reflecting on everything she had learned and witnessed in the last few days.

Luke couldn't have brought her to a better place. The Pengarrons had been kind to her, although Sir Oliver seemed rather aloof. Alicia felt he neither liked nor trusted her, and he had made it clear to Jack that he suspected he and Luke were lying about their London venture; Alicia had supposedly been a governess to a family visiting the capital. If a certain name – Trenchard – was mentioned, she noticed Sir Oliver became scornful, unpleasant even, and her ladyship appeared to become impatient with him. She must ask Jack what was behind this. She did not want to make an indiscretion.

The servants were friendly, not pressing her for information after she had lightly warded off their first curious attempts, but she could hardly make out a word they said. Their dialect, especially the hideous old woman's, was less distinct than even the broadest cockney she had heard. She was bemused at the close-knit community she now found herself in, but it worried her that the anonymity she had taken for granted in London, unless in the social sense, was almost entirely lacking. The Cornish were a superstitious race and employed all manner of odd sayings and practices to ward off bad luck, poverty and divine judgement. No matter, she didn't intend to mix with them beyond the daily excursion to the kitchens with Jack to eat a cooked meal and collect fresh food for the remainder of the day.

She missed the noise and bustle of the city. It was strange to notice the weather conditions every day, and although she found the wide expanse of the sea awesome with its changing colours and constant movement, the mist that sometimes came suddenly rolling in off it was somehow frightening. The smoke and fog of London had given only nuisance value, it had never seemed alive and threatening.

She shook herself out of getting fanciful like the locals, and she tried to laugh at herself for believing the claim of the charlatan actress back in the capital: *three, strangely connected, would die*. She, Jack and Luke were safe. She placed a hand over her stomach where her precious baby was growing. Safe and protected.

Her new home, although small and ill-equipped, was welcomingly secluded from the great house and its everyday business. Luke had been the first through the front door on the morning after their arrival at Pengarron Manor.

'You don't hate it, do you? I know it's only a tiny cottage but it's thoroughly waterproof, quite warm in winter, isn't it, Jack? And every room has a fireplace, hasn't it, Jack?'

Luke had fastened an anxious expression on her as she had gazed about the one and only living room of Jack's home. A short time earlier she had succumbed to a fierce bout of morning sickness, and although a little rested after a night in a proper bed with clean linen and feeling more secure, she had been glad to sit down on one of the oddments that made up a trio of chairs. She had worn a cotton day dress of a delicate floral pattern, donated by Lady Pengarron, a pretty affair but very ordinary compared to what she was used to.

Before she could reply, Luke had prattled on, 'The manor's attics are full of furnishings, all good stuff. I'll have some sent round. Or you and Jack can climb up there yourselves and choose anything that takes your fancy. I'll arrange for it to be sent round immediately. Or I can buy new, as much as you want. Absolutely anything, just say. What's in the other room, Jack?'

'The kitchen, but I've always eaten with Esther and Ruth, so I use it to store a few belongings in,' Jack had said, smiling at her in a way that sought her approval. 'I'll move it all out today, turn the room into a little parlour for you, Alicia.'

'That is good of you. Thank you, Jack.' To her relief, at Luke's insistence Jack was not to return to work for two or three days, until his hands were quite healed. Sir Oliver had agreed to this, on the proviso Jack oversaw the stables twice a day. Jack was home, with time on his hands and, he had told her emphatically, he wasn't about to fritter it away as he'd done in London.

'Good,' Luke said. 'You see, Alicia, there will definitely be no skivvying for you. I'm afraid you'll have to do without a maid. That would raise too many eyebrows, eh, Jack?'

'Yes, Luke. I'm sorry, Alicia.'

'Don't be sorry. I can't forget that I lost my maid in the fire, and I've managed without one before. In fact, I've had to attend to many of the duties of a servant. My father had a little land near Alex's estate, but there were no comforts in the house.'

'My dear Alicia,' Luke was suddenly all sympathy, 'I've never really thought about your family. Where are your relatives? Would the Society know of their existence?'

'My father was all I ever had. I changed my name after I left home to protect his honour. He died two years ago. I thought it best that I be thought to be dead too; his small means went to the poor of the parish.'

'I'm sorry you have no one, but in the circumstances it's not such a bad thing, if you understand my meaning,' Luke reflected grimly.

'I do,' Alicia said. 'This cottage is limited but I'm sure, thanks to the manor's servants, it's clean and comfortable. I have observed the esteem with which Jack is served here. But Luke, you mustn't do too much for us, surely so much patronage will bring unwarranted attention.'

'I promised Alexander I'd look after you,' Luke returned, as if that was the end of the discussion.

'I did too,' added Jack quickly, and Alicia knew her husband was thinking that here, in his own home, he should be in charge of the proceedings.

'What are you saying?' Luke had glared at Jack. 'That you don't want my help, that this is how Alicia should live from now on?'

'No, of course not,' Jack replied mildly. Alicia had grasped that he had learned long ago to ignore Luke's prickly nature, which weeded out criticism where there was none. 'Alicia deserves and'll get everything she needs. What I meant is we'll have to make another cover story as to why she's getting it. I am but a groom, with small savings. If you provide all that you plan, questions will surely be asked.'

'Simple. Did you not save my life?'

'No, Luke. You saved mine.'

'Don't split hairs, man! We'll put the story about that you saved my life in the fire, of course I'd be generous. Anyway, you saved me from many an undesirable situation, especially in the case of Sir Decimus

Soames. That monster would've ... well, you know his tastes, then after the perversion, a spot of torture.'

'We don't need reminding,' Jack said sternly, glancing at Alicia. She had looked back at him with a perfectly straight face, then had given him a small smile of encouragement.

'Oh, so it's back to total sobriety, is it?' Luke playfully cuffed Jack's upper arm. 'The juice of the vine is no longer to pass your lips and the unmentionable must not be mentioned. Don't be such an old maid! Alicia knows what's what, don't you, my dear?'

Alicia watched as Jack turned pale and became quiet. She knew he did not wish to be reminded that she had been another man's mistress.

'You must not tease Jack, he does not deserve it,' Alicia reproached her benefactor. Then fear had returned as a companion, making her glance all around, as if Sir Decimus Soames, the acknowledged head of the shadowy Society, a ruthless, violent man, who must have ordered Alex's assassination, might have spies in the place. 'Jack's right, I've left my old life behind and it must never be mentioned again. All our lives may depend on it.'

'I agree we must be careful,' Luke was suddenly impatient, 'but on the other hand it was common knowledge that Jack and I were about to return home for my nephew's baptism. My father's reputation for family observances and loyalty is well known. The Society has no need to assume you went with us, Alicia. Indeed, they'll think you perished along with Alexander. Remember that diamond necklace you were wearing the night of the fire? You think you lost it in the melee, but I took it off your neck and placed it on your maid's. Her clothes will have been burnt off, no one will believe that you survived.'

'Say no more.' Alicia had rammed her hands over her ears. Jack had flown to her and she had turned to him, sobbing. 'This is not a game. Alex is dead. The Society is extremely dangerous, they never forgive and they'll do anything to protect their interests.'

'Hush, now. Luke and I have vowed to protect you, Alicia.' Jack held her close. 'No one will hurt you, you can trust us.'

Alicia pulled away from him and faced Luke squarely. 'I thank you for all your considerations, Luke, but I can't accept them. To ensure that I and you and Jack are in the least possible danger, from now on I must live simply as a groom's wife, as Mrs Jack.'

Since then she had lived in the tiny cottage with the extra comforts sent round by Lady Pengarron and the extravagant things Luke had provided under the guise of wedding presents. He'd had his way, after all.

A young child's voice floated towards her on the warm, dry air. Master Samuel Pengarron was heading her way on his sturdy legs, and with him the one member of the genteel family who, after an initial mutual reserve, she had something of a friendship with. Miss Cordelia Drannock made a point of calling on her every day and Alicia looked forward to her visits.

'Good morning, Mrs Jack,' Cordelia hailed her in her unsure voice. 'I went first to the cottage, but I should have known I'd find you here while the fine weather lasts.'

'Oh?' Alicia rose and dropped a perfect curtsey. Cordelia motioned for her to sit down again and joined her on the bench. 'Are we to expect rain then, Miss Drannock?'

'Just a light shower or two this afternoon, I should think, but a heavy downfall tonight. It should be fine for Master Harry's baptism on Sunday afternoon. You missed attending church last week – understandable that you should desire more rest – but you'll find it a splendid occasion. St Piran's is small, but my uncle's patronage sees it's kept in excellent repair.'

'I shall go to matins with Jack, although I confess I am not keen to attend this Methodist meeting house which he has an interest in, but surely I'm not to be invited to the baptism? It will be for the gentry only.'

81

Alicia had sewn a cloth ball for Master Samuel, and anticipating this visit produced it from her apron pocket and held it out towards him. Already a few inches taller than the average child of his age, having inherited his father's advantageous height, he ran up to her, chuckling, said thank you in toddler-talk, then tossed it up in the air.

'That was very kind of you,' Cordelia said. 'Of course you will be at the baptism. The whole estate and parish will turn out for it. My uncle will lay on a feast here, another in the village of Perranbarvah and another on Ker-an-Mor, the home farm. Not a soul will be left out, and illness or infirmity apart, my uncle will see it as an affront if anyone does not attend.'

'I see.' The Pengarrons would be the main spectacle, but Alicia felt anxious about being on public display. 'I can see why my dear Jack was so anxious to return home and have me meet his friends.'

'I wish my cousin had missed all of us as much,' Cordelia said forlornly, causing Alicia to look at her downcast face. 'Tell me, Mrs Jack, did Jack ever mention why Mr Pengarron had failed to visit his two cousins in London, my elder brothers, Mr Charles and Mr Jack Drannock? Was he too busy, do you think?' Samuel was trying to knock buds off a tree with the ball.

'Sammy, dear, be gentle now.' The child

stopped, grinned cheekily and carried on as before.

'I recall no mention of those names,' Alicia said. 'I didn't know you had brothers. You must miss them.'

'I have another brother, the eldest of the family, Bartholomew. He left the estate many years ago to travel the world and I've not seen him since. I also have two married sisters with children of their own, Hannah and Naomi. They have also moved out of the county and I've stayed with them occasionally. Now I'm too busy looking after Master Samuel to go far.'

'Master Samuel is a wonderful little boy. Now I am expecting a happy event, perhaps we could swap notes on child care.' Alicia had never taken care of a child in her life, but she had the art of making a conversant believe whatever she wanted them to. Anything she learned from Cordelia would be useful for her impending motherhood.

'Yes, indeed. If I may say,' and Cordelia blushed, 'you and Jack are obviously a love match. Did ... did Mr Luke meet anyone special while in London?'

Jack had filled Alicia in on Cordelia's background. Born to a poor fisherman, who had turned out to be Sir Oliver's half-brother, something Sir Oliver had not known himself until after the unfortunate fisherman had been lost in a storm at sea, Cordelia had lived at the manor since her mother's untimely death. It had not taken long for Alicia to see that Cordelia, a thoroughly likeable little soul, transparent and honest, her accent very much like Lady Pengarron's, in pointing to her origins, did not entirely fit into her uplifted station, that she felt gauche and uneasy around men, and that she was hopelessly in love with Luke.

She said what the other young woman wanted to hear, 'No, Miss Drannock, he didn't seem to enjoy much of London at all, and I can vouchsafe he spent very little time with any lady. He enjoyed the theatre, was always enthusiastic about the plays.' She added swiftly, 'So Jack informed me.'

'He's been offhand, secretive and more bad-tempered than usual since his return. He's hardly strung two sentences together for me, and we used to be so close.'

'Take heart, Miss Drannock, give him a little more time. I'm sure he just needs to readapt to his old ways.'

What a lot of lies I've just told, Alicia reflected. Quite the order of my new life.

Eight

Unaware of the various emotions simmering inside some of those gathered around the ancient granite font, Kane and Jessica Pengarron presented their baby, Harry Oliver Clemow to God, the Reverend Timothy Lanyon and the invited assembly.

While having a fondness for his daughter-in-law, Oliver felt it a pity Kane had fallen in love with her. He was furious his grandchild should bear Clem Trenchard's name. Trenchard was behaving as the wretch should, humbly, politely detached towards Kerensa, attentive to his own wife. He had better not step out of line, not once!

Oliver stood slightly in front of Kerensa. He knew she was vexed about it, but he had the right to keep Trenchard out of her line of vision.

Luke was bored and irritable, and felt aggrieved rather than honoured that he'd be chief godfather, and he mumbled his responses throughout the service. When his brother-in-law mentioned the part about fighting evil and the devil, Luke scanned the cluster of manor servants for Jack and Alicia, anxious to satisfy himself they were safely present, not victims yet of the evil devils they had escaped in London. Why couldn't he shake off the feeling that they might all still be in danger and why bring the word 'yet' to mind? That was a worry on its own.

It was a hot steamy day, stifling and airless inside the church, and although Luke was near the door, a sudden wave of claustrophobia threatened to overwhelm him. In a vivid flashback he saw the town house in St James's Street on fire. He felt himself running towards it, saw Jack frantically keeping apace. He smelled the thick smoke and felt the scorch of the flames. He heard the desperate screams and the cries for help.

He realized that a small gloved hand was holding his and it brought him back to the present.

Staring down, he saw his mother had forsaken his father's side. Her lips were moving, but at first he was incapable of understanding her words. Then he made out her whisper, 'Do you want to go outside?'

He shook his head. Faced straight ahead. Took a deep breath back to composure.

Kerensa had to force her hand out of Luke's crushing grip or a cry of pain would have been inescapable. She and Oliver had tried to talk to Luke about his experiences in London, more in an interested way than as an examination, but each time he insisted there was little to report. Always he had looked harsh, angry, resentful.

She became aware that Oliver was watching her, a grave scrutiny for a moment, then his expression lightened. Mood swings, such as she had endured in their early days together. Those old, cruel cat and mouse games. It was as if time had regressed twenty-four years. And gallingly, somewhat pathetically, just because Clem was back in Mount's Bay. Several times since Oliver's apparent clash with him, she had felt her husband's eyes piercing into her, as if in accusation. He had no reason to be jealous – but she had no doubt that this was the trouble.

From here she was directly across the font from Clem. On one side of him was Catherine, on the other his sister, Rosie, and her husband, Matthias Renfree. The Renfrees' and Catherine's eyes were also occasionally aimed her way. She was mindful to attend only to the proceedings, while casting anxious glances at Luke.

Careful to keep smiling, Catherine was comparing herself to her husband's first love, his great love. Catherine accepted, in all grace, that she, herself, would only ever look nicely presentable in the finest apparel, while the other woman would look gorgeous in rags. Even though the baronet's wife was seven years older than she was, she could be a sister to her two lovely daughters.

How did Clem find her? He had mentioned her only in regard to the baptism. Given her only a respectful bow when arriving at the church.

Her brother was intoning, 'I name you Harry Oliver Clemow, in the name of the Father, the Son and the Holy Ghost. Amen.'

Clem turned straight to her and smiled affectionately, and she melted with happiness there on the spot. She had just received a public declaration of his love.

Cordelia had again taken charge of Samuel. Her aunt had objected at first, saying she wanted Samuel with her throughout the service, but Cordelia had pleaded the boy's adventurousness. Her uncle had agreed with her, and she stood now, with Samuel wriggling and trying to free his hand from hers. A short time ago her aunt had changed position to comfort Luke. A strange affair. Luke was usually in total control. Why didn't Luke want her own company any more? I don't care, Cordelia tried to convince herself.

It had taken much persuasion on Jack's part to get Alicia to attend the church today. She had argued that the parson and the Pengarrons wouldn't want her there if they knew her true circumstances. That is was possible that someone among the gentry might recognize her.

'But that's all in the past. You're my wife now, you've a new future,' Jack had said. ''Tis not very likely anyone down here's connected to the Society. 'Twas only Luke's headstrong nature that got him involved in their clubs.' His final inducement had been the suggestion that they remain in the church after the ceremony to say private prayers for Lord Alexander. Her constant lament was not having been able to attend his funeral.

Jack had wanted to show off his lovely bride, unconcerned now after his initial misgivings about her carrying another man's baby. With Lord Longbourne dead there would be no complications. Only one thing could make him happier and that would happen in due time. Although he was thinking about this delicate matter in the church, of all places, he was confident that when the time arrived, he would take Alicia in mastery and sensitivity, thanks to his seduction by the Countess of Kilwarth, and their subsequent unions. Until London, his previous experience had amounted to one failed encounter with a whorish bal maiden.

When Luke started to cough he kept his eyes on him.

Alicia, too, was watching Luke, sorry for his discomfort. Would he allow her one small, private favour? In a quiet corner of the graveyard, a proper, although anonymous, memorial to Alex.

Luke tried a deep breath to stop himself coughing, but was unsuccessful. The hacking sounds echoed from pillar to pillar, seemingly from each individual granite stone.

Timothy Lanyon had nearly completed the service but paused in respect of his brother-in-law's distress.

Luke reached for his handkerchief, his eyes watering, breathing noisily. 'I'm sorry.'

He met Kane's gaze across the font. No! He wanted none of the concern shown in those soft brown eyes. Damn Kane. He and Jessica made a striking couple, full of health and purpose. He, straight and commanding, neat reddish-brown hair, his work-roughened hands claiming how content he was to work his own land. She, vivacious, strong in spirit, a mass of golden curls cascading below her simple beribboned hat.

Olivia had crept round to his side. When he felt her hand massaging his back he was livid that she should treat him as an invalid, embarrass him in front of society and the rabble. He had to get away, but the churchyard was choked with more gawping estate workers and villagers. Pushing roughly through the family party, his handkerchief to his mouth, he hastened up the aisle to the vestry. A long humiliating journey.

Leading Alicia by the hand, Jack skirted the packed pews and benches and those standing in the congregation, and caught up with him at the tiny arched door. He closed it behind them. Luke sat down on the single hard chair. Alicia poured him water, from the tray set out in the event any of the gentry had such a need.

Luke sipped, his hand shaking. 'Thank you. If only I could escape this damned place!'

'Stay here 'til everyone's gone,' Jack said, sensitive enough not to stare into his red face.

'I didn't mean the church.' He looked moodily about the cramped confines, then swore shockingly. 'The register will have to be signed.'

'Only the reverend and the captain and Sir Oliver need come in here.'

'We've got to get away again, Jack. Or I'll go mad.'

'But I—'

'Shut up!'

Luke knew what Jack's protest involved. His parents' disapproval and the thought of leaving his new wife. Jack had not merely fallen in love with Alicia, he had plummeted down an abyss of adoration and not a little lust.

Luke stared at her. She was standing at a discreet distance. Her clothes of powder blue and fawn were of a quality and style suited to her reduced status, but it was impossible to mask her graceful deportment and handsome face. Her hair, although mainly hidden by a delicate straw affair and a lace snood at the back, was a golden sheen of feminine wile and beauty. She was spring and summer, promise and hope.

Where could he find himself such a woman? He was suddenly wildly jealous of Jack's fabulous gain and the rights and privileges that went with it. She never made a man feel less of himself by inappropriate fussings. When the grieving for her lover was over, she was going to make an ideal mate.

God, why didn't I marry her? At least it would have given me something else to think about.

Pain stabbed through Luke's crippled arm and he groaned in misery. 'Don't worry, Jack, the three of us will go away together. And soon. On that I am adamant.'

Nine

'Go and speak to your brother, Kane,' Kerensa urged the more agreeable of her elder sons. 'He's feeling awful about coughing like that in church.'

'Feeling awful about making a spectacle of himself, more like,' Jessica announced tartly.

'Don't let him hear you say that,' Kerensa cautioned. Jessica should show more understanding. Luke was suffering.

'Where is he anyway?' Kane was always willing to be on good terms with anyone.

He looked for his brother along the length and breadth of the great hall of the manor house, where a mountainous spread of food, port and wines was laid on for the guests. From portraits ascending the mighty stairs, Pengarron forebears, dating back to Sir Arthur, titled in King Henry VIII's reign, gazed down on the gathering; not, it seemed, in their usual dark-eyed disdain, but with approval at the newest of their prestigious line.

'If you're looking for Luke,' Olivia said, arriving at Kane's side and fixing Harry, who was reclining wide-eyed in Kerensa's arms, with an artistic eye, 'he's outside in the stable yard with Jack and a few other of the young gentlemen. Harry's got a fascinating little face. When can I paint him?'

'Come over to the farm whenever you like,' Kane replied. 'Why are they in the stable yard? Has Father placed an interesting piece of horseflesh there?'

'No, they're making wagers on the races at Falmouth next week.'

'Not silly amounts of money, I hope.' Kerensa frowned.

'Oh, Mama.' Olivia tossed her head impatiently.

Oliver joined his family, with him were Kelynen and his closest friends, Sir William and Lady Rachael Beswetherick, landowners of the next parish. Oliver enclosed his married daughter in his arms and spoke in her ear, 'So, beloved, when are you going to present your mama and I with the next precious little bundle?'

'There's plenty of time for that,' Olivia muttered testily. She was becoming increasingly impatient with this question, asked by just about everyone she encountered nowadays. Damn it, she wasn't a brood mare. 'Excuse me, I promised to take a turn round the hall with Mrs Ralph Harrt. She needs an arm to lean on, her arthritic ankles, you know.'

She flounced off to present herself to the middle-aged wife of the local coroner and master of hounds, a woman of sharp tongue and ill-nature whom she would normally shun. She found her husband Timothy in her path, looking at her gravely. Not his habitual animated self.

Olivia met his disapproval at her behaviour with challenge and scorn. They had quarrelled last evening on the matter of her apparent infertility. She had been hurt by the injustice of it, she wasn't doing anything to prevent conception. Why all this fuss simply because she did not desire the ties of motherhood yet?

He offered her his arm. She thrust hers to jar against his elbow and allowed him to escort her to Mrs Harrt who was surrounded by a gaggle of frivolous gossips. Timothy promptly left her there. He looked a little lost, until Kane suggested he accompany him to join Luke.

'It appears Olivia could well learn to do a little obeying of her husband. Methinks your son-in-law is desirous of fatherhood,' Lady Rachael observed in her high-pitched voice. The same age as Oliver, she tried, sadly unsuccessfully, to disguise the effect it unfairly made on her gender, with powders, rouge and face patches. Her extravagant gown was too tight at the bodice and the panniers on her waist ridiculously wide.

Spying the tall, blond farmer who had stood across the church font from Oliver, she was intent on a little mischief.

'My word, what pretty infants over there. Twins! Like two adorable cherubs. I must get Olivia to decorate the ceiling of my bed-chamber with their likenesses. Whose are they?'

'You wouldn't want their likenesses any-where but in your water closet,' Oliver observed dryly, while staring at Kerensa for her reaction. He was angered to witness her flinch.

'They're my half-brother and half-sister and Harry's uncle and aunt,' Jessica cut in, looking loyally at John and Flora, who were sitting at a side table, napkins tucked in under their chins, eating morsels of food with delicate manners, their parents in atten-dance. 'Harry's waking up for a feed. I'll take him along to Beatrice's room, Mama-in-law. She's expecting me. Thank you for Harry's gift, Lady Rachael.'

'Oliver!' Kerensa rounded on him the instant Jessica left. 'You've upset Jessica. Why must you keep up with these sort of witticisms against the Trenchards? They're sarcastic and unkind. Clem's only going to be in the house a little longer.'

'He's already been here far too long.'

Kerensa had been careful to give Clem very little attention. Now she looked his way, and it was too bad if Oliver objected. Clem was beside a window and appeared to be discussing the gardens with Catherine. He pointed something out to his children, a kindly, interested husband and parent. Clem had not made a wrong move, said a wrong word all day, while Oliver's conduct was tiresome. And now he was doing it again, deliberately blocking her view. Exasperated, wishing the day was over, Kerensa pushed on his body, but he stood resolute.

William Beswetherick watched them, bemused. Rachael was thrilled, her glassy eyes flicking to and from the Pengarrons and Trenchards.

Of a sudden, Oliver grabbed Kerensa's arm and then Rachael's and bowled them along towards the clutch of Trenchards.

'Come along, William,' he mouthed in a dangerously jaunty manner. 'Allow me to introduce you to someone you'll find most interesting.'

Clem and Catherine rose at once, bowing and curtseying. Setting his jaw, squaring his feet, Clem placed a protective hand on Flora's chair.

Uneasy for Clem and his wife, angry at Oliver, peeved with Rachael, for the silly woman's ploy had worked and might well mean trouble, Kerensa smiled pleasantly at Catherine. She was going to get in the first word. 'You are enjoying yourselves, I hope.

Do say if there's anything you need for the children, Mrs Trenchard.'

She studied John and Flora, unsurprised to find that like all Clem's children they bore his fairness and handsome features. Jessica's touch of wildness was not evident in the twins, nor Philip's brawny toughness. They were temperate like David, Philip's twin, currently upcountry in Yorkshire, preaching on the Methodist circuit. They also had Catherine's sense of propriety, having stopped eating and eased themselves off their chairs to stand in respectful silence in front of their parents.

'We are content, thank you, my lady,' Catherine replied politely. Then she looked at Sir Oliver, and waited for him to belittle Clem in front of his friends, for surely this was the reason he had herded them and his wife here. She prayed Clem would not allow Sir Oliver his fun.

Oliver said in a commanding voice, 'William, Rachael, this is Clem Trenchard, Harry's other grandfather, and Mrs Trenchard, his step-grandmother. Trenchard, Mrs Trenchard, allow me to introduce Sir William and Lady Rachael Beswetherick.'

'Pleased to make your acquaintance, Trenchard, Mrs Trenchard,' William said, true to his sincere nature.

Clem and Catherine bowed and bobbed to the couple. Rachael took her time savouring

Clem's hard-set face. She knew all about Kerensa's childhood sweetheart but had always expected him to be typically rough-cast, of small intelligence, with a common weathered face. She was taken aback by the frank appraisal from his vibrant blue eyes. He knew Oliver's game and he knew her own, and he was not about to be made a fool of. For once, brought to embarrassment, she said nothing, merely giving a slightly conde-scending smile to save face.

'Likewise, Sir William, ma'am,' Clem said, a shielding hand on a shoulder of each twin. He wished now he had agreed to Rosie's suggestion, and Catherine's plea, to allow John and Flora to go to Ker-an-Mor Farm after the church ceremony with Rosie and Matthias, to join their four young children for the celebration there. He'd never come to terms with the fact that Philip and David had been born in this house. He looked only briefly at Kerensa. There would be other times...

'You have business interests hereabouts, Trenchard?' William enquired, not astute enough to ascertain Clem's position from the cut of his clothes, tanned skin and heavy, calloused hands.

Oliver was smiling derisively.

'No, sir,' Clem replied levelly. 'Do you know of any I might speculate in?'

Touché, Oliver allowed him.

'Well, the Roscawen Mine – I am its main owner – is yielding well presently. New investors are always welcome.'

'Trenchard is a yeoman farmer, William. He deals with dirt of a different kind.' Oliver caught sight of Cordelia walking close by, holding Samuel's hand. 'Ah, here comes my baby. Cordelia, my dear, bring Samuel here to me.'

Cordelia did so, while scanning the crowds for Luke. Oliver swept his son up into his arms. 'What think you of the latest addition to my family, Trenchard?

'He's the dead spit of you, Sir Oliver,' Clem replied, with an expression that told exactly what he thought of the black-haired, robust child.

'I'll take that as a compliment,' Oliver mocked him. Then he handed Samuel over to Kerensa. 'Well, my beloved, I think we gentlemen are done with family duties. William, shall we seek out our elder sons?'

'Indeed, yes,' William rejoined heartily, quite bored.

Oliver made to walk away, stopped, flashed his white teeth at Clem. 'Care to join us, Trenchard? Perhaps our children could amuse themselves together on the lawn. I'm sure Miss Cordelia will supervise them. It will allow the ladies time for repose.'

'I would,' Clem said immediately. He was a guest at the manor today and he wasn't going to allow Pengarron the joy of him declining his insincere invitation. Not that he had the intention of spending time in the direct company of the man he likened to the hated dark, bastard-crows. Looking at Kerensa, he said in a melodious tone, 'I understand Jack's with the young gentlemen. I'm curious to learn something about his bride.'

Left with the sight of the men's retreating backs, and relinquishing Samuel again to Cordelia, who, for once, seemed disappointed at the idea, Kerensa prepared, while hiding her reluctance, to entertain Rachael and Catherine. The whole day was becoming increasingly trying, thanks to one member or another of her family or friends.

Rachael declared she was hungry and Kerensa led the way to the food tables. Catherine admired the enormous bowls of exotic imported fruits, and Kerensa thanked her. Polite, stiff talk.

Rachael, still thinking about the effect of Clem's fine blue-eyed penetrating gaze, bit into a peach and piped up, 'Heavens, Kerensa, now I understand just how distraught you were all that time ago when forced to give up your young farm boy. He's simply divine, isn't he? Don't you keep just a tiny notion for him in your heart?'

Kerensa shot a look at Catherine, who had whipped her head round at once to do the same to her.

101

Ten

In the scrubbed-down stable yard, Luke and
his male entourage were smoking their pipes
and taking their snuff. The topic of the
summer's forthcoming country races had
been exhausted, the wagers placed, the
somewhat ludicrous amounts, encouraged
by Luke's frequent taunts, would be kept
secret to the circle. A sense of sloth and dejection had set in, due to Luke's impatience
or indifference of anything anyone else had
to say.

Kane had spoken occasionally to his
brother, but receiving no positive response,
had decided to confront Luke about his
unwillingness to let bygones rest when next
they were alone. Sweating under the raw
sun, Kane waved away troublesome horse
flies. He was chatting to Jack. The smell of
horses, leather and fresh manure was over-
whelmingly strong in the noses of the two
men who usually did not notice it. Jack
wished he could strip off his coat and cool
down with Alicia in the apple orchard, where
she was likely to be.

'So London holds no appeal for a return

visit for you, Jack?'

'No, sir. I hope never to leave Mount's Bay again, nor the estate come to that.'

Jack glanced anxiously at Luke, hoping he had not meant his temperamental declaration in the church vestry. His neckcloth pulled off and lying dirtied on the cobbles, an empty bottle of wine dangling in his hand, Luke was drunk. In danger of slipping off the bale of hay he was sharing with a dozing gentleman in regimentals, Colonel Martin Beswetherick, Sir William's heir.

'Congratulations on your marriage, Jack,' Kane said. 'If I may say, she's a rare catch. Where did you meet her? Oh, come along, Jack, you can't bring back such a sweeting and not expect people to be curious, especially as you showed little interest in the fair sex before.'

'I met Alicia while waiting to escort Mr Luke from a house in St James's Square.' Jack hoped his flushed cheeks would be blamed on the stifling heat. 'She was governess to a visiting family. Luck would have it we met again and then again and formed an attachment. She was unhappy in her post and longed to return to the country, but she had no one in all the world. I took courage and offered her marriage. Mr Luke approved of the match, and ... well, here we are.'

Kane slapped the groom's shoulder. 'Good for you, Jack. I hope she makes you very happy.' Then he looked sharply at his brother, whose dark face was now squashed against Colonel Beswetherick's shoulder. Jack's explanation sounded just a little too well articulated, as if it had come first from Luke's mouth.

The colonel suddenly roused himself and pushed Luke upright. He had noticed Kane looking their way. Why was he acting so familiarly towards the groom, who should be sent about his business? It was curious, the Pengarrons' penchant for closeness to their servants.

'I say.' He shook Luke to wakefulness and hissed into his ear. 'I've noticed that your groom's wife is a comely piece, quite a work of art. She's a stranger, so I'm informed, and a cut above her husband. Brought back from the capital, I presume. What's behind the story, eh?'

'There is no story!' Luke retorted, rubbing at his bleary eyes. 'And I have no care for servants' affairs.'

'Hardly the truth, me dear,' the colonel, of an amiable nature like his father, guffawed loudly. 'You keep your groom always in close attendance.'

'And what is that to you?' Luke snarled with a few choice swear words, pushing the colonel away from him so violently that he hit the cobbles in an ungainly heap. 'Mind your own damned business!'

The older men joined them at that moment.

'Martin!' Sir William hurried along on his short thin legs to help his son regain his dignity. 'That was most uncivil of you, young Pengarron. Apologies are in order, methinks.'

Luke was up on his feet, staggering to keep his balance. Jack was there in an instant, supporting him.

'Think what you damned well like, I couldn't give a gipsy's curse for the lot of you.' Profanities and blasphemies came fast and ugly. 'Bastards you are, one and all. God damn it, even the heathen serf Trenchard is here.'

Clem had walked slightly behind the two baronets all the way, his hands held jauntily behind his back. Once, twice, thrice, Sir Oliver had glared round at him, and each time he had raised his head higher. He took a step backward now and bowed his head, as if in respect, but in reality jubilant at Luke Pengarron's disgraceful behaviour and the lord of the manor's discomfort and wrath.

'Jack!' Oliver exploded. 'Take Mr Pengarron up to his chamber and stay with him. On no account allow him to leave before I join you.'

The news of her son's monstrous disrespect

flew rapidly through the manor, and Keren-sa was discontented when Oliver forbade her to accompany him to confront Luke about its cause. The Beswethericks, thankfully a forgiving family, were ready to forget the whole incident on Luke's apology, putting his outburst down to illness. Kerensa was grateful for Rachael's observation, 'The dear boy hasn't looked well since his return from the capital.' It brought Kerensa little comfort. What was ailing Luke? Was it possible for him ever to settle, be content?

She wanted to apologize to Clem for Luke's abuse, but Catherine was keeping him at the other end of the great hall, and who could blame her after Rachael's unfortunate remark. She had hoped all day for the chance to speak to him alone.

Oliver had stayed in the stable yard long enough to placate the guests – most thought the incident a social hilarity, ripe for repeating at future events. Arriving at Luke's door via the back stairs, he ordered Jack to leave the room, despite Luke's protests that he stay.

Oliver glared at his son and heir. Luke had tidied himself, or Jack had done it for him. He stood with his hands on his hips, as if mocking his father's often used stance. The expression on his dark face was so insolent, so cruel, that Oliver, who had rarely taken a hand to any of his children, wanted to shake him into sense and submission.

'Well?'

'Well, Father?'

'Sit. We shall speak for as long as it takes, for you obviously have something on your mind.'

Oliver seated himself in one of the armchairs beside the double window, replacing his sternness with an air of one willing to listen and counsel.

Luke thought to disobey, but this would make him appear a sulky child. He wasn't willing to own that label – one often thrown at him. And he could no longer keep up his devil-may-care attitude.

He sat, facing his father. 'Sir, you have my apologies for disturbing the peace of your house.'

'Good. On that respect I'll say no more, after you have made equal recompense to my guests.' If Luke was not so intent on his own miseries, he would have gleaned his father had some of his own, as he added tightly, 'Including Clem Trenchard.'

Luke nodded his assent and gazed glumly out of the window, letting his worn-out eyes roam over the panoramic view of the grounds, where a glasshouse for exotic plants and a bowling green had been built in his absence. Always his father planned and improved, leaving less that he might do.

Oliver waited until he looked at him again.

'I take it I was included in your spleen just now.'

'Of course not.' But he could not lie. 'Yes, I'm sorry.'

Oliver employed the softest voice of his life. 'I understand.'

'You do?'

'You're my son, Luke. I've foolishly allowed you too much sway all your life and have turned a blind eye to your recklessness, but I've always known your mind, and all these years I've been hoping you'd purge your sense of despair. I should have spoken to you long before this, I've failed you and for that I apologize. I know you're as desperately unhappy now as when you went away. That you've always felt jealous of Kane and I, perhaps even feel you hate us because we're able to do the things that require two good arms. That you feel you have no challenge of your own.' Oliver paused, greatly saddened. 'Perhaps even that you have no future to invest in?'

Since his return, Luke had planned to hurl all this and more at his father, but his father's astuteness astounded him. He stumbled for words to describe his desperation but none would come, so he confessed his soul. 'I wish I was dead.'

Oliver's eyes misted at the corners. The depths of Luke's despair meant he had lost the emotion to weep for himself.

'I've realized that too. So, have you a notion what to do about it? Throw yourself off Pengarron Point? Drink yourself to death?'

'I might, I really don't care.'

'Have you never had a dream, Luke? Isn't there something you'd really like to do?'

'Yes, I suppose.' His voice was flat, defeated.

'Well, that's good. What is it?'

'You wouldn't like it.'

'Try me.'

'I want to get away from here, do something of my own.'

'There's nothing wrong with that. Every man wants to make his mark on the world.'

'You wouldn't object if I didn't live here? I thought it was expected of me to help manage the estate until I come into it one day.'

'I would prefer that you were here, I won't deny that, and of course so would your mama, but we'd never seek to frustrate your wishes, Luke. Every man must have a vision to follow or he wilts and dies. What exactly would you do?'

'You'll think me foolish, you'll laugh at the very idea.'

Luke shook his head and blew out his feeling of desolation in one deep shaft of breath. He could not bear the thought of his one burning desire being ridiculed, seen as a pathetic secret.

'I might, but that should not be your main consideration.'

Luke chewed this over. His father understood him completely, he was prepared to listen fully and sympathetically. He'd throw his passion back in his face, of course, but perhaps he'd go away and think about it, even come round to the idea in time.

Leaning forward, a spark of energy igniting in his dark eyes, Luke started hesitantly but grew ever more enthusiastic. In the end, it was as if he was on fire. 'While in London the only thing I really enjoyed was the theatre. I loved the drama, the atmosphere, the costumes, the faces of the audience and their reaction. I even loved it when the productions were awful and abuse was hurled at the players. I found I could lose myself in the themes behind the plays. I felt alive somehow. I'd go back to my lodgings and remember everything I'd seen and heard and somehow feel elated. Jack enjoyed them too. We'd talk for hours about them. I wish they had theatres and playhouses on such a scale in Cornwall.'

'You're saying you want to be an actor, Luke?' Oliver kept his face straight. He didn't want his son and heir to follow this course, but thinking of his despair, how could he not give his blessing?

'No, no.' For the first time in ages Luke

laughed with true humour. 'I want to write plays, good ones, tragedies and comedies and fantasies and love stories, stories that people will enjoy and remember all their lives. I want to entertain people, make an impact on their lives. After watching a play I used to restructure the plots and scenes in my head, knowing I could do better than just about anything I'd seen. I'd even started to write a couple but left them behind, thinking...'

The old melancholy regained its grip. Feeling stupid, and even betrayed, that he had share his deepest yearning, he gazed down at the Turkish rug beneath his feet.

'Thinking you'd have no use for them, that I'd not release you from the estate,' Oliver finished for him. Rising, he stood directly in front of Luke. 'Well, my son, I think you should give your ambition a try, live where you will until you come into your inheritance. Here's my hand on it, or are you too grown up to give your father a hug?'

Luke didn't ask his father if he really meant it, he never said a word he didn't mean. He was up on his feet and in his father's bear-hug embrace. He was crying a river of release, a flood of joy and gratitude, and regret. For being so full of his own desolate self for so long, he had not realized the depth of his father's compassion.

'I don't know what to say.' He wiped away

his tears, shaking in excitement. 'Except that I'll never stop thanking you, Father.'

Oliver smiled. 'Where will you move to? Not a hundred miles away, I hope.'

'No, definitely not. I'll give it some thought, but I shall stay in the county, near the sea. What better place to gain the inspiration I shall need? And Mama will not be distraught, she can come to stay whenever she wishes. All the family can.'

'Find yourself a house then. I advise one that is established and needs little attention, perhaps with a retained staff. I'll arrange for the money to be released whenever you wish. Only remember this word of caution, there's just one person who can ruin your opportunity to make well of yourself, Luke, and that is you.'

'I know that, Father. There's no need for you to fund me, I have money. Twenty-five thousand I've brought back from London.'

Oliver pierced Luke with a steady gaze. 'And how come you by that? From nothing legal, I'll warrant.'

'I won some at the gaming tables.'

'The rest?'

Luke went quiet.

Oliver became grim. 'Were you involved with a certain Lord Alexander Longbourne? And is Jack's wife Longbourne's presumed-dead mistress?'

'I should have known you'd be acquainted

with the facts of Longbourne's death and the surrounding circumstances. But Alicia was more properly Alex's common-law wife, they were very much in love and only her lower rank prevented their marriage. Alex had huge gambling debts and knew he'd not be spared, so he charged me and Jack with Alicia's safekeeping.'

Luke recounted the true facts of how he and Jack had come by their burns and injuries, their flight to Cornwall, and how he had slipped back to his lodgings and obtained the twenty-five thousand from its hiding place.

'Alicia was in equal peril from these men – you must know their title – the Society. After Alex's murder, I felt marriage to Jack the best course for her. It was easy to talk him round. You must have noticed he's in love with her. Alicia complied, she needed a father for her child.'

'Dear God, Luke, you've tempted the devil even more than I in my youth!' Oliver swept his hands up in the air. 'This Society of which you speak is saturated in evil. To benefit from their dishonest business practices, or their fixed race meetings, or one of their great number of other unlawful connections, means one is likely beholden to them forever. They arrange death by duels, they'll stop at nothing to further their ends. They're in commerce, government, the royal court, even the clergy.

'Typical of you to make alliance with someone like Longbourne, a weak-skinned wastrel. Pray God, that sleazy set never seeks you out to call in a favour. Even I would not wish to cross swords with Sir Decimus Soames. You realize that by yoking Jack and yourself to this woman it would be ill-advised to show your face again in the capital, at least for a very long time, and you must always keep one eye looking behind you? It's a good thing you wish to live quietly. I'm relieved you've told me all this, it enables me to look also to your protection.'

'Thank you, Father.' For the very first time Luke blushed in disgrace.

'Well, all is done and you have chosen your next course. One other thing, how do you propose to promote your plays? It might be unwise to have them performed under your own name.'

'I shall think of that when the time comes.' Luke was too excited to let anything dampen his enthusiasm. He already knew his first play, act by act, scene by scene, word for word. 'Of course, when I find somewhere to live I shall take Jack and Alicia with me.'

'You have a need of Jack's companionship – I accept that, but I feel sore to lose him. He is more than a servant to me also,' Oliver said quietly. 'You wish to live by the sea, you

114

have the wherewithal to consider the Polgissey estate, it's been on the market for some weeks. Write your plays, and then we will see how things stand in London. Now wash your face, allow yourself ten minutes and go downstairs and do what you must in respect of my guests. And Luke, there's one lady you especially need to make repair to.'

'Mama. I know. I'm sorry I've given her so much worry.'

'Your mama, yes, but I was thinking of Cordelia. You've hurt her more than you know.'

Alone in his room, Luke covered his mouth to forestall a whoop of joy. He hadn't felt like this, dizzy, kind of silly, ecstatically excited, since boyhood. So many years had passed since he'd had something to look forward to. Splashing his face with water from the pitcher on the washstand, he fell down on his bed laughing, bubbling over with sheer happiness, making his father smile as he left his door.

Jack was hovering further along the corridor, out of earshot. The instant he saw Sir Oliver emerge he marched straightway to rejoin his younger master.

Taking his arm in a firm grip, Oliver dragged him back to a discreet distance. 'I now know the truth of what occurred in London. Explain to me why you saw fit to repeat the lie about a fire at an inn when we

115

talked soon after your return?'

'Mr Luke asked me to, sir.'

'And that's it, is it?'

'Yes, sir.'

'I thought I would always have your first loyalty, Jack Rosevear. You're a good few years older than my son, and there is none other I would trust with his welfare, perhaps even his life. I charge you to put him first from hence, even above this wife that you love. Do I have your oath on it?'

Jack was devoted to his wife, but he said, 'I swear on God's holy name, I'll do what you ask of me, sir.'

Looking up from the rug where she was amusing Samuel with wooden building blocks, Cordelia watched as Luke and Kane, who was holding Harry, approached them. For once, Luke's handsome face was a wreath of smiles. Hope pricked Cordelia's heart, but she was wary. Quicker than the weather, his moods could change.

The men sat down beside her. 'We thought we'd join you.' Kane smiled. He greeted Catherine and Cherry, who were conversing nearby about the twins' routine. Luke ignored them and built a brick tower with Samuel.

Cordelia looked at the two men inquisitively. Why was Luke suddenly so cheerful, so friendly, after the shameful goings-on in the stable yard? If she had not been given custody of Samuel again, she would have slipped away and spied on Luke and the young gentlemen, and witnessed the proceedings. Obviously, her uncle had worked some magic on Luke, but then, Uncle Oliver was capable of anything.

'Yes, sweeting.' Luke grinned. 'I've made my peace with Kane and introduced myself properly to young Harry, and I've got something for you.'

Her small, dark face lit up at his longed-for renewed interest. 'Have you brought me back a doll from London for my collection?'

'No, it's this.' He kissed her cheeks and held her a long time in a warm embrace. 'I'm sorry for being such a miserable crosspatch. Forgive me? Can we go back to the way things were before?'

'Oh, yes, yes, I've missed that so much, Luke.'

'There's something I want to discuss with you, Corrie. Will you come with me now to Jack's cottage?'

'Of course.' She was up and on her dainty feet in an instant. 'Why to Jack's cottage?'

'Because what I have to say involves him and his wife.'

Informed by Oliver of the details, excluding the unsavoury ones, of Luke's former adventure and new venture, Kerensa took his arm

117

and breathed an audible sigh of relief. 'Pray God he stays this full of purpose.'

Oliver raised her hand to his lips and kissed it. Society was used to his public displays of affection. He was satisfied, as was his intention, that Clem Trenchard should observe him perform this one.

Catherine came rushing from inside the great hall with John in her arms. 'Clem! Flora's missing!'

'Eh?' Clem, standing alone, for he had no desire to mix with this sort of company, had not heard her. His concentration had been all on the Pengarrons.

'It's Flora. She's wandered off. The nursemaid and Captain Pengarron and I have searched everywhere in the immediate vicinity. I only turned away for a moment, and now there's no sign of her.'

'Worry not, Mrs Trenchard.' Oliver, who had overheard, took charge of the situation. 'An infant can't have wandered very far. There's nowhere she could come to harm. Nonetheless, we will mount a thorough search.'

'Oliver, the lake,' Kerensa said urgently. 'It's a long way off, but I think we should look there first, just in case.'

Oliver organized the servants to make a search in every direction.

The panic was over quickly. Mounting the wide stone steps at the front entrance of the ancient house came Kane, carrying Harry and holding Flora by the hand.

'There's no harm done. Harry and I came across this young lady in the rose garden.'

'Thank God!' Catherine gasped. 'I'm sorry for the alarm, my lord, my lady. It's unheard of, Flora slipping away like this.'

Clem ran down the steps and lifted Flora up, kissing and hugging her. 'You scared us, sweetheart.'

'I suppose you and your family will take your leave now, Trenchard. I'll have your mount and the trap brought round.' Oliver's voice resounded from the top step and all around the courtyard.

Clem was infuriated by his dismissive tone. Did the arrogant swine care nothing about his wife's fright? He climbed back up to confront him.

'You suppose wrong, but as we're obviously not welcome here I'll say goodbye to my grandson, and we'll walk round to the stables. Come, Catherine, say goodbye to your brother. Bring John.'

'Sir, I think—' Timothy Lanyon was cut off by Kerensa.

'Clem, please don't leave like this,' she begged. 'Oliver, you are impolite. Tell Clem he's welcome to stay as long as he likes.'

'I'll not be told what to do regarding this individual, especially by you,' Oliver replied darkly, hurt and angry. She had humiliated him by her immediate support for the whining oaf.

Guests were gathering behind them and cramming the massive doorway to witness this altercation.

Clem looked at his enemy levelly. Then covering his daughter's ears, he said, 'How dare you speak to Kerensa like that, you bastard-crow, Pengarron. You care nothing for her wishes, never have and never will.'

Oliver let out a mighty roar. He reached out with the intention of frog-marching Trenchard, even though he had a child in his arms, to the stables and off his property.

'Father, don't.' Kane was now there, seeking to intervene by warding off his grasping hands. Oliver's momentum was too decided and its strength upset Kane's balance.

Kerensa screamed as Kane and Harry were sent crashing down to the bottom of the steps.

Eleven

A week later, Luke presented himself in Kane's bedroom at Vellanoweth.

Jessica, who was sitting in vigil beside the bed, jumped to her feet, motioning at him not to make a noise. 'He's sleeping. He's still in a lot of pain and I don't want him disturbed. The servants shouldn't have allowed you to come up.'

Luke met the hostility in her wide blue eyes with an air of solemn sympathy and a softened voice. 'I understand your concern, sister-in-law, that is why I've left it until now to come here. I promise not to wake Kane. I've brought news. Perhaps I could sit with him awhile, and if he opens his eyes I'll tell him quickly and leave.'

Against all advice and Kerensa's pleadings, Jessica had insisted that Kane be moved home almost immediately following the accident. She had travelled with him and Harry, who was uninjured, in the Pengarron coach, and she had rarely left his bedside since. Her father had taken Catherine and the twins back to the parsonage. He was delaying their return home until Kane was much recovered, and able to oversee the farm; Philip was completely capable of running Greystone's Farm on his own for a lengthy time. Jessica was relieved to have Clem at hand, she needed him.

'I've no welcome for you. You never got in touch with Kane once during the year you spent in wantonness and waste. You didn't want him near you at the baptism, nor our son – your godson – not until you'd got your own way again with this playwriting thing. You're only here now, Luke Pengarron, because, no doubt, you've something to boast about. Too much like your father, that's your trouble!'

'I understand your bitterness, Jessica—'

'No, you don't!' she hissed. 'Before *your* father nearly killed my husband and son he'd spent the whole day making jibes at *my* father, even at the twins and they're infants! You're both cut from the same cloth, selfish, proud and insufferable. I don't ever want to see Sir Oliver again and I want you out of my house.'

'Jessica.' A low hoarse voice from the bed filtered through her anger and resentment. 'I don't want this unpleasantness. Let Luke stay and say his piece.'

'You're in no state to listen, dearest. Rest now. In a while I'll fetch up some broth,' Jessica cooed to Kane as if he might be her baby son. She wrung out a cloth soaking in a bowl of cold water and replaced it for the hot, sweaty one lying across his brow.

Kane had plunged down the steps backwards, striking his head against the last step, knocking himself unconscious. His collar bone had been cracked and his left leg broken. The leg was in splints, resting heavily on a bolster and covered with a bread and herb poultice to draw out the impurities.

A soothing smell of lavender and sandalwood, heated by a mass of candles, overwhelmed the farmyard smells coming in through the open window and provided mental and spiritual comfort for the invalid. Even so, the smell of human flesh in crisis, similar to that which had assailed Luke's nose from those sick and dying in the poor areas of London, pervaded the room. Luke felt afraid for his brother. His nightmares about the family physician labouring to thrust back his dislocated shoulder after his own accident had made a dreaded return.

'He will recover?' he mouthed quietly across to Jessica.

She stared at him grimly. 'By God's grace.'

Kane tried to stay awake, but racked by pain and fever, slipped back into the land of fantastical dreams, twitching, occasionally moaning.

'If you think I find pleasure in seeing my brother like this, Jessica,' Luke said soberly, 'you're very much mistaken. I can't begin to tell you how sorry I am to see him suffering like this. Thank God, some instinct made him hug Harry against his body. Is there anything I can do for you or Kane?' She made no reply, so he went on. 'Jessica, I've come to say that I've purchased a property and I am going away very soon.'

'Go on,' Jessica said a little less harshly. Despite her hurt and anger at the heartless treatment of her father and the consequences to her own little family, she wasn't indifferent to learn of Luke's plans. There had been times in the past when they had shared moments of friendship.

'I'm moving to the opposite coast, the Polgissey estate on the North Cliffs. Cordelia is coming with me, and I'm taking Jack as my steward and his wife as Cordelia's companion. I shall keep myself informed of Kane's progress, and I hope that if you ever have need of me you won't hesitate to send word. You have my assurance I'll come to you at once. Kane will understand my desire to make my own mark in life.'

Jessica was holding Kane's hand and she looked down at him to see if he had heard. His eyes were closed. 'I hope Cordelia doesn't come to regret it. You are two and twenty, Luke, but too young yet in the head for such a responsibility.'

'Can you not find it in your heart to wish

her, Jack and I well, Jessica?'

She thought for several moments, impressed that he had included Jack in his question. 'Yes, I suppose so, and I'm sure Kane will too when I tell him. He's the one member of your family who doesn't bear grudges, even after what's just been done to him. Write to him when you're settled.'

Bending over the bed, Luke kissed Kane's burning cheek. A grim thought made his hand fly to his constantly aching shoulder. 'Will he be crippled? Please God, not that.'

'We must pray not.' Jessica smoothed Kane's damp hair. 'But Dr Crebo says he'll definitely have a limp. It's infection I'm worried about.'

Pressing his lips together, Luke shook his head. 'Pray God it gives him no lasting pain. Kane didn't deserve this, but Jessica, please heed my next words. My father couldn't feel more wretched about the accident if he tried for all eternity. Won't you relent and answer his letters?'

Jessica looked away.

'Very well. Mama will be riding over tomorrow, is there anything you'd like her to bring?'

Jessica shook her head.

'I'll go now and leave you in peace, but first may I take a peep at my godson? Livvy's going to give me the first likeness she paints of Harry. Do you think she's happy? She seems to have lost her spirit. I suppose this sorry incident has affected her as deeply as the rest of us.'

Luke rode slowly home. He was about to make a new start but was taking a heavy anxiety with him. He had just received a letter written by Lord Longbourne a short time before his death. In it, Alex had actually compiled a list of all those public figures he'd threatened to expose as members of the Society. What a fool the man had been to imagine he could bargain his way out of paying his enormous debts. He'd told Luke it was the only way he could think of to protect Alicia. How could he not have foreseen that the Society would search for the evidence he'd told them he had secreted away and murder them both anyway? Why, Luke asked himself, had he not begged Alex to take Alicia and flee? But at that point he had not realized just how ruthless the Society could be.

Luke had assumed the Society had found what they'd been looking for before stabbing Alex to death. The names on the list had shocked him. The letter contained meticulously gathered details of over fifty dates of national criminal occurrences, of blackmail in high places and of murders. Evidence that could not be ignored by any seriously minded person, or nobleman of impeccable character. The King qualified for this distinction and Alex had even bandied his name in his threats. He had also stated in his letter that he would be willing to give first-hand evidence in the law courts.

Luke's immediate reaction was to destroy the letter. It was the safest, the obvious way to protect Jack, Alicia, his family and himself. He had told Jack that the letter contained only goodbyes and Alex's wishes for Alicia should he be killed. But on second thoughts he decided it might be wiser to keep it, at least for a time.

Unlike Alex, he would hide it very carefully and keep total silence. Wisdom also argued that he should seek his father's judgement, but he had got into this sorry state of affairs by himself, and if he wanted to go his own way and not have his father put all manner of guard and restrictions on him, he must carry on with it alone.

Twelve

Oliver was sprawled at the desk in his study, scratching at an indentation left on the mellowed wood by a long-dead Pengarron.

Important papers had been left unattended for days. He had cancelled the local court he was due to take today. Let the petty thieves, poachers and drunkards go free! How could he look a miscreant in the face when he had performed such a heartless, offensive act himself?

It was hard not seeing Kane and Harry. If it had been for any other reason he would have ignored Jessica's prohibition, but she had the right to exclude him from her home and family for what he had done.

He now saw his attempt at hauling Clem Trenchard off his property in the same light as everyone else, mean and unnecessary. And, as certain others did, despicable and unforgivable.

Trenchard had come out on top.

His attempts at humiliating him had not got under the wretched man's skin, instead Trenchard had succeeded in getting under his: behaving like a saint in church; a loving husband under the manor roof; pretending he wasn't the slightest bit interested in Kerensa; eating and drinking like a gentleman; speaking with care; unruffled and proud in his fine clothes; comfortable and composed. And watching and waiting: watching Kerensa without seeming to, waiting for the first opportunity to lay claim on her again, to rekindle their former feelings. Trenchard was no longer a fool, a loser. He was cunning and sly and dangerous. And what had he, himself, now done? Given Trenchard the respect and sympathy of the county. And with his indefinite presence at Vellanoweth and Kerensa's regular visits there, he had given them the ideal chance to meet, to be alone, to form a new attachment. And there was nothing he could do about it without sounding exactly the same as he had done on that fateful day. A pathetic, jealous husband. If only he had never come across Kerensa's secret things.

How much of Kerensa's loyalty and love did he still have?

The morning after the accident the family were in the great hall; no one had gone to bed, they had kept a vigil of prayer. He, Kerensa, Luke, Kelynen, Olivia, Timothy and Cordelia, dotted under the decorated high ceiling, the rafters, banners and hangings. Oliver had stared at the shields and crossed swords of some of his forebears. The sword he had fought with at the battle of Dettingen many years ago was among them. He should take it down, he had lost his honour.

Only Kerensa had stayed on her feet. Pacing up and down all night, wringing her hands. She had seemed not to want to be close to anyone, certainly not him. He had hardly dared speak to her. There was very little talk at all, only those disturbing whispers that seemed so difficult to get past the throat, only to emerge garbled, needing an invasive repeat. The longer the night had worn on, the more a sense of pessimism and misery had pervaded the house. Every stone and timber seemed weighed down with oppression and accusation.

Oliver had been waiting for the accusations to begin. He deserved them, but when they came he wasn't prepared for the quietness and dignity of the onslaught. Passion and fury he could have dealt with far better.

Suddenly Kerensa had announced, 'I'm going over to Vellanoweth. I'll leave instructions with Cherry about Samuel's care. And, well, you're here, Cordelia.'

Oliver had got up off the chest he was languishing on. 'Jessica doesn't want me there, but I'll accompany you for the ride, my dear.'

She stayed put. So he had started climbing

the stairs to change his clothes. No sound of light footsteps followed him. He turned round.

Kerensa was at the foot of the stairs, looking up as if she were elsewhere, her face marked with horror. He sensed that in her mind she was outside, remembering how it had looked as Kane and Harry came hurtling down the steps. Then she saw him. Her ice-cold expression froze his every fibre.

'How could you do it?' Her voice came out low and cracked and full of despair.

'If only I could roll back time, Kerensa.'

'Even now our son could die! Our grandson may never get over the fright. You may have ruined his life. I'll not go to Vellanoweth with you! I'll ask Polly to ride with me, we'll take the things Beatrice has prepared for Jessica to nurse Kane with. I'll only come back when I'm sure our son's life is out of danger.'

Kerensa had stayed at the farm for three days. It had been an agony of loneliness without her. An agony wondering what might be happening between her and Clem Trenchard.

Recognizing Kelynen's springy step heading his way, Oliver sprang up and met his younger daughter at the study door. Rex bounded into sight, his heavy pads thudding down on the polished oak of the floor. The big black retriever was always several steps behind her, or did the girl's matchless energy make her several steps ahead of Rex, and everyone else? Although tomboyish in nature, she had the knack of anticipating the unexpected, saw events with a mellow philosophy. She had pointed out that he must accept that the two families, the Pengarrons and Trenchards, were always going to be connected. If only he had listened to her. Now he was being forced to accept cool attitudes from friends and servants. The Beswethericks were staying away from the manor, and Beatrice had dared ask him if he wanted 'a bleddy medal fer what 'ee just done?'

The stony indifference to his feelings from Kerensa was crushing him.

'Shelley, beloved, do you know where your mother—'

'Kelynen, will you please keep Rex under control in the house,' came Kerensa's vexed voice behind her. 'Have a care for Beatrice. I don't want to see another nasty accident.'

'Sorry, Mama,' Kelynen said, taking hold of Rex's collar. 'I'll ensure he walks to heel inside the house from now on.'

'I'd appreciate that, my dear.'

Oliver's heart plummeted, the chastisement had been aimed at him more than Shelley, and Kerensa was already walking off towards her sitting room.

'Kerensa, Shelley and I are about to discuss her taking over full responsibility of the charity school. Would you like to sit in with us? I'm sure you'd agree her first action should be to remonstrate with the men over its leaky roof. It was an unforgivable act to use broken slates.'

'Very well,' Kerensa replied at once, coming back. 'I'm sure Kelynen will make a very good job of anything you allow her to do on the estate.'

Oliver felt a little hopeful that she was thawing towards him. To make the discussion less formal he did not sit behind his desk.

Then Kerensa muttered in tones steeped with meaning, 'Now what was that you said about the builders? An unforgivable act?'

'Kerensa.' Oliver knew she was awake. There was a long silence. 'Kerensa, please speak to me.'

In the lavish bed, where she had given birth to her children, Kerensa lay with her back to him, as far away as she could without falling over the edge and making the long drop to the floor. Miserably hot, her head aching, she had pushed the light covers off her body long before, in the small hours of the night, but she had kept her hands wrapped round herself in a cutting-off gesture.

Oliver usually rose before this and Kerensa longed for him to leave the room. She felt

133

him move and his hand come to rest on her upper arm. She stiffened.

'Please, beloved.' He leaned over her and looked down on her face.

Unwillingly, Kerensa turned round to him.

Oliver was careful not to put his weight near her.

'We can't go on like this, Kerensa. Surely it's not what you want? You're hurting yourself too. Samuel will suffer if he becomes aware his parents are estranged, and Shelley's desperately unhappy. I beg you, sit up and talk to me.'

Sir Oliver Pengarron begging? This was a rare occasion, Kerensa wanted to snap at him. She had never thought she could feel this way. The depth of her bitterness over Oliver's contemptible actions rivalled Jessica's.

'I don't want to speak to you now,' she replied, unyielding.

'When then? Just say.'

Another flashback of Kane and Harry plunging down the steps outside, possibly to their deaths, slammed into her mind. Kerensa couldn't bear it and leapt out of bed. Kane did not deserve to be laid up in terrible pain, possibly crippled, fighting off infection, missing out on so many joys with his new son. Kane might be able to forgive quickly, but she could not.

'Maybe never. Leave me be. I'll go over to

see Kane early today. I'll take Samuel with me and stay all day. I might stay all night. In fact I might never come back! Now Luke and Cordelia are leaving, and with Kelynen spending all her time with you, there won't be any reason for me to be here.'

She thrust her arms into her dressing gown, pulling silk threads in her haste.

Oliver swallowed the bile in his throat that formed at her outburst. 'You can't mean that, Kerensa. I know I've done a terrible thing, but you're not going to let it tear us apart, are you? By God, don't you think I feel just as wretched as you do? Even more so? I know what I nearly did, that Kane or Harry or both of them could have died, that Kane has a long fight yet until he's hale again. I'd cut off my own leg if it would undo the damage to his. I understand why Jessica can't forgive me, I insulted and then very nearly harmed her father and half-sister.'

Oliver paused, staring at her unresponsive face. Had he not good reason to be angry too? 'Why do you feel this strongly? You must know I'd never wish to hurt any of my family, and I only sought to put Trenchard in his place. Does it mean nothing to you, what he said to me in front of our friends?'

'No, nothing whatsoever. I've no care about keeping the right appearance in society,' Kerensa said, from halfway towards her dressing room.

What did he mean, put Clem in his place? All Clem had ever done was to love her. She had given him her promise to marry him. Was it so unthinkable that he should have been heartbroken? She and Clem had shared a love stolen from them. They had not drifted apart as sweethearts sometimes do. Marriage for them would have been a wonderful, fulfilling success, not something that would have faded or died in the course of time. It was this that stuck in Oliver's craw! This man, who, for all his excellent ways, sometimes behaved as if all that mattered were his wishes, his desires.

All the emotion and resentment building up inside her burst out in a dam of bitterness. 'You make me sick!'

Thrusting himself off the bed Oliver strode towards her, his long legs bare beneath the nightshirt he rarely wore. He yanked the dressing room door from her hand, forbidding her entrance.

'Get away from me.'

'I'm sorry to use my strength against you, Kerensa, but before I let you go I will have it out of you, what exactly is on your mind. It's because it was Clem Trenchard and no other, isn't it, that you're so angry with me? Do you still love the man? Is this what it's all about?'

'Don't you dare look at me as if I've wronged you. It's your damned arrogance, your damned pride that's resurfaced again that's making me want you nowhere near me. There was enough to endure as it was on the day of the baptism with Luke's conduct and our worries about him. There was no reason for you to mock Clem or his family. You gave no thought to Jessica's feelings or Catherine's and they've never, ever, done anything to you. When I pointed out Jessica's upset, you couldn't even take it upon yourself to apologize to her. Clem didn't do a single thing to show you disrespect or to try to humiliate you as you did him. And you gave no thought to my discomfort when you hauled me off with Rachael for that sarcastic introduction.

'Right from the beginning, when you forced me to marry you over that cruel bargain you made with my grandfather, there was no need for you to cause further distress to Clem. But over the years you've never stopped abusing him or making slurs on his character, even when he moved on with his own life and away from Pengarron land.

'You think you're a great man, Oliver Pengarron. Lord of all you survey, with a God-given right to proceed exactly how you like. But you're spiteful, nasty, vindictive and malicious. That makes you very small in my eyes.'

Kerensa had forgotten to breathe through-out her tirade and she nearly fainted for lack of breath. Oliver put out his hands to catch her. She pushed them away, using the door for support.

There was another silence, only the sound of her harsh breathing echoed in the room. The silence grew grim, heavy and charged with acrimony. He was looking at her as if he had never seen her before.

He moved back.

'Up until a few days ago, when by pure chance I discovered your hoard of keepsakes from Clem Trenchard–' he stabbed his index finger in the direction of the lowest drawer of her dressing table – 'I would hardly have been able to believe you've said all this, that you'd dare to threaten to leave me! To take my son to live at the same farm where that bastard dirt-farmer's presently working! And, not only do you refuse to forgive me for our son and grandson's accident, no matter how much I plead how sorry I am, you now see fit to tell me you've never forgiven me for taking you away from your pathetic sweetheart. That was over twenty-four years ago, for God's sake! I've thought for many years there was absolutely nothing wedged between us, Kerensa, but again I find you've been keeping secrets from me, just as you did for the first eight years of our marriage when you kept it from me that Samuel Drannock was my half-brother, and by the time I found that out the man was dead!

'And I see, as I'd feared, that the love you've professed for me has never been as strong or as exclusive as you'd have me believe. Your words tell me that you do indeed love Clem Trenchard. Well, I don't want your flawed love, your half-love any more.

'You've had your say, Kerensa, now heed this. It won't take a foreign trip on my part to bring about a reconciliation between us this time. From now on you can have this room to yourself.'

Kerensa had listened carefully. In their early days together such a strong harangue from him would have unnerved or humiliated her. Even until recently she had hated to receive his disapproval. Now, she couldn't care less.

'As usual, nothing's your fault, is it? Don't you know that I would have been as upset over your wicked behaviour if it had been any other man standing on the steps with his child? As for Samuel Drannock, you choose to forget he swore me to secrecy, because he despised your wanton, pig-headed ways.

'Listen to me one more time, husband, and try to take this in. It wasn't so much that you wished to harm Clem, it was your boorish attitude towards him then and so it is now that angers me so much. So what if I'd kept his love tokens? If you'd have come to me on the day you'd seen them, I would've felt guilty about it. I always meant to do away with them, I just kept forgetting to. In fact, I did so the very next day. Now I wish I hadn't!

'If you honestly believe my love for you is so fragile, so lacking, then you're every bit as bad as Samuel Drannock thought you.'

'Well, we both know where we stand,' came Oliver's blistering reply. 'I ask for mercy and you see fit to taunt me!' He came towards her. He did not touch her, but nevertheless his bearing pinned her back against the door. 'You are my wife. Think not that this will give you an opportunity to find more time to be alone with that bastard dirt-farmer, to give him the chance to get what he's always wanted from you. Whenever you go to Vellanoweth, I shall see to it that an escort goes with you and never leaves your side.'

Kerensa refused to be intimidated. 'That will cause me no injury. For your information, Clem and I have never been alone on my visits to Kane and Harry. Be sure to keep your own self in order. Just go, Oliver, there's no last word for you this time.'

He stalked off to his own dressing room, saying over his shoulder, 'We'll see!'

Returning to the great bed, she climbed up on it, shaking uncontrollably. She and Oliver had said many things in hurt, frustration and temper. And they had acknowledged a truth that, despite the intensity of the love they shared, someone had always been there like a shadow between them.

Clem.

Thirteen

Catherine Trenchard was having breakfast alone with her brother.

His housekeeper brought a letter into the dining room. Timothy Lanyon held out his hand for it, but Nancy Wills placed the silver salver beside Catherine's untouched plate.

'For me? Thank you, Nancy. It must be from someone connected with one of my charities.'

'I don't think so,' Nancy replied, eyeing the abandoned bread and butter.

The writing above the red wax seal, bearing Catherine's own mark, was barely legible. Only someone home at the farm could have written it. She hid her dismay at what she read.

'Come along, Mrs Trenchard, you're eating less than the twins these days,' Nancy clucked round her. 'And you, Reverend. You've hardly eaten a thing yourself.'

141

Timothy wasn't listening, his mind was on Olivia. She was spending more time than ever about her paintings. If she wasn't upstairs in the studio, which Sir Oliver had arranged to be converted from the attics for her, she was taking her easel and water-colours or oils out to field, wayside, beach or cliff top, sometimes accompanied by an animal or human subject. She was adept in any medium, and he was proud of her achievements, but she was sorely neglecting him and her parish duties. It was receiving comment and he was feeling a fool. If he ever brought up the matter of babies, and as a husband he had the right to, she immediately became unresponsive, eventually breaking into a temper that could out-better the fiercest of her brother Luke's.

It seemed to Timothy that Olivia had out-grown their marriage within its first year, and he ached inside, thinking she might feel she had made a mistake. She admitted that she found matters of the church and the parish something of an annoyance, getting in the way of her pastime – ambition, as she put it. She longed for wider acknowledgement for her talent, and he couldn't make her see that she ought to be putting her duties to him, and those under his cure, before her own desires.

'Once a week is enough for this,' he had stabbed a finger at the painting gear she

142

carried downstairs an hour ago. 'You've a meeting to attend this luncheon-tide at Tolwithrick, of the Gentlewomen's Charitable Trust.'

Out of Olivia's grey-green eyes came a vixenish glare. 'I intend to do no such thing. I haven't painted outside for four days owing to the inclement weather. I'm not about to waste this promise of good light by being cooped up with a roomful of gossiping old biddies, who'll soon twist all the conversation round to my parents' troubles. And news of that,' she accused him bitterly, 'wouldn't have got abroad if you'd acted in due haste to wipe out the rumours.'

'Livvy, you are being unfair. I had no idea there was such talk. If Sir Oliver had seen fit to inform me—'

'Don't blame my father for your own failures! The old Reverend Ivey would have had my parents reunited by now.'

'That's unjust, Olivia, and you know it!'

'Oh, get out of my way, Timothy, and let me get on. Then I might be back in time for this stupid meeting.'

'What are you thinking about, Timothy?' Catherine repeated a third time since Nancy had left the room. He looked up, his brow furrowed. 'It's obviously something very serious.'

'Oh, it's Olivia. She's gone out in one of her moods again.'

'Except for the unfortunate son who bore the brunt of Sir Oliver's sickening exhibition at Harry's baptism, the Pengarrons are a most moody, quarrelsome family.'

Catherine rarely gave vent to passion of an irate kind. She willingly forgave others their transgressions towards her, even without being asked, but not on this account. The hurt, the sense of degradation suffered by her family and herself on that dreadful occasion, was like an open wound to her heart. Clem and Flora could also have ended up at the base of those steps and John would have witnessed it. The twins had been fractious and anxious since then, and Clem had shut the greater part of himself off from her again.

'Aren't they just.' Timothy had never before issued a negative word against the lord of the manor, who had been responsible for giving him the living of the parish.

'They must be handled carefully.'

'I'll try to remember that the next time I ask my wife to give heed to her priorities.'

'Could you not have a word with Sir Oliver? Olivia's attitudes reflect the nature of his indulgences on the upbringing of his children, but he is strict about the observances of one's duties.'

It would suit Catherine's mood if the haughty, crass-mouthed baronet was given a morsel of contention to chew over. He

144

thought his family so perfect.

'My dear, I wouldn't ever dare utter a word of the kind to him. And what advice or understanding could be gleaned from a man who spends days at a time, quite unnecessarily, away from wife and home. I can't go into the details of my recent interview with Miss Kelynen, of course, but he's refused all her pleadings to him. I'm afraid Sir Oliver follows no one's direction but his own.' He sighed in dejection. 'Olivia does too for that matter. Who is your letter from?'

'I cannot say, it bids me to secrecy. Timothy, I'm afraid it means that I'll have to go home, today.' She gave a sigh similar to his. 'I must not delay, and I may not be able to return before Clem will leave here.'

She picked up her dish of tea, sipped but didn't taste it. She kept her gaze low over its delicate gold-trimmed rim. 'Would you keep an eye on Clem for me? I mean, it will be all right if he stays on here after I'm gone?'

'Of course it is, Catherine, but I think you meant the implications of your first question.'

Catherine glided over his remark. 'My presence here has meant Sir Oliver has been keeping away, preferring to see Olivia elsewhere. The instant I leave, I fancy his lordship will order Clem out of your house, perhaps in person, and there will be another terrible clash. I fear that one day he will physically harm Clem.'

'And you have no other fears about Clem, Catherine?'

'No. What could there be?'

'My dear, do you not think Clem will move into Vellanoweth anyway? Jessica will be glad to have more of his company.'

'Yes, of course.' Catherine looked down. 'It will be more convenient.'

Timothy knew what Catherine was thinking: that his deserted mother-in-law might now turn to Clem, and without herself and the twins to come back to every night, Clem would not tarry in seeking her exclusive company. However, Lady Pengarron never went to Vellanoweth without the company of Miss Kelynen or a female servant nowadays, and Clem had taken Catherine there himself, not the act of a man intent on an illicit affair.

He said suddenly, 'Take heart, Catherine. I have observed Clem's affection for you. Out of the two of us, it is not you who has made the wrong marriage.'

Comforted a little, for Clem had never lacked in devotion to either branch of his family, she reached round the table and clasped Timothy's hand. 'Thank you for that, Timothy. I have a word for you, my dear. Olivia is headstrong and I've observed that women such as her need strong men in their lives. Don't you think it's time you

146

took control of your marriage?'

Clem was fetched to the parsonage to see Catherine and the children off for the journey back to Greystone's Farm.

It had been a long farewell. Catherine, whose customary actions would have been a gentle kiss or two, had clung to him, kissing his mouth repeatedly. Her reluctance to go was on a par with his reluctance that she should stay.

He climbed the parsonage stairs to collect his own belongings. Timothy Lanyon was out on urgent parish business, his housekeeper in Marazion for the market, the maids nowhere about, and he thought the house was empty. A sudden crash coming from the floor above, followed by thuds and bangs made him fear the house had an intruder.

Investigation told him the noises were coming from Olivia's painting room. He could hear her crying and uttering violent phrases. He opened the heavy panelled door and yelped as something cut into his cheek. A broad canvas hit the floor at his feet, bounced and fell across his leg, hurting his shin. The bright light from the windows, which took up almost all of the south-facing wall, hurt his eyes and he shaded them against a scene of wanton destruction.

'Hey! What on earth are you doing?'

Olivia, tear-streaked and distraught, a beguiling spectacle with her red hair in wild disarray, already had another of her works in her hands and was about to send it smashing against the door. Clem hopped aside in case she did just that. She let the painting fall to the floor and, trembling violently, stood where she was and howled like an infant in the direst distress.

'What's the matter, sweetheart?' Clem slipped into fatherly mode with her, as he had done on those occasions when she had played with Jessica as a child and had come to some hurt. Reaching her, he took her into his arms and she fell against him, sobbing in great uncontrollable gasps.

He guided her to the couch, having first to shovel off a heap of ripped-up sketches so they could sit down. Holding her tight, he soothed her with quiet words. She rested her face against his chest until her sobs turned into an unrestrained heavy breathing.

His shirt was soaked with her tears, his skin made hot by her contact. He used a fold of his sleeve to mop her face. 'What is it, Livvy? What's brought you to this?'

She looked up at him. Her voice came out as a croak. 'Timothy's forbidden me to paint any more. He followed me to Trelynne Cove where I was at work and ordered me home. I refused to go with him and we had a terrible quarrel. He got really angry and shouted at me, something he's never done before.'

With tender fingers Clem brushed straying hair off her damp face. 'And this upset you so much you felt you had no choice but to destroy your work? That's a pity. I've been taking a look at it. It's very good, in fact I'd say you've a touch of genius, Livvy.'

'Really? You're not just saying that to appease me, Clem?'

He traced a fingertip around her face. 'I promise you, sweetheart. Thank the saints you haven't destroyed the lot. That picture of the castle up on the Mount is just wonderful. My wife's spoken of your talent many times since we've been here,' he lied. Catherine thought Olivia a poor wife and her painting an unjustifiable waste of time. 'The way I see it, Timothy's got no right to deny you this pleasure, to stop you using your gift, which he should know is a gift from God.'

Some of the tension left her, but she stayed pressed against him. 'Others have said that. I gave one of my miniatures to Jack and his wife as a wedding gift, and Mrs Rosevear made some fine, and I thought, informed comments about it. She said she had seen works of the same quality in some of the grand houses she has worked in.' A thought made her want to cry again. 'Dare I think I can produce paintings that might be welcomed further abroad than the few I've sold locally?

'Clem, there was something I was going to put before Timothy but it's out of the question now. There's a well known artist, a Mr George Spears, recently come to the county, who is presently staying at the Mount, with Sir John St Aubyn. I thought if I was to meet him, if he agreed to a request to look at my work, I would know then just how well my talent is. I was going to say to Timothy, that, if Mr Spears slighted it in any way, found it laughable, say, or immature, then I'd be content to carry on with it as a relaxation only, as Timothy wants. I should have pleaded with him differently in Trelynne Cove. Now all is ruined. My dream quite gone.'

'You mustn't give up, Livvy. Is your brother not busy about his dream that many would see a foolish fancy? And your father,' how he hated mentioning him, but Clem was appalled at the thought of Kerensa's daughter being so miserable, 'has given you his approval. He didn't build this room specially for you because he believed it was a waste of time, did he?'

'No.' Olivia immediately regained her usual confidence, her sense of power. 'Thank you, Clem. I haven't been thinking about things from my father's perspective. He knows a thing or two about art. He's always encouraged me. Timothy's opinions and lack of support have been confusing me, making me feel guilty.'

She dried the last tear, knowing she should pull away from Clem, but she liked his soft touches. They were doing astonishing things deep down inside her, giving her sensations of delight she never experienced with Timothy. He never showered her with affection as Clem sometimes did his wife, and in bed he acted as if their intimacy was something he should be apologetic about. She had suffered some anxiety on their wedding night, a legacy from her ordeal of the evil designs of one Captain Hezekiah Solomon, once a friend of her father's, a barbaric murderer, who had very nearly raped and slashed her to death. Even though the ageing sea captain was dead, by her father's sword, her terror had remained cruelly fresh in her mind. Timothy had been thoughtful towards her and remained so, but now she was frustrated in every sense that he never tried to make progress with her.

She touched Clem's cut cheek. 'I did this to you. I'm very sorry, Clem.'

'No matter.' He took her fingers in his hand. And she locked them together tight.

'Do you feel better now?'

'Yes, if I could just stay like this for a while.'

Every minute he had been under her roof, Olivia had watched Clem. He seemed to fill any room he was in, moving with an animal ease. He had a way of reclining in a chair in an indolent manner, his long legs stretched out, masterly, inviting somehow. His hands were big and rough, always scrubbed clean yet work-stained. They drew her eyes whatever he'd been doing. His smile, and it was rare to see it at its fullest extent, was beautiful to behold and she had longed to put it on canvas. His eyes were his best feature, at times soulful or secretive, or lazily surveying whatever caught his attention, or laughing with fun when he played with the twins. Sometimes they had alighted on Catherine, transferring messages that he desired her. Aware of this, Olivia had felt jealous and so very lonely.

He was a man of carnal need. He had taken pleasure with Catherine the first moment alone on the day of their arrival, in the daytime too. He would have no one to fill that need now. Olivia pushed aside the belief that he might like nothing more in the world than her own mother to take Catherine's place. Instead she concentrated on the sinful stirrings her thoughts and his nearness were giving her.

'What're you thinking?' Clem asked.

It was a pleasure to hold this young woman close to him, so similar in mould to Kerensa. Her body shape was sealed against him, she was pleasingly feminine and she smelled delicious. It appealed to him to think how

152

outraged her rotten father would be if he could see them now, the dark-faced monster who had so very nearly killed his flesh and blood. He would never ever forgive Pengarron for that.

'That I will talk to my father. Timothy wouldn't dare go against him.'

'Good for you, Livvy. There's only one thing ever to be afraid of and that's not following your dream.'

Still, she wanted to linger close to him.

'Clem.' She took a long length of his hair and twisted it around her finger. 'Why did Catherine have to leave for home so suddenly? I'm afraid I didn't say goodbye to her.' Olivia was pleased her duty-conscious sister-in-law was out of the house. So much easier to make Timothy eat a surfeit of humble pie.

'A problem with Kerris, my brother's wife, I think. Something only a woman can deal with, by the sounds of it.'

'I think I'll ride over to the farm with you. I'd like to talk to Jessica. I know I can't mention my father to her, but we need each other's support.'

'It'll be good timing. Your mother and sister are there. First, I'll help you clear up this mess.'

Yes, Kerensa was there. Now he had a better opportunity to pursue what should rightfully be his.

Olivia ran down to the kitchen and fetched a broom. She swept up all the splinters while Clem made a pile of the larger broken pieces, then they disposed of the evidence of her broken-hearted fury.

'A good job you didn't start on the paints.' He grinned, tweaking her hair.

'Thanks for all your help, Clem. And for what you've said, I'll never forget it.'

'I'm glad to have helped, Livvy.'

She reached out to him for what he thought was to be one last hug. The feel of her lips on his made his breath lock in his lungs. He kissed her back, meaning to for just a second. She tasted so sweet. The offer of forbidden pleasure was so powerful, and because she was so much a part of Kerensa, he helped himself to more and more. He sensed she had not fully yielded herself, had never reached a full flowering.

Then he remembered that she was Kerensa's daughter and in no way a substitute for her and he pulled her arms off him, holding her gently at arm's length. 'No, Livvy, it's wrong.'

'But, Clem—'

'Don't say anything else, whatever it is you'll end up regretting it. I don't know what your problems with Timothy are, but you need to talk them over with him. Just do whatever it takes for you to be happy and never let go of it.'

154

Before leaving the house Clem dashed off a note to Kerensa. He'd had very little chance for direct contact with her. They had managed to exchange a few rudimentary words and trade sympathetic glances, but always, it seemed, someone was watching them. Banking on a bustle of tea-making when he and Olivia arrived, he intended to slip the note inside Kerensa's riding gauntlet.

Fourteen

On the first Sunday after he moved into Polgissey, Luke took his household to church.

With Cordelia on his arm and Jack and Alicia following, he progressed down the narrow aisle, bringing all the talk, much of it inappropriate for the hallowed setting, and speculation as to what the new landlord looked like to a swift end. Luke kept a solemn countenance but nodded to anyone who sought his eye, which was almost everyone; the nosy, the eager, the aghast.

Trotting importantly behind came the retained staff: the cook at the big house for the past twelve years, Mrs Amy Curnow, a somewhat fetching widow of youngish years and good deportment; the four housemaids, of varying ages, their looks ranging from plainly discreet to insolently common, for whom Luke had ordered material of dark blue and white linen for new female uniforms; at the rear was quiet, respectful, under-sized, Cal Barbary, the gardener; his pole-thin wife and seven, young, minuscule children behind him. Jack had quickly taken to Cal Barbary for he too was of the Methodist connection, and hitherto had been unwelcome in the church.

The church smelled musty, the congregation smelled worse. Dirt littered the floor of cracked slate; mould and worm made free with the woodwork. For the most part the worshippers were equally unkempt, and scratching from flea bites. Luke eyed the high rafters and grimy rough stonework, all copiously occupied with cobwebs, and hoped they were sound. In the corner of one high window ledge was the remains of a small bird.

Luke inspected the foremost pew. *His pew.* He felt a leaping sense of satisfaction. A threadbare runner, and the evidence suggesting its accumulation of dust had recently been shaken on to the floor, covered only half of the hard wood. He ushered Alicia and Jack and Cordelia into the pew then sat down at the end. He held his three-cornered hat, irritated about the state of the church, on his fingertips.

The man who showed such disregard for the building he had charge over, the Reverend Simeon Thake, took his place. First adjusting his ragged white wig, secondly knocking a mummified insect off his frayed black sleeve, thirdly stamping on the heels of his dusty shoes, as if he was following some ancient ritual, he began the service of Holy Communion. Luke and Cordelia kept their prayer books in their hands, loathe to place them on the dirty ledge in front of them.

Thake was the sort of over-humble curate, wont to lament his own woeful position and plead poverty, who Luke despised. Thin of body, beady of eye, lax of bodily hygiene, he had arrived at Polgissey the day after Luke had moved in, while he was busily lining his bookshelves with the volumes he had brought from Pengarron Manor.

Luke had glared at the curate from the ladder in his library, with a case of instant dislike. 'You'll understand if I carry on with my task?'

'Indeed, Mr Pengarron. Indeed, indeed. It's good fortune, if I may say, that Mr Cecil Doble left the house so adequately furnished. I came in all haste to welcome you, and ... and ... and Miss Drannock, isn't it? To the parish of Porthcarne. I would be delighted if I was to see you and the good lady at St

Colwynne's next Sunday. Do you think there's a possibility you will attend?'

Luke put a copy of *The Four Books of Andrea Palladio's Architecture* next to his horticultural books by mistake. 'Perhaps, whatever the good Lord wills!'

'Yes, yes, yes, of course.'

After allowing the curate a sip of port, but not a comfortable seat, Luke ordered Jack to show him the far side of his door.

The service lasted unendurably, the Reverend Thake lapsing into his habit of repeating three times many a word in his sermon, which didn't teach, preach or make any sense.

Luke gave him only the briefest hand at the church door. 'Did I spy a dead sparrow inside, Reverend Thake?'

'Um, dead, Mr Pengarron? Sparrow?' The curate squirmed.

'Every little sparrow is numbered by God.' Luke raised an ironic eyebrow. 'Yet you have no notion that a bird has lain dead for some months inside the church and rotted away. Indeed, I'm wondering if anyone has put brush, cloth or polish to the building since its origins in 1162. Cromwell's men couldn't have done a better work at reducing the building. I don't expect to see such a state of affairs next week! Good morning to you.'

The mortified curate crept away, ignoring the remainder of his flock – an unusual number of worshippers today.

Luke escorted Cordelia to the gates of the weed-infested churchyard. Jack took Alicia after them, muttering how disgraceful the curate was, and she agreed.

Luke suddenly turned round to address the villagers, sure he would find some following in their wake, like gulls after a fishing boat. Nearly all of them were close up behind Jack and Alicia and they froze on the spot. He smiled, it reminded him of a childhood game, 'What's the time Mr Wolf?' He hastened to assure these people that he wasn't a wolf, about to shout out 'dinner time!'

The people, except for a group of black-haired men, one of giant proportions, all in uncommonly fine apparel, at the back of the gathering, were sadly undernourished. Among these men, women and children he would find more workers for his house, his garden, his stables, his fields and properties.

'Good morning to you all. I'm sure you are aware of who I am and who these people with me are. Mr Rosevear is my steward, and you may contact him with any concerns you have on the estate. I hope in due course to call on every home and get to know you.'

While Cecil Doble had kept high standards in his house, he had sorely neglected his land, tenants, and Porthcarne, which nestled where the land fell away in a deep hollow

159

cove off the eastern reach of Polgissey. Leaving Jack to answer any immediate enquiries, Luke strode out through the rusty iron lychgate and peered over the assembly of huts and cottages. Singly and in haphazard rows, on either side of a wide rough thoroughfare, the dwellings included an alehouse and other makeshift businesses, the last solitary hut standing in foolish defiance near the edge of the beach, brazen to the elements.

Luke knew the minds of these sort of people. They hoped that he, as their new landlord would do something, anything, to better their lot. But if he did not, they would simply accept it was their fate in life to be in want and need of even the basic necessities, and they would settle down to exist as best they could. Well, he was here now and he would do his best for them, show his father that he too was of a charitable heart.

He took a second look. Here and there the thatch or slate or cob had been attended to on the buildings. Ashes, rubble or pebbles filled in some of the potholes on the road. He was gratified. It was easier to help those who helped themselves. Days of settling in, attending to his duties and ascertaining what were his responsibilities, had meant little spare time for writing his play.

Luke ventured down into the village next day. He and Jack, accompanied by Cal Barbary for advice on who was trustworthy,

160

signed up workers to start immediately. Cordelia was there too, taking every opportunity to be at Luke's side, but also genuinely curious about the inhabitants.

Infants fretting half-naked in the dirt were cheered by the biscuits, cake and sweetmeats Cordelia doled out to them. Triggy-toffee, fuggan and sugared almonds soon disappeared down ravenous little throats, grubby hands reached out for second helpings.

'Very kind of 'ee, miss. Young uns do never get t'have a treat.'

Cordelia looked about for the owner of the humorous, mature voice. It was a tiny elderly woman, wrapped in a faded tartan shawl, with a frilled cap too big for her head. She was sitting on a stack of ragged cushions on a three-legged stool, outside the last of a straggle of cottages, where the sun reached her kindly, crumpled face. A small whiskery dog lay snoozing nearby. Her minute hands leaned on the knob of a walking stick, and Cordelia noticed she had only one foot. She had seen her outside the church yesterday, supported by two women, like a withered root between two upright trees.

'Would you like something?'

'Bless 'ee, miss, give it t' the babes. Begging your pardon, miss, I don't stand up easy, lost this to blood poisoning many a year backalong.' She indicated where her black hose ended. 'My name's Minnie Drew. I'm ninety-three, outlived my man and five children and I'm the oldest living here.'

'You must know everything there is to know about Porthcarne, Mrs Drew. My cousin, Mr Pengarron, is eager to put the village into good repair.'

'That'll be sumthin' to behold afore I go up yonder, never seen it afore from the big house. Couldn't get a meaner spirit than Cecil Doble where we down here was concerned, unless you went by the name of Kinver.'

'Kinver?' Cordelia was surrounded by every child for miles around now word had got round about her gift basket. She passed out the contents, listening avidly to Little Min, as she was to learn was the old woman's affectionately given title.

She could impress Luke with the details she learned about his property. While his desire to emulate his father as an approachable and benevolent landlord and master was genuine, she knew he was desperate to find a whole day to settle down to his play. Class distinction was to Luke a fact of life. There was only a certain amount of affiliation with these ordinary folk he could stand. Coming from the same degree of background of these villagers, Cordelia felt a sympathy for them that overruled her natural shyness.

'You must have seed 'em after church

yes'day. Half a dozen squires with hair as dark as a dog's guts, one with the build of ole Blamey's ox! Mr Doble sired the lot. Found a welcome, he did, most nights in young Becky Kinver. Pretty as a dove she was, had hair as black as night and skin like silk. All the men wanted her, but she wanted finer things. Got 'em too. Mr Doble built her a fine house, gived it her outright.'

'The first house you come to when you reach the village? It's up high, with a goodly piece of land to it and must have a fine view of the sea. My cousin was surprised when Cal Barbary told him he didn't own it, and that it wasn't the Reverend Thake's. I noticed those men were well dressed.'

'Mr Doble didn't leave Becky no money – she'm long dead – but those boys of hers'll turn their hand to anything. Grows crops and keeps goats and goes crabbing. Fine craftsmen too. 'Spec' the young master will be glad of 'em for a thing or two. Born half quality they be, and they'm always busy reproducing the same kind. Some here would've starved but for they. One of 'em mended my leaky roof t'other day. Put a hand's turn for anybody, they do.' Little Min curled up her face in a shrewd smile. 'Reckon tes going t' be Porthcarne's year.'

'You do?'

'Seven's a lucky number. If you can't be lucky in 1777, when can 'ee be?'

The tiny dog woke up and Cordelia broke off a piece of spiced biscuit for it. Her basket was now empty and she promised the disappointed, sticky-faced children to come again with a newly laden one soon.

Polgissey House was half the size of Pengarron Manor, the acreage of land a quarter of the estate, but Luke intended to make his property as progressive as his father's. He had set men and boys to constructing proper roads. The more skilled were charged with erecting a conservatory and a summerhouse for the ladies, others in building high dry-stone walls, a Cornish expertize, to protect the fields.

Oliver arrived while a train of mules and ponies were delivering supplies of wood and stone to the back of the house.

'What goes on here, Jack?' he enquired, while Jack reached for Gereint's reins. 'Most of these labourers appear to come from one family.'

After giving his former master a brief outline of Luke's plans, Jack repeated the details Miss Cordelia had learned about the six men unloading the building materials.

'Cecil Doble never married, I've heard tale of his litter. All sounds well thought out. The house is a noteworthy prospect.' Oliver looked inland. 'You can see St Agnes Beacon, Carn Brea and Carn Marth.' He pointed up the coast, 'That's Trevose Head.' Then down

coast, 'And that's Navax Point. Hidden beyond it is St Ives.'

'Where they catch great big fish?' Jack's
eyes widened at his education. Before his
great adventure with Luke he had lived in a
radius no bigger than two or three miles. St
Ives had once sounded like the other end of
the world.

'As big as houses.' Oliver grinned. 'Are you
enjoying living here, Jack?'

'Yes, sir.' Jack deemed it disloyal to say he
had, at first, missed his own little cottage and
duties on the Pengarron estate. 'My wife's
not so sure. A cottage along the cliff top
burnt down last week. No one was hurt and
Luke's promised the tenant he'll have
another, better one built, but she sees it as a
bad omen. Won't walk that way, no matter
what.'

'Otherwise she is well? And all else?'

'Yes, sir...' Jack was smarting over strong
words he had exchanged with Luke over his
and Cal Barbary's request to build a Methodist meeting house. 'I'll not have dissenting
rabble on my land!' Luke had snarled.
'Forget that nonsense and see that the
weasel of a curate puts right our proper place
of worship.'

'You want to confide in me, Jack?' Oliver
eyed him closely.

'Oh, no, sir. Mister Luke's out writing
today. First chance he's got since we've been

here. Only going to write indoors when the weather's bad, he says. I'll go fetch him for 'ee.'

'No, Jack. Let him be. I'll wander about on my own.'

A short time later, standing alone on the cliff, gazing down solemnly on his son's dishevelled village, Oliver reflected grimly that Kerensa and he should be here together to view this.

Fifteen

Luke was sitting on a carpet of springy grass, so close to the cliff edge that his feet were suspended in air. He looked up from his writing, at the only thing which could hold his attention from the world he was creating in his head and on paper: the Atlantic Ocean, stretching away to the horizon.

The setting sun was laying down a shimmering silvery-gold path of magic over the busy waves. Where they neared the shore, gigantic rollers were forming and exploding, then sweeping in on the pale-golden beach of the tiny cove, a hundred feet below. As the water hit the sheltering rocks, flurrying white spray was sent up high, then it retreated to

166

rejoin the glorious assault. This was the grandeur, the magnificence of the coast opposite to that on which his father had his estate: the dark and dangerous North Cliffs. The sea was rarely completely calm here, and was more outrageous in its beauty. Up the coast, not far out in the waters, off St Agnes Head, he could see a huge rock and a smaller one at its side. They were named Man and His Man. Like he and Jack.

His cliff, his beach, his village, his people. His play. It all felt good. So good.

He began writing again, furiously adding to his tale of bitter-sweet love in a realm of fantasy. Act II, Scene i, he wrote. Lia moves centre stage. She's lost, nervous but enthralled, looks all around. Sasken, hiding behind the enchanted trees, moves forward. His expression shows his deep, unbearable love for her.

Luke was unaware that someone was watching him. Speaking to him. He did not feel the arms that came about his neck from behind.

'Luke, you've been here all day. It's time to come home. Uncle Oliver is here.'

He thought the voice had come from his mind, part of his play he had yet to write down, or to retrace and include in an earlier page.

'What?' he asked his inner voice, pen hovering over the paper.

The quill was pulled out of his hand. 'Luke, wake up, time to come back to reality.'

His head followed the direction of the pen, and he was surprised to see Cordelia's small face an inch from his. She was smiling, 'Home, my dear. You haven't eaten a thing since breakfast nor touched the wine you've brought with you.'

'What?' Her face was in shadow, it would soon be dark. 'Have I been away so long? It seems but a minute.'

'Be careful how you get up. You're too near the edge and you'll be stiff all over.'

Luke worked his hand, it was stiff and cramped from writing for the best part of the day. 'Ow! My shoulder hurts. Everything hurts.'

'You were wise to keep your hat and shirt on, or you'd be burnt badly by the sun,' Cordelia said.

They walked back to their new home, hand in hand, climbing up the fern-fringed cliff, following the somewhat precarious path he had flattened out that morning through the gorse, heather and bramble. Using protruding rocks as steps, they took care where sudden dips and rabbit holes might cause a stumble or twisted ankle.

'How long has my father been here?'

'Hours. He said not to disturb you. All's going well then?' She was carrying his

168

leather folder of writing implements. 'You'll finish the whole play by the end of the week at this rate.'

'Not so, sweeting. Better ideas come into my mind all the time and there will be restructuring and amending to do, but I'm satisfied today's work will do mainly as it is.'

'Have you based your main characters on anyone?'

'Not really. I've led no romantic life to have formed such creatures. They love too deep, too ardently.'

'May I read what you've written today?'

'No, I'll read it out to you some time. Saints be, I'm famished. What are we eating? I trust not a menu you and the fair Alicia have concocted between you, especially with Father here.'

'No, we'll let Mrs Curnow have sway with the kitchen from now on.' Cordelia's heart dropped like a rock, Luke never called her 'fair'.

'Don't be disappointed, Corrie, you were both brave to try, nearly as brave as my Lia, who faces all manner of heartbreak and danger.'

Soon the roof and chimneys of the house came into view, and with each step they climbed, more of the building was seen. At one end was a tower-like construction, the windows containing over five hundred panes of leaded glass, a view-point from the sea and something of a landmark. Luke paused to savour his cliff-top home.

With its hint of stately importance, Polgissey excited his blood like nothing else had before. Bought from the last of the Dobles, an old Cornish seafaring family, Mr Doble now permanently resided in Bath. Luke felt it was his presence that had breathed first life into the house. As if he had lit a bright candle of hope inside its solid walls that would last a lifetime. He felt empowered by it, and with its feeling of being a safe haven, he wouldn't be surprised to see angels hovering over it. Here he would weave his dreams and build his fantasies.

'You hold Alicia in high regard,' Cordelia said, hiding her jealousy as they approached the rough path to the front door. Luke was expecting a consignment of gravel so the ladies would not be troubled by dusty or muddy shoes or skirts.

'You've not let that fact pass you by then.' Luke hugged her playfully.

Cordelia felt enriched to be an important part of his life, and she was enjoying her new position as mistress of the house, but she despaired that he would ever see her as anything other than a former childhood companion, the little cousin he liked to protect and cosset, or as someone to lean on and take for granted. She had not the slightest notion how to go about changing the situation.

Then he made her soul soar up to meet the colour-splashed sky. 'But you I hold the highest of all, Corrie.'

That evening, entertaining his father at his table and then up in the tower room, which he used as his study, and with Jack fidgeting in a chair near the door, Luke proudly talked of his play and his plans for the next one, then gave the history of Polgissey and its last owner.

'I got it for a very agreeable price. According to our family lawyer, Cecil Doble was an inbred fool anyone could exploit. His wealth was in steady decline and he'd been forced to sell his shares in the East India Company and just about everything else he owned. There's a few pieces of eastern art in the house Livvy might find interesting. I shall add my own things in due course. By the way, Father, how are your shares?' Luke didn't pause to find out. 'This coast is savagely wild, isn't it, Jack? Never experienced anything so stimulating. The village will celebrate a very noisy festival as well as the usual bonfires on Midsummer's Eve. Something about the legend of a sea monster. Needs to be kept at bay or it'll annihilate the village or something, eh, Jack?'

'Tis the evil spirit of a dead pirate the folk of Porthcarne sent to a deserving death a century back. Must be drummed out to sea

171

every year or it'll eat the babies and carry off the women,' Jack said, shuffling his feet.

'It's the custom of the landowner to provide the ale and rum, so I've been informed. Well, I don't mind that. Should be good fun,' Luke rejoined enthusiastically. 'Might prove useful inspiration of a sort for my plays.'

'Absolutely fascinating,' Oliver said, and not as he could have done: 'Yes, I know all this.'

Helping himself to more brandy, he noticed Jack watching the clock. 'Looks as if Jack's about ready to retire. I take it I'm welcome to stay the night?'

'Tonight and any other night. I intend to stay up late and write,' Luke replied, then, 'Yes, Jack, off you go. Tomorrow will be a busy day for you.'

'What will he be doing?' Oliver asked, when he and Luke were left alone.

'Carrying on with an inspection of all my properties, but first he'll start the training of one of the Kinver brood as stable boy.'

'I'm so pleased you're all happy here. I've noticed how well Cordelia gets along with Mrs Rosevear. Now Luke, I've had some discreet enquiries made in London about Lord Longbourne's death. The official verdict is accidental death, also of his mistress. He's been buried on the family property. There is very little talk about it now.'

Luke looked grim. 'We can rest easy then.

I'll inform Jack and Alicia tomorrow.'

Oliver was serious for several moments. 'Does the woman make Jack happy? She is hardly his kind.'

'You sound as though you don't approve of her, Father, but let me assure you she's a very remarkable person. Sometimes I wished I'd married her myself.'

'You are lonely in that respect?' Oliver puffed on his long clay pipe.

'Not for the cares and burdens of a wife. I don't want to socialize until I've accomplished my play and offered it to the theatres, but I miss having a woman available. I don't want the bother of running a mistress, and after some of my experiences this year of brothels they no longer hold appeal.'

Wryly, Oliver shook his head. 'Do you know how hard done by you sound? The answer to your problem is obvious, it stares you in the face.'

'What? I can think of no solution.'

'Just wait awhile, son, it'll come to you.' Holding up the empty brandy bottle, Oliver swapped it for a full one. 'This is good. Untaxed, I presume? Did you know there's a really good smuggler's hide on your land?'

'Hal Kinver, the villager you saw today who shares your height, has mentioned something of the kind. I've assured him his operations will get no opposition from me, but God help him if my name is attached to any.' Suddenly Luke became forthright. 'Father, we've talked of many things tonight, about all the family, but you haven't mentioned Mama once. When are you going to make your peace?'

Sighing, Oliver hunched his thickly muscled body over his knees. 'Have you not seen her of late?'

'She was here two days ago, with Polly O' Flynn and Beatrice – the Lord alone knows how her old bones stood up to the journey. They brought us a wealth of gifts and household things. I couldn't get a straight answer out of Mama either. Surely you've not fallen out of love with her?'

'That, Luke, is impossible.'

'I'm relieved to hear you say so. I suppose you don't want to talk about it?'

'No, there would be little point.'

Luke was alarmed. 'But surely this estrangement is only temporary?'

'I hope so.'

'Hope so?' Luke was on the edge of his seat, fervent, waving his hands in exaggerated circles. 'Make it so! You and Mama have a love most others would never find if they searched a lifetime. You can't possibly let her go. No amount of achievement, lands or titles could match having a woman like Mama. Damn it, Father, I was going to write a play based on the love you both shared.'

Long, dull moments ticked by. The bracket

clock on the ebony mantelpiece ticked and tocked, striking a boom at one o'clock. A candle guttered out. Luke watched the wisp of smoke evaporate. Oliver sat forward, hanging his head.

Luke said, 'What are you going to do about Clem Trenchard?'

Oliver knocked back the remains of his drink. 'It was doing something about Clem Trenchard which brought me to this loneliest of states. What I'd like to do, and I don't mean this as a jest, Luke, is to choke the breath of life out of him. He's being very clever, playing a waiting game. Using the continuing infection in Kane's leg as an excuse to stay on at Vellanoweth. I shall have to ensure that I am more clever than he.'

That same night two gentlemen were setting up the pieces for a game of chess, in a public house in Duke Street, a few streets away from the burnt-out Longbourne house.

The walls were mirrored, enabling Sir Decimus Soames to keep himself informed of all arrivals and departures without actually appearing to. Pale-skinned and fat in a soft, wobbly manner, and delicately scented, he was dressed in crimson, the coat floral-panelled with silver frogging. Huge jewels glittered on all his fingers and thumbs, more were pinned on his neckcloth. His wig, casually understated in design, gleamed brilliant

175

white in the glow of the rich candlelight.

'You missed my thirtieth birthday bash, dear boy,' he said in his highly cultured voice, putting his knee against his companion's under the small square table. 'I threw a magnificant masked ball. Such a pity you were out of the country again. I'll make it up to you tonight.'

A large, deeply tanned hand, completely unlike Sir Decimus's, carefully weighed a black marble pawn. 'Running guns and provisions to the highest paying cause in the colonial war is a risky business. You're lucky to see me here alive and well, sir.'

Sir Decimus reached across and stroked the tanned hand before its owner had time to withdraw it. 'Quite so, and now we're sending you off on another little task so soon after the St James's Street debacle. I know you and the others searched Longbourne's house for this evidence he boasted he had and found nothing, but it's occurred to me that your cousin may know something. He was one of Longbourne's favourites, the only friend he had in the end – the others were all heartily sick of his pleas to lend him money. I've had Pengarron's lodgings searched but found nothing. But I want to be sure, and who among us can get as close to him as you? You were going to Cornwall anyway, you say. Why?'

'Just family business. It's many a year since

I set foot in the county.'

'What's it like all the way down there, Barty?' Sir Decimus ran circles with a pointed fingernail on the other man's wrist, where the end of a tattoo depicting a bird's tail was evident. 'Your cousin couldn't wait to scuttle off home with his precious servant chappie. They spent so much time together, you know, I thought they were of my persuasion, but on the only occasion I managed to prise them apart, darling Luke disappointed me. After that he left his chappie at Longbourne's house and made a point of plundering every bitch he could lay his hands on. Such a waste. Luke is,' he kissed his fingertips, 'simply divine.'

Bartholomew Drannock withdrew his hand, his dark face stern. 'Cornwall has its own beauties, sir.'

'Oh tush! You continue to walk the straight path too, eh? Shame, shame, you're nearly as delicious as Luke. Your dark colour spoils you a little but I like the gold earring. You wouldn't consider coming over to the other side just for one night?'

Bartholomew Drannock kept a heavy-lidded expression.

Letting out a deadly laugh, Sir Decimus beckoned to a youth of about thirteen who had been lolling against the wrought-iron spiral staircase and giving him his eye for several minutes.

'So be it. Bitches for you and whelps for me. You know what to do when you see your cousin? You'll not be swayed because he's kin?'

Bartholomew Drannock leaned back in his chair, grave and unyielding. 'I know where my loyalty lies, Sir Decimus.'

'Excellent, if only I could be sure all our members were as reliable as you, Drannock. You've borrowed enormous sums of money over the years and always repaid it promptly. Go, I shall expect word from you shortly.'

Sixteen

Ben Penberthy helped Kerensa climb up into the Vellanoweth trap, then got up into the driver's seat of the four-wheeled carriage.

Reluctantly, Jessica handed up Harry to Kerensa.

'Don't worry, I'll take very good care of him.'

'I know.' Jessica reached up and arranged her son's bonnet to keep the sun off his face. She was worried to be letting him off the farm without her for the first time. 'You'll bring him back in plenty of time for his next feed?'

'I promise, Jessie.' Kerensa's smile also fell on Clem.

Because she had his grandson in her arms, he was within his rights to come forward, and watchful eyes could make nothing wrong out of it. 'You're taking him to the manor, m'lady?'

'To Ker-an-Mor.'

Clem said nothing. His eyes flickered to her face conveying a chaser to his note. *Where can we meet?* She had destroyed the note for safety's sake but re-read it in her heart every day. So far she had given him no answer.

The more she saw of Clem, during brief moments in the house or yard, the more she found herself responding to his longing to be with her. Each time she left Vellanoweth she saw the hope die in his eyes, the sadness in his expression grow stronger, and she wanted to be with him, to reassure him, give him her affection and her love.

To be alone with Clem would be dangerous. She feared Oliver would find out and the inevitable confrontation that would follow, but it wasn't her main concern. Since their marriages, she and Clem had twice ended up in situations where they had nearly made love. She knew neither of them would hold back now.

She did not look away from Clem quickly, even though Jessica was eyeing them. She gave him a half smile, left him with half a hope.

Rosie Renfree knocked on the office door of Ker-an-Mor Farm and entered the spartanly furnished room.

Sitting grimly at the desk, Oliver growled irritably, 'I thought I'd made it clear I didn't want to be disturbed.'

He was throwing himself into work, going meticulously over reports of every concern of the farm and estate, and then going over it again, no matter how trifling the issue. Nit-picking. Tossing away plans and re-forming them. He had to keep busy, give himself no time to think or his misfortunes would overwhelm him.

Ignoring him, Rosie said, 'I think you will for this young man, sir.'

Looking up, Oliver stared at her and the child she was carrying in her arms. A fair-haired child with striking blue eyes, presently yawning and stretching with strength and vigour.

'Is it Harry?'

'Yes, sir, he's come for a visit.' Oliver sprang up to claim hold of his grandson, Rosie's great-nephew.

'It was good of you to ask Jessica if you could bring him here to me, Rosie.'

He gazed down at Harry. A month had passed since the accident and the baby had grown in breadth and length. Oliver kissed his chubby cheeks.

'I didn't, sir.'

Someone else came into the room. 'Hello, Oliver.'

He raised his brows. 'Kerensa! You are responsible for this? Jessica has relented at last?'

'I was able to make her see it wasn't fair to keep him away from you.'

'I'll see to some tea.' Rosie left, closing the door carefully.

Left alone with his wife, Oliver set stern eyes on her. The gulf between them had iced over part of his heart, as it seemed, on the few occasions they were now together, it also had hers. The sense of betrayal over what he saw as her fickle love for him sat in his guts like a hard rock. Then Harry gurgled, and he remembered that except for Kerensa's thoughtfulness, his grandson would not be here.

'Thank you for bringing Harry to me.'

'He was as alert as this all the way here, enjoying the view of his grandfather's land.'

Kerensa moved across to her husband and grandchild and took off Harry's bonnet. She was so close to him that Oliver could smell her soft perfume, feel the warmth of her body. He had missed this more than he had admitted to himself. It made him agonizingly aware of the gaping chasm in his life, and having Harry here forced him to fight back a show of emotion.

Looking closely at Oliver's face Kerensa saw his eyes misting over. 'I'll take my tea in the parlour and leave you alone with him. Where's Kelynen?'

'She's at Rose Farm. Did you want her for anything particular?'

'No. She left this morning without saying where she was going, but I took it for granted she'd come here.'

Kelynen had refused to divulge her plans but she had not been shy at using her direct tongue. 'Mama, when are you going to forgive Father? I think you're being too harsh with him. And please don't tell me I don't know what I'm talking about. Two people can't be as much in love as you and he one minute and not the next. I won't accept it.'

'I haven't fallen out of love with your father, Kelynen. I never will.'

'So?' the girl demanded in a rare show of adolescent impatience.

How to explain? Kerensa didn't know herself. 'Our situation is complicated.'

Kelynen studied her as if she were an ancient sage, her eyes at that moment as penetrating as Oliver's. 'Please, Mama, don't let it become more complicated. You know what I'm referring to.'

Kerensa had baulked at being under her daughter's disapproval, while she was sure Oliver was getting her wholehearted support.

'Kerensa, could we talk afterwards?' he said.

She nodded and left the room.

Oliver held Harry close. Not for a second had the impression of the accident or the shame of the aftermath left his mind. He might have too much pride, but he wasn't heartless. This baby may not actually have his blood in him, and he was very much a Trenchard in looks, but he was Kane's son and Oliver loved him for that. He wept softly so as not to disturb him.

Kerensa forgot the tea, preferring to avoid Rosie and the servants and the unasked questions they would have in their eyes. Rosie would also be concerned about Clem, wondering if, despite the fact that others were always about at Vellanoweth, they were meeting elsewhere. She had seen the same question in Oliver's eyes.

Nipping along the passage, she quietly mounted Ker-an-Mor's stairs, intending to look out across the fields which swept all the way down to the cliff edge, but instead she found herself in the bedroom where Oliver had been sleeping recently. Where they had slept together during the harvesting most years, when he worked alongside the men and she helped the women with the food and ale. The bed, on which they had fallen exhausted and content, or made love in, staying all night in each other's arms, was neatly made.

Her things were not quite in place, as if someone had picked them up and placed them down without thinking where they actually belonged. Oliver was carelessly untidy but everything was in order. It didn't seem right. Nothing was right.

Downstairs just now, Oliver had looked lost and soulless, and emotional in the way of one not being in control as he had taken Harry in his arms. She wanted to descend the stairs and beg Oliver to come home, to suggest they reconcile even if they couldn't make up their differences, and resume their marriage with whatever each had to offer.

But Clem would be there in some form or other, in the way. She knew why she had kept Clem's things, part of her had always wanted him and always would. Oliver's reaction to finding those simple gifts of twenty-four years ago was understandable, but it did not excuse the extent of his jealous behaviour.

A feeling of oppression closed in on her. What was she to do about the two men she loved? Her feelings for Oliver were just as strong. So were those she had felt for Clem when they had first fallen in love. She had been suppressing them but now no longer could. If she was to turn to either of them, duty should make Oliver the obvious choice, but she had given her first promise to Clem. She felt as if she was being wrenched in half.

She rejoined Oliver, knocking first on the door and waiting for his call. He was sitting in an armchair with Harry laid on his knees, making him chuckle by tickling his tummy. Oliver had played with all his children in this way. Kerensa was reminded what an attentive and loving father he was – few men gave this kind of acknowledgement to their offspring.

She sat down on the deep-cut window seat. 'He likes you.'

'Yes, I believe he does. I'm missing Kane so very much. How is he today?'

'Much the same. Dr Crebo says the wound looks a little less anguished, but Kane is still very weak. I'm afraid I'll have to take Harry home soon before he gets hungry.'

Oliver gazed down at Harry. 'Of course.'

'You said you wanted us to talk?'

'Yes, to ask you if you have everything you need?' His tone was conversational, nothing more or less.

'Yes, thank you.'

'Are there any problems you'd like to discuss with me?'

'Not at the manor. Michael and Conan are coping at the stables. Will you replace Jack?'

185

'In time. I sensed that Jack's not totally content at Polgissey. Luke doesn't see this, but he'd never countenance releasing him.' Harry started to fret and he got up with him. 'You'd better take him home. Thank you for bringing him, it's meant everything to me.'

'Kane can bring him next time. I'll try to make sure Samuel is here and they can begin learning to play together.'

Thinking of his own black-haired, black-eyed little boy made Oliver angry that he was being denied the daily pleasures of him, even if he had chosen to spend more and more time away from the manor. Kerensa's loyalty to the dirt-farmer had a lot to answer for.

'Yes,' he said gruffly. 'The children mustn't miss out on family life.'

Kerensa read Oliver's statements as arrogant assertions that he was blaming her for their problems, and she found this intolerable. Taking Harry from him she left without saying goodbye. On the drive back to Vellanoweth she worked out where she could meet Clem and safely leave him a note.

Going up to his room to change for an overnight stay at the parsonage, Oliver bawled down the stairs for Rosie Renfree to come up to him.

'What's the matter, sir?' she asked cautiously. He was in quite a temper.

'Someone has been in here. Who?'

186

'The maid tidied the room and made your bed, that's all, I swear. I checked it myself.'

Kerensa! How dare she snoop on him. Did she think he might be entertaining another woman here in her place? Had she lost all trust and respect in him? He did not deserve that.

'I'm sorry, Rosie, don't look so worried. I'm not accusing anyone of a crime. Forgive a prickly old man?' He smiled to placate the young woman he had always had an affinity with, as he'd also once had with her late sister-in-law, Alice Trenchard. It was a strange fact that he had always been close to the women in Clem Trenchard's life. He had got so close to Rosie, in her maiden years, just before his steward had wooed her during the first estrangement from Kerensa, that he had taken her into his woods and very nearly made love to her. She was still an exceedingly attractive woman in her mid-thirties. Three of her children were presently at the charity school, the youngest, presumably, taking a nap.

Without actually saying a word, Rosie had been sympathetic towards the reason for his presence here, even going as far as laying a hand of solace once or twice on his shoulder.

'You're not old.' She smiled back at him.

'I seem to remember you saying that to me once before.'

His reference to their intimacy made her

blush prettily. 'That was a few years ago now.'

'I've never forgotten it, have you?' He leaned back against the washstand, staring straight into her eyes, enjoying the old memories, feeling again the warmth of their current friendship.

'No, Oliver, I have not. A woman likes to remember the special times in her life.' Rosie had many years of contented marriage behind her, but this man had never ceased to draw her devoted admiration. Staring back, she moved next to him, straightened the clothes brush beside him on the cold marble top then refolded the towels.

'You've helped me more than most these last few weeks, Rosie. I'll always remember that too.'

Rosie carried on unnecessarily rearranging the items on top of the washstand. It was madness to stay here like this. Until a few moments ago they had been master and servant, with no thought on her part of there being anything different between them. It was madness to allow those old feelings to be recaptured. His look of vulnerability when her ladyship had left with young Harry, and now his physical closeness, was increasing his attraction.

It would be so good to be kissed by him again, just once. A wicked thought! But it excited her beyond any experience she had known before. She could not leave the room any more than she could stop breathing. When she looked at him again he was still regarding her.

'If I can do anything to ease your way, Oliver, you only have to say.'

A moment of unspoken sinful longing re-formed the old connection between them. Then abruptly, he moved away. He couldn't do what his body wanted. He mustn't seek comfort with Rosie again. His hand gripped the door latch.

Humiliated beyond measure, Rosie hung her head and made to leave the room sideways so she wouldn't have to look at him. All she wanted was to make her escape.

Oliver felt the hard iron latch digging into his flesh. He made it hurt him. But instead of pulling the door open wider for Rosie to leave, he closed it, tight.

He cupped her face in his hands, and brought his strong mouth down on hers. She was to get her kiss, just a kiss.

It had been he who had halted their first amours, but this time as their lips made contact, Rosie knew he wasn't going to stop. He was the one who had reason not to be thinking rightly, and it was up to her to break away, to prevent this wickedness spiralling into the inevitable.

She kissed him back, then again and again, allowed him to take her to the bed and push her gently down on it, to pull open her stays and lower her shift and kiss her breasts, and soon afterward to enter her body. The pleasure was so intense, she could not stop him now if heaven showed itself and forbade her the rights of eternity.

Seventeen

Kenver Trenchard was busily employed in his workshop, which was built on to his small, formerly tied, cottage a short distance across the valley from Greystone's Farm. Crippled from the waist down from birth, Clem's younger brother earned his living producing fine crafts, but the piece he was currently working on was not for sale. This was the most important thing he'd ever make.

His wife came in to tell him the midday meal was ready, and they lingered proudly together over the baby's cradle that was taking shape.

'It's going to be perfect.' With delight, Kerris Trenchard inspected the expert joinery, the delicate carving of the cradle. She stood behind Kenver, who was sitting in the special wheeled chair of his own making, and hugged him tight. 'Never thought you'd ever be doing something like this for a child of our own, Ken. Wish the poor little soul was coming into the world in better circumstances, but at least we'll give it a good start.'

It had always pained Kenver that his disability meant he could never give Kerris, whom he had married shortly before leaving Mount's Bay, what she desired most. Now, thanks to an indiscretion of Philip, his lust-driven nephew, he and Kerris were soon to become adoptive parents. Kenver was worried about Clem's reaction, for it was no ordinary sin Philip had committed to beget the child.

'Aye, we'll give it all the love it'll need, but I wish Philip hadn't involved Catherine in the way he did. It's not fair. Poor soul, she's all on edge. He shouldn't have sworn her to secrecy until Clem gets back. I know it sounds cowardly, putting all the facts on paper rather than to Clem's face, but we don't know how much longer he's staying down there, now he's saying that Kane's still very poorly and Jessica's begging him to stay on.' Kenver knew this was true, Clem did not write well and Jessica had finished the letter for him.

'Well, we can't do anything about it. We must prepare for the baby's arrival. Perhaps we should offer for the girl to come here. I'm

191

worried about the baby being born in a hovel.'

'You know her mother won't hear of it.' Kenver kissed the hands resting around his neck affectionately. 'We must pray for a live birth, and that no one puts the law on to Philip. Clem's not going to be at all happy about it, even if he's finally presented with a healthy grandchild. I hope he doesn't take his ire out on Catherine.'

᠂'Me too, but, when all's said and done, beloved, and God willing,' Kerris touched the smooth warm wood of the cradle with maternal tenderness, 'it will soon be our baby sleeping in here.'

It was a grey, cloudy night.

Two-score men, wearing dark clothing, faces smeared with earth, hats pulled down tight and scarves up high around their necks, guided a long line of mules and borrowed ponies along a little-used track at the back of Polgissey land. The animals' hooves were swathed in rags to muffle the sound of their steps and their backs were weighed down with bundles of lace, silk, tea, spices and half ankers of brandy and other spirits. Tense, sweating, each man carried a stave or weapon of some kind. Their leader, looming in width and girth, gripped a musket, primed and ready to fire.

The three-masted ship had anchored a safe

distance offshore in a little nameless cove next to Porthcarne. The crabbing boats and other small craft that had been rowed out on the heavy swell to offload the contraband, had all safely made their withdrawal. Thanks to the efficiency of Hal Kinver, the immediate coastline was left only to rock and water, the unlit beacon built on top of the cliff as a danger signal, dismantled without a trace.

The lights of the big house were left behind and gradually the travellers veered towards the cliffs. Almost silently, they passed behind the recently burnt-out cottage; one of their regular hides now lost, the cleverly concealed trapdoor in the single downstairs floor made obvious. The thatched roof had been burnt away and the charred stones stood out as an eerie silhouette, and Hal had to dampen down a sudden urge to hurry. Too much haste could lead to too much noise or an accident – give them away if the Revenue men were about.

Twenty minutes went by. A certain place was reached in the curve of the cliff. Not far below, hewn out by nature, was the chief hide. In daylight it would be in view as a small black indeterminate shape, the favoured spot where a privileged young gentleman sat and scribbled away, supposedly creating a form of entertainment. A coddled life, some folk do lead, Hal thought fleetingly. Cecil Doble had charged fifty pounds from the smuggling operator, a wine merchant who resided at a secret location, each time he shut his curtains and kept indoors on nights like this, and then a steep one hundred and fifty pounds when his fortunes deserted him. The new master of Polgissey seemed uninterested in making such profits.

The train was brought closer to the long drop. The men's concentration was so intense they did not hear the forbidding boom of the breakers whipping into the aptly named Hell's Mouth, a little further down the coast. Sharp winds snatched at their bodies. The lookouts took up their stations and became even more vigilant. Now the group was at its most vulnerable.

A long stout rope was already tied round Hal's broad waist, so he could act as anchorman. He let the other end tumble over the cliff-face. One of his brothers, Morgan, vigorous and wiry, climbed down, soon out of sight. Reaching the deep opening in the rock he swung himself into it, then tugged on the rope. Another man braved the perilous descent. The smuggled goods were lowered down one by one and they stowed them well back in the hollow, covering them with oiled tarpaulins weighed down with lumps of rock.

So practised were the free traders that only half an hour had passed before they were all away, disappearing into the night.

In the Crabber's Port, Porthcarne's shanty of an alehouse, situated at a right angle across a narrow thoroughfare to Minnie Drew's home, six men assembled around an upturned, empty ale barrel that served as a table.

Hal Kinver, a tankard of ale in a meaty paw, grinned at his brothers with double meaning. 'Nice t' be sitting here, eh?'

'Aye,' said Malachi, next to him. 'A toast to a good job done!'

All the Kinvers had the same fine bearing, deep-set grey eyes and thick coal-black hair inherited from their mother. Hal wasn't the eldest, but his build and greater intelligence made him the undisputed leader.

In view of the other side of their parentage they liked to dress well, eat well and drink even better. They were fiercely loyal to their blood. 'Cross one Kinver, cross 'em all,' was a well-used local remark. Aged from mid-twenties to late thirties, none were married, but a scattering of illegitimate like-featured children gave witness to one of their favourite pursuits. A little respect was gained by their ready financial support to the forsaken mothers, and the fact that they had taken in a son of Hal's, now training as stable boy at the big house, and another of the eldest brother, Branwell.

Harvey Kinver, the most headstrong of the

family, spoke in a culled whisper. 'Made a tidy sum 'night, I do reckon. What about Mr Pengarron and his lot? What if we get trouble off they?'

The brothers looked at Hal for his consideration.

'Don't reckon on that. He's hinted if there's any free trading going on round here, he'll turn a blind eye. Don't come across, he'll make the same demands our father did. Be up for sport of any kind, if you ask me. Going to put a goodly sum on me any time I get in the wrestling ring, so he said. Besides, Boy Hal can keep an ear open for trouble.'

Morgan, the quietest member in temper and talk, spilled his ale. 'Oh dear.'

He was slapped on the back by Tom and all the brothers laughed. 'Did 'ee hear that? Fancy bleddy manners again. Been like this since he fixed eyes on that sweet little Miss Cordelia. The heat's come over him again sure an' strong.'

Morgan just smiled and carried on drinking.

'Nothing wrong in that,' bawled out Branwell. 'She's a comely little piece, will fill out nicely time she gets a first babe in her belly, eh, Morgan? Watching you, she was, more than once. I caught her eyes on you when you was up there building the summerhouse. You'll be home and dry there, certain, sure.'

Morgan had an unusually well-honed

voice. Tonight his tone was slow and melodious. 'You think so? I mean, you're sure she was watching me?'

'Gived 'ee a second look and a third and a fourth,' Tom broke in heartily. 'You could find yourself actually living in our father's house, Morg.'

For a moment the brothers supped their ale in repressed mood. It was something of a sore point to them: while Cecil Doble had adored their mother and lavished her with gifts, he had been indifferent to them, insisting they must never turn up on his doorstep. When Becky died of pneumonia ten years ago, he had grieved openly for her, erecting a fine headstone over her grave, but he had shunned his sons henceforth.

'You'll have to marry that one,' Harvey returned to the original theme. 'Don't reckon she's the sort to lie down for anyone this side of the church.'

Morgan made no reply, settling himself into his own thoughts.

Hal was worried. Morgan didn't lay women at random, more than one at a time, like the rest of them did. He waited between bouts of celibacy for a woman to take his fancy and then nothing would set him on a different course. Seducing the quiet young lady up in Polgissey House, whom Hal had noticed pined after her cousin, would mean trouble, without a doubt.

Luke Pengarron might appear soft, with some silly notion about writing plays, but Hal sensed he was as hard as a ship's nail and he had never witnessed a man as protective of his kin and his servants. Then there was his father to think about. Sir Oliver Pengarron lived far away, but even before Hal had seen the baronet at the big house, he had heard of his reputation for hardness and revenge on anyone hurting his family. It was legendary.

'Wonder how come that Jack Rosevear's got himself such a fine wife? A bit of quality there, if I'm not mistaken. Mighty strange,' Malachi ruminated. 'She's quite a beauty. Got a full belly too.'

'Congratulations to the steward then.' Harvey raised his tankard of ale in a toast in Morgan's direction. 'The other young lady will shortly be joining her, eh, brother?'

Eighteen

It had been an overcast day and would soon be dark. The winds for the month of June were unusually fractious. Chilled through and nervous, Kerensa shivered inside a small private building on the Tolwithrick estate.

Once a gamekeeper's cottage, about to be demolished, Rachael Beswetherick had ordered its ostentatious renovation and turned it into a hideaway for herself where, as mother of fourteen surviving children, she sat and sewed or read or played the spinet. Everywhere there were embroidered cushions and tapestries and hangings on the walls, and piles of the fashionable *Lady's Magazine*, a sixpenny monthly.

Rachael had offered the cottage to Kerensa soon after the day of the baptism. This was Kerensa's first time here. The place where she had chosen to meet Clem.

Unlike Rachael, she could not rest. Pacing up and down, her heart jerking, her stomach churning, she avoided looking at her reflection in the many showy mirrors. When she thought of Oliver she headed towards the door. When she thought of Clem she turned in the opposite direction towards the moulded fireplace.

'What am I doing here?'

She should go, get away before Clem knocked on the door. It was madness to stay. Could she really turn away from Oliver so much and let the inevitable happen? She should not even be thinking about Clem. They were both married and loved their partners. But they loved each other too and always had. It was an inescapable fact and always, always, circumstances brought them back to it.

When he arrived she let him inside, cloaking her nervousness behind warm smiles. 'You had no trouble finding the place, Clem?'

'No, my love. Was quite easy, only had to follow the Withy river like you wrote.'

He took off his overcoat and hat and the dark blue scarf he had worn to hide his face.

He wanted so much to kiss Kerensa, but sensed she didn't want to be rushed. He glanced about.

'I was beginning to lose hope we'd ever be alone. What is this place, Kerensa?'

She told him about the cottage.

'Does Lady Rachael know you've invited me here?'

'I'm sure she suspects, but she'll say

nothing. Where does Jessica think you are tonight?'

'Marazion. Said I wanted to see an old acquaintance.'

She was wearing a graceful dress with delicate trimmings, no jewels and nothing in her hair. She looked so much like the girl he had fallen in love with in Trelynne Cove.

'I've never seen you looking so beautiful, Kerensa.'

'Thank you. You are good to me, Clem.'

'I mean more than that to you, I hope.'

'Yes, you do, much more.'

He reached out to her.

She turned away. 'I'm sorry, I'm feeling strangely shy. I've just spent the most nervous time of my whole life waiting for you. I ... perhaps...'

'Don't, Kerensa.'

He came up behind her and put his arms around her waist. The instant she felt his warmth she leaned against his chest.

'I might sound confident, but my insides are all knotted up,' he said. 'I was so afraid you'd change your mind. We were meant to be together. 'Tisn't wrong. You don't believe it is, do you?'

She shifted her head so she could look up at him. 'No Clem. I want you here.'

'Thank God! Please, Kerensa, turn round to me.'

Slowly, she did so. He moved his hands up

over her arms. She reached up and touched his hair, so fair and silky, a lock of it was hidden in a quiet place in Trelynne Cove. His summer-blue eyes were hunting her face for signs that she loved him. He wanted her to say something tender to him, to say he could stay and love her all night.

'It means more to me than anything in the world to be here like this with you,' he said.

'Clem, you know we aren't the same people of our youth, don't you? We can't pretend there aren't others in our lives. We have ties, responsibilities, other people's feelings to consider. We just can't step into an affair. We must think very carefully about the price we may have to pay.'

'I know, I know,' he said softly. 'I've thought about all that as much as I've thought about you. And I know about paying the price. It's all I've been doing since the day that man took you away from me. I'm here because I can't help myself. I have to be with you, Kerensa.'

Her fingers traced his brow. Clem's expression was open and honest, revealing simply that all he was doing was loving her. This was how it should have stayed. The years in between the very first time she had touched his face disappeared.

While he clasped her other hand and kissed its fingertips, she explored his fine cheekbones, his strong jaw and down his neck. She smoothed his hair, loosening it from the ribbon at the back, all the time gazing at him with tenderness. She wanted to discover him all over again and know him completely.

'I can't help myself wanting you, Clem. I've nothing left in me anymore to push you away.'

'I love you so much,' he whispered.

'I've never stopped loving you.'

He placed a gentle kiss on her cheek, then covered her face with more. Soft kisses on soft skin. Then he brought his mouth down on her lips. Soft and slow and tender, but only for a moment. She opened her mouth to his devotion and they let love turn into want and need.

Clem glanced around for a comfortable place. 'Is there another room?'

'Upstairs.'

Taking her hand, he picked up a three-light candelabra and they climbed the stairs together. She opened the door at the top and they stepped into Lady Rachael's private bedroom. It was steeped in affectation and smelled strongly of the woman's extravagant perfume, but they didn't notice. Kerensa closed the door and Clem put the candelabra on the bedside cabinet.

'This is the wedding night we should have had long ago,' he said.

'Yes, this is our time, Clem.'

Kerensa kicked off her shoes, then smiled at Clem when he stumbled pulling off his boots. It released their last feelings of tension. Laughing with undiluted happiness, they closed in on each other and hugged and kissed.

While kissing her mouth, he unfastened the hooks and laces of her simple dress, sliding it down to the floor. His lips moved down her neck and along the top of her shoulders and she loosened his shirt, her palms gliding up over his skin before pulling it off over his head. She kissed his bare chest and the hard muscles of his stomach. Their breathing grew faster. Their fingers pulled open and pushed down clothes. Their desire now was unstoppable. Lifting Kerensa up off her feet Clem dropped her gently across the bed. Kerensa let out an intense cry of pleasure, a moan of released emotion. Clem wept in absolute bliss, in total joyfulness. His flesh was on her flesh, and inside her flesh, and his heart was over her heart. She was in his arms, clinging to his back, keeping perfect time with his rhythm, matching his passion and his tenderness. At the right moment he lifted her up round the waist to go even deeper into her. Clem took his lips away from hers and looked down at her. She had her eyes shut, her face torn with pleasure, the pleasure he was giving her.

Their last moan came at the same breathtaking instant, their bodies convulsing, shuddering again and again with rapturous release and completion.

He lay down beside her, their limbs in a tangled warm embrace, his face next to hers on the bedcover. Panting, swallowing to regain their breath, they smiled and smiled into each other eyes.

'My love,' Clem gasped, his voice grazing his throat, 'my precious, dear love, are you all right?'

She caressed his hot damp face and kissed his moist lips. 'Oh, yes, my beloved. Are you?'

He kissed her back. 'I've never been so happy. For the first time in my life I feel I am really alive.'

He held her close. So this was what it was like to make love to Kerensa. To make love with total self-giving. So many times he had tried to imagine how it would be with her. It was like drinking from the sweetest cup. Knowing the joy of the entire world.

He moved his head on to her breast. 'I don't want this night to end.'

'It never will because we'll never forget it.'

She stroked his soft hair, ran delicate fingertips down the centre of his back. She closed her eyes to the immeasurably exquisite sensations of his warm breath as it fanned over her perfectly moulded shape. To have Clem make love to her, who by first right and conscience should have been the man she made holy vows to, felt as right as her claim to put breath in her lungs.

His hands began to give devotion to her again and she gave herself over to worship him back.

Nineteen

Luke and Jack were down in Porthcarne before first light. A spray of purple and pink heather was pinned to their coats, one of the local customs of Midsummer's Eve.

The village was alight with torches. Green foliage was tied to the well and draped over every doorway, along every window sill and pushed into every eave and crevice.

Gathered outside the Crabber's Port, the fiddlers were ready and the drummers, men and boys, were making the last adjustments to the leather straps or rope that bound their instruments to their bodies. Some players had tied greenery to themselves, others had streaked their faces with green dye. All had bunches of strong-smelling wild garlic pinned to their hats.

'Looks as if you're all set to see off this pirate, Kinver,' Luke said eagerly. 'What was his name?'

'Tobias James, sir,' Hal replied, twirling his drumsticks in his chunky fingers. 'Was a nobleman, come over from Ireland, so we believe. Stole from merchant ships and murdered fishermen just for the fun of it. Came ashore and took the women and they was never seen again. Put mortal fear in this part of the coast from 1662 till 1669, then we got the bugger! His ship run aground on the reef just out to sea there on this very day. He and bravish few of his men got ashore but we showed 'em no mercy. Hung Tobias James within the hour, then threw his remains back in the sea. He died cursing and we've been drumming him back out ever since. There's no women about, as you can see. They stay indoors for their own protection till we've drummed round all the boundaries.'

Luke produced a flute out of his coat. 'Jack's brought his pipes. I take it we are welcome to join in?'

'We'd be honoured indeed, Mr Pengarron,' came a different voice. 'Did you know that safely locked away in the church is a gold ring of Tobias James's?'

'Oh, it's you, Reverend Thake,' Luke returned bitingly, spotting the simpering curate on the periphery of his vision. 'What do you play?'

'Nothing, nothing, nothing, sir. I'm here to

207

start the proceedings with a prayer on what we often simply call James's Day.'

Luke looked up, inland. Light was showing its first beginnings in the eastern skies. He gave the curate a curt nod.

'May God the Father and God the Son and God the Holy Ghost bless this special day in Porthcarne's calendar.'

The Reverend Thake had good reason to rattle through the prayer, for Davey Endean, a sharp-faced youth, now in regular work as cowman for Luke's new herd, drawn by lot for the right to beat the first drum and head the procession, wasn't going to wait more than a second or two. He walloped wood to animal hide, and to roars and whoops and whistles, marched off towards the seashore.

As squire, Luke followed next. Jack was going to fall in somewhere within the ranks of the players, but Luke pulled him alongside him.

'We'll take a day out to enjoy ourselves!' Luke shouted above the noise. 'Why isn't Barbary here?'

'Too pagan for him,' Jack bawled back.

'It's just a bit of fun!'

Once the two friends caught the gist of the catchy tune they joined in.

Cordelia and Alicia joined the festivities at ten o'clock, wandering through the sideshows and stalls of the fair, watching the street entertainers, avoiding the pedlars and the same unfortunate dancing bear that could seen on market day in Marazion. A fortune-teller suddenly offered her services to Alicia.

'Get away from me!' she screamed. She hated being reminded of the actress in London. The woman had forecast that three people connected to her would die. It made her afraid for her baby.

'I'm sorry,' she said to Cordelia. 'My condition sometimes makes me feel out of sorts.'

'You need to sit down in comfort,' Cordelia counselled. She wondered why Mrs Jack had looked so afraid.

They found Luke taking a drink at the trestle tables and benches outside the alehouse, where his gift of half a dozen barrels of ale and jars of rum were set up. Jack was drinking water sweetened with honey. Happy faces, grateful from a break in their hard existence, were to be seen everywhere, and the two men were laughing too.

'My dears!' Luke rose gallantly. 'The weather has done us proud, although it might become a little too fierce for you, Alicia. Sit down with Jack. Mrs Jewell, bring out something for the ladies!' he shouted through the shanty's open window.

Cordelia sat and sipped a tot of rum, and watched Luke eyeing the females, many of whom were parading up and down for his benefit. The girls were in white or light colours. Wild flowers were braided through their hair. The women had prettied their best wear with ribbons and lace.

'It's a pity they aren't in a position to really dress up,' she said, then deliberately leaned on Luke to whisper, 'I wish I'd thought of it before, I've got some old petticoats which could have been cut up for the little girls.'

'Excellent idea for next year.' Luke smiled. 'I've decided to start the festivities two days early in future, by introducing a three-day miracle play. I wonder if I could find a band of players among this lot.'

'You'll have to write something yourself, Luke,' Jack said.

'I could organize the making of costumes, which could be kept at Polgissey and added to each year,' Alicia interjected, moving about uncomfortably on the hard bench.

'The people need to be taught new skills,' Cordelia murmured thoughtfully. 'Some here even lack the basics in their homes. A school should be set up for the children, perhaps two or three times a week.'

'There you are, Jack, food for thought. We shall all pool our ideas.' Luke raised his replenished glass. 'To another year's casting out of the spirit of Tobias James, and the future of Porthcarne.'

While Luke joined the squash watching the wrestling matches, Cordelia joined Little

Min in her usual place nearby.

Alicia, somewhat bemused by the day's events stayed put, a little more comfortable on a makeshift cushion of materials bought off a trader. Jack stayed and held the parasol over her.

'Seem a nice couple,' Little Min deliberated.

'The Rosevears are devoted to each other,' Cordelia agreed.

She envied Jack and Alicia, chatting so naturally together, looking forward to the birth of their baby; although, and she couldn't work out what exactly, sometimes there was something strange about Mrs Jack. She seemed to cut herself off from everyone with a severe determination, even Jack. She would hug her swollen middle and look tragic. Perhaps she was sad she had no family to present her child to. Luke had erected a small Cornish cross in the churchyard and she often laid flowers at its foot, making it clear she wanted no company as she stood and remembered whoever it was she had lost.

'Good morning, Miss Drannock. Mrs Drew.'

'Good morning, Mr Kinver.'

'Enjoying yourself, boy?' Little Min chuckled. 'Made 'nough noise this morning, old Jamesie'll be too 'fraid to show hisself round here for a whole cent'ry!'

211

'I think Mr Pengarron's presence gave us encouragement. It was very good of him, what he did for the children.'

'What did he do?' Cordelia looked from his fine dark face to old Minnie's tiny wrinkled face.

'Young master gived each of the childer a shilling piece!' Little Min slapped her knee, making her tiny dog shuffle awake and yawn widely. 'Never seen such happy liddle faces. Never had sumthin' to spend on themselves on James's Day afore.'

'Mr Pengarron is very kind.' Cordelia was a little astonished. Now that Luke had a dream and the reality of his own responsibilities, he had become exceedingly generous towards the sort of people who, before, he would have viewed as nuisances, creatures to be taken for granted to wait on him, or at the best, poor unfortunates. Luke had more than a dream, he had those wonderful feelings of being needed and belonging. If only he needed her in the same way she yearned to belong to him.

'He's some polite,' Little Min said, when Morgan had excused himself to watch Hal wrestle. 'I reckon he listened carefully to his father and learnt a thing or two.'

A group of ragged children crept towards Cordelia, plainly hoping she had brought her basket with her. Her study of them revealed two girls who bore the Kinver black hair and soft grey eyes. Had either or both just seen their father leave?

At twilight, Luke was at home standing in front of a full-length mirror. He was having the usual difficulty, because of his stiff shoulder, in tying his neckcloth, but, for once, he was not swearing about it. He was in high spirits, even though he had not long ago had strong words with Jack.

'I've done with the revels,' Jack had announced on the ride back to change their clothes for the next round of events. 'Think I'll stay home tonight.'

'You'll do no such thing,' Luke had said airily. 'There's the ceremony of lighting the bonfire and the ox roast still to come. Don't be so prissy.'

'Alicia needs to take things easy for the rest of the day. You've promised the servants they can go to the bonfire, I won't have her staying on her own.'

'Then one of the maids will have to stay with her. Not another word about it!'

There were two sharp raps on the bedroom door and someone came in with a soft rustle of skirts.

'Corrie? Mrs Curnow – Amy?' He swung round. 'Oh, Alicia. What's wrong? Why do you look so angry? Do this wretched neckcloth for me, please.'

Alicia advanced on him then remained quite still. 'I'm here to take issue with you over the way you spoke to Jack earlier.'

Luke grinned broadly, letting the two fine embroidered ends of the cloth fall from his hands. 'Well?'

'It should be Jack's decision whether he goes out again today.'

'My dear Alicia, Jack is—'

'Your friend,' she arched her perfectly shaped brows, 'or so you keep saying.'

Taking his time, Luke regarded her with pleasure. Resolute, coolly divine, flourishing like a rose at two-thirds through her pregnancy.

'Your loyalty towards Jack is commendable, and how protective you've become of him. Do you now allow him all the rights of a husband?'

'Do you wish to know about my and Jack's private life as titillation because you have no one better at present in your bed than Amy Curnow? Granted, the cook is reasonable of face but she is, to say the least, most second rate. You need to grow up, Luke.' She stepped forward swiftly and saw to his neckcloth, her eyes following his angry ones.

'Now I understand some of Alex's downcast moods. Until now, I thought your attributes to be only benevolent. You have a particular way of humiliating a man. So, Jack is not to accompany me. Quite right, if it's what he wants. Don't wait up for Cordelia and I, I'll ensure she gets home safely.'

214

Alicia was holding out his dress coat and helped him shrug into it. 'I didn't come here to hurt your feelings, Luke. There are times when things need to be said, that's all.'

Luke allowed her to arrange the lace-edged overflow of his handkerchief in a side pocket.

'It's also no wonder to me why Alex loved you and needed you so much. The most foolish of the things he did was his way of trying to protect you. When I took Jack to London with me, I had no idea he'd be bringing back such a treasure. Please allow me to envy him. I suppose you and he have had very little time to yourselves. Enjoy a quiet night together.'

Jack was waiting gloomily for Luke and Cordelia at the foot of the stairs. Alicia floated down to him and he guided her the last few steps.

'Come with me,' she said and led him into the dining room.

The table, an oval-shaped walnut piece, once belonging to the Dobles, was laid at one end for two people, food upon it.

'What's going on?' he asked.

'This is for us. You don't have to go out.'

Careful to avoid her bulging middle, Jack hugged her, then grew sombre. 'You've spoken to him? What'll Luke think of me, not standing up for myself?'

'Oh, you men.' Alicia raised her eyes mockingly while taking his hands. 'Just enjoy the quiet meal we're going to have. We won't have to listen to Luke rambling on about his plays or watch Cordelia making doe eyes at him. We can play master and mistress of this grand house.'

'I wish it was our house, Alicia. I'd give anything to set you up in a place like this, just the two of us, and the baby.'

'Well, she's going to enjoy living here.'

'You've made up your mind it's a little maid then?' Jack's expression showed he was impressed and proud of her. He looked at the table. 'You were sure you'd talk Luke round, weren't you?'

'Luke's still a boy.' Quite easy for her to manipulate. 'One day, when he's finally a man I hope he'll see that Cordelia would make a good wife for him.'

She poured cordial for them both, raised her glass. 'A toast to the baby, the success of Luke's first play, and success for Cordelia in getting him to the altar.'

'Aye,' Jack agreed, then ventured, 'And to us.'

Alicia met his steady gaze. 'Yes, and to us, Jack.'

She played the charming hostess and attentive wife all evening.

When they were lying in bed, Jack, emboldened by her affection, kissed her goodnight on the cheek as he always did, then he kissed her lips and whispered in her ear,

'Please Alicia, I'll be gentle. We can arrange the pillows, I'll be careful with my weight...'

Running a light finger down his face, she let him become aroused and allowed him to touch her and kiss her.

When he made his move, she restrained him with a hand pressed to his shoulder.

'I want us to be a proper husband and wife, Jack,' she whispered in the moonlit room, which showed her his face, 'but there must be no secrets between us. Tell me, what has Luke done with the list of names of the Society members that Alex threatened to give to the authorities?'

This was the best evening of Cordelia's entire life. How important she felt to be at Luke's side on the top of Polgissey cliff where the towering bonfire was about to be lit.

Glancing at her, he took a burning rag from a youth, who had been swinging it in a circle over his head to emulate the sun's passage through the skies. Luke threw the rag into the base of the bonfire, the twigs crackled then flames burst up through the timbers and dried furze.

Cordelia clapped her hands and cheered as loudly as the villagers. If Jack and Alicia were watching from a principal window they would see the flames in the near distance.

As the bonfire settled there was much

leaping over it and when the fire was lower still, a token cow from Luke's herd was driven, practically unscathed, through it, as acts of purification against crop blight infertility, diseases and witchcraft. Cordelia held her breath as, for their protection against disease and other ills, the children were swished over the embers. This was done so skilfully that only a singeing or two of clothing resulted. Alicia had donated the material she'd bought for the cushion to the children, and all were decked out in something from it.

Luke kept Cordelia close, threading her arm through his, making sure she had enough to eat and drink. She declined all calls for her to join in the dancing – it was rather unseemly – wanting only to rest her face against Luke's arm and for the world to see that she belonged to him.

' 'Scuse me, sir,' Hal Kinver was suddenly there, chewing on a mouthful of hot meat. 'Can 'ee spare a minute? Little matter of...' and he silently mouthed the rest of the sentence.

'Oh, yes. Stay here, Cordelia, I'll be gone but a minute. You'll be safe close by the spit, and the Reverend Thake is just over there if you want someone to talk to.'

Cordelia most definitely did not want to pass the time with the obnoxious parson, now gorging himself at the spit as if he was eating his last meal. She turned from his direction lest he try to pursue her company. He had done so before in his ingratiating manner. How dare he see her as a possible bride!

Hoping to find someone she was well acquainted with in the village, she found herself face to face with Morgan Kinver.

He gave a perfect bow. 'Miss Drannock, I hope you'll not find this an imposition, I'd like to collect some ashes for you from the bonfire. It will act as a talisman against the evil eye.'

'I thank you – Oh!' She shuddered. A live rat and another small animal had been thrown on the fire. Others would follow, a necessary sacrifice if the ashes were to have full power. She was horrified to see and hear the animals suffering, but she was as superstitious as most of the county's breed. 'It's very kind of you, Mr Kinver.'

'It'll be my pleasure.'

She could make out his pleasant smile in the glow. Every time she saw him she was struck by his rich voice, smart appearance and quiet manner.

Someone threw an arm round her waist and she shrieked in fright.

'It's only me.' Luke laughed in her ear. He stared at Morgan Kinver. 'I've just done the necessary transaction with your brother. Good night, Kinver.'

Morgan watched as Cordelia was swept back into the festivities, then he went off by himself to wait for the bonfire to turn into ashes.

It was two o'clock in the morning when Luke and Cordelia crept back into Polgissey House.

Giggling and shushing each other, for they were certain the servants were all back and the household was in slumber, they decided on a nightcap before going up to bed.

'Happy Midsummer's Day,' Luke blurted out, quite drunk.

'I forgot to ask, what did Hal Kinver want with you?' she whispered in the hallway.

'It was only about a wager. The villagers can't afford heavy sums. I won five pounds on Hal winning the wrestling tournament, but lost ten on the quaint tradition of who could sit longest on a greasy pole, but no matter. Nothing can spoil what was a wonderful day.'

Luke was holding her hand, and Cordelia had high hopes that he would turn their relationship on to a different footing. She would share his bed this night if it turned out that was what he desired. All she needed now was a little courage to encourage him.

Luke opened the drawing-room door and Cordelia almost let out a scream at seeing a figure blocking their entrance.

It was Jack and he was furious. 'I want a word with you, Luke, and another time will not do!'

Twenty

There was a Midsummer Night's ball at Penzance's assembly rooms.

Olivia, lovely in a gown featuring a ruched, fan-shaped bodice, whispered to her father, 'That's him over there, Mr George Spears. I recognize him from a self-drawing in a broadsheet.'

'He's talking to Sir John, this will lead to an easy introduction, my love,' Oliver said, his dark eyes homing in on the gentleman like a bird of prey's. 'Are you ready, Timothy?'

'Of course, sir. This will be Livvy's night of triumph.'

After a frank discussion with his father-in-law, in which Sir Oliver had pointed out the foolishness of denying Olivia's wishes in respect of her painting, and in light of her renewed interest in the marriage bed and their compromise that she refer to her duties in the parish no less than three times a week, the young parson was a happy man.

Ecstatically happy, for this morning the wife he adored had announced she was with child.

Oliver conveyed his elder daughter to join Sir John St Aubyn and the man he had invited to his castle home to appreciate its collection of famous paintings.

'My dear Pengarron, Reverend Lanyon and Mrs Lanyon, this is a pleasure. And now it is my honour to introduce you to the artist, Mr George Spears.'

The gentleman bowed with a flourish, and Olivia returned a sweeping curtsey smiling with all her charm. Mr George Spears was perhaps about forty, and his looks and his voice fully masculine. She found him forthright and fascinating.

The talk consisted entirely of the world of art, the artist expounding his approach to this and his attitude towards that, what he held in high estimation and what he scorned. He was well-informed and sound, and from the fluid motions of his hands one could almost see the subject he was talking about appear as a brilliant masterpiece. Next came a long catalogue of the wealthy, the noble and the famous who had sat for him.

In any other circumstances Oliver would have found George Spears, as an individual, inconsequential and boring. The artist's facial lines seemed set a little too high and Oliver felt there was a lot about him that needed dragging down. In his current mood, dejected and morose, he would have liked to set about the task with unequal ruthlessness.

'My daughter is gifted on canvas and on any other medium, Mr Spears,' Oliver interrupted the monologue.

'You paint, Mrs Lanyon? Well, how splendid for you.'

Olivia was so engrossed in Mr Spears that she missed the next announcement of who was entering the hall. The master of ceremony was intoning, 'Sir William and Lady Rachael Beswetherick.'

Rachael strode straight up to Oliver, rudely ignoring the rest of the group. 'Oliver, I wish to speak to you.'

Oliver surveyed the matron who had been shunning him as he would a fly who had landed on his person. 'I'm presently engaged, ma'am. It will have to do another time.'

'It must do now!' Rachael risked her extravagantly decorated wig by tugging on him until his ear was on the same level with her lips.

When Oliver righted his head he looked grave. 'Will you all please excuse me? I shall hope to continue with our fascinating discussion in a short while, Mr Spears.'

Oliver went into a small anteroom in the vestibule, undecided if he was furious or delighted to be summoned here by Kerensa. To walk back in with her on his arm, as she had requested via Rachael, would silence one line of gossip and open up another. Many people would see it as a sign of reconciliation. It's what he wanted more than anything – when all was resolved. Could that ever be with a certain detestable individual still skulking within her easy reach? A reach she may have closed up entirely. He knew he could not reasonably expect her to stay away from Vellanoweth, yet saw her continuing visits there as disloyalty to him, and uncaring and selfish. She had shifted a lot of ground away from him, a distance which might never be re-established.

'Thank you for coming out to me,' Kerensa said. She was nervous but set proud, and she found herself moving several steps closer to him. 'I can hardly go in without you, Oliver. I would like to be at the ball for Livvy's sake.'

'Perhaps for her sake it would be better if you had stayed away.' He kept his gaze severe, yet was admiring her. She was wearing a fur-trimmed cloak, pearls were threaded through her hair. Strong yet delicate, fine and lovely, and somehow elusive, she looked as if she had stepped out of a legend.

Kerensa took a moment to calm her thudding heart. 'I know there will be tittle-tattle, but she's my daughter and I want to give her my support. If you send me away I'll simply go. I wouldn't dream of disgracing you by entering alone.'

The sound of his harsh breathing filled the small room.

'Please, Oliver...'

The option of her leaving was one he did not want. Enter the gathering and damn the county! It's what he would have thought at any other time, but it wasn't his priority. To send her away would be to broaden their rift and that scared him. 'And I would not dream of denying your request.'

They left the privacy of the small room and he waited for her to remove her cloak, greeting more arrivals with cool politeness.

'On your own, eh, Pengarron? Eh?' Ralph Harrt enquired with underlying sarcasm, while his silly, petulant wife giggled behind her fan.

Oliver fixed the coroner and his spouse with a hard stare. 'Most definitely not.'

When Kerensa rejoined him, he saw her in the full light of the chandeliers, in all her excellence. Her gown was of russet-coloured watered silk and gold lace, the colours which suited her so well. A ruby necklace sat enchantingly round her throat. The Harrts too saw her exquisite beauty, judging from their gasps and mutterings.

It wasn't just to save face that Oliver put his lips close to Kerensa's ear. 'I have never seen you looking so beautiful, Kerensa.'

'Thank you, Oliver.' He looked statesmanlike and handsome and appealingly

225

vulnerable. She thought about the women who must surely be vying to take her place. A horrible, undesirable thought.

She felt the familiar firmness of his hand. Strong his fingers were as they folded around hers, but not warm and not affectionate. She missed that so much it took her breath away. Tonight he was unyielding, indifferent. Or was he, like her, feeling the loss of their usual intimacy and crying deep inside, while keeping restrained? This was difficult for him and it would be difficult for her. She must think only of Olivia.

He heard her nervous intake of breath. 'Are you up to this?'

'Yes. Shall we go in? Livvy will be wondering where you are.'

'We have been introduced to this George Spears fellow,' he said conversationally, 'but were making little headway with him when I left.'

'If necessary then we must make a fresh address,' she answered, determination for Olivia giving her courage to see this night through.

Olivia was angling for an invitation to join Sir John's supper table, to give her more opportunity to talk to Mr Spears. Mr Spears was relentless at talking only about himself and his works.

Timothy had been unsuccessful at bringing the subject back to Olivia's art. He felt that the artist, who was sending suggestive glances at a lady who was fervently giving similar reply, had not the slightest interest in Olivia's pastime. *The chap probably gets this sort of thing thrust on him all the time, is sure it's only infantile dabblings or something,* Timothy thought, galled on Olivia's behalf. He sent up a quick prayer. Help was urgently needed or Livvy wouldn't be worth getting near to when they got home.

'I get a lot of inspiration from the great da Vinci,' Olivia pursued Mr Spears, trying to get him to look her way again. 'I—'

'Upon all that's holy, who is this?' George Spears suddenly broke away to stand alone and stare towards the entrance.

Olivia was struck immobile as her mother was announced. As her parents progressed towards her, looking to all the world a perfectly happy couple, she was aware of the lowered fans, the stage whispers, the titters, the embarrassed fidgeting and the smirking.

'Mama, I'm delighted you could come.' Olivia dashed forward to kiss her mother then, linking her arm through Kerensa's, introduced her to her quarry.

'Captivated, ma'am.' George Spears gazed blatantly into Kerensa's eyes. 'Well, Sir Oliver, fortune rains on you indeed. May I say that you have two of the most beautiful ladies in this superlative and mysterious county. May I ask if you and your good ladies and Mr Lanyon will do me the honour of joining me at supper?'

'You've saved the day, Mama,' Olivia said, not for the first time, as the evening wore on. 'Mr Spears is besotted with you. Dance with him one more time and arrange a definite time for him to come to the parsonage and view my paintings. Don't promise to be there unless he absolutely insists. Your presence would be too distracting.'

'I'm full of food, Livvy, and my feet are aching,' Kerensa protested. She was also a little lightheaded. For the purposes of the occasion, she had forsaken her Methodist origins and had drank the two glasses of wine George Spears had pressed on her.

Kerensa was sitting with Rachael. She had retreated to her side during the moments she had been able to tear herself away from George Spears.

'Don't make such faces, Olivia, dear. You'll give yourself wrinkles,' Rachael chastised.

'You should take a rest yourself, Livvy,' Kerensa said, peering through the dancers for a sign of Oliver. After supper he had excused himself to go to the games room. She wasn't sure what his mood was, he had put on a starkly contrasting choice of them all evening. 'The first few weeks are the most likely for anything unfortunate to happen.'

'If you mean miscarriage then why not just say so,' Olivia returned airily, thinking such a happening would prove a blessing in disguise. When her mother still made no move in George Spears's direction, she went on tetchily, 'Are you going home with Father?'

'Olivia, please don't get difficult,' Kerensa answered tightly.

'Oh, the answer is no then. I thought – I'm sorry, Mama. Excuse me, I'll go and rescue Timothy from the hateful Sarah Harrt.' Olivia didn't want to think about the tragedy of her parents' rift. She could think of nothing she could do about it.

Rachael gave her friend a sympathetic glance but said nothing. It was plain Kerensa wanted Oliver back and her marriage to be as strong as before. It was also plain that she and Clem Trenchard were meeting in her little hideaway.

Sir William approached Oliver where he had just resigned from a card table. 'No good fortune tonight, eh?'

'What? Oh, I had no concentration.' Suddenly weary and impatient, Oliver signalled to a footman for a drink. 'What do you want with me, William? You've made yourself poor company these last few weeks. Damn disloyal, I call that.'

'It's been difficult, Oliver, with Kerensa spending so much time with us.' William bobbed about like a pecking bird. 'I thought all would be resolved posthaste. I did not want to become involved with taking sides.'

229

'I would not think you so immature. I want her back, plain and simple! But not until she gets that bastard out of her head.'

'You'd let horrid old-fashioned jealousy destroy your marriage? You shock me, Oliver. I never took you for a fool.'

Oliver finished the brandy brought to him.

'You take no exception? You cannot even defend yourself? God in heaven, what has become of you, Oliver Pengarron? I am astounded. I don't know what to say.'

'Good.' Oliver thrust the empty glass into William's hand.

Back in the ballroom, Oliver watched Kerensa dancing with George Spears.

William arrived at his side. 'You can see the way the fellow's looking at her. Do you find it so hard to believe this Clem Trenchard could ever forget her?'

'It's she who should have forgotten him!'

'She did, you complete and utter fool! He might have retained a little tug on her heart, but you had the whole of it as tight as this.' William held up his balled fist. He opened it out flat. 'If it's laid out like this now you are the one who made it so! Wake up, my friend, before it's too late.'

Turning under George Spears's raised arm, Kerensa caught Oliver's eyes on her. They were so harsh, she snatched at her breath. Had he grown to loathe her?

When she repeated the full circle he was

230

there, tapping on George Spears's shoulder. 'May I dance with my wife now, sir? I have neglected her for far too long.' What did he mean exactly, and what was behind his grim smile?

Oliver bowed regally to her. When they joined hands and began stepping the way lightly down through the line-up of ladies and gentlemen, he said, 'How goes it with Spears?'

'He's agreed to call at the parsonage next week.'

'Excellent. Wonderful news about our next grandchild, is it not?'

'The very best.'

He turned her slowly under his arm and she circled around him, then he brought her in closer to his body than the dance dictated. 'We still have much to tie us together, Kerensa.'

She couldn't tell if he meant it as a loving statement or as a threat. 'We always shall, Oliver.'

He wasn't sure how her response was meant. They needed to talk at length and alone.

'Excuse me, ma'am, sir,' George Spears cut in on them. 'Sir John and I are about to take our leave. I would like to thank you for helping to make this a most entertaining evening.'

Oliver and Kerensa left the dance floor

and, joined by Olivia and Timothy, entered into a round of extravagant farewells. George Spears lingered too long over Kerensa's hand.

'Hell's teeth, what an obnoxious fellow,' Oliver said as if he had something sour on his tongue.

'That doesn't matter.' Kerensa embraced Olivia. 'Not long for you to wait now, my love. You must be so excited.'

'It's like being in a wonderful dream. I'm so thankful and proud of you, Mama. It wouldn't have happened without you here. Mr Spears was quite dazzled.'

Left out of all the talk, Oliver bowed silently and went looking for another drink. Kerensa looked about for him. So this was how things still stood between them. He would rather head off back to the dance or the card table.

'Can we leave now, Rachael?' she said miserably.

Twenty-One

Up in the tower room, Luke's brow was furrowed over the manuscript on the shabby desk, a relic procured from Pengarron Manor's attic. Try as hard as he could to focus on his writing, the words leapt about or blended together.

'Damn, I drank too much yesterday. What think you of this, Jack? A woodland setting for the final scene. Twisted black trees with huge soulless eyes and branches that reach out like grabbing hands, mist wafting upwards and ... and ... What was I saying? I've lost the thread.'

'You're tired, you write every minute you're not about your pleasures, you can't expect to keep thinking clearly,' Jack replied gruffly. 'And that's not what I call a new idea. Think of something else.'

'I will!'

'And take a wash and shave and get dressed. 'Tisn't seemly for Miss Cordelia or the maids to see you slopping about in your nightshirt.'

'By the devil's teeth, how dare you speak to

233

me like that!' Then Luke recalled Alicia's comments on how he managed his friendship with Jack. He smoothed his tone. 'Listen, Jack, I've explained why I kept the true nature of Lord Longbourne's correspondence from you. I'm sorry if you saw it as a betrayal of our friendship, but I considered that if only *I* knew of the document's whereabouts there was no risk of us ever talking about it and being overheard. I had no idea Alicia knew of its existence. We all talked at length about it last night, we've all agreed that I alone should bear the burden of the document's hiding place. What is wrong now? Don't you trust Alicia? Is there something else?'

'Course not. I'm off to the stables, Boy Hal and I are going to exercise the horses.'

Luke was left to ponder Jack's dark humour. Had more hurt been done to him last night than that which he himself had been unwittingly responsible for? Exactly what had Alicia said to him when she'd brought the matter up? Could Alicia, after all, be trusted?

She had declared that as Alex's common-law widow, she had the right to know everything connected to him. Her explanation for her silence over the document amounted to her having taken it for granted that Luke would inform her when he received it. Had she secretly been searching for it? If so, what had she intended to do with it? Retain it, as Luke was, as a form of leverage if circumstances ever dictated it?

Greatly disturbed, Luke made haste to his chamber, stripped, washed, shaved and dressed. Needs dictated he must keep on the highest alert. Was she Sophia Glanville, Alicia Rosevear or someone else? Who exactly had he and Jack brought back to Cornwall with them?

At the same time, Cordelia's presence was being requested in the back courtyard.

'Who is it, Mabena?' she demanded crossly. Her hopes for a closer union with Luke having been dashed, she was in no mood to speak to anyone.

' 'Tes a gentleman,' she was informed by the kitchen maid, a flippant sixteen-year-old, whom Cordelia suspected was with child. 'Come 'n' see. I'd be pleased to have he calling on me.'

A gentleman would not arrive at the back door, but curious, Cordelia followed Mabena outside, and found Morgan Kinver standing next to his delivery of goat's milk and cheese and vegetables.

'Is there something wrong, Mr Kinver? I'm sure I gave Mrs Curnow the right amount of money.' She avoided looking into his face but knew he was looking at her.

'That lot's too heavy for me to carry

indoors,' Mabena cut in, winking insolently at Morgan.

'I'd be pleased to do it, Miss Drannock,' Morgan's full soft tones brought Cordelia's eyes to his face. What a quiet expression he always wore. He had a coat on and a neck-cloth despite the morning heat – a man of standards.

'Thank you, Mr Kinver. You may return to your work, Mabena.' It was improper to remain alone with this man, but Cordelia did not want to be under Mabena's impertinent eyes, and she was intrigued to know what Morgan Kinver's business was with her.

When Mabena flounced off, Morgan took something out of his coat pocket. A small leather pouch.

'This is for you, Miss Drannock.' At her perplexed look he went on quickly, 'Ashes from the bonfire, as I promised last night.'

'Oh, really? Thank you very much. You took some for yourself?'

'I did.' He smiled. 'I know we don't really need a talisman, having the Almighty to watch over us.'

'Yes, I agree, but I suppose we can't help our nature.'

'No.' Another smile. 'That we cannot.'

After luncheon, Cordelia and Alicia were out walking, with parasols and wide straw hats

236

protecting them from the strong overhead sun, which burned periodically through the patchy clouds.

'It's good to get away from the house. The atmosphere is most disagreeable. Why was Jack so angry with Luke?' Cordelia said.

'It was something to do with Luke not informing Jack about a matter of the estate, I think.' Alicia was not in the mood for conversation. 'It's not our concern, thankfully.'

'But I've never known Jack to fly at anyone the way he did Luke. I was banished upstairs, but I listened from the top. Jack's tone was explosive. He only became quiet when you went down to them.'

'Whatever it was, Jack was quite happy when he took the horses out,' Alicia lied.

She was sorry she had offended Jack so much last night. It had been unfeeling of her to ask him about Alex's letter while he was at the very point of consummating their marriage. She had meant to question him afterward, but at the last moment she could not go through with the thought of Jack making love to her before Alex's baby was born. Jack had immediately pulled away from her and sat up, hunched over, on the edge of the bed.

'So that's the way of it,' he had accused her, humiliation thick in his voice. 'You want to know something about your lover and the only way you think you can find out is by seducing me. Why couldn't you just ask me

237

straight out? That was cheap of you, Alicia. Do you think me cheap too, that lust controls me? I'm not like the men you're used to!'

Her thoughts then had not been with Jack's distress. 'My maid put Alex's packet into the post to Luke. I've the right to be kept informed.'

'So've I!' Jack had dressed and left her. She had been forced to wait in the bedroom until Luke had come home.

Cordelia detected the impatience in her voice and changed to Alicia's most favoured subject. 'When will your confinement be?'

'Late September.' Alicia smiled a little, imagining how it would feel to hold Alex's child. 'So there will be new life in the house at Christmas. I confess I am a little nervous about the birth. There isn't a doctor for miles.'

'Don't worry, Luke will ensure you'll be properly looked after.'

They had left the grounds of the house and were strolling along the cliff path. The land was almost treeless, but heather grew in extensive bursts and intermingled with golden-flowered gorse. Long grasses swayed in the playful breeze. Alicia fell silent and Cordelia gazed out to the horizon, where the blue of the ocean met the blue of the sky.

'Minnie Drew's a sweet old soul. I like to hear her tales, she knows all about the shipwrecks on this coast. There's a ghost ship, a Spanish galleon, with a figurehead that protrudes oddly, and if it's seen a terrible misfortune falls upon the village. Little Min's told me a lot about the big house too. She worked there from seven years of age. Did you know that Mr Cecil Doble was a wrecker? That is, he deliberately led ships on to the rocks so they'd come to disaster?'

Alicia was saddened at how immature Cordelia sounded. 'If you don't mind, Cordelia, I'll not venture much further. It was foolish to come out at such a hot time of day. I must say, you are obtaining quite a curiosity for this area and its legends.'

'But it's sort of romantic, don't you think?'

Alicia laughed kindly. 'I don't see how. My dear, the only romantic notion you ought to entertain should involve acquiring yourself a real live man.'

Cordelia blushed hotly. 'What do you mean?'

Was Mrs Jack referring to Morgan Kinver? Had she noticed how long they had spoken together this morning? Afterward, Amy Curnow and the silly gaggle of kitchen maids had made free with her feelings.

'Better watch out, Miss Cordelia. He can catch a maid, but like his brothers, he can't be caught hisself.' Mrs Curnow had giggled. 'Must reckon, because he lives in a finer house than we, he stands a chance with 'ee.'

239

Cordelia intended to demand Luke reprimand the cook severely, even though he called her 'a treasure' and an 'ideal servant'.

'Please don't take exception, I meant no unkindness,' Alicia said, regretting her remark. Such a pity Luke was so wrapped up in his play writing. It would take the most shameless femme fatale to harness him, and in Cordelia's case she had the added difficulty of Luke taking her for granted. Luke was not missing out on the intimate side of life because Alicia had witnessed Amy Curnow slipping out of his bedroom with a sly smile, clutching a shilling piece. According to gossip, Mrs Curnow had a Kinver offspring, being reared at her mother's home. If Luke got her pregnant, a dark-haired Kinver could take the blame.

'Oh!' Alicia cried out suddenly.

'What is it? The baby?'

'No, we're almost at the cottage ruins. They give me the shivers. We must go back.'

'Very well. Wait a moment, what's that colour over there?'

'I don't know.' Alicia turned and started to retrace her steps.

'It's flowers,' Cordelia exclaimed. 'Can you not wait a moment while I pick them? They'll die and be wasted with no one to water them.'

Alicia looked over her shoulder. The charred stone walls of the cottage, the windows like huge discordant eyes, made her think how Alex's house now looked. Very soon she would have nightmarish thoughts of how the flames must have devoured his flesh. She was about to break down in grief and needed to be alone. 'I'll carry on, Cordelia. You can catch up with me.'

'I'll only be a minute or two.'

Breathing hard, Alicia walked fast, soon leaving Cordelia and the burnt-out cottage behind. She was nearing the grounds of the house, relieved Cordelia had not joined her, for she needed to find a secluded place to weep for Alex and herself.

The sight of a man in her path startled her. She let her parasol drop from her hand. Then she was afraid. The man was tall and dark, richly attired with a gold-topped walking cane, and although he looked familiar, she could not place him. Someone from London? From the Society? Pray God, no!

'Forgive me, ma'am, I've alarmed you.' He bowed elegantly. 'You must be Mrs Jack Rosevear.'

'Y – you know me, sir?'

'I have not had that pleasure until now. I was just speaking to Jack, we are acquainted of old.'

Her face contorted in shock and fear, Alicia fought to clear her mind. Then she had it. He looked familiar because he had the distinct features of the Pengarrons. A turn of the blanket of Sir Oliver's? But no such person had been mentioned to her. Her fear turned to terror. 'I – I do not know of you, sir.'

'My name is Drannock. I have come to visit my sister. I was told she was walking this way.'

'Drannock? Oh, you're one of Cordelia's brothers, I had not thought ... I had not...'

Her vision grew hazy and she felt a strange lightness in the head.

'Ma'am, are you unwell?'

She heard nothing more. Blackness engulfed her and she did not feel the stranger's arms preventing her from hitting the ground.

There were only a few grape hyacinths growing in the patch of back garden of the cottage. Skirting the rubble and ashes, Cordelia snapped them off on their long stems, feeling she must return quickly to Alicia, considering her condition.

A shadow fell across her, making her rise nervously to her feet. It was Morgan Kinver. Where had he sprung from? Had he followed her here?

'Good afternoon, Mr Kinver.' She claimed the superior position by getting in the first word. 'I did not think to see anyone else hereabouts.'

He performed a faultless bow. 'Good

242

afternoon, Miss Drannock. I often walk this way.' He, or one of his brothers, occasionally wandered about the cliff to see if anyone was loitering near their hide.

Cordelia had a sudden thought. Considering the reputation of the Kinvers, the most likely reason for him being here was an assignation. He was dressed finely, as always, and he smelled of fresh soap.

'They're lovely.'

'Pardon me?'

'The flowers.'

'Oh, yes. I thought they would look very well with some carnations from the gardens. I didn't like to leave them here, abandoned.'

'I understand.' He eased his footing, drawn even more to the gentle young lady's transparency and honesty. 'I keep a little brown rabbit at home. I happened across it last year. Separated from its mother it was about to become a meal for a sparrow hawk.'

'My uncle, Sir Oliver Pengarron, has a hut in the manor grounds kept solely for injured wildlife. I've seen all manner of animals and birds, even insects released, fully recovered, into their habitat. Miss Kelynen Pengarron healed a partially blinded kitten there quite recently. I would have loved to have had it, but my uncle has an allergy to cat's fur.'

'My brothers and I have three cats on the smallholding, all of an agreeable nature. One is about to produce a litter. You are very welcome to a kitten. If you have a care, I will bring the basket to the big house and you may choose one for yourself.'

'I shall consider it, thank you. My cousin, Mr Pengarron, was only saying last week we should have some animals about the house.'

He smiled his soft smile.

Cordelia became aware of how he was looking into her eyes and that she was doing the same into his. He was virtually a stranger, yet she felt at ease in his company.

Then she remembered Alicia. 'Oh, I really must go! I've deserted Mrs Rosevear and she is walking back alone. It's been – goodbye, Mr Kinver.'

'I'm going home to the smallholding. May I not go along with you part of the way, Miss Drannock?'

There were improprieties and implications to consider, but suddenly Cordelia did not care about them. She was tired of being thought of as a 'dear little thing', she was tired of being indulged as if she was still a child and, most of all, she was tired of being ignored.

'Well, you have to walk along the same path, so of course you may.'

They walked off, enjoying more conversation. When he offered her his arm, she accepted it.

Twenty-Two

The same afternoon, another young woman was fainting and another was holding flowers.

Rosie Renfree was in St Piran's church, on her knees, lying limply over the communion rail. When she came to, her vision clearing slowly, she didn't know where she was, then with a groan she recognized the colourless stone flags she was looking down on. Her head buzzed frighteningly. Somehow she dragged herself up on to leaden feet. The shawl around her shoulders had fallen off and she was cold, shivering uncontrollably.

Staggering to the front pew, the Pengarron pew, which she wouldn't even have dared touch before this, she fell down on it, clinging to the figure of the patron saint carved in the dull wood at its end. Bowing her head she wept wretchedly, hoping desperately no one would come inside.

Her lips trembling, she repeated her earlier prayers. 'Please God, I'm sorry for sinning against You and Matthias and the children. I am utterly lost if You don't forgive me. I swear I'll never commit the abominable sin of adultery ever again. I beg You, forgive me also for sinning against Lady Pengarron. I couldn't confess this to anyone, not even the Reverend Lanyon, even if he wasn't Sir Oliver's son-in-law. It's too terrible, too wicked!'

She repeated the prayer twice. She had committed the sin three times and felt she must. Racked with guilt after her first coupling with Sir Oliver, she had sworn she'd never do it again. But when her lover had crept up behind her in a secluded spot in the rambling farmyard, and softly put his arms around her and nestled his mouth on the back of her neck, she had turned round to him at once. Renouncing the devil and taking an oath of penitence and carrying Matthias's Bible everywhere she went, had not saved her a third time.

Yesterday, Oliver had met up with her at Marazion market after she had completed the business of selling her own eggs and other produce and, as fate would have it, the dairymaid she had taken with her so as not to be alone, had given her the slip to meet her own favourite.

As if she had no will of her own, no tongue with which to deny him, she had allowed Oliver to take her to a large house in the town. Whose it was or exactly where it was located she couldn't remember now. Only that he had said they were in no danger of being discovered, and he, pleased at the prospect of making love in comfort for a prolonged period, had plied her affectionately with gifts and compliments and tender encouragements to undress completely and give herself to him without reserve. He had taught and she had learned. To her everlasting dishonour, he had taught her to touch and kiss in ways she had not even imagined before. To her bitter shame, after her preliminary uncertainties, she had enjoyed every moment.

Now for the remainder of her life, she would bear the invisible stain of deceitfulness and corruption. She deserved it, welcomed it. She wanted to be punished. What she was finding unendurable was her betrayal of her gentle and loving husband, a committed Christian, who ministered to an ever increasing flock of members at the Methodist meeting house: tinners, fisherfolk, farm labourers and estate workers, the destitute and dying, people who called him Preacher Renfree.

She had no idea how long she had been inside the church, she must hasten home, before Matthias became worried and sent someone looking for her. Drying her tears of repentance, making sure her hat was pulled down to conceal her face, she edged out of the church door, through the tiny slate-roofed porch and out of the lychgate. Straight into the path of the Reverend Lanyon and Mrs Lanyon, an unknown gentleman and Sir Oliver.

Crying out, she crumpled against the wrought-iron gate.

'Rosie!' Oliver rushed to catch her. 'What is it? Are you ill?'

In her despair, she tried to push him away from her.

'Mrs Renfree, do you need the services of the Reverend Lanyon?' Olivia asked. Handing the bouquet of red roses George Spears had just given her to Timothy, she took Rosie's hand, pulled off her net glove and began rubbing her wrist. 'She's quite overcome, we must take her into the house.'

'No, please,' Rosie gasped weakly. ' 'Tis only the heat. I must go. My husband will worry.'

'It is a soporific day,' Oliver said, aware of her struggles to free herself from his support, 'but you are actually cold, Rosie. I'll carry you into the parsonage and you shall have a hot drink. Miss Nancy Wills can attend you in the kitchen, if you prefer.'

Rosie had no choice but to capitulate, she would be too weak to ride for several minutes. 'Yes, yes, that will do, thank you. I don't want to be a bother. I'm feeling better already,' she lied, and afraid Oliver would carry her and she would be brought into contact with his masterful body, she added swiftly, 'I can walk, please, I am quite embarrassed.'

Olivia took precedence and escorted her into the kitchen. Seated in Nancy Wills' comfortable chair, she sipped steaming hot tea, laced with honey. Nancy prepared a cloth soaked in lavender water for her forehead, and while tip-toeing about her domain, told Rosie the reason for George Spears's presence at the parsonage.

'I wish Mrs Lanyon well,' Rosie said, not caring the slightest.

She slipped away ten minutes later, riding at a slow trot to clear her mind. When on Ker-an-Mor land, the sound of the distant sea was a little comforting and she closed her eyes, letting the pony walk on.

Her eyes snapped open a second later and she turned round at the sound of heavy hoof beats. She knew who it would be before the rider came into view, and although dismayed, perhaps it was best she talk to Oliver. She dismounted beside a stand of oak trees, which gave welcome shelter from the tortuous heat.

Oliver left Gereint at a short distance and walked up to her. 'Rosie, my dear, I was concerned for you. As soon as I was able I excused myself. You have no need to tell me why you were so distressed. It's all my fault, you would never have been tempted if I had not encouraged you.'

'I knew exactly what I was doing, Oliver. But it must never happen again. I love Matthias. There was no excuse to stray from him and somehow I must make amends.'

'I'm so very sorry, Rosie. I'll keep away from Ker-an-Mor for a long while. If it's agreeable with Matthias, Shelley can become even more involved with the business side of things. That should make it easier for you.'

'Thank you, it will make my burden lighter. You haven't been home for some time. Will you go there now?'

'Yes. I thought at the Midsummer Night's ball that I might return there, but Kerensa had already arranged to stay at Tolwithrick and didn't seem interested in changing her plans. It will, of course, take more than a social event to put things right between us.

'You know the whole story, Rosie. I felt betrayed by her, but I should not have allowed my jealousy to show in such strength and so publicly. I do understand, from her perspective, that what I did to Kane and Harry is an entirely different matter. It won't be easy to become reconciled with Kerensa, and that is what I want more than anything. I love her so very much. I can't bear this loneliness without her. She loves me still, well, a part of me, I hope. She's distant in so many ways now. I irritate her. She examines and judges everything I do and say. When we first quarrelled, she told me that she saw me as small, and that is exactly how she makes her feel now.'

'And that doesn't rest easy with you, does it? You've had your own way all your life.'

Only a friend, a confidante, a lover, could say something like that to Sir Oliver Pengarron. 'Yes, I am desperate to regain her respect.'

'Oliver, you don't often listen to anyone, but will you allow me to tread where even an angel would fear to? Me, the woman who's been closest to you in a certain way, except for Kerensa?'

'Have your say, Rosie, please do. I need to hear some plain speaking. I thought Kerensa would soon come running back to me, but I treated her with too much disrespect, and now I'm at a loss as to what to do.'

'It's very simple. You must understand Kerensa's feelings for Clem. A first love is a strong love. She didn't break her pledge to Clem, you came between them.'

'Simple? Understand that she loves another man, one she professes to have emptied out of her heart long ago?' This was the last piece of advice he was expecting. 'You ask too much. God save me, but I wish your brother dead! If I find out he's been having an affair with Kerensa I'll kill him, I swear nothing will stop me.'

'Then it's no wonder you are the cause of your own misery. Can you not see it? What if they are having an affair? Is gaining retribution on Clem more important than regaining Kerensa? You say you love her more than anything. How do you? Even now, you're letting your jealousy rule you. Before you found Clem's love tokens, you couldn't even bear to think Kerensa might have kept even the slightest affection for him. You can't demand that much of people, Oliver. We all have the right to our own feelings, indeed we cannot help them. And have you not been unfaithful to Kerensa? You very quickly took me to your bed, without a thought for her or Matthias. You're eaten up with gall just thinking she might have been untrue, while you went ahead and did the wicked deed moments after she left your presence. You couldn't help your feelings then, could you? Didn't even try.

'If you really want to win her back then use your great intelligence to do it. You must forget your hatred of Clem and forget your jealousy, but first...' Rosie swallowed, should she go even further? He had been her lover but he was still her lord and master.

He pursed his mouth, eyes set grim, 'First?'

'First let your heart grow to the size where it can accommodate Kerensa's feelings for my brother, even if they have grown too close since he's been at Vellanoweth. Clem will soon be returning home. Perhaps you should have a word with him, a public word. A *clever* word.'

Oliver gazed at her, made his eyes widen, sighed and shook his head.

'I know it asks a lot of you. It's your decision. Your life. Your happiness. I'm going home to my husband now, he's worth everything in the world to me, he's my future. I'll leave you to think about yours.'

Rosie's brother and niece were washing their hands at the iron pump in Vellanoweth's yard. Clem had been holding the head of a cantankerous billy goat while Jessica had given him a purge.

'That'll teach the old misery not to break free and drink the starch for my linen.'

Jessica dried her hands and hugged her father. 'I'll miss you when you go home, Tas. Sell Greystone's Farm and come back to the Bay. I hate you being so far away. I'm sure Catherine would like to be back near her brother.'

'I'd love to, sweetheart, but Philip wouldn't have that. Your stepmother and me and the twins will come back before Christmas, I promise.'

'Livvy must be somewhat excited today. I hope this George Spears character likes her paintings.'

Receiving no answer, she stared into her father's face. She was used to his silences, when he went off into his own thoughts. Before, he had always looked drawn, morose, sadly lost, now his eyes were bright and he was smiling from somewhere deep within. There was only one person in the whole world who could make him look like this. Jessica was deeply worried.

She shook his arm. 'Your bed wasn't slept in last night, nor many a night before. Where do you go?'

'What a strange question.' He wiped his hands down his shirt front to dry them. 'I've always gone off to be alone, you know that. I miss my dogs, it'll be good to have their company again.'

Jessica flicked a fly away from her. 'But whose company have you been keeping? My mother-in-law's?'

'Don't be foolish.' Clem gave a sharp laugh.

'Oh, Tas, you're seeing her, aren't you?'

'Oh, look, Kane's managed to get to the doorway, and he's got Harry with him.'

Jessica waved to Kane. He was regaining his strength quickly now the infection in his leg was finally gone. He was leaning on crutches, and had Harry tied to his body in the same manner Jessica did. 'We're on our way in, dearest,' she called out, but she had not finished with her father. 'Dear God,

254

don't you know what danger you're in? Sir Oliver will flay you alive!'

'He can try. I hope he does. Then Kerensa will start to hate him.'

'She won't leave him. He wouldn't let her.'

'He's got no hold over her.'

'She wouldn't leave Samuel.'

'I haven't asked her to. Do you think I'd leave John and Flora? I have more love for my children than he has for his. I don't behave in a manner that could kill them.'

'What about Catherine?'

'Jessie, I'm doing nothing wrong. And I'm eager to see Catherine again. I'd like to stay on and help with the harvest here but I've my own fields to see to, and now Kane's so much better, I'd be getting in the way.'

'Yes, it's time you were leaving us.'

Jessica led the way indoors, regretting her need to have her father close all these weeks, and she wished, how she wished she had not challenged him over her suspicions. She kept nothing from Kane. What would he say, how would he feel about what his mother and her father were doing? Jessica was scared, if Kane told Sir Oliver...

Kerensa was in the manor gardens, playing a hide and seek game with Samuel. She had hidden three tin soldiers under the bushes and he was running about, squeaking with delight as he looked for them.

'Be careful you don't scratch your face on the twigs,' she called to him. The two soldiers he had already found were in her hand. He was taking a long time finding the third and for several seconds she had not heard his excited voice.

'Sam? Samuel, where are you? Shout to Mama. Do you want me to help you?'

The silence continued. She listened for him. There was the sound of Beatrice bawling at someone in the kitchen. Clip, clip. An under-gardener was trimming an ornamental hedge round the side of the house. Next came a bark from Rex. But no answer from Samuel.

'Sam! Tell Mama where you are.'

She weaved her way in and out of the shrubs, darting round to the rose garden, back again to the rug, where the rest of his toys lay forsaken. The garden furniture, where they were shortly to have tea together, before he went up for his bath in the nursery, was undisturbed. 'Sam!'

Panic rose in her. Her youngest son was wilful at times and would often hide away, but he had never kept quiet this long. She tore off to find him, was about to shout his name again when she heard his voice, loud and excited and chuckling with gusto. Wherever he had wandered off to, he was now only on the other side of a massive hydrangea. She ran round it.

'There you are—' she stopped in her tracks. 'Oh, you're with Papa, I thought you'd got lost.'

Oliver was crouching down, tickling his son, the reason for the chuckles. Samuel liked to play rough and suddenly whacked his father on the head. Kerensa laughed and Oliver laughed, pretending it hurt him.

'Right then, you little ruffian.' Lifting him up high above his head, Oliver whirled Samuel round and round until, quite breathless, he set the boy on his shoulders.

'He's the roughest and the toughest of our brood,' Oliver said to Kerensa. 'Don't you think?'

He was looking at her with his great dark eyes, a soft look, studying her. Alert to what his intentions might be, she answered, 'It's true to say he wears me out more quickly than the others.'

Samuel held out the third soldier to Kerensa. 'Ah, clever boy.'

'You've been playing hiding the soldiers. Kane and Luke both liked that game. You are well, Kerensa?'

She walked round the bush to the rug and Oliver kept pace with her.

'Yes, thank you. How went it for Olivia with Mr Spears? I've been on tenterhooks all day for her. Have you come with news?'

Oliver had to think hard for a moment. After his harrowing talk with Rosie and the painful suggestions she had made, the interview with the artist seemed hours and hours ago. 'He did not mince his words. He thought much of her work juvenile and cared not at all for her land- and seascapes.'

'Oh, poor Livvy. She must be feeling distraught. It's a good thing she has a child to look forward to.'

'Hold there, my dear,' Oliver smiled engagingly. 'He did however approve of her portraiture. Said it showed a certain fluency and promise and boldness, and some other such language his ilk uses. He plans to stay in Cornwall another week or so, says he's very taken with the particular light of the county and its spectacular views, and he has kindly said he'll allow time to give Livvy instruction.'

'That's wonderful.' Kerensa clapped her hands, and Samuel copied her and sang an appropriate nursery rhyme. 'She must be delighted.'

'Yes, she is, but disappointed about the other things he said. I think it will work well for her and Timothy as a couple, she won't be traipsing about the countryside so often now.'

'She is good at portraying people, the miniature of Luke shows his personality exactly. Is Mr Spears staying on at the Mount?'

'No. He's taken a room at Sealey's Hotel.'

A stillness came upon Oliver. He had not ridden here straightaway after leaving Rosie but had gone to Pengarron Point, the place where he went to think. Was it really possible for him to follow Rosie's suggestions? Could he dismantle that much pride and allow Kerensa to retain her feelings – the feelings he himself had brought back into focus – for Trenchard? The thought of her having loving relations with Trenchard filled him with horror, disgust and a pain too unbearable to dwell on. If Kerensa was innocent, she would feel something similar if she knew about his affair with Rosie. If she was seeing Trenchard, would she understand that he had needed someone else? Could their marriage survive the unfaithfulness on his part? Unfaithfulness by both of them? He knew that if they were to ever trust each again there must be no more secrets between them. At some point he was going to have to make a confession to Kerensa.

Looking at her now, he knew that, whatever may have happened between her and Clem Trenchard, he couldn't bear their rift turning into an unbridgeable chasm.

Somehow he got his voice to emerge in a natural tone. 'Kerensa, I have something to tell you. No, don't look worried, hear me out, please. Today, I've decided to come home for good. I hope that will be agreeable to you. For Livvy's sake, I thought perhaps,

259

in a day or two, we could invite George Spears here to dine with us.'

Kerensa felt a lift to her heart. With an aching despair, she had been expecting Oliver to leave again soon. Was he coming home for Sam's sake, or to reassert his claim on his property? Was she involved in his reason? Pray God, she was. Then there was a tightening in her chest as her thoughts flew to Clem. She was due at Rachael's cottage tomorrow night for her last meeting with him, before he left for home the next day. She was missing him already.

She cleared her throat. 'This is your house, Oliver. You may please yourself when you come and go. Sam has missed you, and Kelynen the constancy of your company.'

'I've missed them both, and Beatrice. And I've missed you most of all, Kerensa.'

Their eyes met. Was he reaching out to her? Their love had once been so strong, she found herself wanting to give way to him, but there were many barriers between them.

'I've missed you, Oliver, but we have – there's a lot – we've both said things, and—'

'I'll sleep in the other room, of course.'

Their boundaries set, they talked more about Olivia and George Spears. Samuel was pushing on Oliver's chest and he allow-ed him to ease him down flat on the rug. The little boy sat astride him and set about smacking his face and tugging his hair.

Kerensa knelt down and restrained him. 'No, no, Sam, you'll hurt Papa.'

Samuel giggled, then grabbing Kerensa in a stranglehold, he pulled her down with them. Wrestling with him brought her into contact with Oliver.

'Now that's what I like to see. A really happy family.'

Kerensa looked up at the source of the voice, a tall, dark-skinned young man. Beatrice was with him. Oliver lifted Sam's sturdy body out of his line of vision.

'See whom 'tes?' Beatrice said, watchful of what had appeared a happy scene.

'Bartholomew!' Oliver bawled out jovially. He sat up, his face almost touched Kerensa's and he had the overwhelming desire to kiss her.

She smiled at him, then got up and went towards the newcomer. 'What brings you here, Bartholomew, after all this time? Welcome home. You look so well, I take it you've not brought bad news.'

'Are you sure you don't mean I look like a pirate, Aunt Kerensa?' He flicked his earring and pointed to his tattoo, much amused. 'It's what Luke accused me of not too long ago. My sudden appearance to visit Cordelia frightened the other lady residing there, Jack's wife, and Luke was absolutely furious with me. I'm happy to report I've done Mrs Rosevear and her child no lasting harm.

Luke's estate is well kept, is it not? I did not stop long, with the commotion over Mrs Rosevear. She was put to bed with such a fuss. I thought it very strange; a servant's wife.

'My dear Aunt, you are more beautiful than ever. Uncle Oliver, are you not the most fortunate man in all Christendom? And who is this? Samuel! My father's namesake. I had quite forgotten you'd had another son. A true Pengarron there.'

Bartholomew, informed of Cordelia's new address by his brothers in London, had hoped to stay the night at Polgissey, but he had brought someone with him, and in view of Alicia Rosevear's condition, he had travelled on to the manor. Luke's ill humour with Cordelia for not being present with Mrs Rosevear when she had fainted, had caused her to accept Bartholomew's invitation to accompany him.

Oliver shook his nephew's hand. 'Where have your travels taken you? You're as dark as a native.'

'As I've written you, to the South Seas mostly, over the years. Fairly recently, I'd been running vital provisions for our troops in the Americas – duty to king and country. Very occasionally, I've been in London. Apparently, I'd just missed Luke and Jack.'

Cordelia appeared carrying a child of about a year old, wrapped up in shawls. As she came closer it could be seen the baby had the true skin of a native.

'Whose is this child, Bartholomew?' Oliver asked, glancing at Kerensa then at his nephew.

'Meet my daughter, Uncle. This is Tamara Drannock. Her mother is dead, tragically taken by the smallpox some weeks after her birth. I had to smuggle her away on to a ship to Portsmouth with a wet nurse, and have kept her a secret ever since. Don't worry, there's no risk of infection. Beautiful, is she not? Well, Uncle and Aunt, how do you feel about taking over the care of another child?'

Twenty-Three

In the depths of the night, there was a loud battering on the back door of Greystone's Farm.

Philip Trenchard went downstairs in his nightclothes, a gun hanging over his brawny arm, a staff clutched in his other hand. Catherine, who had slept little in the past weeks, rushed out of bed and followed cautiously after him.

'Who is it?' Philip demanded gruffly.

'Open up!' came the terse reply.

Philip motioned to Catherine to stand back as he unbolted the door.

'Can the missus come at once?' a scruffy, haggard female hissed in a hostile tone. 'The maid's gone into labour.'

At the sound of this particular voice, Catherine showed herself. 'Is Mrs Roach on her way?'

'She won't come. You'll 'ave to 'elp 'er. The maid's terrified. Won't let me near 'er. Get a bleddy move on, or you an' 'e will 'ave a death on your 'ands.'

'Wait there,' Philip snarled, thrusting the woman off the doorstep and slamming the door in her face.

He and Catherine exchanged worried looks then got dressed quickly. Wrapped up against the thick mist and fretting wind that always seemed to linger on the moors, he held up a lantern to light their way across the yard and along the muddy lanes. He guided Catherine by the hand as they picked a way over hazardous marshy ground to a make-shift dwelling.

It was a hovel, partly a natural cave, no more than scavenged timber and boulders of granite and scraps of furniture and tatters of cloth. Stinking moisture was running down over the stones. All that served as a fireplace was a makeshift grate of moor stone and, with no proper chimney, the peat-burning fire gave some warmth but filled the air with smoke, making them cough.

Catherine looked down in horror at the girl writhing in agony on a filthy sack of straw. They had heard her screams for quite some distance back in the lane. She was just twelve years old, her child conceived before the legal age of consent. A simpleton, a child herself. Yet her body was developed past puberty and it could be seen, even in her anguished and unwashed state, that she was extraordinarily pretty and, to Catherine's eternal shame, one of her stepson's conquests.

'I gave you money, Nollie Skewes, to look after your daughter,' she rounded angrily on the woman who had fetched them here. 'What did you spend it on? Gin? I was a fool to expect different. There was enough to provide her with bedding and warm clothes and food. Oh God, Philip, why didn't you let me come here? Why didn't you tell me it was this bad?'

The girl, and that was how she had always been referred to, so Catherine had no knowledge of her name, howled with pain and blubbered in fear.

'Hold the lantern up high, Philip. Nollie Skewes, have you no candles? I need more light if I'm going to help her to deliver this baby safely. What on earth is her name?'

'Ruth, and that's the truth.' Nollie Skewes cackled at her joke.

She lurched aside to avoid Philip cracking her across the neck with a blow of his hand. She scrabbled about in the semi-darkness and finding two candles, lit them and placed them on a granite ledge.

Catherine was on her knees, trying to comfort the girl. Ruth had no understanding and fought her off, kicking and punching and scratching, her mouth opening and clamping down as she sought to bite her helper.

'Ruth, can you hear me? My name is Mrs Trenchard. If you'll just become still it will lessen the pain. I'm here to help you. The sooner we can get your baby out the sooner the pain will stop.'

'Waste of bleddy time talkin' t' she,' Nollie Skewes scoffed. 'She don't understand a bleddy word what's said, never 'as. Only good for one thing, an' Philip Trenchard 'ere knows what that is. I 'ope you've brung the money you promised with 'ee, or 'e's off to prison for rape. Won't get away with it whatever either of 'ee tries. Everyone round 'ere knows 'e can't keep 'is breeches up and no one else 'as been round Ruth while 'e's been 'aving 'er. When the brat's born you can take it with you like we agreed. Leave it 'ere and I'll kill the little bastard.'

With a roar of rage Philip flew across the hovel and grabbed the woman by the throat. He began to choke her.

'Not if I kill you first, you evil bitch.'

'Philip, stop it,' Catherine shouted through the struggle and Ruth's agonized screams. 'You've threatened to kill her so often the whole district is holding its breath waiting for you to do so. Do you want to end up in Bodmin gaol hanging from a rope? Leave her be and help me bring your child into the world, from this poor girl you've abused so sinfully.'

Philip let her go, but unable to tolerate her presence pushed her out of the hovel. Another scream brought him to his knees beside his stepmother. He ducked to avoid being kicked by Ruth.

'How much longer?'

'Not long, I think. Pass me the parcel of clothes I brought for the baby. When Ruth pushes it out we'll have to act quickly, for I fear she'll kill it in her struggles. Hold her still.'

'God, this is disgusting.' Philip turned his head from the sight of the bloodied something emerging from between the girl's thighs. Catherine fought to keep her scrap of dress up out of the way.

'Not as disgusting as the act that brought this poor girl to this. How could you, Philip? You've women enough eager to be with you, why go with a child of simple mind? You disgust me.'

While Catherine accused him she got a

267

grip on the baby's head. She feared it would be difficult to keep her hold, but Ruth, either worn out, or some instinct warning her she could cost her baby its life if she continued to thrash about, went limp.

Philip looked round. 'She's stopped pushing. You'll have to pull it out like we sometimes do with a calf or a lamb.'

Catherine sent up silent prayers and set to work.

Dawn came and Philip stepped out from the hovel, holding aside the planking that served as a door for Catherine. She had a bundle in her arms.

Sprawled on a boulder, an empty bottle of liquor beside her, Nollie Skewes took the dirty pipe from between her ragged lips. 'Is it dead? Save a lot of trouble for 'ee.'

'No, but your daughter is. I've laid her out, and Philip will stay here until I can send for someone to take her away and give her a decent burial, for which I'll pay. You'll never be able to exploit that poor child again.' Catherine threw a purse at the foot of the boulder and the woman scrambled down to get it. 'There's your money, enough to buy your grandchild and your silence about my stepson's paternity. You'd better be on your way, Nollie Skewes.'

'How'd ya make that out? Why should I go? 'Twas 'im what done the dirty deed.'

'The locals have turned against Philip for fathering the child, and the law, if his crime was reported, may require him to be brought to account over it, but what will people say if I was to tell them you kept your simple-minded, pregnant daughter starved and covered with bed sores? They have a particular way of showing their contempt, you wouldn't be the first to suffer under a hail of moor stones.'

' 'Ad enough of this place any'ow. Can live somewhere a mite more comfortable now.'

As she swaggered off Philip shouted at her back, 'Stinking rotten bitch! I hope you drop dead before you can spend a penny.'

The baby gave a weak mewling sound. Catherine lifted the woollen shawl that had once wrapped one of her twins and gazed down at the tiny puckering face.

'Is it normal?' Philip asked as if he had a lump in his throat.

'Appears to be. I must get back and see about providing it with nourishment.'

'She didn't even ask if it's a boy or cheeil. Think it could be mine?'

'This little girl, even so newly born, looks very much like young Harry Pengarron.'

'Well, it's all worked out in the end,' Philip said, almost nonchalantly. Nollie Skewes was already out of sight, taking the trouble she could have caused him with her.

'How do you consider that to be so?'

269

Catherine snapped.

'Uncle Kenver and Kerris are going to bring her up as their own. Make them happy.'

'Your father might have something to say about that, as you see fit to shirk your responsibility. And have you forgotten that you and I have to face him as to why we've kept your sordid affair a secret? He will not be pleased that you have dragged our name through the mud. The locals have long memories, we will never live this down.'

Twenty-Four

In the grandiose bed, Clem gave Kerensa a final kiss which turned into many. When he lay down beside her, she touched his face.

'You watch me when we make love.'

'You're so beautiful, I don't want to waste a single moment.' His hand traced out her slender contours.

'Have you not enough memories to last you?' she whispered softly.

'You know I'll never have enough of you.' He sighed. 'It'll seem like forever until we can find a way of being together like this again.'

'Clem, I've got something to tell you.'

'No, don't say whatever it is, my precious. You look serious, I don't want to hear anything serious.'

'I'm afraid you'll have to, beloved. Oliver has moved back into the manor.'

'Oh God, no.' He wrapped her tightly, possessively, in his arms. A mountain of trepidation and jealousy surged through him, making him shudder. 'What does that mean?'

'I don't know. He's being very polite and pleasant but he's not saying much.'

'Is he back in your bed?'

'No. He stills sleeps in the other room.'

'Thank God! You'll not let him make demands?'

'Clem, you know I can't promise that. He's my husband. If he wants to ... and Catherine will expect you to be with her.'

A searing pain entered Clem's heart as he thought about the other man enjoying himself with Kerensa's body. 'But there's giving way and there's the giving of one's self.'

'Yes, there is.'

To speak about Oliver in this way, as if she could merely lie with him, disassociated from him, in the bed she had shared with him for so many years, suddenly hurt her more than she could ever have imagined. She felt disloyal. As if she was hurting Oliver

271

in an unforgivable way. She should not have been so hard-hearted with him over the terrible event at Harry's baptism. If the accident had never happened would she have had this affair with Clem? No, she told herself, most definitely, no. The accident had made her concentrate on Oliver's faults, taking all the wonderful things about him and her life with him out of focus.

The last thing she wanted to do was to go on punishing him. She pictured his noble face when he had told her he had missed her the most during his absence. Tears welled up in every chamber of her heart.

'Please, Clem, let's not talk like this.'

'I don't want to, nor even sully my thoughts with him. I'll not think of you with him and you must not think of me with her,' Clem said, in a voice that sounded as if he was trying to be brave.

He needed the comfort of Kerensa's touch, the welcome of her lips, to have her give herself to him again. He trailed kisses from her mouth down over her neck and her body.

She lay still. Clem wanted her again. My dear wonderful Clem. She thought like this every time they shared this closeness.

Clem made love this time with all his power, as if he was trying to stamp himself inside her. Tenderness gave way to passion and went on and on until his terrible need ignited the same need in her. They journeyed together and came together, the exquisite moment exploding in their bodies and splintering fantastically into their souls.

'Remember this,' he pleaded with her when at last he could speak.

'Don't worry, my dear love.' Taking his hand she pressed it against her heart. 'I have you safe in here, forever.'

They dressed slowly, both dreading the moment when they must say goodbye.

At the bottom of the stairs Clem suddenly pulled her to him tightly. For the first time since they had begun their affair he was thinking realistically, suddenly afraid these wonderful times they had spent here were all they were going to get.

'I love you so much. This has been the best time of my entire life. Why can't it always be like this?'

He knew the reason. He had a cunning, ruthless enemy. A man who loved Kerensa as he did. If the reason Pengarron was back home was because his love for her had outstripped his damnable pride, and if her feelings for him broke through her anger and horror over the accident, then his own cause would be lost again.

He clamped her face in his hands. 'Kerensa, we can never tell what might happen. If for some reason we can't meet like this again, you will seek me out? Even if it's just to talk awhile? I couldn't bear to be without your acknowledgement that we had something special.'

She reached up and tenderly smoothed out the furrows in his brow, then took his hands and kissed them. 'Clem, beloved, I promise from my soul that there will never come a time when we must consider ourselves as unequal. When we come together as Harry's grandparents, we will speak naturally, as we should. I'll always love you, Clem.'

After a last emotional kiss, Clem left before the darkness turned into day.

A few hours must pass before she could leave. She went back upstairs and sat down on the bed, wrapping herself up in the bedcovers and pretending Clem was still there. Next time Clem came to Vellanoweth he would be bringing Catherine and the twins. It would not be easy to meet him like this. From his frantic words it seemed he doubted it would happen again. Only time would reveal what fate had in store for them.

And for her and Oliver.

Twenty-Five

Oliver was enduring a second sleepless night at home. On his homecoming, Kerensa had spent a long time acquainting herself with Tamara, then after a quiet supper with him, Bartholomew, Cordelia and Kelynen, she had gone up to the master bedchamber alone. Tonight, she was away at Tolwithrick, having informed him of her invitation just prior to leaving in the afternoon.

When he remarked to Kelynen that it did not appear to be a party her mother was attending, she had explained that Kerensa had taken to going off for quiet reflection.

Reflecting what?

Please God, let her be thinking about me. What we once had. What I could still give her if she'd only give me another chance.

Quietness? In Rachael's raucous company? One had more chance of calm seas for a whole year. It had been the Tolwithrick carriage that had collected Kerensa. Was Tolwithrick her true destination? He really was terrified he had lost her.

He clenched his fists and beat them against

his face. He paced up and down his study, drinking half a decanter of brandy, then stared out of the windows at his grounds, made strange and ghostly in the silvery moonlight.

'Don't go, stay here with me. Love me again,' he had wanted to plead, but he couldn't risk annoying her, driving her even further away.

He was almost amused at the thought that he was pining like a lovesick fool. Yearning after her like – like the young Clem Trenchard had once done.

'Am I such a bad man?' he asked himself aloud. Bad enough to have almost killed two members of his own family in a spell of jealousy, bad enough to bed the first woman available and risk destroying her happy marriage.

'What's wrong here, Uncle? I never thought to find the house under such a mood of despondency.'

Bartholomew was standing in the doorway. He had brought two bottles of claret, their necks dust-laden, from the well-stocked wine cellar.

'Bring those in, Bartholomew, and I'll relate what the others have been unwilling to say to you.'

'The servants don't quite know what to make of me after such a long absence,' said Bartholomew. 'Even Beatrice, who I must add, I'm astonished to find is still this side of the grave. Can't understand why Cordelia is being mysterious, but she is somewhat distracted. In love, I suppose. It's time she was. The way she croons over Tamara says she'd make a wonderful mother. This smells divine.' Bartholomew handed Oliver a large glass of the ruby-red wine. 'Well, what goes on here? Obviously you and my aunt have quarrelled.'

'It's much more serious than that. Sit down and prepare yourself for a shocking story. You have not been to visit Kane yet, or you would know he's recovering from a broken leg and other injuries, for which I am entirely responsible.'

When Oliver had finished speaking his voice was hoarse and both bottles of wine were empty. His head felt as if a storm was raging inside it. It was as if he was out on the great seas, all alone in a tumult, being slapped this way by a thundering wave called Loathing, and that way by another called Unforgiven. No one wanted to climb into his boat, no one wanted him to reach a calm port. Kane had not written for over a week, and even Shelley had partly deserted him for the excitements of her new responsibilities in the affairs of the estate.

'The servants are polite to me and all Beatrice says is,' he mimicked her, ' "Tes yer own bleddy fault!" She regards Kerensa much more affectionately than she ever did me. So, nephew, there you have it. How the mighty have fallen. Have you heard a greater tale of woe?'

'A tale of tragedy, yes, for I loved my late wife as much as you love my aunt, but as for woe, you have first place, I'm sorry to say, Uncle. Like all women, even my sainted aunt gives way to what I call aberrations of the mind. She'll come round. It's hard for you while you're waiting, but it will happen. I know enough of the good and generous lady who took my mother's place to be certain of that. And then all will be well. There's too much good history between you and Aunt Kerensa to be otherwise. Don't worry about Kane, he doesn't bear grudges and why care what his wife thinks of you?' Bartholomew smiled as if sharing an amusing secret. 'Take heart, that fair-headed piece of scum will never match you. You'll win the day and with every honour and all the glory. I always do, no matter what is before me, for it is you I emulate every time. No man has ever taught me better. No man has ever outstripped the pride I have in you and, on my honour, none will ever surpass the loyalty I owe you. If I can do anything for you, just name it and I'll do my outmost to accomplish it.'

'By the singing of angels, Bartholomew, you encourage me. You can do something for me right now. Revisit the cellar and return with a whole armful of spirits, then drink with me until we cannot stand up.

'Tomorrow, I shall ask your aunt to ride with me to Vellanoweth. She has no plan to go there but she'll not refuse, she goes at every other opportunity. She can hear me say a special farewell to the man who dares call me a bastard-crow before he leaves for his moorland dirt-farm.'

Twenty-Six

The rose garden at the manor was at its best. Set out in a rectangle, the beds were arranged in arcs and scallops, then four oval shapes around a central circle, every rose bearing both buds and fully opened blossoms, which filled the air with their strong intoxicating scents and gratified the senses with their dazzling colours.

Neglecting her dress by sitting on a corner of one of the dew-laden grass paths, Cordelia's mind, however, was on the grape hyacinths she had picked before talking and walking with Morgan Kinver. Like the grape hyacinths he was not completely cultivated, yet not wild or uncouth. She liked his calm speech and thoughtful ways. She liked his clean smell better than the cologne Luke splashed on himself. More often Luke stank of spilled alcohol – he drank too much.

Cordelia was still smarting over his unjust anger with her. 'Where the hell were you when Alicia fainted? Anything could have happened to her. Don't you care?' he had shouted. Who on earth had he thought he had been talking too? A bone-idle servant? A woman of the streets? Those were the sort of people who deserved such reproach. Not she, who worked herself tirelessly in running his house to a well-timed efficiency, so he was able to go about his writing undisturbed. And why must Alicia always come first? She did, every day and in every way, even if Luke said she did not. He must be in love with her. What other explanation was there for the way he cared about her comfort and her whereabouts, and the special way he smiled at her, the soft voice he kept just for her. He was always looking at her, when his mind wasn't on his play it was on her.

All the devotion she, herself, had given him over many long years counted for nothing.

Well, I have another man interested in me now. How do you like that? she asked Luke's arrogant image in her mind.

Before parting with Morgan Kinver after their walk, he had asked her politely, 'May I take the liberty of asking to see you again?'

She had not replied and he had conceded

his improper suggestion by dropping his eyes, stepping backwards and giving an apologetic bow.

'Perhaps you will think about it.'

Perhaps she would.

'Perfect, don't move, hold that pose exactly as it is. Never have I seen a more beautifully melancholy expression in such a heavenly setting.'

The voice had a similarity to Morgan Kinver's and for an instant Cordelia thought she must have conjured him up across land and air to this very place. However, Morgan would never speak to her so condescendingly, be so personal.

She looked up slowly, irritated and insulted. Who was this man who had the impertinence to address her so?

'Madam, or is it miss? Forgive my audacity for speaking to you without being introduced. My name is George Spears, you may have heard of me. I am here to call upon Sir Oliver and Lady Pengarron. I have been instructing their daughter, Mrs Timothy Lanyon, on how to perfect her portraits. We are all to dine here on the morrow. I have the habit of exploring a location before the host shows me about, so I may pick an ideal spot myself for a sitting rather than one that's pressed on me, which is usually totally unsuitable.'

George Spears swept his soft pale hands

about as if he was conducting a slow symphony. 'You would be just the very thing for Mrs Lanyon, just there, precisely how you are. We shall demonstrate for her when the time comes. And who might you be?'

Cordelia felt the greatest rage of her life boil up in her. Of all the rudest, insufferable braggarts in the world, this white-haired individual was the biggest of them all.

'I don't care who you are, and who I am is none of your business. Sir Oliver would certainly not approve of you tramping over his property without the courtesy of being invited. He and Lady Pengarron are abroad. Mrs Lanyon is a fool if she accepts anything you say about her art work. I doubt if you could teach her anything worthwhile. Now go away, I do not wish for your company for another second.'

Kane was leaning on his crutches, gazing into the meandering stream that ran down through his land. He was debating what to do about his mother and his father-in-law.

If only Jessica had not asked Clem if he was having an affair with his mother, he would not now have the awesome duty of deciding what to do about it. Clem may not have actually admitted it, but there were too many signs for he and Jessica to believe otherwise.

Telling his father was out of the question,

blood might be spilled and the whole family would be destroyed. Should he approach his mother? How does one mention such a sensitive thing? Should he show the anger he felt, or the understanding? Her affair with Clem was not the usual kind of sordid thing. Surely, he must confront Clem? It was his duty. He had no other choice. He must warn Clem that he would not be welcome again at Vellanoweth if he intended to see his mother. The affair, the madness had to end.

If only his father had not tried to grab Clem that day. If only he, himself, had not tried to intervene, then the accident would never have happened and his parents would not have quarrelled and Clem would have returned to Greystone's Farm long ago, and the affair would never have started. If only life and love were simple.

Kerensa kept glancing anxiously at Oliver on the ride to Vellanoweth, but apart from giving her the occasional warm smile, he said nothing.

His horse had a longer stride than her pony and he kept Gereint in check so that they rode together.

She couldn't bear it. 'You haven't told me why we are to see Kane today. Is there some special reason?'

'I think it's time I spoke to Jessica directly. I want to end the bad feeling between us.'

'I don't trust you.'

'Do you not, Kerensa?'

She reined in. He stopped also, waiting patiently.

'Oliver, look at me.'

He did so, turning Gereint round so he was facing her. 'My dear?'

'You obviously know Clem is leaving for home today. Do you intend to cause trouble?'

'No, Kerensa, I do not.'

She narrowed her eyes. 'Give me your word.'

'It's not necessary, but you have it. Shall we carry on?'

Kerensa took Kernick forward at a trot. Oliver stayed back a few strides then came forward and took his place beside her again. 'Is that a new riding habit, my dear?'

She knew she cut a fine figure in the velvet two-piece habit, crisp white lace flowing from her wrists and throat. 'Do you mind?'

'Absolutely not. Buy as many dresses as you please. You look very beautiful. I'm proud of you.'

She felt increasingly nervous at his possessive undertones. 'Thank you.'

By the time they rode into the farm yard, their mounts' hooves clacking more loudly over the cobbles than her ears could stand, as if announcing to the whole world they were here and had come together, Kerensa felt she was collapsing inside.

Clem was at the side door, dressed for riding, holding his packed bags. Kane, Jessica and Harry were gathered on the doorstep and Ben Penberthy was bringing Tally forward. Servants and farm workers had gathered to say goodbye.

When Oliver lifted her down off the sidesaddle, Kerensa felt chilled through to the bone and couldn't stop shaking.

As her face passed his, she whispered, 'Oliver, please don't...'

She looked across at Clem. He came forward, head up, tight-lipped. Please don't say anything, her eyes begged him.

Jessica was more feisty than her father.

'If you've come to cause trouble, Sir Oliver, you can just get back on your horse, turn round and go back the way you've come.'

'I'm here to see your father, Jessica.'

'You couldn't possibly have anything to say to me that I'll want to hear,' Clem hissed, dropping his bags and balling his fists. 'You're the man who nearly killed my grandson, who terrified my little girl.'

'I know, and I accept all that, and I take full responsibility for all the unpleasantness that happened at my house. And it's time I told you to your face how sorry I am. I apologize unreservedly to you, Clem Trenchard, for all the hurt I've caused you and your family,

285

and even back to all those years ago when I took my wife away from you as your intended bride. The circumstances of the last few weeks have caused me to search my soul and I've come to the conclusion that I have much to be ashamed of. I have already written to Mrs Trenchard with a full apology.

'Here's my hand, you may choose for yourself if you take it.'

Clem looked with anger then horror at the large dark hand held out at the level of his heart. This was no act of contrition. The clever bastard was employing tactics in the most underhand of ways to reconcile himself to Kerensa. He had left her with nothing to reproach himself with. If he didn't take his hand, accept his apology, then Pengarron would successfully change places with him where wrong attitudes were concerned. And if, while accepting his hand, he whispered how much he hated him, wished him all the harm under the sun, Pengarron would later tell this to Kerensa.

Kerensa watched them in abject misery. These two men who she loved so very much in different ways, were locked in a silent battle over her. If they asked her to choose between them right now she would not be able to. She could not have them both and she could not bear to be without either one. Putting the back of her hand to her mouth

286

she let her tears fall, dropping down over her wrist and the snowy white lace.

'Make your decision, Clem,' Kane said briskly. 'My mama is quite overcome.'

I won't let you take her back from me, Clem's blistering glare conveyed to his enemy. Then his expression softened as he pictured Kerensa in his arms, he loving her, her loving him. Whatever the outcome of this sham, nothing could change the fact that he and Kerensa had been as husband and wife.

'I agree with you, sir, it's time to put the past behind us.' The future was a different matter. 'I accept your apology. For the sake of our children and grandchild let all be considered forgotten.'

Kane hobbled forward and clamped his hands on their shoulders. 'This is the act of brave and honourable men. Well done.' Not that he believed for an instant that either man was sincere. Aware of each other's battle plan, they were merely shifting their defences. Pray God there would not be a fresh onslaught. Suggesting they drink to their public announcements would be going too far. He hoped Clem would not complicate the situation by lingering.

Turning to kiss Jessica and Harry goodbye, Clem strode away without another look at the baronet.

When he got to Kerensa, he bowed, 'Goodbye, m'lady.' There was no one close to overhear and he mouthed, 'I love you.'

He swung up on to Tally's back and Ben passed him his bags. He rode away.

Kerensa watched him for several stunned seconds. He was leaving and she had to tell him he was taking a part of her with him.

'Clem!' she called out from where she stood in the middle of the yard, alone.

Clem halted and brought the mare round. He took off his hat and waved it to her.

'Have a safe journey, Clem. Goodbye.' Kerensa was aware that Oliver was coming up fast behind her, but she stayed looking at the man on the horse.

Twenty-Seven

Alicia Rosevear had not been an early riser in her old life, but with Cordelia away she had taken over the responsibility of running Polgissey, and could now be found up and about before the tenth hour each day. Her easy manner, and her sympathetic concern for the pregnant kitchen maid, had quickly brought the servants to respond in kind.

Amy Curnow brought this to Luke's attention during one of their bedroom unions.

'Mrs Rosevear has made it clear she wants

to concentrate on her child after her confinement,' Luke muttered. His sexual energy satisfyingly used up, he had reached for a page of manuscript and was editing in a better phrase. *Lia: Live, I cannot, without my dear Sasken.* 'My cousin will be home soon and the house will be run in her equally well-organized manner.'

'Of course,' Amy Curnow said quickly. As she always did after their vigorous couplings she was massaging his stiff shoulder, careful not to interfere with his jottings. 'I weren't saying nothing 'gainst the young lady. Though Miss Drannock do seem a little unsure of herself at times.' And sanctimonious in the way of the nervously virginal, Amy Curnow thought spitefully. 'I do miss her.'

'So do I, very much,' Luke said truthfully, although he was annoyed at Cordelia's defection and the fact that she was delaying in answering his letter of repentance.

The massage done, he gave Mrs Curnow her shilling. 'Thank you, Amy. You do better to ease my pain than any other.'

'I'm some glad of that, sir. Mr Luke...'

'What is it?' He motioned to her to leave, his play taking over his mind. It was almost finished. When he had written the last word, he would go after Cordelia and apologize again for blaming her, as much as he had her cocksure brother, for Alicia fainting that day. With the air cleared she would come back

289

and life would settle down to normal.

He had charged Bartholomew, who had turned up with tiresome regularity these past two weeks, to convey his regret to Cordelia every time he left. What more did she want him to do? Why must she play silly female games and go on ignoring him? And damn Bartholomew. Why didn't he bugger off on his travels again or at least leave Polgissey in peace. He took far too much interest in Alicia. Well, Alicia was married. Bartholomew must think again if he hoped to entice her away from Jack. Strange behaviour for a man who could see the lady was happily awaiting her confinement.

His thoughts slipped away to Alicia. Apart from an unexplained slip on Midsummer's Eve, she treated Jack with kindness and respect. She had not set foot outside the grounds since her cliff-top walk, sewing for her baby and visiting the kitchens twice a day. He was no longer suspicious about her, and he no longer wished he had married her. He was happy with the way things were, and would be even more so when Cordelia was back.

'Sir.' Amy Curnow reminded him she was still there. Attired once more, she was standing in respectful attendance by the door. Not a light-brown hair out of place under its cap, her dextrous hands folded primly in front of her apron. Somehow characterless, but

290

comely, sluttishly comely.

Luke frowned. 'Did I not pay you for your consideration?'

' 'Tisn't that. I thought you should know that Morgan Kinver keeps turning up, even when he's got no business here, asking when Miss Drannock's coming back. He's got an eye on her, you see, sir. And, well, I don't want to be a teller of tales, but did I overhear un ask Mrs Jack to write her for un.'

'I see, you did right to inform me, Amy.' Luke yawned. 'Did you overhear Mrs Rosevear's reply?'

'Aye, sir, she said she couldn't do that, not her place to and he best forget the young lady.'

Overcome with an awful weariness, Luke fell back on the pillows and closed his eyes. This news wasn't anything to worry over. Kinver could be easily dealt with, but perhaps it was a good thing Cordelia was being churlish at the moment. Feeling feebly amidst a handful of coins on the bedside table he tossed one to Mrs Curnow.

'Thank you for your trouble. Close the door quietly behind you.'

She snatched up the florin where it had landed at the foot of the bed. Passing on information to the young gentleman was going to prove more profitable than servicing him.

She delayed her departure to watch him

sleeping, creeping closer. His breathing was heavy, unwholesome. Shame he didn't look after himself properly. He was a skilled lover but he was losing his energy, and, worried for her savings for her old age, Mrs Curnow feared he might start losing his desire. His ardent resort to the bottle most nights might steal his good looks. Shame he had a slightly malformed arm, be a greater shame if he ever returned Miss Cordelia's love. The girl hated her and would soon have her out of the house.

The cook looked at his writings. It was all a mess of scratchings and ink blots to her. Sheets of expensive paper lay everywhere, in bundles, scattered singly, torn in half, screwed up. The maids weren't to tidy it up, on pain of death! Shame, such a fine gentleman wasting his time on something so frivolous. Shame, that for so much of the time he was lonely.

An hour later, Jack sought out Luke on a matter of the estate and decided to let him stay asleep.

Bartholomew arrived and had no such resolve.

'Wake up, Cousin, you have a journey ahead before night fall. It's Beatrice's ninetieth birthday on the morrow, and your father has charged me with summoning you to a party he's giving for her. All the family will be there, and you can at last meet my daughter. Oh, and he said if you cannot do without Jack and Mrs Rosevear, bring them along too.'

Twenty-Eight

A large bruise stained the greater part of Clem's chin, made all the more obvious by its few days of healing. He looked down at the cause of the disfigurement, his two-week-old granddaughter.

Content after her early morning feed of goat's milk, Rebekah Trenchard lay awake and yawning in her cradle.

While a keen wind hugged the corners of their house, Kenver and Kerris Trenchard were proudly showing her off in the well-ordered kitchen. Kerris reluctantly tore herself away from the baby to rescue her washing from a sudden shower of rain.

'You should've told me about her, Kenver,' Clem huffed over the breakfast Kerris had prepared for them. 'You've learned to write, there's no excuse.'

'Not this again, Clem,' Kenver replied patiently. 'Can't you be pleased for me and Kerris? You've got five children, you know how empty it's been for us having none. And Rebekah's not just anybody's blow-by, she's got our blood in her.'

The baby murmured, a soft piping sound, bubbles forming on her tiny lips. Clem's sternness fell away into a half smile.

'See,' Kenver said, putting a gentle index finger into his daughter's grasping fist. 'You're beginning to fall under her spell. She's a charmer.'

'Unlike her real father,' Clem returned, as if he had ice between his teeth.

He had arrived home late in the evening – missing Kerensa so much, yet eager to see his family. For the first time, he was seriously pondering why Catherine had been called away from Perranbarvah. Her letters had given no clues. For a short while he had been delighted with the pretty girl-child presented to him as Kenver and Kerris's, at his home-coming meal. Then the full story had emerged.

'How could you go with that poor girl?' he stormed at Philip. 'She was a child, an innocent and you've cost her her life! I don't s'pose for a moment it entered your head to offer her security and marriage, no matter what the condition of her mind. And how could you leave yourself open like that to blackmail?'

His shouting woke up the baby and she'd cried in fright. Kenver pleaded with Clem to calm down.

Clem ignored him and grabbed Philip by the coat collars. 'How dare you involve your stepmother in your sordid doings! You must've had her worried out of her mind.'

Philip's build and strength outmatched Clem's and he pushed back hard. 'Let me go, Father, or you'll be sorry.'

'It's you who should be sorry. You're worse than a bleddy he-goat. You've got the devil in you. You're a disgrace!'

The more Clem went on, the more Philip threatened him. After hurrying John and Flora upstairs, Catherine, scared and weeping, begged Clem to stop and let him go.

'Not until he learns the word honour. From now on—'

'You can't order me about!' Philip snarled, thrusting Clem off him. 'It's not you who owns me. You own nothing round here and don't ever bleddy forget it. I didn't need you when you was off helping Jessie and I don't need you now.'

Father and son faced each other like two warring stags, their expressions dark and ugly.

Clem said cuttingly, 'But you went whining for help to a woman, after probably raping a helpless girl. You're no sort of man, Philip Trenchard.'

'And what are you? Living off your wife and your son!'

Catherine and Kerris screamed in unison as Clem swung his hand towards Philip's face, but Philip moved out of reach with the fleetness of his wrestling expertise and smashed his fist into his father's jaw. Clem was sent hurtling nearly the length of his sitting room, smacking in to a sideboard and sending the ornaments and other things crashing to the floor.

Clem was stunned, shocked and horrified at his son's words and violence. Barely able to get to his feet, rocking and blinking, he wiped at the blood that ran from the corner of his mouth and dripped on to his coat.

Kenver had wheeled himself and Rebekah to the doorway, out of harm's reach. He spoke with grim emotion. 'This is madness, everything's got out of hand. We're a family and have a new member in it. It doesn't matter now who actually fathered Rebekah. She's here and she needs to be brought up in a loving home, and that's what me and Kerris are going to do. Philip's signed her over to us, Clem, and as far as I'm concerned there's no more to be said.

'You two are going to have to make things up. Think of Catherine, this has been a dreadful experience for her. We shouldn't have kept you in the dark, Clem. It might have been easier for you if you had known about the baby's birth, but we thought you had enough on your mind with Jessica, Kane and Harry.'

Clem said nothing. Glaring with revulsion at Philip, he dodged Catherine's reaching hands and fell out into the darkness. He heard her shouting after him, but, gathering his three dogs, he went on to the moor, to one of the sheltered spots he favoured to be alone.

'I know Philip's still refusing to say sorry and ask your forgiveness,' Kenver said carefully when he had caught up with him, 'but what's hurting you the most, Clem? What he did or what he said?'

'I've come to terms with Rebekah's existence, you and Kerris rearing her is the best thing for her. I feel better about the dead girl now I know she's had a decent burial. What I hate, Kenver, is the fact that a son of mine could take advantage of a half-witted child. As for his jibe about me not owning the farm, of course it's a blow to my pride, always has been, even though everyone's been careful not to mention it. I can't do anything about that, but it's brought home to me something I must do. I have to get Catherine and the twins away from Philip. If I were to die, they'd be at his mercy. Catherine herself and her money. I don't doubt for a moment he wouldn't try to force himself on her. I can't take that risk.'

'But what will you do? Could you really give up all you've worked for here? Speaking plainly, as we are, you'd only have what's left of Catherine's settlement. Could you bring yourself to live only off her money while you look for something? To p'rhaps not even be a tenant, but a farmhand? Catherine and the children won't like living in a tied cottage.'

'I've got no choice, Ken, and at least they'll be safe. I'll think of something.'

'You...'

'What?'

'You aren't thinking of returning to Mount's Bay, are you?'

'What if I am? Jessica lives there. I enjoyed working on Vellanoweth. Kane would give me work, and when it comes to my pride, there's not much difference between working for my son or son-in-law. And Catherine will be near her brother, she'd like that.'

'And Kerensa Pengarron lives round the Bay. Would Catherine like you living near her again?'

'What're you getting at? Has Catherine said something?'

'Give me credit, Clem, I didn't just come out of the misty wet. For years I've seen you gazing into nothing, your thoughts always in Pengarron Manor; you didn't stop that just because you moved away. And Catherine doesn't have to say anything, I've seen it in her face every day of your marriage, that she knows she's second best. Even more so since she came back, leaving you down there.

Even Sir Oliver's letter of apology has been little comfort to her.'

'I told Catherine everything that happened at Vellanoweth. I love Catherine and want for her to feel comfortable.'

'Did you and Catherine talk about Kerensa?'

Clem gave a smile so guarded that Kenver had no idea what it meant. 'I worked hard on Vellanoweth, nothing more.'

'Did you see Kerensa alone?'

'For a few odd minutes.'

'And?'

'And nothing, Kenver.'

Kenver shook his white-blond head. 'I don't believe you, Clem. Best we say no more about it. So, have you spoken to Catherine about leaving, and have you definitely decided it'll be the Bay?'

'No, I haven't spoken of it yet, but I will today. And Kenver, let me assure you that whatever I do, it'll be for the best for my family.'

Kenver went to his workshop, sifting through Clem's statements for the truth and the lies. Somewhat downhearted, while sawing and planing, he contemplated life at Greystone's without Clem and his second family. Clem was taking away the only playfellows Rebekah was going to have, and while Philip had always been respectful towards him and Kerris, he rarely ventured to see them.

Kenver's disability meant he had spent his entire life surrounded by family. He felt a mild panic at the future loneliness, and at how much he would have to rely only on Kerris. Was this fair to her? He made a good living, enough to strike out on his own. Should he leave with Clem? Clem would like that.

He could keep an eye on Clem. There would be many eyes on him if he returned to Mount's Bay, particularly a pair of sharp, black ones.

Twenty-Nine

Catherine led the way into the sitting room after supper.

'You've got something to discuss, my dear?' She smiled, hoping to lighten Clem's morose mood.

Philip, who had not eaten with them, suddenly banged his way out of the kitchen door and she flinched. Then looked uneasily at Clem. He seemed angrier and more impatient than ever with his son. How much longer was she to regret keeping Philip's sordid secret from Clem? If only she could

300

get one of them to back down, but they bore the same stubborn line.

'We've got to leave here, Cathy,' Clem said suddenly. 'You do see that?'

'Because of Philip? Surely, you and he will restore your good relationship?'

Clem explained his reasons. 'He can't afford to buy your stake in the place, we'll just have to leave him with everything.'

'This is all so unsettling, and it's my fault. I should have told you about Ruth Skewes and the baby.'

'Yes, you should've, but it's brought up these new concerns and I won't have you and the twins living in possible danger. What to do, where to go, that's hard to know. I thought I could ask Kane for work, or look for something different, although I don't know what, I've only ever done farming.' He waved his hand in a deflated way. 'I'm sorry, Cathy, I've given you nothing in our marriage and now there's all this.'

'If you feel we really must leave here, we can at least afford to buy a house, Clem. I have the means.'

The whole sordid situation, the injustices of life was getting him down and he snapped, 'I'm trying to protect your money, not spend it!'

'I'm not taking my children to some pokey, ill-made tied cottage,' Catherine protested indignantly. 'And we're man and wife.

What's mine is yours. Can you not see that you've worked hard on this farm, that you have an investment in it, that it belongs to you as much as Philip and I? I found the moor disconcerting at first but I've come to love this place. It's isolated but I've moved about the area and made friends. I'm settled and so are the twins. I thought we'd have a lot to live down when Rebekah was born, but in time people will forget.

'Do you really want to leave here, Clem? Or is what you really desire to simply move back to Mount's Bay?'

'I won't deny I'd like to live near Jessica. Yes, we have made this place our home, and I've felt a sense of freedom here.' Of a sort he had not experienced under Pengarron's landlordship. 'But we must leave because of Philip, and that's all there is to it.'

'Clem, I know things are difficult for you, and what man wouldn't be justified with what you're feeling with Philip's actions, but I don't agree with your—'

'There are no buts, Catherine!'

'Yes there are!'

The frustration was getting too much for her and this became one of those rare occasions when she angrily and emphatically raised her voice. A voice to be attended to, and Clem listened in sullen silence.

'Philip sinned and fathered a child, but that child is now being brought up in a loving and secure home. The mother died in pain and fear, but she's better off in heaven, never to suffer again by living with a vile mother who sold her body to men. Oh, yes, Clem, it's true. I've made enquiries into the life of the wretched Nollie Skewes. Philip struck you, but it was out of temper and embarrassment, and isn't it only your pride that's making you so unforgiving? He has his faults and his constant chasing after women is to be deplored, but he's been a good son to you, and while I accept your concerns about him, I think you are allowing them to get out of perspective. I'm aware that Philip has looked me over, but that is all, he respects my position as his stepmother.'

'So, I'm just a bloody fool, am I?'

Catherine ignored his self-pity. 'There's one more thing I will say to you, Clem.'

'A pearl of wisdom from the Bible, parson's sister?'

'Not once in the two years we've lived here, and not since your quarrel, has Philip mentioned that it's his and my money that bought this farm. To people round here it's you who is Farmer Trenchard, not your son. I call that loyalty, respect and sensitivity on Philip's part. You need to stop living inside your head, Clem!'

Catherine stalked out of the room, march-ed up the stairs, and for the first time in her life forgot she was a lady. 'Damn you, damn

303

you, Clem!' She kicked at his work clothes, which he had dumped on the floor.

She'd had enough of fretting over his moods and his broodings, and enough of the torment at wondering, while he'd been entrenched in Mount's Bay, whether he had contrived to re-establish old ground with his old love. This desire to move had nothing to do with Philip. It was *her*. That red-headed picture of mock innocence, that unrelenting siren. Kerensa Pengarron was still succeeding in keeping her hold on Clem.

They were having an affair! Why else had she engineered her husband's exit from his fine house? She was a ruthless tactician, to get an autocratic, arrogant swine like Sir Oliver Pengarron to desert his own house, even temporarily.

In one fierce arc, Catherine swept everything on top of her dressing table on to the floor.

'Cathy—'

Clem leapt aside as brushes, jewellery, lace runners, china receptacles and scented missiles crashed and smashed, thundered and rolled in all directions about the room.

'Go to her, go on, go now if it's what you want so much!'

She faced him in the biggest fury of all time. She wasn't crying, just shaking from head to toe, scarlet-faced and claw-fingered. It seemed she would bring down every drape with the wind of her breath. 'If you want to move back to your precious Kerensa, then just go to her. Don't give another thought to me or John or Flora or Kenver or your newest grandchild. Just get out of the house, go to her for good, and – and take your blasted dogs with you!'

'Stop it! What's got into you?' This violence, this rage, this loathing was so out of character. Her accusation neither nettled or disturbed him, but he was concerned for her.

He had told the truth to Kenver about loving her. He held her in every high regard, she was an excellent woman, her heart kind and true, empty of any hypocrisy. And now she had showed her vulnerable, human side, he loved her all the more.

'I'd just come up to tell you I agree with everything you've said about Philip. I needed a good talking to. I wasn't seeing things in the right light.'

'Oh, shut up,' she gasped almost inaudibly, but in such a way it gained his attention even more.

The ferocity, the moment of madness went out of her. She stood in the middle of the mess and breakages, shocked with herself for creating such chaos. 'You're cruel, Clem, and your pride is so often misplaced. You and Sir Oliver Pengarron are much alike.'

What! Clem nearly exploded, then caught himself. He resented the comparison. 'Why talk of him? What's he got to do with Philip, or whether we stay or leave here?'

'Because,' she drifted down on the bed, absolutely miserable, 'you want to move back there. Because, just like Sir Oliver, you can't bear not to be near his wife. I saw how happy you were the moment we arrived at Timothy's house. You've never been as happy as that here with me. And don't lie about it. I couldn't stand it.'

'Cathy, my love.' He went to her, picking a path through the damage. Sitting close, he wrapped his arm round her trembling body, trying to make her feel safe and wanted. 'I'm telling you the truth. I got my worries over Philip out of perspective. I love you, Cathy. Listen to me,' and he repeated the three most vital words in the world very, very slowly. 'I love you.'

She fell into a heavy quiet, but allowed him to bring her face against his neck. He held her in his arms, kissed her fever-maddened brow. Soon he would suggest, for a second time in a few short weeks to a distraught woman, that he'd help her clear up a mess of her own making, of her own things.

'I'll talk to Philip, make things up with him. I owe him my forgiveness in view of his loyalty. We'll stay here, build on our life together, Cathy. Everything will be all right, I swear.'

Despite his tendency to set himself apart,

he knew Catherine as well as any devoted husband knew his wife. He did not doubt that she was already shamefully sorry for her loss of decorum and for the wilful destruction, and that she was too steadfast and humble, and wholly dedicated to him and his hopes and needs, to continue the argument. Now she had dispelled his fears about Philip, improved his confidence and given him every reason to hold his head up in local circles, he felt a little at peace.

Downstairs, he had realized that his plan to live closer to Kerensa was a stupid one. Jessica and Kane knew the truth about him and Kerensa, they would never allow him to live and work at Vellanoweth. Even if they did, Pengarron would never let Kerensa out of his sight, and continuing their love affair would have been impossible. At least this way he might be able to see her alone occasionally. It was all he could settle for. He must act more wisely from now on, his desires for Kerensa were blanketing his good sense.

He became aware that Catherine was staring at him. Kissing her lips, he smiled to reassure her. He owed her that. He owed it to her to make her happy, feel wanted and cherished. To feel the love he was able to give her.

She had powder on her shoulder and splattered down the front of her dress. He rubbed at it gently, pulling free the fine muslin fichu which uncovered the upper swell of her breasts. He loved this part of her. Flawless, snow-white warm skin and he kissed her there.

Catherine decided to bind him to her exclusively with whatever means it took. She pushed him down on the bed. He looked stunned, she had never initiated familiarity in the bedroom before.

'I've missed you, I've missed being with you, Clem.' She crawled up the bed and sat astride his body. 'I'll show you how much.'

Thirty

'What are 'ee thinking 'bout, my 'an'some?'

'Oh, Bea.' Kerensa was startled and sat up straight in her chair. 'I was just taking a few quiet moments before your party gets under way. You should get ready. You don't want to be late celebrating your special day.'

Beatrice stubbornly made acquaintance with a chair. 'You forget I knows thee. You was thinking 'bout someone in pa'tic'lar, weren't 'ee?'

'None of your business, my dear.' Kerensa

smiled in a way to humour the nonagen-
arian. 'Now off you go. Polly and Cordelia
are waiting for you.'

'I reckon you def'nit'ly 'ad someone on
your mind and I do reckon 'is name begins
with a C.'

'You think I've got Clem on my mind?'

'I never said nothin' afore, 'twas better to
let you an' Oliver work out yer strivings yer
own way, like 'ee did backalong. You was
different this time. You was un' appy just the
same and you missed un, but I also gleaned
'ow full of spirits you was each time you
come 'ome from Tolwithrick. 'Ad to be a
reason fer that, and usually when a maid
looks that sort of 'appy, it's 'cause she'm in
love. You've 'ad yer time with – won't say 'is
name out loud – and now both 'e and Oliver
are back in their own 'omes. What're 'ee
goin' to do now, Kerensa? I'm not askin' 'ee
to tell me, 'tedn't really my place to ask, but
my dear gurl, you'm as precious to me as if I
birthed and raised 'ee myself, and I'm takin'
the liberty to warn 'ee to think carefully.
You'm in an impossible place, do the wrong
thing and you could find yerself without
either of 'em, out in the cold, in a living 'ell.'
Tears flooded down the old woman's
raddled cheeks. 'I didn't live all these years
to see you brung to that.'

'Oh, Beatrice, don't cry, not on your
birthday, not for me.'

Beatrice caressed her lovely, concerned face with a motherly finger. 'You can't 'ave 'em both. I know you want to, mebbe even think you can, but it's not possible, my luvver. Think on it, promise me you will.'

'I've been thinking about very little else except Oliver and Clem and my feelings for them, Bea.' Kerensa took her ancient gnarled hands and kissed them both. 'I promise I'll think about what you've said. Now, dearest, what about your party? Oliver's gone to such trouble for you.'

'I know that. I'm goin' now, and I'm goin' to ferget this sad business till the party's over. Then we'll talk again, eh?'

'Yes, Bea, we'll talk again.' She hadn't been thinking only of Clem just now.

Two nights ago she had found Oliver in the master bedchamber. Her assumption that he was there to ask if he might join her had not been the case. He was standing, slightly stooped, next to her dressing table, holding her hand mirror, staring sightlessly down at the carpet. He seemed mesmerized, and so sad. Gradually, the mirror was slipping from his grasp.

She had raced across the floor and had taken it out of his hand.

'Oh,' he'd said as if in a dream. 'I just came in to ask you something about Beatrice.' After explaining his idea for a momentous celebration for his old nursemaid's ninetieth

310

birthday, he had said goodnight quietly and left her.

Sitting up in bed she had stayed awake half the night, feeling all alone, her emotions thawing towards the man with whom she had shared so many, many loving nights here. Oliver had not left the manor grounds since they had journeyed silently home from Vellanoweth. He had stayed polite and kept his distance, keeping company with Kelynen, Samuel and Cordelia, and drinking and playing chess with Bartholomew when he was here.

Not for a second had she believed that his apology to Clem had been sincere. Kerensa's heart had followed Clem down the farm track, and her opinion of Oliver, out of a need for self-preservation, was hard and suspicious. She believed he had a scheme to lull her, to make her drop her defences, then he'd do something brilliant and deadly to ensnare her, to bind her to him again with the unbreakable calls of loyalty, honour and obedience to him. She had even been a little afraid of him.

Yet the man who had stood only feet away from her, without the strength or forethought to keep hold of her mirror, was not the proud villain she had once so deservingly slated, had found so hard to forgive.

Slipping out of bed, she had put on her dressing gown and padded out of the room.

311

Creeping along the corridor, she stopped at the door of Oliver's room. It was the dead of night. The silvery glow of the moon breached the tall windows behind her, illuminating the bare boards beneath her feet, turning the hand she put on the door knob a cold steely hue and her dressing gown into a shimmering flow. She felt nervous, apprehensive, shivered, and opened the solid oak barrier.

She could feel the disappointment as acutely now as she had done then, of finding the room empty, the bed untouched.

Her hands had flown to her face in desperation. She loved him. Dear God, how much she loved him, she had never stopped, never could. And she liked this new Oliver, at last it seemed he had grasped how it was to be a mere mortal, not having the right to abide to his own code of behaviour.

She had run to the top of the stairs. He was most likely with Bartholomew, but she had to know. She had to know if he was all right.

A laugh, a typical laugh of male bravado from Bartholomew came floating up the stairs. 'Come now, Uncle, you'll never beat me at chess if you don't concentrate. I'll away to the cellar and fetch us something rousing.'

Kerensa listened. Bartholomew's steps were coming away from the study, where Oliver had his chess set; his papers had been pushed aside for days. Matthias Renfree and

Kelynen were entrusted with all estate affairs after a brief weekly audience. Bartholomew was heading in the direction of the cellar.

As if some notion had informed him she was there, he looked up at her. His words drifted up to her, full of meaning. 'When you're ready, you'll find him waiting for you...'

Ready. That word, heavy with import, still hung under the ancient beams of the house.

Oh, dear God, what a position to be in. Choose, Beatrice had begged her. She had, and it meant she was going to suffer the loss of one of the two men she loved.

Thirty-One

And so Pengarron Manor was astir with activity of an unprecedented kind, and the talk throughout the establishments of the local gentry was that Sir Oliver Pengarron had gone quite mad.

'He's giving a party for a servant and, me dear, can you believe, it's to be outside of the servants' quarters, in the great hall?'

'Have you heard of such a thing? But, of course, one can't forget that he married a ... well, I don't know exactly what she was

313

before the wedding but she's of the lower orders.'

'It's outrageous! He'll be giving the working class dangerous ideas.'

'The man's clearly unstable. All this accident and separation business has driven him to a course that's extreme even for him.'

'It's said he has even suspended his harvesting for half a day. Unthinkable!'

Beatrice would get to hear each and every comment by and by and would be greatly amused by them all.

In view of her age – she retired most evenings at nine o'clock – the party was being held throughout the day, with guests coming and going at their leisure. In the manner of a dowager duchess, to the accompaniment of stringed instruments, she held court from a barrel-shaped chair raised on a specially built platform. She was gruesomely resplendent in a new dress of shades of blue, the divided skirt criss-crossed with tiny silk flowers, a white wig, not too tall or heavy and flowered and feathered by Polly and Cordelia, and new shoes with shiny brass buckles, all gifts from her master and mistress. A lace handkerchief hung importantly from her wrist.

With a never empty glass of the highest quality gin, she grinned hideously while receiving the gifts or good wishes from the

314

manor's servants, the Renfrees and estate workers, and invited servants from other great houses – her gossip machine. There were also those she numbered among her friends, like an equally haggard-looking crone known as Painted Bessie, who kept a cliff-top kiddleywink, where smuggling operations, Oliver's among them, had been arranged for over three decades.

Oliver and Kerensa kept attendance on either side of Beatrice's chair. When she was given a present, she said regally, 'How kind. Thank you for coming.' Then after taking a sharp-eyed look at it, humming her approval or not, she passed it to Oliver, saying in her usual dribbling rasp, 'Put un on the table with the others, boy.' For every good wish, she said, 'Well, I've the good Lord and these two dear people 'ere to thank for livin' long enough to see this day.' Then, in most cases, she leaned confidentially towards Kerensa and whispered what she really thought about the well-wisher.

Kane, limping with the aid of a stylish ebony stick, gave Beatrice a box made from Pengarron oak, the size of a small wall cabinet, with compartments inside and a handle attached for carrying, for her awesome collection of herbal potions and medicines. Throughout the rest of the proceedings he kept a watchful eye on his parents.

It was half past two when Bartholomew brought Tamara, and Jessica brought Harry down from the nursery so that Beatrice could dangle them, with help, one at a time on her knee.

Bartholomew teased the old woman. 'You must be about ready to take a little nap now, eh, Beatrice?'

'Gis on with 'ee, not a weary bone in me ol' body t'day. I'm not goin' to miss a moment of my birthday.'

Luke and Jack had ridden over to Marazion in the morning to buy something for Beatrice. Luke chose a pretty cameo brooch and Jack the old woman's favourite selections of sweetmeats.

Jack didn't have quite the heart for the occasion. Sir Oliver had employed a new head groom and it hurt Jack to think of someone else living in his cottage. Worse than that, he and Alicia had had another quarrel that morning, and it had been a very fierce one.

On his return from Marazion, he thought he would try his best to forget her ruthless treatment of him on Midsummer's Eve and attempt to resume the full warmth of their easygoing relationship. Alicia was too big with child now to consider intimacy again anyway.

While she had been tying his neckcloth for him he had placed his hands on her swollen waist and kissed her cheek. 'My love, before we leave on the morrow, and when Beatrice has got over her carousing, I'll ask her to look you over.'

'Why?' Alicia had nearly spat out the word, her face aflame.

'Well, you know she's an authority on childbearing.'

'So you say! How dare you assume I'd let that disgusting, filthy old witch touch my body, or my child!'

Rocked by her venom, he'd had a hard task to find his voice. 'I – I'm sorry, Alicia. Don't be upset. I made a stupid suggestion. I meant no harm.'

'Harm! I'd never let anyone harm my baby.'

'Nor would I. Surely I'm to have some say in how it's reared. Beatrice has attended all the births on the estate, even her lady-ship's.'

'It's my baby. It's not for you to say what happens to it in any way. Do you understand me?'

Jack had finished dressing in heavy-hearted silence. He had been spoken to as if he was his wife's servant, no, less than that. He wasn't sure any more how he felt about becoming stepfather to the offspring of the weak-spirited, undeserving Lord Alexander Longbourne.

Throughout the party, Alicia refused to go

near Beatrice, even if she did smell of rose-water and not grime and perspiration.

Tamara began to fret and Cordelia carried her back up to the nursery and handed her over to her nursemaid.

Luke went with her. 'We should talk, Cor-rie, and I mean properly. You still haven't explained why you won't come home to Polgissey with me. You're not letting Bartholomew's brat keep you away, I hope.'

'Don't you dare speak about Tamara like that.' Cordelia rounded on him. 'Who do you think you are? She's a beautiful, sweet-tempered child and she's my niece. I feel as close to her as I do to Samuel.'

'Please come back, sweeting, I miss you all of the time.' He tried one of his old tricks to manipulate her, by looking up under her chin with puppy-dog eyes. 'Don't stay angry with me. I promise not to shout at you like that ever again. You can have anything, do anything you want. And the good folk of Polgissey are missing you too, they were all asking about you after church on Sunday. Surely you've not forgotten Little Min?'

'Don't look at me like that, Luke,' she cried indignantly. 'Do you think I am five years old?'

He straightened his back. 'Sorry. Look I am really sorry for everything, Cordelia.' He thumped his fist to his forehead, truly serious now. 'I know I've got to rethink how I treat you. I will, I promise. Just please come back with me!'

Her small mouth pursed, she smoothed over her skirts and patted her hair, and Luke noticed how pretty she looked. She was wearing rose-pink, with gauzy trimmings, her black hair sparkling with diamond clips. Finally he realized she had grown up.

'I'm missing some of the people of Polgissey too.' Especially Morgan Kinver and his fine voice, the sensitive way he looked at her, their interesting conversations, and more. 'But I've other things to consider.'

'Such as?'

'Well, I might want to get married one day and you would be reluctant to let me go. Bartholomew will be returning overseas soon and he's asked me to take charge of Tamara while he's away on his long journeys. Uncle Oliver wants her to stay here, but he's said if I feel I'd like to strike out on my own, which is something I'm seriously considering, he'll give me one of his houses in Marazion.'

'You can't really want to be a glorified nursemaid!'

'It's better than being an unappreciated housekeeper! Whatever I decide to do it will my decision and mine alone.'

'What's happened to you, Cordelia? You've turned into a tough little madam. Did I upset you so very much?'

Tears sprang to her eyelashes. 'More than you could ever know. I said I'm considering all my offers. One thing is certain though, Luke, if I was to return to Polgissey that dreadful Amy Curnow would have to go!'

'I should think Olivia and Timothy will arrive soon, my dear,' Oliver remarked casually to Kerensa, across the celebrator's chair. He was in fact annoyed with Olivia for being so late. Beatrice's party was in full swing, the classical musicians had been replaced by those suited for country dancing. Beatrice's gin was being watered down but she was becoming inebriated nonetheless, clapping her hands, swinging her legs against the chair, singing rude ditties to the raucous tunes.

The waterwheel was announced, a noisy circular dance involving much clapping, foot stamping and hooting, and tossing and swinging of the women. Kerensa came round the back of the chair to shout in Oliver's ear. 'Livvy hasn't been out of the house for days. She's been in a strange mood since Mr Spears suddenly left for London. She said he was a hard taskmaster then he suddenly lost interest. I don't think her painting is going well, either that or she's getting childbearing moods.'

Oliver rested his hand on her shoulder, a

gesture as natural as breathing to him, and while he listened to Kerensa, feeling her sweet breath on the side of his face, he prayed he would not feel her stiffen and move away from him physically or mentally. 'We must make allowances for her then.'

Aware of his hand, the discerning lightness of it, Kerensa felt a strong desire to close her eyes and enjoy the familiarity of his nearness. 'Perhaps Timothy has been called to a sickbed or something and she's waiting for him to return.'

'Yes, perhaps.'

As the music gathered pitch and pace, Beatrice chuckled all the louder and clapped her hands all the faster.

Kerensa was worried that all the frivolity would wear her out and make her ill, but Beatrice, catching her piercing inspection, waved her away. 'Get out there an' enjoy yerself, an' I mean both of 'ee.'

Oliver still had his arm about Kerensa. He put his lips to her ear. 'Dance with me?'

Kerensa glanced at the wild scene of laughing, frolicking dancers. Red-faced, hot, relishing every moment, they were making the most of the free entertainment and food and drink: those given time off from the harvesting on Ker-an-Mor Farm were still being paid. The frivolity was addictive. Nodding her assent, she stepped out on to the floor with her husband.

In respect for the lord and lady of the manor's entrance into the circle, the music halted for a second then carried on at its strident speed. With the other revellers Oliver and Kerensa galloped round and round the great hall, twirling, cavorting, stopping at short intervals to clap their hands and stamp their feet, then pitching off again. When Oliver swept her up off her feet Kerensa laughed; when he lowered her down she flung her arms round his neck to steady herself. He was laughing too.

Bartholomew was watching them with satisfaction. Waiting for such a scene had delayed his return to London, he had planned to finish his errand for Sir Decimus Soames long before this.

Luck was on his side. On rare occasions, Sophia Glanville had been left unguarded. Bartholomew had no doubt that Mrs Jack's true identity was that of Lord Longbourne's mistress; careless of him not to have made sure she was dead. Jack had unhitched himself from his wife and gone to the stables with the new groom. Luke, returning from somewhere in a violent mood, was now slumped on the dais at Beatrice's feet, fast getting drunk.

Sophia, apparently, was taking a turn in the early evening air.

Thirty-Two

Alicia was in the apple orchard, grateful to be away from the noise, the overbearing heat and the activity, which to her standards bordered on the barbarian.

The apples on the trees were swollen in full fruit, windfalls lay on the ground. She was saddened to find her first memorial to Alex was impertinently encroached by long grass and weeds which stung her hands when she tried to uncover the pitiful circle of stones.

'My favourite dog is buried hereabouts.'

The intrusion of the voice made her gasp and look up crossly. Bartholomew Drannock, whom she neither liked nor trusted, was offering his tanned hand to assist her to rise. Alicia allowed the mannerly act but made no comment. She felt the first prickings of apprehension, sure he was about to proposition her. He had made a practice of staring at her, had winked at her once or twice for no reason.

'Her name was Sky, she died as a puppy, kicked by one of the horses. I hate it when something dies young and unnecessarily, don't you?'

'What do you want?'

'An answer to a certain question will do for a start,' he drawled, coming closer, leaning towards her.

'It's no! And if you bother me again I'll tell my husband, Luke and Sir Oliver.' She stepped back, turned on her heel but got nowhere. He wrenched her round then pushed her back against the apple tree.

'You misunderstand me, Miss Glanville.'

Alicia felt her insides shrivel up with terror. She thrashed about trying to get free, but his grasp was too strong.

'Oh, dear God. You're a member of the Society!'

'Intelligent and perceptive as well as lovely and good natured. No wonder the mealy-mouthed Longbourne leaned on you and no wonder Jack adores you. Well, he did. Is he no longer interested in the cuckoo in the nest?'

'If you've come to kill me, do it now. Don't hurt Jack, he's no threat to Soames's clique,' Alicia pleaded.

'And brave. What a remarkable person you are.' Bartholomew lowered his voice dangerously, 'Unlike your lover was. He whimpered to be spared. A pathetic sight. So ungentlemanly.'

'You murdered Alex?' Alicia stopped struggling and glared at him with pure hatred.

With lightning speed he thrust a long blade into the tree, beside her neck. 'With this very knife – the traditional blow to the heart. I'd hardly stepped off my ship when Sir Decimus handed me the contract on him. Sir Decimus thought it would make things more interesting, me being Luke's cousin. Longbourne died quickly, if that's any comfort to you. I'm not a sadist.'

Alicia opened her mouth to scream but did not get the chance to utter it. He clamped a hand over her mouth. 'Longbourne threatened to name names. I'm certain anyone foolish enough to try to blackmail the Society would've had evidence stashed away somewhere. You think Luke has it, don't you? I've seen you searching Polgissey when he wasn't there. Where is it, Sophia? Tell me now or my knife will find its way into your heart, and then Jack's.'

'Stand back from her or I swear I'll kill you!'

Bartholomew turned his head a fraction.

Luke was there, harsh-faced and sober, a short firearm held out at full length, his expression deadly. 'I meant it, Cousin. Move away from her or I'll shoot you where you stand.'

Bartholomew loosened his grip on Alicia. She kept her terror-filled eyes on him. He gazed at Luke with an ice-cold smile. 'You know what I want, Luke. Hand it over and I swear neither I nor the Society will ever bother you again.'

Luke aimed the weapon between Bartholomew's eyes. 'Do you think I trust anything you say? The Society owns you body and soul.'

'Believe this, Cousin. I wouldn't hesitate to carry out the Society's policy and remove all witnesses to Longbourne's death, except for one man. Your father. I owe him everything. He has my first loyalty. I didn't come here intending to kill this woman. If I was forced to, and then had to kill Jack, I might even have to kill you. No, I couldn't murder my uncle's son and heir, nor mar his estate with a Society killing, it would bring him into Sir Decimus's scope of attention, and you know how dangerous he is.

'I've written to Sir Decimus, stating that Jack's married a local servant and you are content with your new estate and pastime. He trusts me, you need never fear him again. You can read the letter, take it to the post yourself, if you so choose. Then the three of you can go on with your lives. But you do see, if Longbourne had written down the evidence he said he had, I can't allow it to continue to exist. Show me, and we'll destroy it together, and you can watch me add to my letter that I'm confident such evidence was just the prattlings of a pathetic man.'

'Why could you not say all this before?' Luke kept the gun on the same level. He had never liked Bartholomew, but he had changed from an insolent youth, who had done his best to care for his younger brothers and sisters when they had lived in poverty, into a cold-hearted killer. 'If I hadn't been so obsessed with my play I might have realized there was more reason for you being in Cornwall than to offload your child.'

'I needed to study your set-up, and because of the affection I hold for your father, I also wanted to be sure this bitch did not mean harm to you in any way, Luke. I'm confident she's only obsessed with her brat, that she took the only way, in marrying Jack, that promised its security. Now, where's the evidence hidden?'

Luke lowered the gun but stayed fully alert. 'I'm grateful you think so highly of my father. If what you say is true, we need fear the Society no longer. First, I'll read your letter and watch you add the appropriate addition. Then, I will send for the document – where I have it kept will remain my secret. You surely did not think I'd have it here or at Polgissey? We will burn it together, and then that will be the end of the matter. After that, Bartholomew Drannock, I hope to never set eyes on you again. You will certainly not be welcome here when I inherit the estate. Stand back from Alicia. Leave the knife, I'll get it.'

Smiling sardonically, Bartholomew did so.

Alicia spat at him. 'You murdered the man I loved. One thing I have learned from the Cornish is the power of ill-wishing. I wish you dead, a violent death, a painful death, and I wish you to feel a hundredfold the terror you made Alex suffer. I shall repeat these words every day and not rest until I hear that you are dead!'

Thirty-Three

When the last party guest had gone, and Beatrice, out of necessity, had been put to bed by Polly O' Flynn and Esther King, the Pengarrons, the Drannocks and the Lanyons gathered round the dining table, set with a cold supper. Oliver dismissed the servants and the family served themselves.

The merry atmosphere in the ancient house was changing into one of disquiet. Pensive and brooding, Luke ate nothing but drank glassful after glassful of wine, and every so often he shot Bartholomew, on the opposite side of the table, a look of utter loathing. He felt sick to his stomach to be facing this man across his father's table.

Short hours ago, he and Bartholomew had stolen away to Trelynne Cove, where they had burned Alexander Longbourne's hateful document, which Luke had fetched from a bank vault at Marazion.

'Also a letter from you to the authorities, Luke!' Bartholomew had congratulated him. 'In the event of your and the others' sudden deaths you were going to bring the Society down. Now let us forget this ever happened. I wish you good fortune and success with your plays. You have nothing to fear now about approaching the premier London theatres.'

Luke did not want his good wishes, and Alicia's counter-wishes to Bartholomew still chilled him to the marrow.

Cordelia was nibbling her food. She had witnessed Alicia turning to Jack, weeping with distress, which neither of them cared to explain. They had retired to their room and declined to come down to supper. She hoped they were not worried about the baby, but her main thoughts were about her own future. If she chose to care for Tamara, should it be here at the manor or at Marazion? Or should she choose to explore something entirely different?

Kelynen tried to raise everyone's spirits with reminiscences of the party, but it was a lost cause and she soon excused herself to slip off to the library. There, with Rex, she would examine the figures of produce and income, the gains and losses of previous harvests.

Kerensa was quiet, thinking about Oliver. Oliver was quiet, thinking about Kerensa. Olivia was there. She had arrived just in time to offer Beatrice birthday wishes, her explanation, morning sickness that had lingered all day. She was pale and wan and temperamental. She was not eating because the smallest morsel would not stay down long inside her.

Only Bartholomew appreciated the food. Swallowing a giant forkful of ham and pickle, he waved his two-pronged fork in the air. 'Tell me about your paintings, Livvy. I regret, that except for those in the manor and on Polgissey's walls, I haven't had time to see them for myself.'

'What paintings?' Olivia snapped back. She was hot and uncomfortable, her back ached and her head ached. Her feet felt too small for her shoes. She dreaded the time when she would waddle about looking fat and cumbersome. From the first week when she had realized she was pregnant, she knew she would hate the entire process of childbearing.

'My dear...' Timothy cautioned her.

'What's wrong, my love?' Oliver asked, glancing at Kerensa. They exchanged a look of parental concern.

Olivia scratched a fingernail along the edge of the enormous table. Her voice dropped to an emotional whisper. 'Everything's wrong. I used to just dash off anything with brush or pencil, now nothing flows, nothing feels natural any more.'

'Why do you think that is?' Oliver asked gently.

'I don't know!' Olivia proclaimed irritably.

Cordelia had been listening. 'Perhaps it's something to do with that horrible Mr Spears.'

'What would you know about it?' Olivia glared at her little cousin, who appeared uncommonly bright, not her usual moping, simpering, dull self.

'Livvy, dear, please don't be rude. Perhaps I should take you home,' Timothy said, embarrassed. Her moods were getting on his nerves. He gestured an apology to Cordelia with a lift of his earth-brown brows. 'Cordelia may be right. You've only been this way since that fellow suddenly lost interest in you.'

'When did you meet George Spears?' Olivia glared suspiciously at Cordelia. Something must have made him forsake her – had she found the reason? She hoped there was a reason, the not knowing why he had suddenly rejected her was humiliating and was destroying her confidence.

'She hasn't met him, only heard of him,'

Luke interjected, bored with the conversation.

'I have met him actually,' Cordelia said perkily. Unusually for her, she welcomed being the centre of attention. 'I happened to be in the rose garden one morning, a few days ago, and he chanced upon me and was very rude indeed, utterly patronizing. I told him of it in no uncertain terms, and, in view of it, that he couldn't possibly be of any help to you, Livvy.'

Cordelia waited for applause from all those around her, but before anyone could respond, Olivia leapt to her feet, sending wine glasses toppling and plates of food colliding in a noisy sequence. 'How could you? How dare you! You deliberately offended George Spears and he will make sure no one ever takes my work seriously. He was my one chance of making a debut into the proper art world, no longer to be thought of as a stupid woman dabbling in painting at a whim to the neglect of her husband, and you, you sanctimonious little bitch, you've ruined it for me.'

Timothy jumped up and tried to stop the tirade, but Olivia thrust him away from her. 'Look at you, preening yourself and believing you're witty and worth a second glance, and what for? Luke hasn't a clue that you've been in love with him for years, and he'd never want a plain-faced, child-woman anyway!'

Luke gasped in horror. Cordelia was in love with him? Too drunk to think past this astonishing revelation, he hung his head.

Humiliated beyond measure at Luke's reaction to her long years of worshipping him and sobbing desperately, Cordelia made for the door.

Simultaneously, Timothy seized one of Olivia's flailing arms. 'That's quite enough! Not another word from you. Home, lady. And tomorrow I'm bringing you back to beg your cousin for her forgiveness.' Careful to keep his wife steady on her feet, he dragged her towards the door at the other end of the room. Olivia was now sobbing wretchedly too. Only the fact that her daughter was pregnant made Kerensa feel she must go to her rather than Cordelia.

'The bloody bitch!' There was the scraping of a chair and Luke left abruptly, furious, embarrassed, dangerously miserable. He could hardly go to Cordelia, so he lurched outside, where he was promptly sick over the top stone step.

Bartholomew said in the manner of his former days, as a rough, hard-working fisherman, 'What gives she the bleddy right to speak to my sister like she's gutter-shit? I'm not having this for Cordelia.' He left the dining room in indignant anger and went to his sister, his face ugly and contorted.

Oliver, Kane and Jessica remained, all

white-faced, speechless, bewildered.

Finally Oliver said, 'What's happened to this family? Was it my fault?'

'It was none but Olivia's, Father,' Kane said. 'She had no right to behave like that. Neither her disappointment over her painting nor her pregnancy is a justifiable excuse.'

Jessica could have said, 'She doesn't love Timothy, not in the way she should. Her marriage was a mistake.' Wisdom kept her mute. She pressed an affectionate hand on Kane's arm. 'I'll go up to Harry and leave you and your father in peace.'

'There's very little peace in this house,' Oliver muttered after she had gone, staring numbly at his empty wine glass. 'You and Jessica are so fortunate. You were deeply in love before the wedding ceremony and you're totally in tune with one another. The rest of us,' he waved a hopeless hand, 'the rest of us just totter along.'

Kane took a while to speak. 'You and Mama appear quite reconciled.'

Oliver stared straight ahead. 'I don't know if a full reconciliation is possible. You see, Kane, I've betrayed her with another woman.'

'My God!' Kane put his face in his hands. Not another disclosure of this kind! He couldn't look his mother in the face without thinking of her lying in bed with Clem Trenchard.

'Who with? Someone in particular or a harlot?' Which would be worse? 'No, don't tell me. I'd rather not know.'

'On no account would I mention her name. It was brief, a spur of the moment thing, all over before I returned home. I can't believe I actually did it, Kane. Unfaithful to your mother. I love her more than my own breath, my own soul. I'd spend eternity in hell if I could only have her back. She's warming towards me. It's easier now your godforsaken father-in-law's out of the way. But what do I do? Confess to her? Pray she'll forgive me this sin, as well as for nearly killing you and Harry? Should I hope to win her back and say nothing? I've used another woman's body, Kane. How can I go to your mother and ... I'm sorry, I shouldn't be talking to you about such matters. I just wish I knew what to do.

'I keep thinking if things were put right between us then the whole family would settle again, be like it was before. Everyone supporting everyone else. No spite, no malice, no lack of forgiveness. Oh, why did Livvy say all those things? It will be hard for Cordelia to forgive her.'

Kane couldn't bring himself to condemn his father's straying, not when he knew his mother had done likewise. If he told his father about his mother's affair, his parents' marriage might not survive the shame, the recriminations and the heartbreak, and within twenty hours Clem Trenchard would be sorely punished, at the least. It seemed cruel to let his father suffer his guilt while his mother clearly did not regret her illicit union. But it was the only course.

'I don't think Mama needs, indeed, I don't think she'd want to know about your wandering. Is there any chance the lady in question would make it known?'

'None at all, she's as horrified as I am.'

'Well then, why say anything to risk the chance that, judging by Mama's manner towards you today, you clearly may have. You and Mama could have as many happy years together in the future as you have had in the past. Leave the past well alone, Father. That's my advice, and you'd be a fool not to take it.'

'I shall take it, son. Being a fool was what brought me down. I've never felt so lonely and bereft in all my life as I have since Harry's baptism. I feel as if my soul has died, and it's hard to put this into words without sending the chills riding up my back, but I'm scared. Scared to live without your mama, without her love and respect. I'd thank God a thousandfold if I could regain just a little of it back.'

'But you have. I've already said that Mama has been more than friendly towards you today. She seemed happy when you danced together.'

'That may only be because she was intent on making a happy day for Beatrice.'

Kane was perturbed at how much his father's confidence had slipped. 'It was more than that, believe me. Take heart, Mama still loves you. A little time and patience on your part and all will be well again.'

A dart of pain seared through Kane's injured leg. He had been sitting too long and kneaded the stiffening of his flesh, flexing his foot to ease away the grumbling discomfort. Unable yet to sit astride his horse with ease on long journeys, he must, nevertheless, on some pretext ride to Greystone's Farm and order Clem to never see his mother alone again, and tell him that he'd use any method necessary to prevent such a reoccurrence. And, somehow, he must face his mother with similar words.

Oliver looked down the length of the table, at the abandoned glasses of wine and uneaten food. Everyone had deserted him. If not for Kane and his beloved Shelley, he would find it hard to be strong.

Thirty-Four

Alicia fought off consciousness.

In her dream, she and Alex were safe in each other's arms, high in spirits after moving into the house in St James's Street. Alex, never thinking beyond the moment, frivolous, innocently trusting. Twenty-three years old, with animated eyes, a perfectly formed countenance and an effortless smile. To awaken now she would be thrust back into the reality of him being dead.

Wakefulness, however, would have her. She groaned in despair as her eyes, heavy and aching, opened against her will.

A hand holding hers pressed a little round her fingers. 'Jack?' She knew it would be him.

He leaned forward and his face appeared between the bed and the ornate ceiling. Candlelight offset the gloom. 'You've been sleeping for hours. Can I get you something?'

Her mouth was dry and sore. 'Yes, a drink please.'

He brought a glass of water to her lips and

she took a few sips. 'Is that monster still in the house?'

' 'Fraid so. There's nothing me or Luke can do about that. Tomorrow we'll return to Polgissey and we'll never have to see him again.'

'If I had the strength I'd kill him!'

'I could kill him myself for what he did to Lord Alex and to you. It's hard to believe what he's become – tainted and evil. He may go on about being loyal to Sir Oliver, but his lordship didn't give him a home and opportunities to see him turn into a treacherous murderer.'

'Do you trust Bartholomew Drannock to keep his word and not tell Sir Decimus I'm alive?'

'He'll have to, or he'll pay the Society's price himself, for lying in his letter. We must forget him, Alicia. We must try, for the baby's sake.'

'You're such a good man, Jack. Allowing me to turn to you after the way I've treated you. I can't tell you how relieved I am to know you still want to be a father to the baby. I'll never forget Alex, but I'll try hard to make it work between us.'

Jack nodded. 'We could have a good life together, Alicia, and I'm making a promise to you in return. I have a duty to Luke, but I'll never let his demands override my cares for you. Me and you used to talk for hours up in London, but we've never talked frankly as husband and wife. I'm devoted to you, Alicia.'

'There was too much in the way, of course, for me to marry Alex. My poor sweet love, he couldn't see that we wouldn't have been able to stay together forever, his family and the wife they had planned for him would have seen to that. But I want to tell you that I've been proud to be Mrs Jack.'

She reached for Jack and they exchanged an emotional embrace. Then Alicia exclaimed, 'Jack, there's something I must do.'

'Let it wait, my dear, you've had a terrible fright and need to rest.'

'No, I won't be able to rest until it's done. If I don't act now, happiness for someone here may be denied.'

Thirty-Five

Oliver was in the great hall, stripped now of all the trappings of Beatrice's party. It seemed ages ago that the place had been packed with revellers and resonated with merriment. He looked up the stairs. Not long ago Olivia, persuaded to stay the night for her health's sake and for the sincere apology she wanted to make first thing in the morning to Cordelia, had climbed them with Timothy two dejected steps behind her.

Then Kane and Jessica had gone up, arms round each other, all smiles, whispering intimately as Kane's clumsiness brought him into even closer contact with her.

Oliver sighed dismally, it seemed a long time since he and Kerensa had gone up those ancient oak treads together, eager for bed.

Bartholomew had come downstairs soon after making haste to Cordelia's room. He had gained no admittance. She had stubbornly maintained that she needed to be alone, and he had reluctantly left her to her tears. A second and third excursion had been equally unfruitful, and he had taken himself off to pass the night with a fretful Tamara.

There had been no success either on Kerensa's part to speak to Cordelia, and she was now checking on Samuel. Shelley was safely abed. Where was Luke? He had no idea.

Oliver was all alone. Prolonged union with the brandy bottle was highly alluring but he had an example to set, a family to soothe, a wife to win back. On heavy legs, he made the ascent and went straight to his room.

It was the room he had used before his marriage, an autocratic rebel then, sure of his life, his right to his opinion, his right to dominate, to reproach all others and indulge himself. His peers, who had once scorned or tolerated his unconventional manner, now thought him gone soft. He had stayed at home for the longest period of his life, had cancelled his last two smuggling runs, runs in which he always participated. He had lost the respect of the Beswethericks, the allies of the Pengarrons from time immemorial. Respect had been all-important to him once.

He cared not what people said or thought about him, only what Kerensa did.

'I'm sorry the end of the day didn't go as you'd planned, Oliver.'

Kerensa's voice made him whirl round.

She was framed in the doorway, a spectacle of heavenly beauty in the light of his single candle. 'It's good of you to be concerned about my feelings, Kerensa.'

'I've looked in on Samuel, and Tamara is now settled. All's quiet.'

'Thank you for informing me.'

Kerensa tried to see his face. His outline was unclear where he was, in the darkest part of the room. He had not moved a fraction. Was this polite interchange about the family all he wanted to hear from her? He had not actually said it, but all his actions and attitudes implied he wanted her back. Had he grown cold waiting for her to come round to him?

Seconds passed.

She took a step backwards. 'Goodnight, Oliver.'

'Kerensa!'

'Yes, Oliver?'

'I should like to kiss you goodnight, if that's all right.'

She came into the room, willingly.

He went to her, feeling a little shy as he placed his hands behind her head.

It was the softest kiss she had ever received. The purest and the warmest. So very, very tender, and it took her breath away. He was draining her, yet he was filling her entirely. He was giving her a once in a lifetime kiss, the salute of someone who loved unselfishly, absolutely, perfectly.

'Goodnight, my dear love.'

After a last fleeting touch on her face, he left her and returned to the window.

Then he felt her arms about his waist and her face resting against his back. Relief leapt out of him in a rush of breath, a mighty gasp. The demon of despair was expelled. He turned and at the same time she moved round to face him.

Simultaneously they cried, 'I'm sorry. I'm sorry. Forgive me. Forgive me.'

'I let my jealousy and pride come between us, but never, ever again,' Oliver swore.

'And I forgot how much I loved you, and what you meant to me.' She mourned for the time they had lost.

'I don't just want to *feel* happiness from now on. I want to give happiness to you, my dear love. I only want to make you happy, Kerensa.'

'And I will only ever want you, Oliver.'

They went to their bedroom, their bed, their bonding place and lay down together, face to face.

In a feather-light caress Oliver glided the backs of his fingers all over her. Kerensa touched the strong muscles of his shoulders, threaded her fingers through his black hair and over the fine silver traces at his temples.

She opened her lips for his next kiss, moving closer to him, placing the full length of her body against the full length of his. While he touched her with a velvet-smoothness, she ran delicate paths down his back with her fingertips, murmuring tender words in his ear.

His body shuddered with desire. She gave a deep, telling sigh. Putting her hand on his hip she angled herself into him and united their bodies.

They rocked gently, heightening the pleasure with loving hands, reacquainting themselves with all the burning and exquisite sensations that were theirs, and only ever could belong to them. They took their time, time was theirs to have. He nestled her face into his neck, whispering his love and dedication until the moment came for him to strive deeper and deeper into her to carry them to the point of utter, unforgettable culmination.

Thirty-Six

The hut that served as an animal hospital in the Pengarron grounds was overcrowded with anxious humans.

Luke was slumped on a sack of grain, not nursing an injured or ailing creature but a sore head. He groaned every time he shifted, having spent the night here intoxicated and brooding over Olivia's cruel comments to Cordelia. His head ached, his throat and stomach felt on fire, his bad shoulder was particularly sore and stiff, but he had neither the will or energy to manipulate it into some sort of ease.

'Everything's a mess,' he complained to his two sisters, glaring at Olivia, who kept dropping her face to the cage where she was giving fresh water to a watchful thrush with a splint on its wing.

'What am I going to do about Cordelia? Should've realized how she felt about me. Even Father knew, said something to me a short time ago which I entirely missed the meaning of. Why didn't you say something, for heaven's sake, Livvy? Always had your say before. Too damned selfish!'

'It's you who's selfish, brother,' Kelynen returned, while stroking a muzzled, pale-brown fox on her lap. The fox, a vixen named Gilly, obviously the runt of a litter, would surely have died if not for Matthias Renfree's soft heart in bringing it to the hut. It had suffered two deep gashes down one side from an unknown source. A certain victim for a stronger predator, Gilly could not be released into the wild and was making an anxious pet. Rex, feeling neglected outside, occasionally whined his displeasure. 'And whenever has anyone been able to tell you something you didn't want to hear? Poor Cordelia, to win you or to lose you, what a terrible choice.'

'How do you see that?' Luke regretted his forceful tone, which made his head pound all the fiercer.

The timbers of the hut creaked as the early morning sun warmed them through, the planked floor did the same as Olivia moved restlessly about, the dry air was filled with animal smells, all adding to his discomfort.

'No, don't tell me, I know what a selfish ignoramus I can be. I hope she didn't spend too wretched a night. Open all the windows, Livvy, I can't breathe in here.'

'I could cut my tongue out for what I said to Cordelia. What exactly am I going to say to make it up to her? She'll probably never forgive me and it's no more than I deserve. I went to her room first thing. I thought she was still refusing to answer the door, then Polly told me she'd risen even earlier and had gone riding.'

'Ask her to be godmother to your baby, she'll be delighted with the idea. More importantly, what are we going to do about Mama and Father?' Kelynen said.

'What do mean?' Luke asked irritably, wondering why he drank so unwisely. He must take care not to turn into a sluggard. 'They seemed quite happy yesterday. I thought they were getting along very well. Didn't you, Livvy?'

'I didn't notice at the time, but in retrospect they seemed almost affectionate.'

'Perhaps, but how much of that was for our and Beatrice's benefit?' Kelynen persisted, grooming Gilly's coat. The fox had settled, its tiny pointed face on her knees, looking down at the floor. 'You haven't been here, Luke, to witness their estrangement first-hand, to feel the tension. Mama has been every bit as stubborn as Father over this. The day Father came home and announced he was staying, obviously with the intention of making full amends, I could see this entirely didn't suit Mama. I asked her directly if or when she was going to let bygones rest. Her words were, "All I can say is I hope to and very soon."'

'Well then,' Olivia said with a sigh of relief. 'I believe she'll do as she says. Why do you doubt her, Kelynen?'

'I don't really, it's just that I can't bear seeing Father so unhappy.'

Luke smiled grimly. 'Why am I not surprised that you should see things more from Father's point of view? I can understand his feelings, although not his actions towards Clem Trenchard. He's been a thorn in Father's flesh for years, but Father should have simply ignored the ignorant fellow. Trenchard stayed under your roof, Livvy. Could you not see that he might have been a threat, that he was planning something in the way Father must have had in mind?'

Olivia felt her face flood with colour. She waved a hand about and blamed her discomfort on morning sickness. She knew better than most women the potent attraction Clem possessed, and there was so much more to him than the usual masculine appeals. If only she could paint his likeness, capture the soulful essence of him, she was sure her talent would be fully restored, but even if she did it from memory, as a gift for Catherine, she was afraid it might somehow reveal something of the secret closeness she had shared with Clem. Could Clem come between her parents? For her father's peace of mind, and her mother's comfort, she had no choice but to evade the issue.

'This is indelicate talk, but I will disclose what I witnessed in my home. Clem paid my sister-in-law every attention. He loves her very much. Perhaps it would have helped if Father had known this, but even if I'd had a notion he'd intended to be so belligerent towards Clem, it was hardly a subject I could bring up.'

'Father should have kept his head, but,' and Luke was thinking about the caring way he had been allowed his freedom from the estate and encouraged to write his plays, 'Mama should have trusted him. What saddens me the most, is that after so many happy years together they still do not know each other well enough.'

'The trouble was,' Kelynen deliberated, for she had thought it all through, 'that there was unfinished business between them and Clem. Only they can break down those old chains and heal their marriage. We must stand aside and say and do nothing to hinder them. They studied each other wrong all these years, perhaps we are doing the same to them now.'

'Well, Miss Clever-little-thing,' Luke grinned at his youngest sister's serious expression, 'first you worry us, then you cheer us and give us hope. Do come here and rub this useless shoulder of mine, and tell me what I must do about Cordelia.'

Putting Gilly on a long lead, which was

fastened to a hook on the wall, Kelynen pushed Luke forward to sit up straight, then set to work on his rigid muscles.

'As usual, I missed the to-do at the supper table; I really must stay around longer. How do you feel about Cordelia? I mean deep down.'

'Yes, Luke,' Olivia eased herself down on the old backless chair Kelynen had vacated. 'Had you no idea at all that she was besotted with you?'

'No, of course not,' he protested at what sounded like an accusation. 'She's always been like a little sister to me. I only realized she'd grown up yesterday. And before you girls call me heartless, let me tell you I've been thinking about her all night. Ah, Kelynen, that's wonderful, don't stop! I need to talk to her when Bartholomew isn't around, he's set on her bringing up his child, which won't be easy in view of her colouring. People will either shun Tamara or treat her as a curiosity.'

'So you have come to a decision?' Kelynen looked at his face.

'Yes, I suppose I have.'

'And?' Olivia asked eagerly. 'You're blushing!'

'I am not! I value Cordelia more than any woman I know and I need her to be with me. Polgissey would be too lonely without her, and in view of her feelings for me, we cannot be there together unless we are married. In due course, when Cordelia is back and I've made myself presentable, I'm going to ask her to marry me.'

'What's going on in here? Planning games like the old days?' Kane appeared smiling in the doorway.

'We've got wonderful news!' Olivia and Kelynen called out excitedly together.

'Not as wonderful as mine,' Kane shushed them with his hands. 'Mama and Father have just come down to breakfast together. They are reunited, and that's official!'

Thirty-Seven

In the nameless little cove under the Polgissey cliffs, which her cousin favoured to do his writing, Cordelia was standing on a high cluster of rocks that jutted deep out to sea. It was low tide and this allowed her the vantage point.

She had been down here twice before, with Luke, the sea coming in both times, slapping against the rough base of the granite. The first time, while he had sat well back near the foot of the cliff and raced on with his play, she had run barefoot on the sand, tossing pebbles into the rushing breakers and peering into the rock pools, hoping to discover marine creatures and seaweeds unknown to her, but the pools had soon filled up, losing their identity and denying her the quest.

The second time she had been forced to retreat quickly to Luke's side as the ocean had greedily invaded all of the beach. She had asked him what his play was entitled. His reply, when finally roused from the world of his imagination, was that he would tell her when he had decided. It would be something very special, extraordinary, unforgettable. If he had thought up a title he had forgotten to tell her what it was.

She was not thinking about Luke today. A small figure in her riding clothes, she was watching a solitary man in a small anonymous boat, out past the drift of the waves that lapped the shore. His jet-black hair was touched by the shine of the sun, as were the oars as they flashed in and out of the water. His powerful arms took him from the crab pots to the lobster traps that bore the coloured buoys of the Kinvers. He was looking seawards, bending over his pots and traps, hauling them in and emptying the contents into baskets.

Cordelia was waving to him with both arms, her hat in one hand, swishing it through the clean fresh air, its bright red ribbons like banners and heralds to her cause.

'Morgan! Morgan!' she shouted his name again and again, and she let out the shrill, whooping cry of the sort her male cousins had made as boys when locked in war games. Morgan did not look round. He could not hear her. Gentle as the sea was today, it retained an unrelenting thunderous roar.

The cove, like the numerous others along the coast was hemmed in on either side by towering cliffs. Many of the coves when fully exposed by the ebbing tides were joined to their neighbours, but the overreach of the cliffs here denied this tiny stretch any such freedom. Cordelia was afraid that Morgan, on his way towards the east point and then Porthcarne, where he would land his harvest, would miss her. He only had to look up to see her but he kept his head down, as if tired, as if defeated.

Scrambling down from the rocks she ran to the shoreline and was splashing in the water. 'Morgan! Morgan!'

He was moving away from her and Cordelia began to scream his name at the highest pitch of her voice. It seemed she would have to climb back up the cliff and ride all the way to the village, and she so wanted this encounter to be just between the two of them. She was sure it would be a reunion, a special time, with this man who was as gentle as the waves that caressed the shore, who had never been out of her mind for a minute since she had forsaken Polgissey. She had needed no persuasion to come to him after Alicia had visited her room last night.

'Cordelia, please open the door to me. I'm bringing you news of Morgan Kinver.'

This, and only this, after the pleadings of almost everyone else in the manor, had got her off her bed of humiliation and misery.

'I should have written to you about this days ago,' Alicia had said. 'He's been pleading with me to ask you to see him. He loves you, Cordelia. You can trust him. You are right for each other. You love him too, don't you? It isn't infatuation this time. Don't let those who only seek to use you influence what you do with the rest of your life. Don't miss this chance to be happy. Nothing else in the world matters.'

Cordelia had never felt entirely at ease in her elevated life, never knew who she really was, what she should do, but she had seen it clearly then. Related to gentry she may be, but she was first and foremost a fisherman's daughter. Alicia had helped her pack the necessary things, and Jack had stolen away with them to a place outside the manor grounds where, shortly afterwards, he had met up with her and escorted her all the way to Porthcarne.

Fate in the form of those two wonderfully kind people had brought her here to this insignificant little cove. Now she was begging fate to intervene again and make Morgan look up and see her waving to him to come to her.

Of a sudden, he stopped pulling on the oars and lifted his head towards the cove.

He saw her, gazed at her a moment as if seeing something only in his imagination, then he waved back enthusiastically, sculling the boat round to row to shore. With every other rapid stroke, he looked over his shoulder, as if making sure she was still there. She leapt into the water, calling his name.

'Cordelia! Wait there. I'm coming for you.'

Dropping her hat to float away, she trawled through the waves until waist high in the water. Streamers of her long black hair, caught by the wind, were soon wet and clinging to her shoulders.

Morgan strained to reach her. Stretching out his long arms, gently and victoriously, he pulled in the most prized catch of his life.

Thirty-Eight

Later in the day, the Kinvers were confronted at their smallholding by the Pengarrons.

'This is our property, Sir Oliver Pengarron,' Hal Kinver stated coolly, standing in front of four of his five brothers and his son and his nephew. 'We've been expecting you. Hope this is going to be civil like, or you can bugger off back where 'ee come from, and take the young master and this other man with 'ee. Begging your pardon, ma'am, Mrs Jack.'

Kerensa and Alicia were waiting, wary and watchful, near the horses.

'I'm pleased we aren't about to waste time, Hal Kinver,' Oliver said in an equally harsh voice. 'I understand you're being protective of your brother Morgan, but I'm not leaving here until you tell me precisely where my niece, Miss Cordelia Drannock, is.'

'Tell us now, Kinver!' Luke bawled in fury. He made to push past his father, but Oliver flung out an arm to prevent him.

'I won't be stopped. Where is my sister?' Bartholomew pulled out the pistol he had

357

nestled in his belt. 'You have five seconds, big man, or I'll shoot you down like a dog.'

'Be careful of him, Hal Kinver. This man is a murdering swine!' Alicia's voice seethed with hate, causing Kerensa to gasp in horror; what did she mean?

Jack shot his wife a look of warning to be cautious.

Oliver frowned, but kept his eyes fixed on the giant.

'I've no need to lie to any of 'ee. She's gone off with Morgan. You won't see she again till they're wed. They're in love. That's the way of it, and there isn't a thing none of 'ee can do about it.'

'Thank God,' Alicia got in before anyone else could comment or make a new threat. 'I'm so pleased all is well for her. It's what she and Morgan deserve.'

'Shut up, Alicia! This would never have happened if not for you and Jack. You had no right to interfere.' Luke twisted round and glared at them with utter reproach. He felt betrayed by their actions, and isolated, excluded, shunned. Eventually, when everyone at the manor had begun to worry over Cordelia's late return from her ride and the fact that Jack was also missing, Alicia's presence had been demanded by the family. With pride, she had produced a letter that Cordelia had written, of her intentions to go to Morgan Kinver. Cordelia had penned many paragraphs on the wretch's character, making him sound like a saint.

'Where did they go?' Oliver advanced on Hal Kinver. Luke and Bartholomew matched his steps. Oliver was in control but he was also angry, annoyed and anxious. In his preoccupation over his personal life he had let Cordelia down, and Kerensa was feeling even more guilty, declaring she should have been aware of all Cordelia's moods. They were afraid she had made a terrible mistake, but Oliver would make sure she was not beyond their help.

The Kinvers crossed over the same length of ground. Oliver and Hal were almost eye to eye.

'If we knew where they went we wouldn't tell 'ee,' Hal curled his mighty fists, widening his aggressive stance. He motioned his great dark head towards Luke. 'She's better off away from he there! Treated her like a skivvy, he did. Snapping her head off whenever the fancy took un. Too busy scribbling away and bedding his whore of a cook to see how unhappy the little maid was. My brother'll make her happy, and come hell or high water, the rest of us Kinvers will see he gets the bleddy chance!'

'It isn't your decision to make, Kinver!' Oliver roared, bracing himself for sudden attack.

'My sister isn't going to spend the rest of

her life living in poverty with some ne'er-do-well,' Bartholomew's teeth grated on the words. 'Tell us where they are or you'll be the first to die.'

'What's all this talk of killing, Bartholomew? We've come here only to take Cordelia home safely.' Oliver was shocked at his nephew's clear intent; was there some truth to Alicia Rosevear's allegation? He was fearful now for Kerensa's safety if a fight broke out. He squared off from the opposing family.

'Hal Kinver, you say my niece is not here. I would like to search your house.'

Hal swept a massive arm towards his threshold. He was not a warring man, seeking only to protect his kin and what was rightfully his. 'Go ahead, Sir Oliver. Look in every room, search every cupboard an' corner. I've told 'ee no lies, but I'm willing to let 'ee look for yourself. And when you do, take a good look round. You'll see this property's not run down, nor poorly furnished, nor are our cupboards bare. Our land is well teeled and our beasts are well cared for. We're humble, but not poor. Not so common as you believe either. This house and land was given to our late mother by our father, Mr Cecil Doble. You'll even find a picture of he on our walls. Like your niece, we've got good blood in our veins.'

'Oliver, perhaps we should listen to what

Mr Kinver is saying,' came Kerensa's careful opinion. She was at Oliver's side, hugging his arm. 'Cordelia is not a child any more, it's time we all stopped thinking of her as such. She's made a decision, and before we try to wrench her away from this man, who Jack and Alicia are convinced she loves, and by their account, who will treat her well, we should think about what Cordelia really wants. Has our love not triumphed across the social divide and every other circumstance?'

'Never! I'll not allow it!' Luke uttered disbelievingly. How could his mother suggest such a thing?

'I'm afraid you have no say in this, Luke.' Kerensa turned to him, offering a comforting hand. She knew how badly he was feeling about Cordelia's elopement, over how he had failed her. 'You had your chance with Cordelia and must now accept she has chosen another man.'

'I won't allow my sister to live in this place, not after what she's used to,' Bartholomew swore.

'She and Morgan aren't 'tending on living here,' Hal said, with meaning in every word. 'Be a bit too overcrowded anyways. They'll make their own way in the world. He's got means put by, she'll not go without nothing.'

'I'll see that she doesn't! And I'll see to it that your brother doesn't benefit from what

361

I've settled on her.'

'Morgan'd insist on that,' Hal said, with the same sort of pride. 'We Kinvers aren't afraid of hard work, we've always made our own way in the world. Mrs Morgan Kinver will still live the life of a lady. My only regret is they won't be able to settle round here, not with the way he's going to be.' Again, he jerked his head at Luke, who was staring despondently down at the ground; it could be thought he was sulking or scowling. 'I just hope he won't make the villagers suffer because of it. My boy will be out of a job for a start and he was enjoying learning all about horses under Jack.'

Luke felt as if he had been smacked in the face. He eyed Hal Kinver, shaking his head. This was unjust and he was hurt to the marrow of his bones. Had he not supported Porthcarne in a great many ways since his arrival in the big house? Why was it thought he could be so vindictive, so fickle, so anxious to seek vengeance? Did no one see any real good in him? Jack seemed to have lost his respect for him, he had brought Cordelia here and had been waiting with the Kinvers for the inevitable conflict.

'Are you really going to allow this, Uncle?' Bartholomew demanded roughly.

Oliver glanced at Kerensa. She smiled up at him and he wrapped his arm round her waist. 'I've known Jack from a small boy and

I trust his judgement completely, as does your aunt. If Cordelia has chosen Morgan Kinver, and it strikes me that at least the fellow is going to marry her, then I will respect her choice, although if he ever hurts her in any way, he'll have to pay me before the devil!

'Hal Kinver, our families are about to be joined in wedlock, and although I'm not entirely happy about it, I shall do nothing to prevent it. Will you take my hand on it?'

'I'll do that gladly, sir. My brothers too.' And with one breath, all the brothers relaxed their hostile stance. 'Will 'ee finish it all off with a drop of brandy, sir?' Hal tapped his broad nose. 'Fine foreign stuff, if 'ee knows what I do mean.'

'Willingly, her ladyship and I shall stay a few minutes. I do not speak for the others.' Oliver raised his eyes in question at those he had brought with him.

Intense, incensed, Luke stalked up to Hal Kinver. 'When you next see your brother and Miss Cordelia, tell them they may settle where they will, with no opposition from me on any account. Also, tell my cousin she and her husband may call on me any time they wish. And also hear this, I am not as small-minded as you would have tell of me. The people of Porthcarne are under my patronage, I will always see them right and do whatever I can for them. But I will certainly not stay and drink with you.' To his parents he said, 'You will rest and dine with me before returning home?'

'We'll be along soon.' Kerensa smiled at him.

To Bartholomew, he said in hushed tones, 'My play is in its final stages. I take it this incident will delay your departure again for London, until you have seen Cordelia and know that her well-being is assured. I'm sure this rabble will get word to her that she need not hide away. By then, I shall be ready to accompany you on the journey up to London. I do not forgive you for what you did to my friend, nor do I admire the man you have become, but I should feel safer, in the circumstances, if Sir Decimus Soames sees, when I present my plays for acceptance to the theatres, that I tolerate your company.'

'I should like to have you with me,' Bartholomew said grimly, ignoring the insult, his firearm now hidden away. 'I'll return to my daughter now and call on you in a day or two.'

On reaching the horses, Luke ignored Alicia. To Jack, he whispered, 'See to it that your wife does not reveal to my father why she hates Bartholomew so much. I suppose you are staying here for the present? I should like to speak to you later – alone.'

Wanting to explain his actions to Luke, but wisely holding his peace until they had this private talk, Jack held his young master's horse while he mounted. He watched sadly as Luke rode off without a backward glance, holding himself erect and aggrieved in the saddle.

Jack's next thought was for Alicia's welfare. She had endured a long ride, taken at a fast pace for a woman nearly eight months' pregnant. She was grimacing and massaging her back with both hands. He shivered. She was staring at Bartholomew with utter malice, her lips moving silently, ill-wishing him again.

He guided Alicia to her pony. 'This is a happy day. Miss Cordelia and Morgan Kinver will be wed and able to live in peace, and at last Sir Oliver and her ladyship are back together. Now it's our duty not to delay in going home.'

Thirty-Nine

'What's this?' Jack asked, looking at the document Luke put before him. Many of the words were made up of more than six or seven letters and made no sense to him.

The two men were up in the tower room. Drops of rain were beating a scattered threat against the windows. A rapid change in the weather saw looming dark clouds forming out to sea. Candle flames were bending in a draught coming from an undetermined source. By midnight a storm would lash the coast.

'It's my signature to hand over to you the sum of five hundred pounds.' Luke eyed him darkly across his desk. 'It's a gift to you and Alicia – who no longer needs my protection – to enable you both to do as you please from now on. I'm releasing you, Jack, from my service and from any obligation you feel you have towards me.'

'Luke, I can't take this! I don't want it.' Jack dropped the paper on the desk as if it was burning his fingers.

Leaning back in his chair, Luke smiled

sarcastically. 'Of course you don't, pious, honourable Jack Rosevear. Mustn't offend your principles, must I? Why are you not sitting with me like you always do?' Luke smashed his fist down on the wood. 'Why do you think I'm giving you this money? As some kind of petulant bid to buy you off? To ease my conscience in some way? I am not in a strop and neither am I feeling guilty, but I am absolutely furious with you and deeply hurt by your actions over Cordelia and Morgan Kinver. After Alicia chastized me about my lack of showing true friendship to you, I've sought to redress my behaviour. I took you as a guest into my father's house. Yet you saw fit to whip Cordelia away in secret. How do you think that made me feel?' Luke was shouting now. 'You are a sanctimonious bastard, Jack! Every bit as shallow in treating people like dirt as I am, apparently.'

Jack stood reeling at the extent of his wrath. 'Luke, I was going to explain. I had to act quickly, and I couldn't tell you about it because you would've stopped at nothing to prevent Miss Cordelia going away.'

'What gives you and Alicia the right to say who she should marry? Kinver might be ill-treating her this very minute.'

'As your steward I've come to know the villagers well, and I like and admire Morgan Kinver,' Jack spoke calmly, hoping to take the sting out of Luke's temper. 'And I saw how happy Miss Cordelia was when Alicia talked to her about him. I'm sorry it made me act disloyally to you. I just did what I thought was right.'

'Right? Oh, you think you know a lot about doing what's right, Jack Rosevear. Well, I will have to manage without my cousin from now on and I can also manage without you.'

'I'll leave if that's what you want,' Jack said coolly, 'but I'll not take your money.'

Luke slashed at the money order with the back of his hand. 'Take it for Alicia's sake! Or are you so selfish you'd deny her a comfortable life in order to keep your sanctimoniousness? Go when she is fit to travel. You are no longer a Pengarron servant or a friend of mine.'

'I accept I've hurt your feelings over Miss Cordelia's elopement, but I don't deserve this much spite from you. I thought that you and I were friends, but I realize I never knew you at all. My wife and I will leave here tomorrow. I'm sorry, sir, that things have ended this way.'

The door crashed open and Jack was nearly knocked off his feet.

'Jack, sir, come quick! Come quick!' Amy Curnow came bursting in, flushed and flapping her hands, so agitated she had not taken in the raised voices. 'She's in labour! Mrs Jack's pains are so bad, it'll be all over 'fore the hour's up. You have to come right now.'

Jack froze. From the floor below there came the sound of a loud groan of pain.

Luke grabbed his shoulder. 'Move, Jack!' The two men shoved Amy Curnow aside and clattered down the spiral staircase and sprinted into Jack's bedroom.

Alicia was on the bed, propped up by pillows, knees drawn up, face twisted horribly as she endured a strong contraction. Mabena, her own pregnancy clearly showing, was holding her hand. Another of the maids was anxiously laying out the things put aside for this event.

'Ah, ah, ah, ah, ahhhhh!' Alicia clutched the pillows.

'Right, right,' Luke said, white-faced. 'You stay with Alicia, Jack, and I'll fetch Dr Leane.'

'What do I do?' Jack panicked, staring wide-eyed at his wife, who was now blowing out through her mouth as the pain subsided. 'It's coming too early, will it be all right?'

'You can get out the room, both of you.' Amy Curnow hurried in after them, rolling up her sleeves. 'There's no time to get that old fool from Gwithian. I'll see t' this, I've done it afore. Don't worry about the earliness of it, my maid was born two month too soon an' she survived. Go on, get! And open up all the doors and windows.'

Jack and Luke exchanged terrified glances. 'Are you sure there's no time to get the doctor?' Luke demanded.

'Oww–ah! I need to push,' Alicia shrieked, 'I need to push!'

' 'Twill be all right, m'dear,' Amy Curnow was at the bed, pushing up Alicia's nightdress.

Jack and Luke fled to opposite ends of the corridor. Jack gazed, unseeing, towards Porthcarne. Luke gazed, unseeing, towards Navax Point. Both were praying and both were shaking.

Alicia was making mighty strange noises which reduced the two men to utter helplessness. They turned and faced each other.

'Why do we have to open all the doors and windows?' Luke asked, suddenly afraid he was omitting to do something vital.

'I don't know!' Jack was frantic. 'Wait! It's to make sure it'll be an easy birth.'

They opened all the windows and doors down the corridor until they were outside the labour room. Alicia screamed again, a terrible sound, which seemed to go on and on. Then there was silence. Worried beyond belief, Jack and Luke closed in on each other.

'What's happening?' Jack whispered, very scared.

'I don't know,' Luke whispered back.

They put their ears close to the door, and

heard the sound of a baby's cry. With exclamations of delight they shook hands, their eyes met and they fell into an elated hug.

'How long should we wait?' Jack was back to whispering.

'You should have stayed in there,' Luke said sympathetically. 'Remember how my father wouldn't allow the midwives to turn him out while my mama was giving birth to Samuel? Or any of us, apparently.'

'It's still crying. I hope Alicia's all right.'

Luke listened. 'She is, that was her voice.'

'I wonder what it is.'

'They could at least shout through the door. You've got the right to know if you have a son or a daughter, Jack.'

'She had backache all day. I should've thought—'

'Shhh, someone's coming.'

The two men quickly smoothed back their hair and fiddled with their coats. They were standing tall and straight when Mabena opened the door.

'Well?' they said together into her chirpy face.

' 'Tes a little maid. All's well. We've rubbed her foot with ta rabbit's foot, so she'll have good luck all her life. She's a brave enough size considerin', an' poor Mrs Jack had a hard job bringin' her out. She'll be more an' a bit sore with the quickness of it. Mrs Curnow says t' give her ten minutes then 'ee can come in.' Mabena bobbed a cheeky curtsey and closed the door.

Jack looked at Luke. 'A girl.'

'Yes, a girl.'

'A girl!'

'You've got a daughter, Jack.' Luke slapped him on the back. 'Congratulations. I'm so glad this happened before I leave for London.' Luke held out his hand, 'About just now...'

'Can we just forget it?'

They grasped hands.

Luke leant back against the wall. 'If your little girl had chosen twenty-four hours later to make her appearance, Jack...'

'There's no need to think about that now. We can all settle down and enjoy life from now on.'

When Jack went in to see his daughter, he took Luke with him.

Forty

Around the Cornish peninsula on the south coast, heavy rain had fallen all night. It eased off at dawn, leaving the sky unsullied, the air hushed and fresh.

The shingle and rocks of Trelynne Cove were drying out at mid-morning when Kerensa and Oliver looked down on them. They were in a pensive mood, worried that there might come another crisis to rock their newly recovered world. Both had good reason to be feeling this way.

'Shall we go down?' Oliver said softly.

'I'll lead the way,' Kerensa replied, taking Kernick forward.

The black granite cliffs of the empty cove had a dramatic shape, like that of a horse shoe, the steep rocky path leading down to it wound in a figure three. Over the years, hardly a week had gone by when Kerensa had not come here, yet this was to be the most poignant, the most painful journey she would ever make down to the place where she had been born and raised in her grandfather's tiny cob-walled cottage.

The cottage was long gone, as were Old Tom Trelynne's neglected rowing boat and worn-out crab pots. Old Tom had been scrawny, cunning, and more wicked than Kerensa would ever have believed. He had hidden contraband and stolen goods in a heavily concealed shallow cave. It was where he had died at the vengeful hands of a tinner, for committing a Cornishman's most grievous sin; betraying a smuggling run to the Revenue men. It seemed part of another life to Kerensa now.

Leaving Kernick, she crunched over the shingle to the shore. This was the beach where she had walked and held hands with Clem in their youth, and where, two years ago, they should have said goodbye, in their hearts, for all time. Tears stung her eyes. Clem would soon know she had let him down again; Timothy or Jessica would write with the news that she and Oliver were once more a loving couple. How many times could Clem bear it?

Was he miserable without her at home on his farm? He had something she did not, a granddaughter. Matthias Renfree had told her of the event, written in a letter from Kenver to Rosie, of Rebekah Trenchard's birth. She prayed Rebekah was making Clem happy.

'This is where it all started for us,' Oliver said, at her side, his words carried across the cove by the ever-present winds. 'I accept that my agreement to Old Tom's outrageous proposition that I marry you to claim the cove back as Pengarron land, was wrong. But, my love, as I've said here once before, I've never regretted taking you as my wife.'

Kerensa took him by the hand. 'Come with me, there's something I must show you, something I must do. I pray you'll understand, but I believe our love is strong enough for there to be no more secrets between us.'

As they walked they looked down at the pebbles, hands held tight, hearts heavy, for both had something that must be told.

Kerensa stopped under a part of the cliff known as Mother Clarry's Rock, a smooth-shaped spur which jutted out and formed the seat of a mythical witch, who was said to have sat there on nights when there was a full moon to plot her evil misdeeds. Had Mother Clarry cast a spell over the inhabitants of the cove, dooming them to unhappiness? Kerensa's parents had died young, her father from typhus, her mother in childbed, her grandfather had been murdered. She was soon to find out if she had been cursed herself, if the happiness she had regained with Oliver was to be everlasting.

Locating a particular large pebble of twisting black and white colour, Kerensa let go of Oliver's hand. Lifting the pebble aside she scooped away fine shingle a foot deep. A tiny sealed leather bag appeared and she picked it up.

Oliver took it from her. 'I think I know what's in here,' he said in the lowest of voices. He guided her to some flat rocks where they could sit down.

Kerensa's heart seemed to rise and choke her as Oliver untied the drawstrings of the bag. He pulled out a lock of blond hair tied round with blue ribbon, and laid it on the palm of his hand.

She took his free hand, gaining courage from the fact that he did not pull it away. The restriction in her throat made her next words come out raw and husky. 'I'm sorry I lied to you about throwing it away, Oliver.'

It was what he had feared for so long, and what he had been working at so hard to make his heart accept. His fist tightened round the evidence. He felt that his whole self was about to explode with rage and hatred. What she had admitted by keeping this lock of hair, hurt him so much he had to fight back the horrendous darkness invading his soul.

'Trenchard has meant everything to you, Kerensa?'

She started to cry, tightening the grip on his hand, afraid he would tear himself away from her. 'Yes, Oliver. Forgive me! Don't let it spoil what we have now, I beg you. It's all over, I swear to you it will never happen again. It's you I love, really love, from the bottom of my soul.'

Tears were in his eyes. While her confession had distressed him deeply, what he was about to confess she had no suspicion of. Why should she? He had not been wrenched away from someone he had loved and could never forget, from someone he could turn to for true love, after a sequence of humiliating and terrible events. His confession might burn away all her love for him.

'As difficult as it is to come to terms with the very thought of you being with another man, I – I do forgive you, Kerensa. Although for one hideous moment I felt I could kill Trenchard, I acknowledge you were in love with him.' He sighed from the bottom of his heart. 'That's more excuse than I had.'

She looked at him, puzzled, then as realization flooded through her, in shock and disbelief. 'Are you saying...?'

'Yes, Kerensa...' his voice faltered, 'it was with Rosie Renfree.'

'What?' The relief that he taken her confession so well was overshadowed by acute emotional and physical pain, as if she had been given a blow to the heart. It had crossed her mind that Oliver might have thought about being unfaithful, but she had dismissed it. There had been no gossip, no rumours. But with him staying at Ker-an-Mor, and apparently being utterly discreet, an affair with Rosie had gone unnoticed. Why did he do it? Why Rosie? Clem's sister! How strange. How terrible.

'I never thought you'd ... Rosie? Was it to get back at me or Clem in some way?'

'Not that, I swear. I was so lonely, so wretched, Kerensa, and I was so afraid. I needed someone and Rosie happened to be there. I beg you not to say anything that will destroy her and Matthias's marriage; her remorse made her ill. I overwhelmed her better judgement, stirred up past feelings. You see, there was a brief, innocent, attachment between us when you and I fell out after the death of my half-brother. I too know how, through terrible circumstances, one can give way to one's needs and, although it pains me to admit it, I can acknowledge that you never lost your feelings for Trenchard. I shall never stop regretting that I helped to push you towards him. I'll not ask if you still love him, only to say that I accept there will always be a bond between you. Kerensa, can you forgive me for my unfaithfulness?'

They were both staring miserably down at their feet, absorbing the appalling things they had heard. Simultaneously, they lifted their eyes to the other's face.

Kerensa was grieved at his despair. 'Yes, I do forgive you, Oliver. I was wrong to hold my resentment against you for so long, and I understand why you turned to Rosie, and loving you the way I do, I understand why she became involved with you. I want you to believe you can trust me, Oliver, I swear I won't ever turn to Clem in that way again. It's you I love more than anyone else in the world, more than my own life. Thank you, for being so understanding towards my betrayal to you. I thank God for that.'

'I believe you, Kerensa. It was Rosie who pointed out to me how I should see things differently concerning you and her brother. I thank God for your forgiveness, and I thank Him with all my heart, that at the end of the terrible time we had been through, you chose me. It's all that matters, I swear to you. On my life, I swear it.'

'It's all that matters,' she repeated. 'All else is dead and buried in the past, forever.'

He lifted her face and they kissed, a long, dedicated kiss. Finally they smiled, enjoying each other's closeness.

Kerensa said, 'Oliver, there's one thing left to say. It's about Clem. Jessica or Timothy will write to him with the news about us. I hope you will agree that it would be cold and unfeeling for me to just leave it at that.'

'What do you want to do, Kerensa?'

'There's nothing I can do until he returns again to Vellanoweth. If I write to him Catherine might see the letter. I think Clem sensed that my love for you was the strongest. All that I ask, Oliver, is that you will allow us a few minutes alone, so I can explain everything to him properly.'

'You have my agreement, Kerensa.'

'Are you sure you don't mind?' She was anxious for both men's feelings.

'Not as much as I once would have done.'

'Thank you, Oliver. I know it's not easy for you.'

'It will be a lot less easy for him.' Oliver turned the lock of hair over in his hand. 'And this?'

Kerensa took it from him. 'It must be blown away like the rest of the past.'

They walked down to the shore and climbed an outcrop of rocks that straggled out into the sea. Untying the blue ribbon, Kerensa rubbed the lock of hair into separate entities, then raising her hand she let them, and the ribbon, be carried away by the wind.

'The past is gone,' Oliver said, enfolding her in his arms.

She leaned into his strength. 'No more echoes.'

Forty-One

'Hello, Luke, busy as usual, I see. I've come to take a look at Jack and Alicia's baby. My brother-in-law, Hal, said I would find a welcome from you also.'

Luke was tying the last knot of string around his manuscript for the journey to London and had not heard Cordelia sweep into the tower room. He studied her. She looked very pretty and somehow taller than before, then he realized she was holding her shoulders back, her head up high.

'You're welcome any time, Cousin. You look happy. The married state obviously suits you. Have you come alone?'

'Morgan's waiting for me downstairs. I wasn't sure how you would receive him. I'll not have him subjected to your less agreeable moods.'

'And I'd not expect you to.'

Luke came forward and enclosed her in a fond embrace. 'I hope you both can stay. Bartholomew is due here at any moment, we could all dine together. It's good having a baby in the house. It's made it a home, like the manor.'

Cordelia stared at him. Since her return from her honeymoon yesterday, people were constantly exclaiming how she had changed. From all appearances so had Luke. He was particularly well groomed and had a glow of vigour about him. A glance round the room showed no evidence of the spirits and glasses that usually frequented the place. He was different. He actually seemed content. Over the years, she had witnessed him in acts of high jinks and merry-making and the ecstatic moments when her uncle had allowed him to leave the estate to write, but contentment had always eluded him.

'I'm pleased to find you in such good health, and congratulations on finishing your play. As to whether Morgan and I should stay and see Barty, I'm worried my brother will be harsh with us. Hal said he'd threatened him with a pistol.'

'My father has accepted your husband and therefore so will Bartholomew. He agrees with everything my father says and does, have you not noticed? He may be harsh with you, but pay no heed to it. He'll feel easier when he sees you. He's been waiting for your return before he goes back up to London. I'll be going with him. Now, my dear, tell me where you're going to live, what Morgan Kinver is going to do to provide for you.'

'I've come to love Polgissey, Luke, and

Morgan doesn't want to leave the village. If you'll allow us, we would like to build a house somewhere near here, up on the cliffs. Morgan will continue to work both the land and the sea. He hopes also to build a fleet of boats and to sell them or rent them, at a low affordable rate, to the local men. It will provide more work hereabouts.'

'It all sounds very honourable. Be assured you have my blessing. I can't think of anything better than having you as my close neighbour. Choose which ever slice of land you care to, I shall consult my solicitor over the legal side of it on the morrow. Why not live here while I'm away? Alicia will be delighted to have your company, but please, Corrie, I would very much like to retain Mrs Curnow's services. It was she who safely delivered little Mary Caroline.'

'I'd like nothing more, Luke. I'll ask Morgan what he thinks, but I'm sure he'll agree.'

'Excellent, how well things are moving. Have you heard the splendid news that my parents are happily reconciled?'

'Yes, isn't it wonderful? I wrote to them from Bath and received an immediate reply. I must say, I am relieved mine and Morgan's beginning was not as complicated as theirs.'

'So all ends well for us, Corrie, dear.' He made a quizzical face. 'Did you really think you were in love with me?'

'Yes, Luke, but I know what real love is now.'

'You may have had more good fortune than you think. I was going to ask you to marry me. Would you have accepted?'

'Let's not waste time over what may have been, Luke. Will you content yourself only with the fleeting comfort Amy Curnow gives you when you come home again? Do you not think it is time you looked for love?'

'Definitely not.' He ushered her to the door. 'It seems to me that love prefers to reveal itself at just the right moment rather than being tracked down. I hope, if it ever shows itself to me, I'll not be too preoccupied with other things to recognize it. Now, let us go down to Morgan and we will all go to see this lovely baby.'

At the foot of the stairs, Cordelia had a sudden thought. 'Luke, what is the title of your play?'

He laughed aloud. 'I've named it with you in mind. *The Strength of Innocence.*'

Forty-Two

Beatrice was plodding along to her room, a jar of gin cradled in both arms. When she neared the dining room, where Polly O' Flynn was stationed outside, supervising the comings and goings of succulent fare and empty dishes, the two women exchanged unrestrained gestures of delight.

Their master and mistress were holding a goodbye supper party for Luke and Bartholomew. All the family and a number of their friends were sitting around the dining table, and the room, indeed the whole manor, seemed to be reverberating with laughter and scintillating talk.

'Goin' t' be all right from now on,' Beatrice grinned and spluttered. 'I don't jus' feel it in me water, I knows it for certain, sure!'

Polly eyed the gin jar and Beatrice bristled in challenge, but Polly laughed raucously, an unusual occurrence for someone normally uncompromisingly strict in all quarters. 'There's something better than that tonight for those of us servants who partake. Sir Oliver has given us half a dozen bottles of his best wine from the cellar. Join Nathan and myself and the others after the meal's over, Beatrice.'

'Well, bless 'is 'eart! Always was a good boy, an' who do knaw that better 'n me? We'll celebrate fit t' lift off the roof! Drink a toast t' the boy an' 'is maid!'

For once, Polly did not correct Beatrice's affectionate term for their master and mistress.

Throughout the evening, regardless of this being a meal in Luke and Bartholomew's honour, everyone's eyes were constantly on Oliver and Kerensa. He sent a secret signal down across the table and she sent him one back.

'You simply must tell me what that meant, dear heart,' Rachael leaned across Luke and squawked at Kerensa. Then she nudged Luke, and winked. 'Or should I wait until I'm alone with your mama for the explanation, eh, eh?'

Luke looked steadily at his mother, who was laughing now at a witty word from Bartholomew. His parents had evidently resolved all their troubles, but did she perhaps have something shattering to tell Clem Trenchard?

Olivia was interested in the newest member to join the family. While occasionally entering the conservation Timothy was having with Cordelia about the various attractions offered at Bath nowadays, she turned often to view Morgan Kinver's strong profile. He was talking mostly to Jack and Alicia, and finally, somewhat bemused, he gave Olivia a full view of his face.

She was immediately drawn to his warm smile. 'Forgive me for staring, Mr Kinver – Morgan. Do you happen to know I do a little painting? I'd like to do your portrait, if I may. Would you have the time to come to the parsonage?'

'I'd be pleased to.' He glanced at Cordelia, who nodded in encouragement.

'Livvy, dear,' Timothy interrupted, and Olivia clammed up, pretending to be interested only in her food. He was saddened to witness once again how George Spears' defection had robbed her of her confidence. This was the first time since then that she had shown any enthusiasm to resume painting. She was despondent about the house and parish, and showed little delight in expectation of the baby.

He went on rapidly, 'I think I might have a better suggestion, my love. You planned at one time to do some painting at Polgissey. There's still weeks yet before you must rest before your confinement. Go to Polgissey, stay with Cordelia and Morgan and paint him there. And why not paint him about his work? Out in natural conditions. Draw Jack with the horses and Mrs Rosevear with the new baby.

'I don't care what that Spears fellow thought about your landscapes, your seascapes, or anything else. I was jealous of your ambitions before, I admit that in company, but I really do admire all your works, as have the people who've bought them in the past. The more you paint the more your style will develop. I've brought four of your best works with me and Luke is going to take them up to London, for a second, a third and even a fourth opinion, if need be. Your talent will grow with the right encouragement, of that I am sure.'

'Oh, Timothy!' Olivia gasped, elated, then she ran round the table to hug him.

'Both our gifts will be put the test, but our dreams need never die, Livvy,' Luke bawled mirthfully down the table.

'Good for you, Timothy! I propose a toast!' Kane rose to his feet, his leg quite improved now. He had drunk a good deal of wine and staggered a little. Jessica grabbed him and steadied him, amid much laughing.

Kane was happy and heartily relieved he did not have to go to Greystone's Farm. In agreement with Timothy, Jessica had been given the unenviable task of writing to her father about Oliver and Kerensa's reunion. 'To new beginnings,' Kane said. 'The marriage of Cordelia and Morgan. The success of Luke's plays and Livvy's paintings and to whatever Bartholomew's latest venture may be. To my little brother, Sam, for a long and happy life, and my new little cousin, Tamara, that she will enjoy growing up in Cornwall. To the good health of Miss Mary Caroline Rosevear and the coming of Livvy and Timothy's baby, and– ' he smiled proudly – 'I would like to announce that Jessica and I will be adding to our own nursery next spring!'

When all the cheers and good wishes had died down everyone rose and the toast was finally drunk.

Then Kane went on, looking down to the foot and up to the head of the table, 'And to you my very dear Mama and Father, whom we all love so very much.' He could not add publicly how everyone felt about their reconciliation, the sudden hush of emotional silence spoke for him.

The toast was drunk and the noise and joyful banter broke out again.

Then everyone watched as Oliver strode down the room. He bowed to Kerensa and taking her by the hand led her up to his chair. 'Sit there, beloved.'

He fetched a chair from beside the door and placed it next to hers and sat down. 'This is how things should be,' he said. 'Equal in everything and always together.'

There were rounds of applause and cheers enough to threaten to bring the ceiling down. Beatrice and Polly and the other servants crept into the room and joined in.

'Speech, speech!' demanded a beaming Sir William. It was good to be back on good terms with his friend.

Sir William's call was taken up by all the others and Oliver obliged them by standing up. A sudden quiet fell over the room.

'If I am to make a speech,' Oliver declared, gazing at all the eager faces around his table and those at the door, 'then Kerensa, your mother, your mother-in-law, her ladyship, your friend, or whatever this wonderful lady is to you, will stand at my side.'

Kerensa was a little stunned. Oliver helped her to her feet and they stood very close, his arm round her shoulders, hers round his waist. 'You say something first,' he whispered in her ear.

'Me? What shall I say?'

'You'll find the right words, my love.'

She took a deep breath. 'I'll say only what I want you to know, and then what you want to hear. All of you gathered here mean everything to me, and I thank you for all the love and loyalty you've shown me over the years. I love you all, and,' she raised her face to Oliver, 'most of all I love this great man at my side and always will.'

Oliver bent his head and kissed her. The noise broke out again to deafening pitch. He motioned with his hand for silence. 'I have no different sentiments to express, only to say I love this woman, this most precious, beautiful woman more than ever. And now, let us go to the great hall and get on with the entertainments.'

'I go up to London with a different heart this time, Cousin,' Luke remarked to Bartholomew, during a break in the dancing.

Bartholomew took his eyes off Alicia, who was sitting with Jack across the hall. She was glaring at him, the same malevolent look he had received with ever-increasing regularity at the supper table. Never before had someone looked at him with such utter hatred, but he was undisturbed. She could do nothing to harm him. Even an anonymous communication to the authorities disclosing how Lord Alexander Longbourne had really met his death would be laughed at. Nothing could be proved.

'And so you should, Luke. Before we set out the day after tomorrow, I have a little personal business to attend to.'

Luke followed Bartholomew's eyes and was alarmed to see them fixed on Alicia. 'You had better not be planning to harm her!'

'You have my word Mrs Jack is safe from me. No, I was thinking of my uncle and aunt. I don't believe anything could ever spoil their happiness again, but I'd do anything to make sure nothing could even be a nuisance to them.'

'I think you mean someone. You're thinking of warning off Clem Trenchard? I'd a notion Kane intended to do that. I say, leave it. Trenchard would only see a warning as a statement that he has some sort of power over Father. Things will be different at the baptism of Kane and Jessica's next child. I'd like the county to see it.'

'You're right, Luke, let's look only to the future and forget the rigours of the past. Before we retire for the night, what say you and I take a ride over to Marazion? I've the desire to call at Madame Frances Nansmere's residence, visit her girls. Then, when we reach the capital, we'll look only to the serious side of our respective business there.'

'An excellent idea.' Luke warmed to the prospect of visiting one of his old regular haunts.

He watched Cordelia dancing with her husband. 'I'm glad for Corrie's sake that you've come round to Kinver. He's hardly suitable for her, undoubtedly not what you'd hoped for her, but she's happy and that's the only ambition the dear girl has ever had.'

Bartholomew looked at Morgan Kinver from keen eyes – an unsettling sort of stare, to Luke's mind. 'I'll wait and see how things go for her. Kinver can easily be persuaded to move on, if the need arises.'

'Bartholomew, how you do like to make threats.'

'I'm not so cold-blooded, Luke. I merely don't baulk at removing a threat to anyone I love or admire. Or doing an unpleasant service to anyone I have a certain loyalty to.' He tapped his chest.

Luke shuddered as he saw again the knife wound in Alex Longbourne's heart, and he recalled the hostile manner with which Bartholomew had confronted Hal Kinver. He wished Jack was going with him to London instead.

Forty-Three

Out on the moor, Clem was hard at work with his scythe, slashing down furze, brambles and ferns for use as the base for the ricks Philip and the farmhands were building in the yard. Ferns would also be used for bedding for the pigs, calves and yearlings. He was content to be doing a labourer's job. In previous years he had organized the rickbuilding, but now he and Philip had made their peace, he was allowing his son to take charge of this.

He would be returning home soon, leaving

his harvest to dry out for a few days, to wash and change to attend a funeral. One of the labourers had lost his wife from a fever; the third victim in a week in the village of St Cleer.

His three dogs were darting about, bounding over granite boulders, sniffing the undergrowth and the bank of the nearby stream. A crow cawed from somewhere. Clem straightened up and looked in all directions but saw nothing except the wild landscape, its dips and tors. He'd slice the bastard-thing in half if he could.

This made him think of Oliver Pengarron. What was happening between that hated man and Kerensa? Being so far away, with no way of knowing, was eating into his guts. If only he and Kerensa had thought of a way to keep in touch.

She loves him more than me, he told the silent moor, miserably. If I could make her turn to me then he can do the same. He'd felt she had been turning back to her husband before he'd left her in the Tolwithrick cottage – her love for Pengarron had always been hopelessly strong. Like his own for her, sadly it didn't just go away. How much more bearable his life would have been if it had been otherwise.

Sighing, he attacked a ridge of fern with fierce, sweeping strokes. He worked on until sweat stung his eyes and ran in rivers down his back. He went to the stream for a drink of water, skirting a patch of peat bog, wide and deep enough to drown a beast, the fate of one of his straying bullocks last winter.

Gawen barked and Halwyn joined in and then Gracie. Clem took no notice, the dogs often took issue with a hare or some other creature, or were startled by the sudden flight of a grouse or pheasant, or just played noisily together.

Gracie, the most faithful of the three, was suddenly beside him, her hackles raised, growling, showing her teeth.

Snatching up his scythe, Clem straightened his back and swung round. 'Who the hell are you?'

The stranger, standing up on a boulder, said nothing, just smirked.

Clem recognized the tall, dark-haired man with Pengarron looks. He was dressed, not like the gentleman he had become, but in the clothes of a gipsy. His deep tan and an earring made the effect complete. Clem was on guard, all his dogs lined up with him now.

'Bartholomew Drannock. I'd heard you were back in Mount's Bay. What ill wind blows you this way?'

'I've come with some news for you, Trenchard. News you're going to hate.'

Clem met the haughty gaze with one of equal contempt. 'Get back to where you came from. You've got nothing to say I want to hear.'

'I know that, Trenchard. You skulked about my aunt to try to get her to turn against my uncle, but it didn't work. You might have won a battle or two but you didn't win the war. They've made up their differences and are happier than ever. She wouldn't have looked at you if not for Kane's accident.' Bartholomew jumped down off the rock and leaned forward, mockingly. 'Do you really think she'd prefer you in the end? Why do you think she married Sir Oliver in the first place? Because she liked what she saw, and she's liked what she's been getting from him all these years. She's over her moments of foolishness. There won't be a repetition. And my uncle is a changed man. If you had been in Pengarron Manor last night you would have seen exactly by how much. He's lost the pride my aunt found so offensive. Face it, Trenchard, you lose again.'

With painful resignation Clem accepted he was being told the truth. He couldn't offer Kerensa anything more than clandestine meetings, and even though she had been wonderfully happy to be with him, making love to him with joy and tenderness, it was so much less than what Pengarron could give her.

As long as Kerensa was happy it was all that mattered to him. 'You're enjoying this, Drannock. You always were a detestable wretch.' Clem spat on the ground. 'I curse the day you were born and the air you breathe.'

'I've been cursed before, Trenchard, it doesn't work.' The sardonic amusement in Bartholomew was replaced by malevolent intent.

Clem saw it and weighed the razor-sharp scythe in his hand.

'That's right, dirt-farmer. I haven't come here to order you to stay away from my aunt but to make sure you do. I won't let you remain a bother to my uncle a moment longer.'

Clem braced himself for attack. Bartholomew drew out the pistol from his belt.

Clem was shocked. 'You're going to kill me? Are you capable of cold-blooded murder?'

A cold, chilling laugh. 'In a word, yes.'

Gracie heard Clem's gasp of horror and leapt towards her master's enemy. Bartholomew fired and Gracie was dead before she hit the ground.

Letting out a cry of rage, Clem hurled himself forward, ready to cut the man down like a crop of brambles.

Bartholomew coolly stepped back and produced a second pistol. 'You're next, Trenchard. Oh, don't look so taken aback. You don't really mind dying, do you? You've said a thousand times since my uncle stole away your bride that you've nothing left to live for. So, I'd be doing you a favour really, don't you agree?'

'Drannock, I—'

'You don't want to die? You've changed your mind? Too bad. Too late. You shouldn't have stayed on in Mount's Bay and seduced my aunt, bedevilled my uncle, the man I admire above all others.'

Clem wasn't afraid to die. Without first place in Kerensa's heart it was back to the old soul-leaching loneliness, but suddenly the most important thing to him was to see his twins and Harry grow up – and he had Catherine and his grown-up children to live for too. 'Please, wait, listen to me.'

Bartholomew was concerned that the sound of the shot would have carried to the farm and someone would come hurrying to investigate its source. 'Throw down the scythe and order your dogs to run off, but not home. We'll talk.'

Clem did this, keeping his eyes on Bartholomew's hard face.

Bartholomew came to within arm's length of him and pointed the gun at his forehead. 'You lied!'

'You're such a fool, Trenchard, I was merely making things easy for myself.'

Clem ducked and threw himself at the other man's body. Bartholomew lost his grip on the gun but smashed both hands across the back of Clem's neck. Clem dropped to the spongy-wet ground. He felt an agonizing pain in his side as Bartholomew thrust his boot there, rolling him over to face the sky. Clem groaned, reaching round to his neck. His vision cleared and he saw Bartholomew now had a long-bladed knife in his hand.

'See this, Trenchard? The natives in the islands of the South Seas use knives just like this one in ceremonial slayings. It's capable of gutting a man in ten seconds. A quick slash across the throat will do for you.' Bartholomew put the blade to Clem's throat. 'Say goodbye to whatever god you believe in.'

In desperation Clem used all his strength to yell out and rear up. The knife thrust missed his throat and seared a deep path across his collar bone. Bartholomew grabbed him by the hair and smashed his head against the ground. Clem tried to fight him off, knowing it was useless. Drannock would pin him down and use his knife on him. He'd never see those he loved again. His last thought was that he was glad that Kerensa was happy.

Of a sudden, his attacker was sent flying away from him, and Bartholomew sprawled among the bulrushes. He looked up and saw Philip Trenchard looming over him. Spying his gun, he reached out for it.

'You all right, Tas?' Philip glanced at Clem before looking down at Drannock, now splattered in black mud, his billycock hat knocked off. 'Bartholomew Drannock? What in God's name are you doing here? And why attack my father?'

'Be careful, Philip,' Clem managed to gasp. 'He's got a pistol.'

Bartholomew had reclaimed the gun and was scrambling to get up off the waterlogged ground. Philip acted quickly, using a wrestler's lunge to launch his brawny body through the air. Bartholomew fired, blasting a hole in Philip's chest. Philip's full weight hit Bartholomew in the head and shoulders, sending them both careering backwards. He landed heavily on top of Bartholomew. Philip stayed motionless.

Bartholomew felt wetness underneath his top half and knew he had hit the edge of the bog. He pushed Philip off him, and in control now, leapt agilely upright.

Clem was halfway up, shouting to his son.

'Looks like I'll have to dispatch two Trenchards in one day,' Bartholomew gloated. He looked about for his knife and saw it glinting where it had landed, on the edge of a low mass of granite. Clem saw it too but wasn't close enough to reach it first.

Bartholomew swept his foot forward to move off, but something was gripping his other leg, making him unsteady. Philip had grabbed him and was unbalancing him. Bartholomew swung his free foot round to kick at Philip's hand and free himself.

It was Bartholomew's undoing. He swayed precariously for an instant, then plunged backwards into the swamp. He felt with his feet to find the bottom, but there wasn't one. The thick cloying mud would not allow him any movement. He was shoulder deep and sinking.

Clem staggered over to Philip, who was lying with a hand on his bleeding, heaving chest. Falling to his knees, he lifted Philip's head up and cradled him. 'It's all right, son. I'll get help. Why did you come here?'

'The post came with a letter for 'ee, Tas. I brought it out to 'ee.'

'Trenchard, help me,' Bartholomew cried out. 'I'm sinking.'

Clem looked at the man who had tried to kill him with no pity. He had shot his son close to the heart, and there was no point in him leaving Philip to go for help. Philip was dying. Because of this murderous brute, he was going to lose his son. Clem fought back the tears, he didn't want Philip to die afraid.

'I feel strange, Tas. All sort of sleepy.'

'You just settle yourself, Phil. Think about your next wrestling match.'

'Long time since you held me like this.'

'Yes, a long time.' And the last time.

'That someone shouting?'

'It's just the wind, son. You close your eyes now.'

Clem watched with tears coursing down his face as Philip's eyelids shut. 'I can see Mother.'

The oozing black mud was covering Bartholomew's shoulders. He was revoltingly, fearfully aware he couldn't get out of the stinking slime. 'For pity's sake, Trenchard. I have a daughter! Please, please!'

'Go to your mother, Philip,' Clem said softly, stroking his son's fair hair, made wet and dirty from the muddy water. 'She's waiting for you.'

Philip's face fell closer against Clem's chest and he died. Clem bent his head over him and wept like he never had before.

'Clem!'

Bartholomew realized that Clem would not help him if he could. He was going to die! He was being sucked down into a thick, wet darkness. The peat would seep into his nostrils and down into his lungs, choking him, suffocating him.

'Oh, God, help me!' he cried as the mud closed over his mouth.

Clem looked into Bartholomew's eyes, they were filled with abject terror.

Bartholomew twisted his neck vainly in an attempt to gain a little height, a little more time. Then he was drawn under millions of years of rotting vegetation, to a deserving death.

Forty-Four

Luke lifted his head off the plump, silk-covered pillows and stared up at the canopy over the bed. Extravagant, lustrous drapes, gold and orange and red in colour, flowed down out of sight.

Where was he? With a struggle, he sat up. He was groggy, his head ached, his throat felt like parchment. Then he remembered where he had gone with Bartholomew last night, but after arriving here in the brothel he remembered nothing else.

He groaned. He had not meant to get so drunk. He had a host of goodbyes to get through this morning before he went home and spent one more day and night at Polgissey, and he wanted to start his long, important journey to London with a clear head. He was thankful, at least, to be alone in the plushly furnished room.

Once dressed, he tossed some coins on a table to join a profusion of spirit bottles and glasses.

'My dear Mr Pengarron. My dear Luke. There's no need for that. Your cousin has

403

'paid most handsomely for both of you.'

'Eh? Oh, Mrs Nansmere. Frances. Good morning. Forgive me, I'm having a little trouble coming round.'

The proprietor of the establishment, wearing a flimsy negligee, floated across the thick carpet of her own bedchamber towards him. Graceful, beautiful in an unrefined way, and once well-connected to one of the county's foremost families, Frances Nansmere curtseyed to him, then fluttered her fingers up to expertly bind his necktie.

'It's long past morning, Luke.'

'Damn! Not that I don't enjoy lingering here.' Luke massaged his muzzy brow, but could not help grinning manfully. 'My cousin and I had a riot last night?'

'Indeed, you did. I should say, your cousin knows a thing or two, he slipped a little something into your wine to make your night ... a little more interesting. And you know I'm honoured to have you here, sir, at any time.'

Frances gazed blatantly into his dark eyes. She took his hands in hers and moved them about in the feathery sweeps that was a custom of hers, reacquainting him with her delicate perfume. 'Even though you're, not unsurprisingly, feeling a little jaded right now, I've never seen you looking so well. Encouraged and positive at last, if you don't mind me saying so. The girls and I missed you greatly while you were away in London, and then on your own estate. I beg you not to leave it too long to come and see us again when next you return.'

The madame kept her personal favours for a select few of her clientele. Luke was one them and he felt privileged, although he regretted having no exciting memories to take away with him.

Ignoring the thickness of his head, he raised her hands and kissed them sensuously. 'I promise you, Frances, you'll be one of the first of my friends I call on. Tell me, is my cousin astir?'

'I've absolutely no idea.' Frances smiled gaily, while fetching Luke's frockcoat. 'Mr Drannock did not spend the night here.'

'He did not take any of his own stuff?'

'No, sir. He said he wanted to keep a clear head. He left Ellie after an hour, saying he had some business to attend to for Sir Oliver.'

'How curious. My father said nothing of the kind to me. What could he want done at such a late hour? And why ask Bartholomew?'

Luke rubbed his brow, recalling Bartholomew's words of the previous evening: his thinly disguised threat towards Morgan Kinver if he failed Cordelia, and his remarks concerning Clem Trenchard. Is that where he could have gone, to warn Trenchard off?

He remembered Bartholomew's violence towards Alicia, his murderous intent towards Hal Kinver, and Alexander Longbourne's blood-soaked corpse. His cousin was a cold-blooded killer. If he had ridden to the moor to confront Trenchard, perhaps his intention was more than to give a warning.

'Frances, this is very important, can you tell me anything else?'

Frances's curling eyelashes flickered rapidly, the only sign of her curiosity at his urgency. 'He seemed to be in a hurry.'

'Perhaps he had a long journey to make,' Luke muttered to himself. Then to Frances he said, 'Order my horse to be made ready. I must go home to the manor without delay.'

Luke found his parents in the gardens with Samuel and Tamara, taking the fresh air.

'There you are. We've all been ready and waiting for you and Bartholomew for ages,' Kerensa said brightly, while noting uneasily his tense strides and that he was wearing yesterday's clothes. 'The others are inside.'

'Is Bartholomew here?' Luke called out, while still at a distance.

'No.' Oliver lifted Samuel up in his arms and advanced towards him. 'Like your bed, his hasn't been slept in. What's wrong?'

'Leave the children with the nursemaids. I need to talk to you both urgently. I fear something dreadful has happened.'

Forty-Five

'What do you mean, Luke, that you fear Bartholomew has gone off to murder Clem Trenchard?' Oliver demanded incredulously, moments later in his study. 'You're not making any sense!'

Luke was watching his mother with concern. She might take this news very hard.

'Why should he do such a thing?' she said, angry that Luke should come up with this ludicrous idea over Clem's safety. It wasn't true. How could it be?

His fingertips together, Luke pointed out the facts as he knew them. 'Bartholomew blames Trenchard for your recent troubles. He mentioned last evening that he'd go to any lengths to remove anything detrimental to the well-being of your marriage. I'm telling you, Father, Mama, that he is fully capable of such a crime. You don't know what he's become. It was he who murdered Lord Alexander Longbourne. He came down to Cornwall to ask you if he could leave his child here while he makes himself scarce and free again, but he was also sent by

407

Sir Decimus Soames, to ascertain if I or Jack knew certain details in connection with Longbourne's death. He's lied to Soames to protect the family, or at least, because he sets such great store by you, Father. Otherwise, I don't think he'd have spared Alicia Rosevear, he's lied about her survival too.'

Icy darts of fear for Clem rode up Kerensa's spine. 'Apart from gossip over this Lord Longbourne's death I don't know what you're talking about, and full explanations can wait till later. If you really believe Bartholomew has gone to kill Clem, we have to do something!' She looked steadily at Oliver. 'I'm sorry, I have to know.'

Oliver nodded and said gravely, 'What we'll say to the Trenchards if Luke's fears prove unfounded, I've no idea, but that's not important. The three of us will set out at once for Greystone's.'

At the beginning of the ride to Greystone's Farm, Kerensa, Oliver and Luke prayed they would come across Bartholomew innocently making his way back to the manor. Later, as their mounts kicked up the dust and avoided the ruts and holes in the narrow, straggling lanes of the moor, they prayed not to find him returning from the violent deed that Luke feared he had slipped away to perform.

'Why did you not tell me the truth about Bartholomew? Do you suppose I'd have continued to welcome even kin of mine under my roof after such a change of personality?' Oliver asked Luke bluntly at one point.

'I was going to tell you once I'd made sure he'd left Cornwall. He was all set to return to London immediately after Beatrice's birthday party, but then Cordelia ran away.'

When they closed in on the placid, solemn village of St Cleer, they halted at a small inn to water the horses. Kerensa paced up and down over the small square of dirty cobbled yard, desperate to continue.

'Stay with your mother, Luke,' Oliver said at the pump and animal trough. 'I'll go inside and ask directions to the farm.'

The landlord, a short, fuzzy-haired man with black teeth, hurried out to meet him, bowing and touching his forelock. He listened avidly to Oliver's request, then gave him brief directions. ' ''Tedn't far, sur. Could see the farm from 'ere, 'cept for the 'ills. Someone t' do with Mrs Trenchard, are 'ee? She'm a fine lady, been some good t' the village, she 'ave. Even more so since we've bin buryin' our dead from the fevers, one laid t'rest only this mornin'. Dreadful bizness though, she'll take it 'ard.'

'What are you saying? Is Trenchard dead?' Oliver lowered his voice, slipping a few pennies into the landlord's grimy hand.

'Ais, dead an' laid out. Constable's been there. Bound to 'appen some day. Serve un right, I say.'

Oliver thanked the landlord and stalked away, lest Kerensa overhear, so he missed the man's last remark. 'Should never 'ave done what 'e did t' that little maid.'

'What was he saying?' Kerensa asked anxiously.

Oliver lifted her quickly on to her pony's sidesaddle. The landlord was heading their way to indulge in more gossip.

'We'll be there shortly, my dear. Try not to worry.'

How was she going to take it when she learned Clem was dead? Oliver didn't know how he felt about it, he would think about it later. Right now he had to be sensitive to Kerensa's needs. He was committed to giving her as much of whatever sort of strength and consideration she asked of him. He hoped Trenchard's death had not been too gruesome.

And what of Bartholomew? The identity of Trenchard's killer was unlikely to be known by anyone in this area. Had he already started the journey up to London?

On his way to Gereint, Oliver whispered to Luke. 'We're too late! Have a care how you present yourself in front of your mother, and for heaven's sake, don't mention your cousin's name, at least not at first.'

They trotted out into the lane and were soon passing through the village. Kerensa tried to ignore the curious stares of those

410

who had come out of their poor housing to see who, suddenly in their midst, was on horseback. They wore stern, subdued expressions and black clothes. Usually she would offer greetings, but she was afraid these people were discussing the bad news she was dreading to hear.

When the houses gave way to open moor again the riders stepped up their pace.

They arrived at the track that led off to Greystone's Farm. All the way along the muddy, stony ground Kerensa glanced nervously at Oliver. Her stomach was bound up and she had to keep remembering to breathe. How would she bear it if Clem was dead? It would be her fault, she should not have agreed to meet Clem alone. Bartholomew had made it known, rather nastily, looking back, that he knew she and Clem had been lovers.

In the course of a busy day on a farm few people would be about the yard, but labourers were loafing about grim-faced and there was a cluster of dairymaids and female servants, red-eyed from weeping. They watched the newcomers with wary interest. As was the custom throughout Cornwall in the event of a death, all the farmhouse's curtains were drawn over.

Kerensa felt a bolt of terror course through her and an overwhelming sense of loss and failure. 'Oh, no. It's really happened!'

Oliver reached for her hand. 'I'm so sorry, my dear.'

Luke chewed on his bottom lip. If he had told his father about Bartholomew's character all this could have been avoided. They dismounted. Luke gathered in all the reins and passed them on to the farmhand who came forward.

The front door of the farmhouse was opened and Catherine appeared, in a black dress and black shawl. The black lace on her head made her skin glow an unnatural white. She held her head high, a picture of strained dignity.

Leaving Oliver's side, Kerensa ran to her, her heart slashed in half, her tears unstoppable. 'We had reason to believe something terrible might have happened here. I'm so sorry, Catherine. Please don't be angry with me. I had to come.'

Catherine gazed at her coolly. For a moment she wanted to order Kerensa off her property. Then the charitable side of her understood her distress, and that she had assumed the victim was Clem. Of course, she would grieve for Clem. She had loved him for over twenty-four years. And how could Clem be expected not to love her still? This woman, as youthful-looking as a girl, beautiful and perfect in every way.

'It wasn't Clem. He's hurt but the doctor's attended to him. Philip was killed trying to save his life from Sir Oliver's nephew. Bartholomew Drannock is also dead, drowned in a bog.'

'Oh, my God!' Kerensa cried out. Her relief that Clem was alive was replaced by a different sorrow, she knew how grief-stricken he would be at losing one of his children. Bartholomew's death meant nothing to her. 'I'm so sorry. Where is – I mean – can I...?'

'Can you see Clem?' Catherine finished for her quietly. She looked at Sir Oliver.

'Mrs Trenchard, I would like to offer you my condolences on the death of your stepson and to express my deepest regret and horror at my nephew's part in it,' Oliver's voice was firm but not without emotion. 'Also, I am willing to agree to Kerensa's plea if you are. I should very much like to talk to you alone, ma'am.'

'He's in the sitting room, with Philip,' Catherine said.

Kerensa looked from her husband's pitying expression to Catherine's pale suffering face. 'Thank you, both of you.' Then she stepped over the Trenchard threshold.

Catherine gave a small cry and made to show she had changed her mind.

Oliver prevented her, gently. 'It's hard for us, ma'am, but I have learned that nothing is to be gained from denying that they have a special bond. I see you have a well-kept

413

garden. Will you take a turn round it with me? We have much to discuss.'

Clem was sitting on Catherine's spinet stool alone. Philip was laid out on a platform of boards and trestles, used only recently for the celebration at the end of the harvest. He had been too tall for the length of a table. Four large candles were lit, one at each end of the platform, giving a passive golden light over the bold, fair features. Philip's body was dressed in his best suit of clothes, his meaty hands crossed over his chest.

Kenver was to make the coffin. He'd been to grieve, to take his nephew's measurements, and had been driven home in the trap to get on with the saddest task of his life. Lydia, the nursemaid, had taken John and Flora to stay at his house. There was a lot of sorrow and anger at Greystone's, and Catherine had thought the twins best not subjected to it.

'This shouldn't have happened to you, son,' Clem's voice was thick with tears. 'It should've been me. I'm the one who should be lying there dead.' He wept, as he had wept almost continuously since Philip's last breath, putting his hands over his son's cold hands.

Forced to reach for a handkerchief, he also pulled the letter out of the pocket of his clean breeches, where he'd put it after the doctor had stitched his bone-deep cut.

'Oh, God, Philip, why did you bring me this?' He studied the sheet of thick folded paper, instrumental in the atrocity. The writing was Jessica's. He broke the seal. 'I s'pose I could read this to you, eh, Phil? Just about, without Catherine to help me.'

With difficulty he made his eyes focus on the spindly writing. 'Your sister starts off by greeting everybody, then it says, "I am sending you all good news, I am having another baby." Hope the next baptism goes better than Harry's, eh, son?'

Clem did not read out the rest of the letter. It confirmed Bartholomew Drannock's news that Kerensa had returned the greater part of her love to her husband. He let out a howl of despair, a terribly savage sound. 'Has my life come to this?' he yelled, face contorted. For a second he almost went out of his mind.

Then he tore the letter into pieces and stuffed them into his pocket so Catherine would not chance upon them. There was no need to add to her grief and misery by allowing her to learn about his unfaithfulness. She had not questioned him about the reason for Drannock's assault, and he prayed she never would.

Checking his emotions, he got up and stroked Philip's cold brow. 'You died a brave man, and all because of what I did. Forgive

415

me, son. You worked hard on the farm, wanting to make it bigger and better. I promise you, from now on I'll forget myself and what I've always wanted, and do everything I possibly can to carry out your wishes.

'I've sent for David. He can say a prayer in the churchyard for you, you'd like that, my dear boy, I know you would. I'll tell Rebekah all about you, how many prizes you won for wrestling, how you were the Mount's Bay champion for a year, and the champion of the moor. I won't let anyone forget you, Philip. You did wrong, that's why Rebekah's here, but we all do wrong. If only I hadn't. It's you who's paid the price.'

If only he had not loved Kerensa so much, yet for all that had happened, he would give anything for her to be here right now. He would tell her he was glad she was happy with Pengarron and to get on with her life and forget him. He longed to hold her one more time. He had always longed for the impossible.

The door opened and he braced himself for the intrusion. He was petrified with astonishment when he saw who came in. To have Kerensa here, now, was too incredible.

'Hello, Clem,' she fought to keep her voice calm. Seeing him so stricken tore at her heart. 'I'm so sorry about Philip.'

'Kerensa, I don't understand.' His voice was hoarse, barely audible after so much weeping. 'How? Why?'

'Can I come in and pay my respects to him?'

'Yes, I'd like to have you here.'

She closed the door and moved to Clem's side. A few months ago they had held hands and looked down on their sleeping grandchild, now they did the same to his lifeless son.

'What happened, Clem?'

'Drannock tried to kill me. He shot Philip, then Philip managed to tip him into the bog. Philip died in my arms, peacefully. Drannock did not. You know why it happened, Kerensa?'

'Yes,' she sobbed. 'Because of us. Forgive me, Clem. If I had been stronger and not—'

'You're not to blame. If I'd stopped being so selfish all these years, looked only to Alice and then Catherine, you would've forgotten me. How is it that you're here, Kerensa?'

Kerensa explained. 'Oliver's with Catherine now. Luke's waiting to see if there's anything he can do. Jessica and Timothy should be on their way.'

'And he didn't mind you coming to me? Can't quite believe that.'

'It was Oliver who persuaded Catherine to let me see you alone. I don't know what will come out of this, but I hope we can all put suspicion and bad feelings behind us, and in future meet as equals. Try not to hate Oliver,

Clem, for the sake of Jessica and Kane's children.'

'Yes,' Clem said bitterly. 'This is the time to be noble, but I'm sorry, I can't feel anything but hatred for the man who took you away from me, and whose kin murdered my son.

'Kerensa, stay and say a prayer for Philip, and after, although I'd like you to stay, I must ask you to leave me, for Catherine's sake. You see, I've changed too. I can't go on putting my own feelings first.'

She felt the tenseness in his hand and took hers away. 'Very well, Clem. I'll do whatever you want.' Bowing her head in a short prayer, she looked at Clem's fierce face and walked towards the door.

'Not yet!' he cried out. 'Not yet, Kerensa. I thank Pengarron for letting you come to me like this. Just don't leave me yet.'

She ran to him and wrapped him into her body. They wept together for Philip and everything they had lost.

In the pleasant little garden, Oliver walked with Catherine, somewhat unwillingly, on his arm.

'What is it you want to say to me?' she asked, her tone dipping and rising, like the hills they faced.

'Forgive me, ma'am, I have to ask you, is my nephew's body still in the bog?'

'It is, for now. The bog is not so deep that

418

a body cannot be retrieved. The constable will arrange for it to be brought up when he's taken away all the evidence he requires. I take it that in due course you will dispose of your nephew's remains?'

'I'll get the body away from here as soon as I possibly can.'

Oliver was aware of her using his arm for support. She was growing weaker, probably from shock and numbness. He took her to a painted wooden seat, and rather than stand sat down beside her. He needed to be close to someone himself right now. For a moment he wondered what Luke was doing, then how Kerensa was comforting this lady's husband.

'I had not the slightest idea my nephew had turned into the sort of man who could so lightly set out to kill another. If I had not tried to manhandle Clem off my property that day, we wouldn't have arrived at this point now. I apologize unreservedly to you, ma'am. You are the only one innocent in all of this. You and Philip, of course. You had a fondness for him, I understand.'

'I shall miss him very much. Clem will have to run the farm single-handed now, although it is to be hoped David, Philip's twin, will stay a while.' Catherine glanced at him sharply. 'You mystify me, Sir Oliver Pengarron. Does it not kill you to know your wife more than likely has her arms around my husband?'

'It gives me real pain, far worse than the physical kind, but I've already let my jealously nearly destroy my marriage. I thank God every minute, that Kerensa realized she loved me more than him. I loathe Clem. How could it be otherwise, when it's not possible for Kerensa to forget him?'

'So, you are saying that we should allow them to fall into each other's arms whenever they meet?'

'No, Mrs Trenchard, of course not. These are special circumstances today and, well, I've put his need before my own.' Oliver was silent for a moment, then said, 'I can hardly believe I'm pleading for understanding in the case of Clem's feelings for Kerensa and hers for him. I'm thinking of the future, when our families come unavoidably together. It would be better if we can meet with some sort of ease. May I call you Catherine?'

'Why not?' she replied tartly. 'Our spouses are on first name terms.'

'Catherine, do not feel disgraced in front of your people here because of what's happening this very minute in your house. Consider this. I don't think that you and I will ever find peace if we continue with our desire to keep Kerensa and Clem aloof. I have had, against all that I believed sanctified, to allow my heart to grow to the size wherein I can accommodate this. You, dear lady, are feeling, quite rightly, abused and pained, yet I am sure you have a heart that is greater than mine.'

Catherine gazed down forlornly. 'But Kerensa loves you more than she does Clem. Do you suppose this notion of yours will stop him yearning for her?'

'I can only hope so. I've never been a man to settle for less than full measure, but now,' he smiled grimly, 'in the odd moment of compassion, I think about what I forced Clem to settle for all those years ago – absolutely nothing. Thank God he had Alice and now you, Catherine.'

'You know that when Clem first asked me to marry him it was because he believed Jessica needed a stepmother. Then, when she fell in love with Kane, he came to me and asked me again, for himself. He says he loves me and I know he does.' Catherine was crying softly. 'But it hurts so much to know he'd rather have Kerensa with him now than me.'

'It's only for a little while, Catherine. We will not be staying here long.' Oliver took her cold hand. 'It's you who will be here for Clem after we've gone and for all the days ahead when he'll need help coming to terms with his grief. Kerensa doesn't want to remain for that. She wants to be with me.'

'How kind you are to offer me comfort,

when in a way, your grief is of the worse kind, knowing your nephew is not only dead but the perpetrator of a capital crime. Come inside the house, Oliver, and wait with me.'

Although most of the workers had drifted away to their usual tasks, Luke wandered off behind the outbuildings, where he could not be seen.

Looking out across the vastness and loneliness of the moor, some of the old, heavy sense of isolation returned to beleaguer him. He could not face journeying alone to London. In the light of what had happened, his play, his hopes for its success, seemed unimportant. He would shelve its presentation, his dream, for the time being.

From the evidence around him this was a well-kept farm. Philip Trenchard had achieved his dream, his life cut undeservingly short by a man who had allowed his wish to be rich and free to wander the world to be corrupted by evil. The cost of his crime would affect Jessica and Cordelia, and to a lesser extent his father and mother, for the rest of their lives. All so tragic and unnecessary.

The sound of horses brought Luke out of his musings. It was Jessica, Timothy and Jack who clattered into the yard, with the farmhand sent as messenger. Jessica and Timothy went into the house. Jack approached Luke.

'I thought you might be glad of some

company.'

'I am, thanks Jack. How's Cordelia?'

'Shocked, upset. She's got Morgan and Alicia with her.'

'Alicia can't be feeling sorry Bartholomew forfeited his own life.'

Jack looked grim. 'She feels she's avenged Lord Alex by ill-wishing it on him. I'm glad, at least, that'll stop. 'Twas getting unhealthy; an obsession with her. Luke, what's Sir Decimus going to think about Bartholomew's death?'

'I was worried about that at first, but he can't connect it to you, I or Alex. I wish Bartholomew had not asked my parents to bring up his child. She's going to be a constant reminder of him and this dreadful tragedy.'

'When will you go up to London?'

'I intend to stay and support the family and look to my property. I've done a few things for Polgissey and the estate but much needs my urgent attention. I'm sure Cordelia and Morgan Kinver will agree we'll all rub along together.'

'Luke, I've been thinking. The Countess of Kilwarth has a great liking for the theatre, she knows a lot about the profession. Why not send her your play and ask her what she thinks about it? That way it wouldn't be gathering dust. Start on the next one too. You need to do that, not just concentrate on work.'

'Thanks for that, Jack. It's good to be back sharing in each other's lives. I'll do all you suggest. Now, let us not give the unfortunate people here more burdens, and see to the horses for those of us who are soon to leave here.'

Forty-Six

Clem and Kerensa had come out from their private vigil and met Oliver and Catherine. There had been no unpleasantness. Gaunt, crushed, Clem merely gave Oliver a curt nod and looked lingeringly at Catherine.

Jessica had flown to her father, giving full release to the grief she had held back on the journey.

'Your brother's at peace, sweetheart.' He had wound his arms around her tightly. 'Don't upset yourself too much, you've got the baby to think about. Perhaps the Reverend Lanyon will take you in to see Philip. Your stepmother and I will join you in a while.'

'Of course,' Timothy said quietly. Leaving Catherine's side, he placed a consoling hand on his brother-in-law's shoulder.

The two couples were left alone. Oliver

wanted to go to Kerensa and take her back, but stayed his ground. He and Catherine exchanged glances of affinity.

'I'd like to express my heartfelt sympathy to you, Clem,' he said in a solemn, sincere voice. 'Please, will you allow me to attend to the matter of my nephew with the constable? That way, you need only attend to your family and your grief.'

Clem stared at him. Pengarron had never called him by his first name or offered him help before. Did he suppose all that had happened gave him the right to patronize him? He felt Kerensa's fleeting touch, reminding him how she had been allowed to go to him. Then she went to her husband.

'I thank you, Sir Oliver. Stay and take a meal, if you will, before you and Lady Pengarron and the others start the journey home.'

'We welcome your hospitality,' Oliver said.

Clem studied him and Kerensa together. The picture he had kept inside his head all those long, lonely years of her and himself like that, close and belonging together, was gone. Perhaps it was because of his grief, or that he had accepted at last that fate had never meant him and Kerensa to be joined.

He held out his hand to Catherine. 'Shall we join Jessica and Timothy?'

Catherine crossed the floor to him. At the door, she swung her head round to observe

Kerensa Pengarron staring after Clem, still keeping her hold on him. Only she wasn't. She had her eyes closed and was leaning into Oliver, for comfort, for support, for love. Oliver motioned his encouragement to Catherine. She thanked him with a small smile.

In the passage, Clem halted as he heard Jessica sobbing wretchedly in the other room. 'I'm sorry, Cathy,' he croaked. 'I need a moment.'

She reached up and touched his face, smoothing at his hurt expression. 'Do you need me to hold you, Clem?'

He nodded. 'Yes, I need that very much.'

The business with the constable settled, the two families were saying goodbye.

Oliver usually ensured he had the first word but left it to someone else.

Clem spoke to him, while sheltering Catherine and Jessica in his arms, 'When next we meet, for the sake of our families, I hope it will be with this same lighter attitude.'

'It is my hope too,' Oliver replied. 'We shall all make the new baby's baptism next year a cause for wholehearted celebration. We shall stand as equals, you and I, Clem Trenchard, and the whole county will see it.'

These were words Clem had never expected to hear from the other man. If Pengarron could change enough to offer to see him as his equal, he would not allow himself to be ruled by bitterness. Leaving the women, he held his hand out to Oliver. Leaning down from his horse, Oliver gripped it.

'We'll stand as equals in the church, and Catherine and I look forward to that occasion, but I shall keep my proper place elsewhere. Wherever we may meet, not as grandparents of the same children, I'll give Kerensa her title. Goodbye, Sir Oliver.' He stood back. 'Goodbye, Kerensa.'

'Goodbye, Clem.' She started off for the journey home with Oliver, the hour so late they would have to spend the night at an inn. She stopped after a few paces and looked back.

Clem had not moved. He waved to her, 'Goodbye, Kerensa.'

'Goodbye, Clem, for now.'

Clem turned round. With his arms outstretched, he walked back to Catherine and Jessica and gathered them in. 'Come, we will eat and then sit with Philip. I'll send someone over to bring John and Flora home. To get through this we need to be strong, and to be strong we all need each other.' He rested his head against Catherine's and whispered, 'It'll be all right, I promise.'

When the returning party had left the sadness of the moor behind, Luke and Jack rode on a little ahead, chatting about their new schemes for Polgissey and Porthcarne.

Kerensa gazed across at Oliver, bringing Kernick closer to him. They had exchanged many tender glances but now she kept her eyes fixed on him.

'Are you cold, beloved?' he said. 'The wind's getting stronger. The inn is not far now.'

'I am a little cold and lonely too. Can I ride on Gereint with you?'

Smiling, he lifted her across to sit in front of him, holding her fast to his body.

'We have a child to bring up now, Oliver, as if she were our own. Tamara has lost both parents. It will not be easy for her when she learns what her father did and how he died, but I believe she should be told. We know the cost of keeping secrets.'

'We will do our best for her, beloved. At least it will be the truth when we tell her Bartholomew loved her.'

'I love you so much, Oliver. Your change of heart, the way you were at Greystone's today, showed me what a great man you are.'

'And how much I love you too, I hope.'

'That too.' Winding her arms round him, she vowed, 'I'll never say goodbye to you, Oliver. Never, ever.'